My Education

My
Education

SUSAN CHOI

VIKING

VIKING
Published by the Penguin Group
Penguin Group (USA) Inc., 375 Hudson Street,
New York, New York 10014, USA

USA | Canada | UK | Ireland | Australia | New Zealand | India | South Africa | China
Penguin Books Ltd, Registered Offices: 80 Strand, London WC2R 0RL, England
For more information about the Penguin Group visit penguin.com

LIBRARY OF CONGRESS CATALOGING-IN-PUBLICATION DATA
Choi, Susan, 1969-
My education / Susan Choi.
pages cm
ISBN 978-0-670-02490-2
1. Teacher-student relationships—Fiction.   I. Title.
PS3553.H584M94 2013
813'.54—dc23   2013001605

Printed in the United States of America
10 9 8 7 6 5 4 3 2 1

Set in Warnock Pro with Fairfield LT Std
Book design by Daniel Lagin

My Education

1992

S ince arriving the previous week I'd kept hearing about a notorious person, and now as I entered the packed lecture hall my gaze caught on a highly conspicuous man. *That's him* I declared inwardly, which of course was absurd. It was a vast university, of thousands of souls. There was no reason these two kinds of prominence—scandalous noteworthiness, and exceptional, even sinister, attractiveness—must belong to the same human being. Yet they had. The man was Nicholas Brodeur, though I knew it for sure only later.

That first time seeing him, even before being sure who he was, it was already clear that his attractiveness was mixed up with a great deal of ridiculousness. He wore a long duster coat, in the heat of September. His filthy blond hair stuck up and out in thatchy spikes from heavy use of some kind of pomade, as if it were 1982, not '92, and he wore Lennon shades with completely black lenses, as if it were outdoors, not in, and overall, in his resemblance to a Joy Division poster, he comported himself as if twenty and not, as I'd come to find out, almost forty. Still he was the best-looking man, by a league, in the room and certainly the best-looking man I had seen in the flesh to that point in my life. I hadn't yet lived in one of the world's great cities, where such specimens congregate, but even now that I have, he still ranks. And he must have realized; there was in his posture a kind of inverse vanity, a suggestion that he engaged in his sartorial ridiculousness out of some impatience with the effects of his beauty.

He stood alone at the back, his feet away from the wall and his shoulders slumped against it. An ambiguous expression that was not quite a smile slightly lifted the sides of his mouth. His hands remained stuffed in the duster's deep pockets. The inappropriate hoodlum charade seemed to chide anybody who stared, as I did.

Casper was the only fellow student in my program I'd managed so far to befriend. When he arrived and dropped into the seat I had saved him, I directed his eyes to the man. "Oh my," Casper said. "Do I want to fuck him, or just be him?" Just being him did seem the lesser risk.

I'd been inoculated against the villain Brodeur before I'd even enrolled. On my visit to campus the previous spring, my informational coffee with a second-year poetry student had been interrupted by a timorous and blushing undergraduate whom the second-year had caught in a fervent embrace, and then presented to me portentously as someone "any *woman* considering coming here needs to talk to." In the course of preparing her senior thesis under Brodeur's direction, the undergraduate had been victimized by him, in what precise way it would victimize her further to ask her to relate. The result, thus far, had been a petition demanding his firing, but the second-year was confident that far more severe retribution would follow. This was only the most recent petition, and the most recent of his sexual crimes. He was rumored to ask female students to read Donne to him while he lay on the floor of his office, in darkness, it was presumed masturbating himself. He was said to recite bawdy couplets referring to breasts while directing his gaze in the classroom at actual breasts. He'd attended, at the repertory cinema on campus, a screening of a late-career, poorly received film by Roman Polanski—the rapist—and unlike the rest of the solemn, censorious house, there to sharpen the critical blades, he'd apparently laughed so hard as to have literally fallen from his seat onto the floor. Amid all this baleful intelligence it came as a superfluous footnote that his relations with his wife, who was also a faculty member, were obscure and chaotic.

I was as susceptible to this sort of gossip as anyone else—it impressed itself on me with more permanence than the titles of the texts I was required to read for my first set of graduate courses. And yet, as opposite as they would seem from each other in worth, the salacious gossip and the scholarly imperatives, they were equally thrilling to me, different-color threads of the same mantle: that of adulthood. Graduating from college, I'd suddenly found I'd Grown Up, and graduate school was my Eden, where I named and possessed all the precious, first things, even those with a taint, like the villain Brodeur. Eagerly I absorbed Brodeur's villainous status as I did the rest of the new esoterica. Rents were cheaper off the hill than on. The better grocery store was Friel's, not Mighty Buy. Nicholas Brodeur was a predator—not to mention a sexist!—whose continuing presence on campus proved the sorry truth of everything we'd learned in women's studies (and so was gratifying, though most of us wouldn't admit it). But for all my initiate's self-importance, about Nicholas Brodeur and the rest, I hadn't been warned of his beauty, which for true initiates went without saying. Consciousness of his beauty, I understood now, thrilled beneath every condemnation. It was the shared secret that lent the condemning its eager subtext.

The assembly of hundreds in the stifling hall was for a series of readings by the writing program faculty to fight world hunger. How the funereal poems, or the confusing prose excerpts, each of which was prefaced by long explanations of context, might fight world hunger had not been made clear. Admission had been free, and no one was taking donations. Yet nonattendance at the reading seemed sufficiently aligned with indifference to world hunger that even acid-tongued Casper did not wax sarcastic, and despite the ravishingly gorgeous day outside, the hall was standing-room only, its atmosphere a strange combination of stultification and a showy self-regard for the good we were doing. I recognized just a scattering of students here and there, and not many more from the group of performers, who took the stage one by one with perhaps a hair too much affectation of reluctant humility, or loose-limbed unconcern, alternating these attitudes almost as consistently as they alternated genres: poet, fiction writer, poet, and so on, each, at the conclusion of his or her reading, giving introduction to the colleague who followed in a wry, collegial shorthand which sometimes provoked scattered outbursts of laughter from the knowing concealed in the crowd. Not a word that was read stayed with me. I could not even recall, once the readers were back in their seats, which had read poems versus prose. Affecting a pose of my own, of enchanted absorption, as if the powerful words drew my gaze far beyond the confines of the hall, I very slowly rotated my head toward the back, but the standing-room area now was so crowded I could no longer see him. Perhaps he had left.

When the reading was over it was a long time before we could even get out of our seats. "I'm very disappointed Byron and the Bunnymen didn't share his work also," said Casper.

"The man standing in back? But he isn't a poet."

"What else would he be?"

"Something made me think he must be Nicholas Brodeur," I admitted, but Casper pooh-poohed. "Brodeur's a Spenserian," Casper explained. "He'll be tweedy. Even if he's a rapist he's going to be tweedy. You're casting too much to type."

Later that week, when I came up the steps at the end of my first day of classes, Dutra was already home, sprawled in the porch hammock with a half-empty bottle of beer. "What an insane day!" I complained and exulted.

"You *obviously* need a drink," he said, swinging the bottle at me so I had to accept it. Dutra had a pouncing way of expressing himself, as if the subtext was always *"I gotcha!"* His voice was generally too loud for its setting, for the porch on this homely, leaf-drowned block of wood-frame houses on this somnolent, hot afternoon, for example, but the oversize voice was well matched with his face, long and lean and not the least softened up at its edges by his five-dollar barbershop buzz cut, its narrow span busily occupied by a large, slightly hooked Roman nose and large, hooded green eyes and a wide, mobile mouth and large out-sticking ears, all of which he tirelessly manipulated as a clown would, launching his eyebrows or stretching his grin from one lobe to the other. Yet in his rare moments of repose it was easy to imagine him leading the Argonauts and clanking his sword in the dust. It was my latest theory that the carelessness with which he carried himself—shambling with his shoulders hitched up, or tossing himself like so much useless scrap wood into a heap in the hammock—was meant to conceal this feline athleticism, to benefit him with a hidden advantage. He seemed to particularly relish being underestimated, a condition which formed the theme of the story he was now telling me, and which had surely played a role in our current relationship. I happened to be sleeping with Dutra. Ten days before, the very night I'd moved in, he'd seduced me, with no more effort and no less presumption than he'd used handing over his beer.

His story had to do with the boot-camp-style orientation he'd just undergone. He had begun his day dismissed as the skinny wise-ass, and wound up unanimously elected team leader: a typical triumph for him.

"It was every kind of kill-the-individual, forge-the-collective, kick-your-ass, boot-camp-type thing they could think of," he went on, reaching over his head for the six-pack to fetch us new beers. "Climb walls, swing on ropes, fall blindfolded off high things into a net someone's supposedly holding. Toward the end of the day, when we were doing that—put their blindfold on, help them up the ladder, talk them into jumping off with no idea is someone going to catch them or their neck's getting broken—one of the residents said to me, 'You're going to make a great doctor. They really trust you.'" Dutra's unabashed braggartliness was like a sedative to me; I was unused to so much confidence. Dutra stated his superiorities because they were facts, not because he required my agreement. It was the same attitude with which he'd stated the idiosyncrasies of the apartment, the day I'd come for a viewing: the apartment was, and would always be during his tenancy, absolutely messy and absolutely utilitarian—he had no time for nor interest in beauty—but it would never be dirty; he had no tolerance for dirtiness. He rolled his sleeves up and scrubbed things, he washed windows and laundry, but he did not waste his time making things neat; it went without saying I'd live the same way. As far as shared space, I should feel liberated to do as I pleased so long as I didn't object to his habits, which were principally smoking marijuana, watching television, and studying to be a vascular surgeon, all of which activities took place at all hours simultaneously, and were necessarily bound to one another. Finally, although the apartment was furnished, as advertised, the two rooms I was offered were in fact absolutely empty. There were not even blinds or lightbulbs.

Arriving in that town I hadn't owned any more in the way of furniture than I had four years previously on my first day of college. I'd circled his ad when I'd seen the word "furnished." "I don't suppose," I'd said tentatively in the course of that first conversation, "there's an old desk and chair, or a bookshelf, or anything. Maybe in the attic? Or the basement?" The apartment was half a wood house: half a front porch; half a first floor, with the living room and dining room and kitchen; half an upstairs, with three rooms, a big one in front which was his and the two small available ones, off the hall and in back just beside the bathroom; half a basement below; half an attic above; and half a small, grassy backyard. The other half of the house—it had been built as one structure, with two identical, symmetrical sides—was occupied by the owners, who regarded Dutra alone as their tenant, and Dutra's housemates as his business. I was to pay my rent to him, and he would take care of all of the bills.

"No," Dutra had said. We'd been standing in the hallway together, regarding the stark, spotless rooms, which I'd had the sense had not been merely cleaned, but sterilized and perhaps exorcised.

"What about a bed?" I'd wondered, hoping to sound breezily unconcerned.

"No," Dutra had said, "but you're welcome to sleep on the couch, or with me, until you get one."

It was a few hours more before I knew I had heard this correctly; at the time I said only, "Did someone else used to live in these rooms?" as we returned down the stairs.

"Yes," he'd said, with emphasis but without elaboration.

Dutra's given name was Daniel Francis Dutra, and the story of his conquest of the university was one he shared more readily, given that it amplified the theme of his hidden advantage. He was from New York City, the only child of a hairdresser mother and a shiftless, perfidious father who left them when Dutra was three. Dutra's mother, whom he adored and berated for her numerous foibles for hours on end on the phone, had raised him to believe in himself, to say the least, the result being that Dutra had gotten into Bronx Science and been met with adulation; had gone from there to NYU on multiple scholarships, patrons verily shoving one another aside to give money to him; had at NYU launched a historically lucrative drug-dealing business; and had in quick succession failed out, OD'd, and gotten a record, because his girlfriend of the time, "in a moment of weakness," had called an ambulance on seeing him turn blue, instead of, as any right-thinking person would have, just walking him and dousing him with water until he revived. His downfall had been total. Stripped of his scholarships, thrown out of school, too disgusted with his girlfriend to forgive her for seeking assistance in saving his life, he had taken what remained to him and moved to the small town of Cortland, where he'd enrolled in community college. Coming among such humble comrades as he met there, most of whom had never set foot in Manhattan, and were dating their cousins and listening to the Allman Brothers Band and struggling valiantly and hopelessly to master the parts of the cell, had been the cure for Dutra's arrogance, Dutra arrogantly reminisced. He'd been thoroughly bored in community college, but careful, piling up his straight A's and his credits, and then he'd presented himself to the university as a diamond-in-the-rough transfer student from wee nearby Cortland as opposed to a prodigal from New York City, and been taken up joyously, and been there ever since.

So this was Dutra's third year in town, though his first as a graduate student in the School of Medicine. These contrasting conditions, of jaded veteran and innocent initiate, rendered Dutra my ideal if surprising companion. In his habitual controlling egotism he was happy to spend hours lecturing me as to where I should buy morning bagels, afternoon six-packs, late-night falafels; with whom I should bank; at what drugstore I could most cheaply purchase toothpaste; which bar had an acceptable pool table, jukebox, draft beer selection; what site of natural beauty among dozens in town was most congenial to drug use, al fresco sexual relations, a bonfire—I had not yet found one category of need, however mundane or abstruse, about which he lacked a bombastic opinion.

Yet at the same time as serving as sage, Dutra was boyishly thrilled about medical school. Without contradiction he both saw it as his due and cherished it as an astounding piece of luck. It merited his delight, a sentiment he generously extended to all other aspects of his new situation, myself included. Dutra possessed a wonderful capacity for alternating domineering, almost bullying speech with a listening so thorough, so rapturously attentive—eyes percolating with interest, clown grin by impossible increments gaining more width—that my paltry resistance that first night had been demolished well before he pulled off all my clothes. No detail, of his new world or mine, was too inconsequential. His orientation thus far had been unlike mine a genuinely harrowing ordeal of obstacle courses and scavenger hunts and overnight camping trips with insufficient equipment, yet he insisted on my full reciprocation. "So I'm exhausted. Too exhausted to talk," he concluded now while still sprawled in the hammock, after regaling me for perhaps an unbroken half hour, his arms and legs gesticulating and his bottle sometimes splashing beer that fell onto the porch with a slap. "Get the other six out of the fridge and tell me all about your *insane* day."

I was very worked up. The first meeting of one of my classes had been disrupted by protesting second-year students who accused the professor, an elderly white male novelist and Faulkner scholar from the South, of perpetuating racist/colonialist sentiment in his most recent book. "They were chanting 'Joseph Conrad, Joseph Conrad'!" I evoked, splashing beer of my own as I mimed a hand waving a sign. "Because, you know, of Conrad's Colonialist Agenda. So we're going to have an emergency meeting to decide if we should boycott his class, or stay and try to subvert it somehow from within."

"Can I ask a really idiotic question?" Dutra said, in a tone that suggested his question would reveal that all idiocy lay elsewhere. "With these people, is that name, Joseph Conrad, supposed to be an insult?"

"Well, yes!—obviously."

"But Joseph Conrad is a fabulous writer." It was the pat declaration of a nonscholar and nonwriter; even Dutra had his limits.

"I don't think they're talking about his writing so much as his politics. And the way his discourse perpetuates the status quo. The inequities in power between whites, who control the discourse, and nonwhites, who are controlled by it—"

"Who cares about his politics?" said Dutra, swinging out of the hammock.

"I think his politics are inseparable—"

"Oh, bullshit. Do you like his books or don't you?"

"Whose?"

"Joseph Conrad's."

Here was a question I hadn't expected. "I've only read *Heart of Darkness* but . . . I liked it," I acceded at last. This was just the sort of double admission Dutra seemed to extract as a matter of course.

"Do you like the other guy's books?"

"Whose? My professor's?"

"Exactly."

"I've never read them." Strike three.

Dutra burst out hysterically laughing. "No wonder you're confused!" he exclaimed, in the exaggeratedly bemused, tenderly condescending manner I'd already learned was his method of shifting the mood. He actually lowered his eyelids at me. Annoyed, I drained the last of my beer and threw the bottle at him, which he snatched deftly out of the air as he followed me into the house. "You don't have any empirical evidence," he went on, pinning me to the couch cushions after sweeping a jetsam of hardcover textbooks and bong components and record sleeves and the leavings of an interrupted penny-rolling project from the couch onto the floor. "You've never read the guy's books, let alone interacted with him— how could you expect yourself to know if he's racist or not?" But by now, with joint effort, we'd unpeeled my sundress from over my head, and freed one of my legs from my panties, and freed his erection, tumid purple and blue, interestingly bent, and logically corresponding in all other ways with his assemblage of outsize mobile characteristics, so that it no longer seemed necessary to make a reply.

Dutra's outsize self-confidence worked its influence on me in more ways than one. At that age I still believed in the malleability of personality, and could imagine myself more competent in fields about which I knew nothing, or more devil-may-care about such competence, than I actually was. Signing up for Nicholas Brodeur's seminar was the sort of thing Dutra, in an analogous situation, would have unhesitatingly done. First-year status in a room full of third- and fourth-years; perfect unfamiliarity with the material; and perhaps most significant, as it turned out, complete lack of aptitude for it, would have only spurred Dutra to lay hold of the qualifications as quickly as possible. And knowing him, within a month he would have learned Middle English and been competing with Brodeur for who had the most lines memorized. But I wasn't Dutra, a deficiency I already suspected.

I told myself Brodeur's beauty had nothing to do with the reason I had, on impulse, added his class as the fourth to an already-respectable roster of courses with no link at all to his Chansons of the Middle Ages. Yet the image of him in absurdly spiked hair and absurdly unseasonal duster was stamped in my mind. With the recent exception of Dutra, to this point my whole sexual history, which I flattered myself to consider quite epic, might have been represented on my tomb wall with a single hieroglyphic comprising the principal features of the Byronic type. All through college with instincts befitting a bloodhound I'd unearthed variations on this theme, boys with long hair and tormented, hooded eyes and a cramp in the wrist from the thick hardbound *Collected Journals of Kierkegaard* they insisted on carrying everywhere without the benefit of a backpack. They all tended to brood and weep thrillingly, they were as sexually suave as castrati, and they were perhaps all in love with one another, not me. But by some accident of my early environment I'd been raised on them, as a person might be raised on an unnourishing, bland home cuisine, and then want to eat nothing else. In Brodeur I'd recognized the paragon of my type. Yet at each visible point he so exceeded the prior examples, I suspected he might be a superior type altogether.

A premature autumn cold snap had blown in, enabling me to dress, with more effort than I'd devoted to most of my undergraduate courses, as a sort of Catwoman of Academe, in circulation-impeding high-heeled black leather boots, and black tights, and a painted-on black miniskirt, and an outsize black cowl-neck sweater on which the cowl gaped so carelessly open in front I required a black camisole. And so it was with thumping heart, clammy hands, and naked sternum that I entered the classroom to discover Brodeur no less transformed, in professorial camouflage of slightly geriatric rimless bifocals, a jacket of actual tweed which vindicated Casper, and utterly unremarkable, even cheap-looking khakis. His leonine mane had been artlessly flattened, as if he had slept in a hat. It was the khakis that most obsessed me. Were they self-consciously mundane and sexless, or unconsciously so? Then he'd stood up from the table to do something baffling and metric on the board, and I had seen that the pants had a horizontal rip high up on the right thigh. It was not recent, judging from the stringy unravelments, and it was wide enough to expose about an inch of the cuff of a pair of white boxers, gone humbly gray from the wash—and beneath this, if lost in shadow, a narrow swath of very pale, hairy, vulnerable skin. Not one of my classmates, all of them pale, slightly hunched, and dressed like elderly clerks or librarians, seemed to notice. Nor, I felt sure, had Brodeur. That fish-belly paleness of thigh was something even a libertine would have concealed. And so already on the very first day I'd encountered the odd contradiction, between the solemnly abstracted Brodeur of the classroom and the Brodeur of notoriety; between the hapless obliviousness advertised by that hole in his pants—like the plumber's ass-crack, like the festive toilet-paper banner waving out of the back of a woman's mis-tucked pantyhose—and the vandal's dark glasses and duster he'd worn at the reading, items one could almost think he had purposely, childishly picked to fulfill others' worst expectations.

No such perversity was evident in class. His pedagogic behavior was formal to the point of anachronism. He called us, unironically, by titles and last names, and we, who had immediately grown accustomed to calling all our other professors by their first names, as if we were truly their colleagues, called him only "Professor," or "Professor Brodeur." His greatness as a scholar, which no one disputed, here achieved preeminence. No other detail seemed to matter. Yet the purely intellectual awe in which he held us—and I include myself despite my bewilderment, for I too was entranced—gave a clue to that degraded persona of his wandering like a rogue in the world outside. For he cast his spell on us by reading aloud, and the way that he read thrummed with sex. He was an almost indecently riveting reader: husky, restrained, oddly sullen. He read like an actor displeased with his part, Brando muffing his lines in the unlikely hope he'd be fired. He maintained an affectation of unnecessarily tenting the text open in tense fingers and pretending to read off the page, but inevitably a surfeit of emotion would ejaculate via his hands, and the book would launch off through the air as he hotly spoke on; or if this didn't happen, coming back to himself at the end of the verse he would spank the text onto the table, as if slightly annoyed by our collective dry mouths and slack jaws.

But my classmates constituted a cabal of highly specialized persons, and once the spell was broken they piped up in an elaborate argot. Dowdy, studious, and translucent as they were they yet somehow held the keys to these cloistered proceedings. Perhaps sex was so little a habit with them they did not even credit it as a distraction. Whatever the case, I was totally out of my depth, more and more with each class I attended. I never spoke, and my silence was increasingly mortifying. Why had I been so stupid as to forget that he also did lectures? This term he was teaching two titanic undergraduate surveys, Shakespeare and Chaucer, from within the anonymous hundreds of either of which I could have gaped at him undetected. Each time he stopped reading to us and asked for discussion I counted the minutes until I could plausibly leave for the bathroom, a remote destination to which even a perfunctory visit would take fifteen minutes. All the women's bathrooms on campus had been grudgingly crammed into unvalued spaces, like former broom closets or the triangles under staircases, sometime in the mid-1970s, in a belated acknowledgment of coeducation, and the one for the English department was interred in the basement, reached by a claustrophobic subterranean passage that had only been meant by the hall's architects to give access to the heating pipes running the length of the ceiling. But despite its obscure situation the bathroom was a nodal point, heavily used for the whole range of female purposes, hygienic and otherwise. No sooner had I settled down onto the bowl than I read, at eye level, BRODEUR IS A HARASSER, HARASSER crossed out and revised—by the same hand?—to RAPIST.

It oddly seemed to confirm my impurity more than Brodeur's. Of course I had come to his class out of prurience. Whatever sort of criminal he might also be, he was committed to his field. I was not; not once in my life had I given a thought to medieval chansons. I was a prurient fraud; unself-consciously slumped on the toilet, I could see myself clearly and feel calm resolve.

The weather at the brink of October had reverted to the stillness and heat of an Indian summer, and it felt apt that on what turned out to be my last day in his class, I'd been obliged to forgo my Catwoman costume and reveal my true self, in a juvenile sundress and sandals. Emerging from the suffocating basement the palatial first floor gave relief, with its long colonnade, in the shadows of which it was cold as a cave, but ascending back up the staircase I rose into the blanket of heat as if into a cloud layer. Down the length of the hall I could hear him, enthralling with his voice; this would be the last time. Slipping back in the room I left the door standing open, as it always remained. He had made this preference clear the first day, when one of the translucents, hurrying in moments after Brodeur took his seat, reflexively pulled the door shut in his wake and was told: "Leave it open, Ted, won't you." In subsequent classes, if someone forgot, he walked over and stood it wide open himself. Was this in response to some past accusation? Professor, or students, reciting unclothed?

I'd tried to return to my chair without making a sound, yet he glanced sharply at me, and then I realized that his gaze had been drawn by a movement outside in the hall. I turned in time to see a very fair, slender woman come into the frame of the doorway; she must have been climbing the stairs just behind me. Without pausing she threw a look at Brodeur that seemed to land on him like a grenade. Then she passed out of sight. His voice, which I'd never heard falter before, died off as if by the flip of a switch. In a beat he resumed, but a little past where he had been.

A few moments later I saw her again, out the classroom windows, passing by on the sidewalk below. Very straight, lank blond hair the confusing color of drenched straw, both dark and pale. Her face a portrait from Wyeth. Her carriage was so narrow and erect, her arms and legs so finely jointed and long, she looked something like an egret stalking past, except for being massively pregnant, so pregnant the prow of her belly seemed to part the air some two feet ahead of the rest of her. She was wearing black leggings and some sort of cheap black cotton slippers, and a white tank top, riding up at the waist, and over it a white Oxford, unbuttoned, the overlong sleeves making donuts where she'd rolled them to her elbows.

She was impressive in that way that preempts every other impression. I had no idea who or what she might be. Her appearance at Brodeur's door, his discomposure, did not serve as clues. Inexplicable apparitions by their nature can appear anywhere, and leave all their witnesses oddly unsettled, and so my unease felt in some way inevitable.

It was unbearably hot in the classroom. The remainder of class oozed away without my even discerning what page we were on. When I heard the translucents shuffling their texts into their arms and departing I looked up and found myself alone with Brodeur, who was fully recovered and even humming an air to himself as he packed his books and papers forcefully and haphazardly into the hard-used, tattered Danish cloth schoolbag—the national flag was embroidered at postage-stamp scale on the inner but now exposed flap—which had lately replaced his far sturdier calfskin briefcase. "Can I meet with you a moment?" I asked, and for the first time he bent that avidly inquisitive, almost delighted gaze on me that subsequently I would so often see.

"Absolutely," he said.

His office was on the fourth, highest floor, almost directly above his classroom. This uppermost floor of the building was all professors' offices, almost every door tricked out, like undergraduates' bulletin boards, for optimal worldview projection. Esoteric photos and postcards and laser-printed sheets bearing grandiose or sarcastic quotations wafted slightly with disturbance as we passed, except for where doors were propped open, and conferences in progress. Then I would hear voices briefly die off, and feel a surreptitious gaze catch at us as we flashed past the door frame. Who knew if my flat hippie sandals and voluminous cotton sundress marked me as less, or even more, quintessentially Brodeur's latest victim. The heat had accumulated with greatest intensity here, captured under the eaves, and in the course of our short, silent transit the contours of my body hidden in my tent of a sundress were streaming with sweat. I kept swiping my hair, which in a gesture toward womanliness I'd worn loose, behind my ears, until just as we came to a halt I gave up and made it into a ponytail with a hair elastic I'd had on my wrist. He rooted at such length in the ratty schoolbag for his key that I had time to wonder if he'd only just moved to this office, for this door compared to the others was almost vacant. Only a postcard reproduction of some severe lunar scene, containing neither humans nor flora nor fauna, was taped in splendid isolation at my standing eye level, the placement recalling that bathroom graffito.

"Caspar David Friedrich," he said as he unlocked the door. "*Das Eismeer.* I adore it." Then I felt I should look more closely, and only realized too late that so long as I did he would not yet push open the door, so that for a moment we stood slightly too close together, our twin gazes hung from the postcard's fulcrum as if weighed in its scales.

"What does that mean?" I asked, to say something.

" 'Sea of Ice.' You don't speak any German."

"No—*oh*," I blurted without meaning to, and then the heat of his smiling gaze pressed on my cheek.

"You've just seen the picture," he said.

I hadn't realized the scale. There were slabs of ice piled on each other I had thought were the size of flagstones, and forming a peak, like a bull-dozed sidewalk. But now I saw the peak was of Matterhorn height, for there, cast off barely noticeably to one side like a shoe lost in snow by a drunk, was the keel of a ship.

"It makes one feel small," he said—or asked, studying me.

"I've had nightmares like this." In fact the nightmares involved not behemoths of nature but impossible buildings—cathedrals like Martian volcanoes rearing miles up into the clouds—but the terror and awe were the same. This was not something I'd ever told anyone, or even something I'd thought about much, apart from in the sweaty bewilderment just upon waking.

"He'd have been pleased that you said that." Now the door swung fully open, and I stepped in the room, made to go before him by a hand briefly steering the small of my back. Here was another vertiginous arctic expanse. The desk was almost bare. Only a jointed lamp and some rocks sat upon it. The desk was a slab of fine-grained, silken-seeming blond wood which perhaps from the lingering spell of the painting evoked in my mind a lichen- and wildflower-dotted tundra where such slabs of blond wood certainly did not grow. The lamp was tarnished chrome and might have served a Victorian dentist in a previous life. The rocks were pink granite worn to the smoothness of eggs. Behind the desk, and an unmatching oak swivel chair, lined up along his windowsill were some little glossy dingy-colored things. He had piloted me with that feather-light touch into a leather club chair that sat facing the desk, but then he spent such a protracted moment out of sight behind my back, apparently grappling with a rubber doorstop to prop open the door, that the whole business of ensuring unfurtive exposure began to feel in itself covertly, preparatorily sexual.

"That was rather stupid what I said about German," he said from behind me. "I was thinking of your name, but there's no reason an American Regina Gottlieb should speak German any more than she ought to speak Sanskrit."

"My father's parents were German," I offered. "But I never knew them."

"And your mother?" with some determined door rattling, still behind me somewhere on the floor.

"Not German. She's Asian."

"Ah. That explains your happy lack of Germanic appearance." At last he stood, his innocence—or his guilt?—secured by the doorstop, and came around the far side of the desk. "My God, it's hot." He now began grappling with the window. He still hadn't asked what I wanted.

"What are those?" I asked as he moved them to get at the sash.

"Inuit carvings. From whale's teeth." He stopped what he was doing to gather them into his palm, then leaned over the desk and transferred them to me, both of us cupping our hands edge to edge in the process, as if we held something alive. Then he turned back to the sealed window and I sat back in the club chair and studied the animal figures more closely than their simplified forms warranted. I was probably blushing. When the window gave way and slid up with a loud smacking sound, the influx of air from outside felt like snow on my cheeks.

"No, I don't speak Sanskrit either. These are beautiful," I added, chasing all conversational threads.

"Aren't they? I want to say they're so pure, but I'm sure that will sound both simplistic and somehow condescending, which will fall very wide of how I feel about them."

"I should probably say why I'm here."

"No rush. I'm very glad to hear your voice. Today is the first time you've used it." I must have visibly faltered at this because he added, "I'm sorry. I've made you self-conscious."

"No, it's true. I'm really out of my depth in your class. I've never taken a single prerequisite. I'm just not qualified."

"Is that all it is? What a relief. I've been afraid it was something much worse."

"That I'm brain-dead? Or amnesiac?"

"I suspected your brain was quite sound. I thought you might be a spy of some kind."

"Sent by your enemies, to monitor you."

He grinned delightedly. "Given that you're not a spy, it's very rude of me to bore you with such stupid conceits. Tell me what you would like to discuss. Though I'm afraid that it's dropping my class."

"It is, but it has nothing to do with you. I just don't know what's going on."

"There's no reason you should. Everyone else in the class is a sorry specialist like me. They've been doing nothing else day in and day out for the past half a decade but reading this stuff. It's not your specialism, happily, because you have yet to select one. When you do, what do you think it might be?"

I hesitated. In college, my interests had always seemed so clear, but in graduate school the unit of measure had switched abruptly, as if from the yard to the pica, and every effort I made to describe what my specialism was sounded dopily broad. "Well, I'm pretty sure my century is the twentieth," I began carefully. "Before nineteen hundred I'm clueless."

"I doubt that, but I also suspect that your exceptional intelligence more than your prior education is what got you into this program. Just because you've taken only twentieth-century literature to this point doesn't limit you to one century's compass. It's clear to me you can wander wherever you choose."

All this time I had been worrying his whale-tooth menagerie in one palm and now I took a moment to set the pieces on the desktop in order to conceal my pleasure at his compliment. "I don't think you have much of a basis on which to credit me with exceptional intelligence," I said. The more seriously we spoke, it seemed, the more flirtatious we were.

"Please don't impugn *my* intelligence." Then as if he knew this was too much he added, "I was on the admissions committee. So I've read your transcripts and yes, they don't suggest much knowledge of my subject, or any subject, perhaps, dating from prior to the First World War."

"More like the Vietnam War," I put in heartily, to cover how his observation chagrined me.

"But I've also read your essays," he went on, cutting short my disparagement, "and they have all the scope that your transcript might lack. They're terrific."

"Thank you," I managed at last.

"Don't take this question as a chiding at all. Take it just at face value. Given that it's far from entry-level, and far from what seem like your realms of interest, what were you hoping to get, signing up for my class?"

I couldn't say "you" or "a moment like this," gather my things, and depart, though that would have been elegant. It also would have saved me much subsequent grief. Instead I heard myself saying, "In college I never read any of the classics, because everyone else that I met had read them in high school, in their elite private high schools, and dismissed them as very uncool. So I dismissed them also, although where I went to high school none of that was assigned and so I never learned it. Which meant that in college as well I never learned it, because I wanted to seem like I already knew it. It's like studying art—you have to do life drawing first before you get to ditch that and just do abstraction. I went straight to abstraction and I've been faking the rest ever since. I've never even read Dickens, or Austen, or Brontë."

"The fun stuff."

"I've started to think that it would have been fun. I pretend that I've read them. I fake it."

"What *did* you read?"

"A lot of psychoanalytic and poststructuralist theory."

"Oh, God! And you understood that?"

I laughed. "I thought so, but maybe all that was faking as well."

My confessions seemed to fill him with admiration. "I always envied and feared such as you in my own school days. Those with nothing but brilliance. Could land on their feet anywhere. I was one of those others you might have envied, if wrongly. Elite private schools, private tutors, and an old-fashioned whack on the ass when you made a mistake. All I had on my side was a tendency toward fearful obedience and a trainable memory. Not like you. Waltzing out of college summa cum laude—remember, I've read your transcript—and as yet you've read practically nothing. I'm terrified what you'll become once you've actually stuck your nose into the books."

"It's nice of you to call my ignorance an asset."

"False modesty doesn't become you. Nor does hyperbole. You're hardly ignorant, you're just not well read. I can help you with that, and in turn you can do me the much greater favor. How's your Chaucer?"

"Nonexistent."

"Perfect. Unimagined delight awaits you. I don't suppose you know Sasha Weill? She was supposed to have been my other Chaucer TA but her plans unexpectedly changed. You'll have four sections, one meeting of each every week, and an avalanche of papers at the end, but I'll teach you the secret of speed grading, for which you will ever be grateful to me."

"This sounds suspiciously like a work-study job, but I've already got one. And there's a rule against holding two."

"What is it, coediting *Tempus Fugit*?" This was the literature quarterly the university published, and with which it occupied all first-year English students. In the forthcoming Winter issue I would appear on the masthead, for which honor, not to mention the stipend I lived on, I was supposed to sit in the *Tempus* office at least six hours a week. "I can reassign you easily," he was saying. "You will not lose your stipend, and you'll be spared the corrosive effects of an editing job on your mind."

"It's not really an editing job—"

"I hope you'll never waste your energy buffing up someone else's poor writing," he interrupted me again, and again I caught a glimpse of the imperiousness that was the flip side of his apparent humility, and to which I admittedly thrilled. "It doesn't only take time from your own work, it hurts your work actively. It infects it with a viral mediocrity. Much better that you should spend your spare time reading Chaucer. You'll still have the students' mediocre papers to guard yourself from, but they'll prey on a less crucial bit of your brain."

"I don't know a thing about Chaucer," I reiterated as a final, if pro forma, protest, though from beneath my damp sundress, my heart telegraphed its excitement. He knew I knew nothing, and still wanted me. By the end I'd know *something*—I vowed it.

"You need only read him." He had gone into a drawer of his desk and for a moment I caught sight of mashed haystacks of paper, like the inside of his Danish schoolbag, before the drawer was shoved shut. He passed a few stapled pages to me, his Chaucer syllabus. "You see I'm presuming consent. Reassure me." He waited so seriously for my answer I felt a finger of pleasure slide down my midline, and so was conscious of seeming as chaste as I could when I spoke.

"I'd love to. Thank you. But I'm nervous. I'll be out of my depth in a whole different way."

"I promise you won't. And as I said, you'll be doing me the greater favor. Since Sasha bowed out it's only been myself and my superlative student Laurence Pumbleton—do you know him?—and Laurence has a baby at home, and soon I will as well."

The penny had dropped. The woman who'd passed by his doorway and tossed the grenade of her gaze at his face—this was his wife, prospective mother of his child. I tried to hide my flusterment by laughing, with too much energy. "You might find me better suited to babysitting than teaching Chaucer," I said. "When is your baby due? And I should say congratulations."

"You're very kind. My firstborn is due in mere moments it seems. Meanwhile Chaucer: the lectures are Thursdays at three. Read this week's tale first and then start from the top and catch up with as much as you can. I'll have Laurence tell you the rest as he understands all of it better than me."

"I'm sure that's not true."

"Oh, it's true, and it will be true of you before long."

There was physical comedy as we ended our meeting. He came out from behind the monumental desk, and I rose from the chair, and then we were left sharing the little square of floor space in front of the door so that contact seemed called for and yet none was appropriate. It would have made no more sense to shake hands than to kiss. And so we hovered a moment too close to each other before I was able to sidle myself just athwart the threshold. Then with one of my feet planted in the hallway I think we both felt a danger had passed, in the same way that, with my dizzying transformation in minutes from dependent pupil to dependable colleague, another and far greater danger had passed. The evocation of his forthcoming baby seemed to ratify this.

Uterine Dystopias: The Legacy of Dora; Pynchon and Postmodernism; Fetishes and Freaks: Strategies of Queering the Gothic; never could I have imagined, filling out my registration at the start of the fall, how quickly these interesting courses could take on the appearance of make-work, of the false tasks of investigation and organization that parents invent to keep small children busy. Only Chaucer seemed to have any substance. His writing felt particularly hard and elemental, like a lump of coal or a potato, a thing of obvious use grubbed up out of the ground. The same afternoon I had met with Brodeur I'd started working through *The Canterbury Tales*, and right away had felt the thrill of mastery, perhaps because having known nothing, I actually doubled my expertise with each couplet I painstakingly muddled out.

"Of course he didn't mean you should catch up with all of the reading before your first day," Laurence Pumbleton said to me now. "Or he probably did, but you don't really have to. Ignore him."

"But I've never read any at all. And I'm coming in late. If the class wasn't so huge and so popular I might be less worried."

"You have nothing to worry about. Each week you'll sit in his lecture the same as they do. I guarantee that's all you'll need. In section you go over his lecture at a remedial pace and you force them to make little comments. You'll be wonderful." Tilting his head back he poured in his mouth the whole contents of the second of two dainty and conical glasses that had been sitting on the table before him, with a last shake to dislodge the olive.

After calling and arranging our meeting Laurence had picked me up in a cream-colored two-seat Alfa Romeo convertible and driven me, as if I'd been Grace Kelly on the coast of Amalfi, to a nearly defunct ski resort on the Tompkinsville Road half an hour outside town. The place seemed neglected for reasons beyond the still-warm autumn weather. Perhaps fifty years earlier the small glacial escarpment in the shadow of which it was built had won acceptance from area farmers as an Alpine landscape, but now the Swiss-chalet style of the buildings only poignantly reemphasized their inadequacies. In the dining room nonfunctioning cuckoo clocks crowded the faux-split-log walls, and a faded motif of red hearts was melancholically repeated on the dingy white curtains and the dingy white lace tablecloths. Where there were not cuckoo clocks there were antlers, or elaborate beer steins with hinged pewter lids. No music played. The scattered other patrons sat hunched over wide plates of shingle-stacked meats overwhelmed by a viscous brown sauce. At noon, not one other table had drinks, but the taciturn woman in a dream-catcher T-shirt and Nikes who apparently served as host, waiter, and bartender had shown no surprise when Laurence, declining the menu, ordered us four gin martinis with olives. Laurence was arrestingly suave, in the Jimmy Stewart mold; his very lack of handsomeness seemed to burnish his charm and make him that much more handsome. He was taller than the average tall man and even so his long, spidery limbs were out of proportion to his exaggerated height, so that his arms and legs seemed to have extra joints, as with expensive umbrellas. His mode of dress, Brooks Brothers everything, was rigorously perfect down to woven leather belt and cuff links. On top he was going bald in an unusual pattern, like a monk's tonsure with decorative fringe. He had a wide gap between his front teeth amid features that were otherwise slightly too narrow. But his close-set eyes were mobile and penetrating, and he was so coordinated in his subtle attentions, holding doors and hanging coats and arranging cocktails and ashtrays with supernumerous, dexterous limbs, and, in sum, he possessed so much more than most men now alive of that intangible, old-fashioned thing we still call chivalry that I had not been at all surprised to learn that his wife was a former beauty queen from Shiraz whom he had met at the Chanel counter at Bergdorf Goodman and swept away to connubial bliss in the space of two weeks.

"There's an expectation that the teaching assistant has *some* expertise in the subject," I persisted.

"The expectation is enough all by itself. I guarantee you, Regina, even if you never read one page of Chaucer and even if you skip every one of the lectures you'll do beautifully because they invest you with all your authority. Just relax and accept it. But you should at least go to the lectures, for your own enjoyment. He's so good. It's why they sign up in hordes."

"Up to this week I was taking his seminar."

"Oh, no, in seminar he's terrible. He's so mumbly and turgid. It's excruciating. All his stage fright comes back in small rooms."

"His stage fright?" I exclaimed.

"Nicholas Brodeur is the shyest, most socially awkward, just-barely-cured-of-stammering human you will meet in your life. No, absolute truth," he cut short my amazement. "I mean, beyond what you're thinking. Special classes for half his childhood—they thought he was retarded! That's where the memorization comes from. They found if he memorized things he could say them straight through." Our second double round of cocktails arrived. "They're so lovely because she pours them so small," Laurence said, draining the first of his second pair, meaning his third overall—I was still nursing the dregs of my second but I was already substantially drunk.

"He alluded to that. To doing poorly in school and getting—whacked, he said."

"I can only imagine. Vicious narrow parents with prosaic ambitions. They really thought he was quite a dim bulb. And then of course there are the other endearing peculiarities, not of mind, of course. More on the side of emotion."

"Peculiar in what way?"

But Laurence had mislaid the thread. "Isn't this place wonderful?" he exulted.

"I'm so glad you brought me. I never would have found it."

"That's the idea. That's the *idea*. That others not find it. Not you. You merit it fully." Laurence had first dined here the previous winter, when during the meal a freak blizzard had blown in and trapped him and his wife and their then-newborn child, by that hour the only customers left. "They went up and prepared us a room—I don't think the hotel at this place has been open since the Vietnam War. And they slept here themselves—by this time they had to—and the next morning cooked us the most magnificent breakfast of eggs and kielbasa. Then we all drank Chartreuse and pear brandy for hours while we waited for snowplows to come. By the time the roads were open Sahba and the cook were weeping on each other's necks they had grown so attached. I'm telling my colleague Regina about the time we took up residence," Laurence unexpectedly said to the taciturn waitress, who unseen by me had drawn near in the course of the story.

"That was a hell of a night," she agreed.

"Carole, meet Regina. She's teaching with me. Regina, Carole here, as you have already learned, is a superlative hostess, and also she is married to Claude. It's their place. It was Claude, along with Marcus the waiter, who took mercy on Sahba and Bebi and me. Of course, you enjoy having us indebted," he play-scolded Carole, who now chuckled and blushed and pshawed.

Before she brought the check they talked awhile, mostly about nearby roadwork—Laurence lived just a few miles away—and her friendliness increased so much compared with at the time of our arrival that once we had paid and were back in the car, I made a comment about it. Laurence said, "She was afraid you were my bit on the side. And then hearing me talk about Sahba, she grew reassured."

It was just what I'd sensed, though I wouldn't have said it so bluntly.

"Don't think I have any such history," Laurence went on, as if reading my mind. "I'm almost comically irreproachable. In fact, among our colleagues it is thought comical."

"What is?"

"Being happily married."

My last night before Chaucer I splashed through *The Canterbury Tales* until the lines loosed their moorings and swam off the page. I crossly refused Dutra's numerous offers of dope, and awoke from a far too brief sleep with fatigue circles under my eyes. But as the hall began to throng with earnest, shambling students hurrying up the aisles, actually seating themselves on the floor in the front of the very front row, the better to gape at their dangerous idol, their arms hugging their knees, their brightly colored hoodies flopping from their waists where they'd belted them on by the sleeves because the hall was too hot—Were they actually college-age students? Had I really been one such, just one year ago?—I felt my anxiety lifting away. With cool professional absorption I conferred with Brodeur and Laurence about copied handouts, standing so near Brodeur's corduroy-jacketed shoulder I could feel his warmth meeting my own. I returned his concise nod of greeting with same, exulting within that he already took me for granted. When he left us, broke away to brood a moment Olivier-like in the lee of the podium before launching on his performance, I felt spotlighted also, Laurence's height, beside me, adding yet more conspicuousness. I too was an object of rapt expectation, pinioned by a thousand young eyes.

Once Laurence and I, like the royal attendants, had seated ourselves in our reserved front-row seats, I was free to devour the lecture, and I feasted on it as the lightning rod feasts on the lightning. Laurence had been right about Brodeur's seminar manner as opposed to his lectures. The man who had held me entranced in the classroom was like this man's fuzzy impostor. Glancing back once, at the mammoth composite half-shell of five hundred identical faces, boys and girls alike with lips parted and feverish eyes, I understood that whatever his sexual conduct, it could never guarantee his sexual reputation—that was subject to forces outside his control. Yet my own sexual interest in him was transposed to sublime incorporeal realms. I could hardly credit the schoolgirl crush I'd felt on first seeing him—as if that man in the vandal's sunglasses had been his own shadow on Plato's cave wall, and myself a poor, silly cave dweller, who had now emerged into the light.

My legitimate feeling took one other form. My style of dress changed, and not just by contrast with the way I had dressed for Brodeur while his student. I had always been as partial to skirts as to jeans; to tall boots as to sneakers; to floral prints, and dangling pendants, and earrings. But now I found myself going to lecture in sober, androgynous clothes. I seemed to want to imply I was just coming from or about to embark on some nonintellectual, macho diversion, so that, for example, I wore black jeans and black V-neck sweaters with a French boating shirt underneath, or a gigantic plaid work shirt of Dutra's with Timberland boots, or a gigantic Irish sweater of Dutra's with wool hiking pants thick with pockets for trail maps and wilderness tools. One morning I found I was wearing a pair of OshKosh overalls I had inherited from an old boyfriend and never previously worn unless painting a house. My hair grew out shaggily from its most recent cut and was left to its own devices so that it often floated strangely in sections from the static of a black knit watch cap.

In late October Brodeur's child was born. I learned of it only when, after lecture one day, Laurence handed Brodeur a slim, flat, pale blue Tiffany box bound lengthwise by a white satin ribbon. Brodeur took it onto his hand as if it were a potentially dangerous creature, a snake or a bird. He seemed not to know what to do.

"A minor congratulatory token, with much love from Sahba and Bebi and me," Laurence gently encouraged. "You can open it now if you like."

Within was a small silver spoon, the end of its handle enlarged in the shape of an apple. The two rounded ends, spoon and apple, gleamed like moons. On the back was engraved in impossibly small yet entirely legible cursive *Joachim Hallett-Brodeur 27 October 1992.*

Brodeur appeared dumbstruck.

"It's beautiful, Laurence," I said to dispel the silence. I felt chagrined for not having a gift of my own, and, what was worse, for not even having remembered the baby was due. But Brodeur, since the day in his office, had not mentioned it.

Now he finally spoke. "This is lovely, Laurence," he said, and I saw he was moved.

"My best to Martha," Laurence continued. "Let us know when you're ready to have people over. We're dying to meet Joachim. Sahba's over the moon." I had so little experience of the sort of indispensable consideration that Laurence now was performing—saluting a dear friend's first child's arrival: what greater pleasure or privilege was there?—that I felt overwhelmed with admiration for Laurence, and hamstrung by my own awkwardness. But so was Brodeur. As if he could not escape the contemplation of his happiness quickly enough, he gave Laurence's hand a rough shake and left us, the white satin ribbon, lost in the transition, floating onto the floor in his wake.

"Poor Nicholas," Laurence, uninjured, said after a moment. "Want to get a quick drink?"

In our usual postlecture place we had our choice of the outsize wood booths, each deep pew of which would hold six or eight drunk undergraduates later this evening as they guzzled Budweiser from pitchers and pored over a century's inane obscenities for some overlooked square inch or two they might claim as their own with the end of a Swiss Army knife. But at five-thirty the faux medieval mess hall was entirely the province of fatigued, poorly dressed graduate students and the occasional youthful professor. Martha: so this was her name. I turned it over in my mind as we carried our pitcher and steins to the farthest-off, neighborless booth. It didn't dent with astonishment, but it rumpled her smooth anonymity, gave her a texture I hadn't expected. "Poor Nicholas why?" I prompted as soon as we sat. Only when Laurence and I were together did I call Brodeur "Nicholas," each time enjoying a transgressive frisson, under cover of Laurence's entitlement, on the basis of their actual friendship.

"I didn't mean anything by it. Just that he's overwhelmed, as who isn't by having a baby. It's overwhelming, of course. The brand-new and unprecedented being confirming one's mortality and one's immortality at the same time. Of course when they're so wee and helpless you can spend all your time having existential crises of one kind or another. Once they start to talk to you and show their personalities you forget all about it."

His shift from the specific to the general failed to throw me off the scent of his comment. "But you think he's unhappy," I said.

"Unhappy! No. No, he wanted this child very much. I think more than she did." Ah, he'd done it again—it was as if I could see his mind, kicking itself.

"And she didn't? Martha," I added, for the interest of speaking her name.

Laurence's endearing tendency toward inadvertent gossip was very poorly matched with me, as I abetted it whenever I could, despite knowing—or perhaps because of knowing—that he constantly struggled to bring it under the dominance of his better—his beneficent, discreet, chivalrous—self. I liked that self of his perfectly well, but no more than I liked the other, which was gossipy and alert to weakness, which did not suffer fools, and which when it disliked anyone, disliked them to the point of contempt. If not for this dark side of Laurence I doubt we would ever have gotten along.

"Perhaps she did," he allowed, "with an effort of will that could render irrelevant whether she didn't."

"Laurence, you're speaking in koans," I complained, which made him laugh but not further explain. "Things weren't going well between them last year," I tried, probing for sharper outlines, for as I'd told Brodeur myself, I had always had the gift of faking greater expertise in a subject than I actually possessed. "What with the accusation against him."

"Actually, that might have made things somewhat better, at least for a while. Had any of it been true it might have been better yet."

"That doesn't make any sense."

"It might have leveled the playing field. Made her less sure of him. It's Sahba's theory, based on no information, that Martha married Nicholas because she thought he was a great deal more wicked. She believed all the hype."

"And she would *want* him to be wicked? That's not the usual reason for marriage," I said, with an awareness of my own hypocrisy. Hadn't I thrilled to that seemingly sinister man in the long duster coat? Though what I'd wanted from him wasn't marriage.

"Remember, all this is Sahba's fantastical vision. It's not based on anything real. Sahba is the kindest, most generous-hearted of women, but she just doesn't get on with Martha."

"Why not?"

"She thinks Martha condescends to her. Perhaps Martha does. I actually greatly like Martha, except for the fact that she wrecks the composure of these two people I'm so hugely fond of, my wife, and her husband." And that was all I could get out of Laurence that day on the interesting subject. But it was not very long afterward that I saw her again.

The Indian summer had held halfway into November, undeterred by the decorative pumpkins all over the town, and then even by the decorative turkeys—but the night Dutra and I threw a party, on no better pretext than that it was warm, the temperature plunged more than twenty degrees some time after I passed out and just before dawn. Now the sky gleamed coldly, scoured of haze; and the trees were simply flinging their leaves to the ground to catch up with the lonely red flags of the sugar maples; and it was, perhaps, the last opportunity for certain seasonal pleasures until the great wheel revolved once again!—"Meaning," Dutra loudly intruded into the hungover fug of my sleep, "two words: coffee-iced coffee."

"Please don't talk," I implored him, for I'd had an extremely good time at our party. "And that's three words, not two."

"Coffee-iced is hyphenated, to qualify coffee. It's a compound word. The second 'coffee' is the second word: Coffee-iced coffee."

"Please get out of my room," I scraped out, with more force.

"It's an amazing day! This is this town's *quintessential* day. Autumn, baby. Better late than never." And what better day to partake of the coffee-iced coffee, Dutra argued, given how badly damaged we were? Of course Dutra didn't seem damaged at all. He was not merely wide-awake and voluble and mintily brushed but extensively clean—I could smell the fumes of Dial and Prell, his no-nonsense self-disinfectants, wafting off his damp flesh. Bustling like a nurse he raised my blinds, ushering yet more hostile light into my room so that I saw now, on the insides of my eyes, livid branches of blood. After some vigorous scraping and straining my window came open and a cold current entered, bringing a faint scent of pine trees and mud and wet rocks—the secret breath of the town that I sometimes discerned late at night, sitting out on the porch while Dutra busied himself with his bong.

"*Ahhh*," Dutra said in gratification. "C'mon, Ginny. Hustle or I'll spank you."

I throttled my pillow as if it was him. "Who's still here?"

"Only your ridiculous new boyfriend Manny."

Manny was not remotely or even potentially my new boyfriend, although he had, during the night, wrapped his arms around my waist and dropped his face in my lap and mumbled incoherent confessions while we sat dizzily on the porch. This intimacy, touching if obscure, had lasted until he abruptly thrust me from him and ran up the stairs to the single bathroom, where after locking the door he had resumed the same position in relation to the toilet, refusing to surrender his hold for the rest of the night, so that our guests, from then on, had relieved themselves on our back lawn.

"Is he still in the bathroom?"

"I was amazed to discover this morning that he was not in the bathroom or even here in your bed, but facedown in the hammock. He's breathing."

I ignored the jibe about my bed except to turn it back on him. "What about your new girlfriend? Where's she?"

"I felt so bad! I've never seen anyone blushing so much. You know I didn't even lie on the mattress with her, I slept on the floor, and then around sunrise I heard something crash in the kitchen and went down and she was standing there, all petrified, hugging her blender the same way you're hugging your pillow. I was like, 'How are you feeling this morning?' and whoosh, her face goes as red as a beet and she just keeps hugging on to the blender like I might try to take it, and runs out the door." Arms clutched to his chest, Dutra mimed desperate, hunkered-down flight. "Next time you see her make sure that you tell her I never touched her, except to put her to bed." The night before, the woman we were discussing had suddenly fainted—had been standing and talking to someone, when all at once her feet flew up and out and her rear struck the floor. I had been in the next room but had seen the whole mishap enacted by the woman's crisp shadow thrown onto the wall by one of Dutra's clip lamps. First head up and feet down, then—*whee!*—feet up and head down. It had looked like an antic performance, except that, in landing, the woman's brassiere somehow caught, through her shirt, onto the latch of one of Dutra's military-issue gun trunks, in which he stored his

LPs. The latch must have gouged her, yet the woman continued to hang like a rag doll, unconscious. Before I could press through our dismayed, milling guests, Dutra had deftly unhooked her and lifted her floppy length into his arms.

"I don't know her," I said now. "It was so odd that she brought her own blender."

"It was sweet! We don't have one."

"But she didn't *know* we don't have one. And we didn't need one. It never even got used."

"No, it did. She made margaritas. You don't remember when she made the margaritas?"

"She *did*?"

Dutra drove a very old, very damaged Volvo sedan the color of calamine lotion where it wasn't afflicted by rust. The car was so barely distinguishable from the countless other aged, rusted, neutral-toned Volvo sedans living out their last days in that town it might have been part of a utopian experiment of ubiquitous, ownerless cars, as with bicycles in some parts of Europe and indeed even here, in the seventies, when the university had apparently paid for a fleet of bicycles for public use on the campus, all of which had wound up within just a few days abandoned at the base of the hill. Such socialistic ideas were nevertheless still in brisk circulation. For example at the farmers' market, where a sort of scrip was accepted that encouraged a barter economy, though who handed it out, and in exchange for what service or object, even Dutra had never determined. Leaving inanimate Manny we drove to the parking lot next to the lake, where the market was held every nonwinter weekend, and was as much a carnival and outpatient clinic for the acutely hungover as it was a real market, although the produce shoppers piously browsed, French-style string bags hung over their shoulders, amid the jug and washboard musicians and the flax muffin vendors and the overflowing crates of tumbling kittens and puppies offered up for adoption by the SPCA. Dutra and I being among the acutely hungover concerned ourselves only with coffee-iced coffee, another of Dutra's discoveries about which he held forth as if he'd been the man who invented caffeine. The coffee-iced coffee was ice-cold espresso poured over ice cubes of frozen espresso and served in ten-ounce paper cups. As Dutra would never grow tired of remarking, it grew stronger the more the ice melted. We sat with our coffees on an unused vendors' table just outside the pedestrian flow, shoulder to shoulder for warmth. Now that the weather was finally right for the season we were underdressed for it, and particularly here by the lake, we were quaking with cold. The coffee-iced coffee vendor had affirmed this was the last day this year he would sell it. "Next week it's hot cider and cocoa. Until then you're gonna have to find some other way to keep warm," this last said with a wink. Of course anyone seeing us here on a Saturday morning, seamed together from shoulders to feet and with wet hair and twin coffee cups, would assume we were lovers. But in fact I'd stopped sleeping with Dutra the previous month, once I realized he'd somehow transformed, from an attractively provocative stranger to an actual friend. I'd worried the transition would be difficult, but the most difficult thing had been getting myself my own mattress, and so of course Dutra had done it, driving me in the Volvo to the department store in Syracuse and roping the mattress himself to the roof of the car. His matter-of-factness about it had made me love him, if not in the way that would have us keep sharing a bed.

An old-fashioned silver-wheeled pram had been making its way through the milling foot traffic, and now I realized the same woman was pushing it forward as I'd seen on that day outside Brodeur's classroom. It was Martha Hallett. Even before she approached very near, and came to a halt just a few yards away, standing revealed and obscured constantly by the traffic of shoppers, I had no doubt at all who she was, despite how transformed she appeared, not just by my knowledge of her but by the change in her body. She was radically distilled, as if she'd been somehow unsheathed from herself and buffed free of a layer of fingerprint grime. The bright luster of her straw-colored hair was restored, though despite this she had pulled the hair into a small bristly knot at the nape of her neck. Her pram was dowdy, it seemed deliberately so. Her clothes were a man's: a dishwater-gray unraveling sweater, a slightly oversize and wash-worn pair of jeans cut as straight as stovepipes, a pair of flat canvas sneakers she wore without socks. The look on her face was remotely allied to the look I'd seen before, that she'd flung through Brodeur's doorway like a grenade, but now it was abstracted: her restiveness and uncertainty weren't connected to anything here. No part of her seemed to be. A heightened quality that I couldn't call flush, or good health, or least of all joy, emanated from her like the heat from a stirring volcano and seemed to set her at odds with the actual air. I wondered if she was aware of this, and hoping to conceal it by standing attached to her pram with one hand, in her blandly unflattering clothes. She was vastly more beautiful than I'd remembered and of course Dutra called out to her, in the unsuitably confrontational tone with which he liked to discomfit strangers, "Don't look so sad. You can get your own right over there."

"Not with decaf, I'd guess," she replied, so little ruffled by Dutra's manner that for a baffling moment I thought he must know her.

Dutra raised his eyebrows in mingled pity and disdain. "If it's decaf you want, I can't help you."

"It's not what I want, but it's all I can have. The plight of the nursing mother." She said this in a tone of mild reminder, as if she and Dutra had often in the past discussed her breasts and their uses.

Dutra lifted his palms in a broad show of helpless apology. "I'd like to say you metabolize all the caffeine before it reaches your milk, but I'd be talking out my ass." He so determinedly hoarded her attention I felt sure she wouldn't notice as, concealed by his bluster, I scrutinized her restored, or redoubled, postpregnancy beauty. I had the idea of committing it to memory, so that I couldn't be surprised by it again. "I don't honestly know," Dutra now surprisingly conceded of the science of metabolization. "I think that's true with booze, though."

"I know it's true with booze," she assured him.

"Nice. So your life isn't all deprivation."

She began to move on. "Not at all. Very full of rewards."

For a few moments we watched her recede, her narrow hips and mannish ass minimally betraying themselves in the loose pair of jeans. She moved along as if she were entirely alone, accompanied not even by the contents of the pram. She was like a farmer conducting some piece of equipment the length of a field.

"Single mothers are so sexy," said Dutra appreciatively.

The market, I had more than once noticed, was not just an undying hippie performance with a bluegrass soundtrack, but a pageant of self-consciously picturesque parents and children. Here was everyone winsomely dressed for the weekend, in their house-painting clothes or their floral sack dresses or pulling their little red wagons, displaying their most heedless, natural selves as if still in the privacy of their own homes. But they weren't in the privacy of their own homes. They were out promenading, and seemed to make a point of it. It was to this intention that Martha seemed so indifferent. It hadn't even crossed Dutra's mind that she might have a husband, at the market or not. I meant to correct his assumption. When had I ever known more about something than Dutra? Yet even more satisfying than trumping his knowledge was keeping my own to myself. And so I kept my poker face and kept silent, and as Dutra did, kept watching her, until she'd passed out of sight.

"What day is this!" shrieked my mother ebulliently when I picked up the phone. Despite a lifetime of habituation and, more immediately, a morning's worth of expectation, I still winced at the sound of her voice. My mother's voice was known to interfere with radio broadcasts and to summon stray dogs; in her late girlhood, when her nuclear grin and her lightning-fast hands had landed her a job as a typist with the U.S. Armed Forces based in Manila, she'd been useful for mustering troops who could otherwise sleep through all bugles and bells. My docile American father, who was descended from speech-shunning Teutons, and so near-anemically pale he could only go out on the march thickly slathered with zinc, had already when he first met my mother been deaf in one ear from a tour in Korea, and in due time would have almost no hearing at all, and this must have enabled their lasting romance more than all other factors combined. Beaming, wordless, my long, pale father with his weak teeth and fine gingery hair married my short, dark mother with her hair like a black horse's mane and her blinding white teeth that could serve to cut gemstones, and brought her unparalleled decibels back to America. Throughout my childhood, my mother was the one-woman honeybee swarm to my father's inert, serene hive; all day long he sat in his little air-conditioned cube of an accountancy office enjoying his columns of numbers in miraculous silence, while my mother, at her receptionist's desk, shrieked at terrified clients all the better to shriek-translate their problems to him. Besides their surprisingly prosperous business, and me, they'd shared a beaming enjoyment of televised golf and stories of entre-preneurial moxie; and an untroubled indifference to literature and the arts. They'd been confused by my turning out bookish, but agreed it would burnish my small talk with customers, once I finally went into some kind of business—"some kind of business" having always been the broadly vague, prosperous future they envisaged for me. They had also shared, and I with them, a blissful absence of any suspicion that my father's extreme elongation might mean a congenital flaw in his heart, which took him from us, suddenly, in my last year of high school. Now my mother, in her well-funded bereaved widowhood, had become a fanatic for organized cruises and tours, though she still hadn't given up hope I would someday make use of my "good head for business" for which glorious turn of events she had promised to leave her retirement.

"Happy birth-day to *queen*, happy birth-day to *queen*, happy birth-day Re-*gi-na* my *da-aa-aar*-ling!" By now I'd settled down at the kitchen table with a pot holder over the earpiece, a magazine to read while she talked, and a bowl of cereal, though even with the pot holder it seemed possible her voice through the line would wake Dutra, still sleeping up-stairs at the opposite end of the house.

"Hi, Mommy. How's Helsinki? Is that where you are?"

"*Twenty-one!*" she was wailing. "My *baby*. I was twenty-one when I met your poor daddy. Oh, I miss him, Regina. He would have loved com-ing here. His homeland."

"His parents were German. Aren't you in Finland?"

"It's all the same *thing*. Europe's all the same thing. Everybody here looks like Daddy."

"Are you having a good time?"

"I sent you an article, Gina. Did you get it? About those Nantucket Juice Guys? They're the same age as you! They did IPO just this year, now they're both millionaires. You must drink that juice all the time, right? On the bottle it says, 'We're Juice Guys!'"

"Are you having fun, Mommy? Are you meeting anybody?"

"You mean *men*."

"I really just mean anybody. Nice people to talk to."

"You're so grown-up! You used to hate it when I asked about your boyfriends. Now, listen to you. Mommy's best girlfriend." From her voice's slight sag off the uppermost end of the scale I could hear she was moved. "I bet *you* must have someone special."

"No, Mommy. I'm just taking classes. Working hard."

"You must be getting tired of school," she said hopefully.

"I like grad school. I've got a new job, working for a professor. He's very brilliant."

"Is he single?" she pounced, her flagging optimism now restored. To my mother, a good marriage was, if not equivalent to going into business, a strong prognosis for doing so.

"No, Mommy, he's married," I scolded, and then, as if I needed to hear this myself, "very happily married. He and his wife just had a baby."

She had moved on already. "What do you want for Christmas, sweetie? This year all my shopping is From Catalog. I leave for my Holy Land tour on the tenth of December. Oh! There's the ship bell! I *love you*. Happy *birthday* my darling!" And whether to obey the bell's shrilling, or competitively out-shrill it herself, with a last fireworks of effusion she ended the call, and I was left with residual bells in my ears agitating the silence. I took three aspirin, as it was always wise to do after speaking with her, and uttered a prayer that she meet a kind, deaf widower on her travels, and later, when the mail was delivered, I found that for my present she'd mailed me a fortune in Finnish tinned fish and stale Danish butter cookies, which that night Dutra and I made the pretext for devoting our scant mingled funds to the purchase of imitation champagne.

Since my earliest career as a student, when I'd gone to preschool in a corduroy dress with a Snow White lunch box, I'd almost always been the youngest in my class, studiously assuming the manners and mores of the already-fives at age four, or the thirteen-year-olds at age twelve, or the legally drunken eighteens while still many months shy of the privilege myself, so that my birthdays persistently suffered from anticlimax. Twenty-one was the same, but somehow even more so: the superior maturity I'd expected that age to confer I now felt I'd acquired already. At least in part I owed the acquisition to my friendship with Laurence, a heterosexual male with whom the problem of sex would not ever arise. I'd never before now been friends with a man who was married, let alone comically happily married, to use his own words. The unself-consciousness and freedom of my relations with Laurence, in which flirting, or the absence of flirting, had no relevance, hearkened back to nonsexual, innocent childhood. And so, though it sounds paradoxical, to me it felt very adult. On the other hand, the particular ripeness of my recent maturity seemed owing as much to Brodeur, who had surprisingly made me his colleague, and transported me out of that world of insinuation of which the bathroom graffito about him had been the chief emblem. From my new elevation that world seemed transparent and silly, which a short time before, from the low rung of twenty, had seemed so esoteric and grave. So it was that my new age felt old, and my childlike, restored wholesomeness new, and despite such extreme inconsistency, which I would have refused to call youthful, an inaudible hum of expectancy seemed to sing up through the soles of my feet.

Brodeur had promised to teach me to speed-grade, and a week or so after my birthday, amid the dread avalanche of the end-of-term papers, he summoned Laurence and me to dispatch them all in one marathon session. "He's exceptionally organized," explained Laurence to me as we drove. "He's already going to have alphabetized all the papers and broken them up in three piles. We'll each get a pile and a roster, with annotations: what each student received on the midterm, their semester's attendance, and, if applicable, naughty behavior, primarily grade grubbing. Just from your glance at the roster you'll know what the paper grade is within four or five points. From there, lavish check marks and question marks, underline, and if you're extremely moved, scrawl 'yes!' or 'why?.' The main task is find one thing to praise and one thing to rebut, and no more than five minutes per paper. That's his ironclad rule."

Brodeur was hosting our so-called grading party in his actual home, and as we approached this unimaginable place, fortressed somewhere in the heart of the faculty Arcadia north of the campus, I repeatedly noticed the hour, which was bracingly early, and told myself Mrs. Brodeur—or it must be Ms. Hallett—would be sitting in the kitchen in her robe, or her drab weekend clothes, with ungoverned hair and a large mug of coffee, if she wasn't still upstairs asleep. I was strangely impatient to see her there, wherever she would turn out to be, whether withdrawn behind a laden breakfast table, or greeting Laurence and me at the door, as if the early-morning domestic tableau would resolve for me some long-standing point of contention. Since the day I'd seen her at the market my scant hoard of knowledge about her had grown, for with the end of her natal seclusion, she seemed to have returned to very limited yet conspicuous circulation—or perhaps it was only my listening for mention of her that made me think she was mentioned more often. If one believed ambient gossip, before her pregnancy she had been known as the sort of professor who, perhaps from a dislike of artifice, continually muddles the distinction between students and self by dressing as they do, in snug jeans and T-shirts and Doc Martens boots; by drinking in their bars; by attending their parties and smoking their dope, or, more often, inviting the chosen of them to smoke hers. For a time she'd been seen a great deal in the company of another enemy of artifice among her colleagues, a junior professor of French history named Denis (silent *s*) Pelletier with whom she was rumored to be having an affair despite the fact he was gay. She'd been known to affect the distinctly student manner of wearing a messenger bag slung across her thin shoulders, out of which was made to visibly protrude, for example, *The Sublime Object of Ideology* by aid of which, she might inform listeners, she was reinterpreting the works of Melville via psychoanalysis—of course her "realness" was the true artifice. She was no slouching, impoverished grad student with a cigarette dangling prelit from her lips and a pool cue momentarily inactive in her hands. She was thirty-three years old, Yale B.A., Berkeley Ph.D., two years in her job and two more until tenure review; she had made a conspicuous marriage and now borne a child, and she apparently lived, as faculty did in this town, like a titan of industry—the limbs of great trees locked their arms overhead of the lane down which Laurence had turned. Our destination was not the largest house within view, but it was equally far from the smallest. As Laurence carefully parked at the outermost edge of the drive I took in with what I hoped appeared drowsy noninterest, and not avid shock, the faux-Tudor mansion, and its complicated multiplicity of fitted gray stones and diamond-shaped panes of stained glass through which, on this heavy gray morning, the interior lamplight just barely escaped, as if guttering weakly toward us from the wastes of deep space. A pair of lanterns denoted a grim obstacle of thick planks and wrought-iron hardware, like something to repulse an invasion, but Laurence led me away from the apparent front door, up the drive to the side of the house. "No one uses the front," he explained, "everybody goes in and out through the solarium," and so we were going, through a wide room of flagstones and glass, and through a door that was already being pulled open.

"I heard that spirited Italian engine of yours coming into the drive. Laurence. Regina," Brodeur greeted us, double-kissing our cheeks, as if we had not seen each other in months.

We now stood in a kitchen the size of the entire first floor of my and Dutra's shared house. In it Brodeur seemed as transitional as a butler. His feet were not even quite touching the black and white tiles. But at the far end, in a deep breakfast nook, I could see where he'd set up his camp, as distinct as if he'd built a small fire and run up a flag. The papers sat squared in three equal-height piles, each centered exactly on one of the three sides of the nook-enclosed table and each with a roster beside it. Brodeur would sit at the narrow end, in a chair, and Laurence and I on the two longer sides, on the deep padded benches. "I've prepared the ground, I've laid in supplies." He beamed as he settled us down at our places and then, like a proud host, added to the table for centerpiece a coffee can of some two dozen brand-new razor-tipped pens, color red, and an egg timer. No Martha Hallett leaned on the gleaming black slab of the counter, nursing her coffee or making small talk to distract us. No sound of any kind reached the kitchen from anywhere else in the house, no footsteps, no voices, no grumbling of plumbing. There was only a silence more profound and palpable than the winter morning quiet we'd left behind us outdoors. And so I assumed that the rest of the house was enjoying the tail end of sleep, and kept imagining I heard subtle movements of waking in far upstairs rooms, and thinking we were about to be joined by Brodeur's wife, or even his child, for I underestimated how large the house was, and how many choices of exit it offered, and how easily persons within it might achieve the objective of not crossing paths.

"Coffee's just finished brewing," Brodeur said as he bustled with saucers and cups. "On the bench between you and the window, Laurence, is a large box of vile powdered donuts, and on your bench, Regina, for later, a large box of assorted fresh-made sandwiches, both delivered this morning. Shall I pour coffee now? And continue with coffee until—what say, Laurence? Noon?"

"Eleven-thirty or everyone's twenty-fourth paper, whichever comes first."

"Good man. And so it shall be. Thereafter wine. Case is under the table."

"And when we're done, God willing, scotch," Laurence said, now revealing a wax-stoppered bottle he'd brought in his book bag.

"May I first propose a toast?" Brodeur interrupted himself just as he'd been making to wind the egg timer. He lifted his coffee mug. "To invaluable colleagues. And friends."

"Here, here," Laurence and I said together.

Brodeur and Laurence could read, write, and banter at once with the ease of jazz masters embellishing on the egg timer, while I had gone mute with the effort, squint-eyed and claw-handedly gripping my pen. The more I raced toward them, the faster the papers receded from me toward a point where I would have been grading them blind—and then just at the brink they abruptly changed shape, and popped open in space like box kites. I realized not what any of them was about, nor if any of them had succeeded in proving its point, but where my red comments, like dabs of paint, ought to go; and what sort of transit through space they should make; and what attitude they should convey. It wasn't reading or writing but music! It didn't matter at all what I said!

"Ah!" I cried.

"She's got it!" said Laurence.

"Of course she has." Brodeur smiled.

Wine was uncorked not at eleven-thirty but at twelve-thirty, on account of my slowness, but from there, perhaps riding the sluice of the wine, I went faster. Calculating for transition time a flawless performance was ten papers an hour; by one-thirty I'd done eight in an hour and by two-thirty, nine. Long since torn open, the sandwich box splayed at the end of the table, and each of us gripped sandwich crust in our nonwriting hand; each time Brodeur wound the timer, Laurence topped off our glasses, and we all tossed back wine like parched soldiers draining canteens. Talk had thinned out, replaced as it was by a sense of meshed power and intricate skill such as I felt I had never been part of before, as if we were airborne trapeze artists, or the sort of gymnasts who form pyramids while water-skiing—the door from the solarium suddenly opened and shut and we jerked in alarm, the trance broken.

"Oh," said Martha Hallett, regarding us. "Sorry to barge in. I meant to come back by the other door."

Laurence was first to recover. "How are you, Martha?" he said while attempting to rise, though his spidery legs were trapped under the table. Something in the moment felt backward, as if it was we who had barged in on her, dressed as she was in a way that seemed private, despite that she'd just come inside from a subfreezing day. She must have just returned from exercising. She was wearing a baseball cap pulled almost to the bridge of her nose so her eyes were obscured; a bomber jacket zipped all the way to the delicate skin of her neck, but no scarf; saggy outsize gray sweatpants with elastic at the ankles; and, without socks, a pair of authoritative-looking running shoes of the sort whose maker I could not even recognize from the symbol on the side, so specialized must they have been. I found I was very embarrassed, as if the fact that I'd seen her that day at the market, and now was ensconced in her kitchen, should rightly excite her suspicions.

"Don't get up, Laurence," she cut Laurence off, and in much the same tone to her husband, "Lucia took Joachim out."

"Paying a visit to some tiny person or other?"

"Something like that. I'm going to shower."

"Gym was lovely?" he called after her.

"I don't know if that's quite the word," she tossed back, and was gone, her footfalls swallowed by some thick carpeting that must have started just outside the kitchen door. The egg timer completed its transit and rang.

"Might be a good time to run to the loo," Laurence essayed.

"Me too," I realized.

"There's a second downstairs, down this hall, near the front of the house," Brodeur directed, Laurence having already gone into the small one we'd been using all day that attached to the kitchen. The kitchen door swung shut behind me and I had the sense of trespassing. Separate from the pressure in my bladder I wanted to hurry, on my own carpeting-silenced feet. I wanted a last glimpse of Martha, of that unguarded early-morning attitude I'd been hoping to find. I imagined her ascending her stairs, her attention drawn frowningly down to some item of mail. That was really all I sought: a quotidian picture I'd already formed in my mind. And I only sought it, I felt, because curious. She had an inverse effect to her husband, whose romantically sinister aura dissolved with each step nearer to him one took, so that, achieving the vantage of the man's breakfast nook, one was forced to admit he was practically normal. Martha, by contrast, grew stranger to me with each viewing—or so I theorized, pursuing her down the hallway, but it seemed that my theory wouldn't be tested. Without having seen her I came to the foyer off which was a small powder room, and my original errand could not be put off anymore.

When I reopened the door moments later she was standing directly outside, looking as startled as I must have, finding her there. She no longer wore the cap, jacket, or shoes and now I could see her green-gray eyes, like seawater on a bad weather day, and, through her thin, limp, too-large white T-shirt—had she borrowed these clothes from her husband?—the outline of her breasts—and also, though I was trying to look in her face, somehow the blue-veined nakedness of her feet.

"Oh! Sorry!" I cried, grinning and blushing that the strength of my mind had transported her there, to her own evident puzzlement.

"Oh, no, I'm sorry. I'd just been reaching for the doorknob when I realized there was someone inside. Sorry. I'm just—"

With exquisite awkwardness we changed our places through the narrow doorway, and then I stood outside and she inside the very small room, where she opened the undersink cabinet and lifted out a tidy stack of thick, if slightly dusty-looking, towels. "Sorry," she repeated, turning to face me with the pile of towels between us, as if she realized her shirt was transparent. "No clean towels upstairs."

"Oh! I'm sorry," I repeated, hardly aware that I'd said it, for here she was, the object of my avid curiosity, and I could hardly hook a noun to a verb—but I didn't *want* to converse, I complained inwardly. I'd just wanted to see her.

"Why sorry? I assume laundry's not part of your job."

I laughed disproportionately, and she added, as if politely hoping to inflate her joke to account for my outsize reaction, "Nicholas asks a great deal of his teaching assistants, but thus far I don't think that he asks them to launder his clothes. You're his new TA, aren't you? Why else would I find you handcuffed to a chair with a red pen in hand? I'm Martha," and here she extended her hand, and I took it in mine for a moment and quickly let go.

"Regina," I managed. "Gottlieb."

"You're a first-year?" I agreed that I was, and this seemed to explain something to her. She went on, kindly, "You must be happy the semester is ending. All my students tell me the first is the hardest. You're still adjusting, and the winter's setting in."

"I haven't minded."

"The semester? Or the winter? Let me warn you, the winter is just getting started. 'You ain't seen nothin' yet.'" To save us both from a repeat of my oversize laughter she added, "Are you going home for the holidays?"

"No. Nowhere to go."

"Oh dear."

"It isn't as bad as it sounds. My father's dead and so my mother likes to travel. She's spending Christmas in the Holy Land this year."

"Ah. Really getting to the bottom of it."

"Yes, going straight to the source. She keeps very busy."

"She must have been happy with your father. She finds widowhood lonely."

"I think she does," I said, entering thoughtfully into this unexpected mood of analysis.

"That's nice. I mean, not that she's alone, but that she was so happy with him."

"And they were an extremely odd couple."

"Were they? Now you've made me curious about them. Wait, let me guess." Very bemused suddenly, she examined me over her pile of towels, her eyes walking like fingers all over me, taking my measure. "Mr. Gottlieb. I'll guess the shy, quiet type. Germanic, obviously. Military? He must be, but I can't guess which branch. He meets Miss X while he's posted in Fill-in-the-Blank. For the hell of it I'll say Jakarta. Miss X is vivacious— she's going to spend her later years running around Palestine—and of course she must be beautiful. I'll guess Mr. Gottlieb is adequately handsome—perhaps he's not a heartthrob, but he has the kind of face that people like. An odd couple, they wed, and find enviable happiness, if it doesn't last quite long enough. Their—two?—children are very fond of them. So how did I do?"

Faintly, from far down the hall, I heard Laurence's donkeylike laughter. "Army," I supplied after a moment. "Not Jakarta. Manila. Just one child. Also, somehow you failed to guess that she has an extremely loud voice, and that he was half deaf. Points off for that." We regarded each other with delighted dismay.

"Goodness," she said. "Points off or not, I'm impressed with myself."

"I'm impressed with you, too," I replied, which was an extreme understatement.

"What about the rest of my clairvoyance? Was Miss X a beauty?" Her first time voicing this speculation I had blushed at the implication for myself. Now I felt the blush return—but if I'd inherited anything of looks from my mother, I'd inherited her robust brown skin, which could conceal a furnace of blushes, even from close observation. That same observer, though, might feel extreme heat, and I took a step backward before I replied:

"It's funny to think of her that way, but I'd have to say yes. In her time."

"In her time," she repeated, as if she discerned extra meaning. "Speaking of time, I suppose you have papers to grade."

"Only another thirty-nine."

"Well, I'll let you get to it."

"All right," I said, very much wishing she wouldn't. "It was nice meeting you."

"And you," she agreed graciously, turning away.

But somehow I could not be content with having regained dignity by the time of our parting, and so I blurted, to her back, "And it's nice of you to have us to your house. It's a beautiful house," realizing too late that this inanity might somehow imply that her husband was also a guest. She looked back at me over her shoulder, and for the first time I saw her disarming, uneven smile, just one corner hitched up.

"Now I know you're procrastinating," she chided, resuming her ascent of the stairs. "Back to the salt mines with you."

In the kitchen Laurence was still shaking with laughter over one of his papers, and Brodeur was rinsing bottles at the sink, and neither of them looked at me strangely despite how long I felt I must have been gone. The spell had broken for good in my absence, if not because of it, and they'd decided to transfer the rest of the party to the Collegetown Inn, so we could have a proper dinner, which it apparently went without saying we couldn't obtain where we were, in that enormous and well-equipped kitchen. And so I didn't see Martha Hallett again on that day, or for months afterward.

Looking back I can almost imagine that all of that time, in my life as a student, I preoccupied myself with nothing else but Nicholas Brodeur and his household, but that wasn't the case. The larger share of my time I spent successfully attending three classes, and writing three end-of-term papers I imagined would not be perused much more closely than I'd perused eighty-six papers on Chaucer. I chose courses to take in the spring, and set myself pious goals in reading unfamiliar classics and in otherwise improving myself. Over the Christmas holidays Dutra, as always equipped with the best in all things, produced from the basement a safety-orange plastic toboggan and took me for perilous drunken sled rides on the hills of the Ag School's Exhibition Plantation, where the sugar maples marched in their ranks down the slope, and the lines for spring tapping were already strung, so that we might, at high speeds, behead ourselves if we didn't first shatter our spines on tree trunks. Now I'd seen every season but one, and was inclined to believe, with Dutra, that our town was the earth's distillation: no place hotter nor colder, no place more purely aflame in the autumn nor palaced with ice at New Year's, nowhere so bathed by its waterfalls, cleaved by its gorges, sexed up in the spring by its shamelessly honey-mouthed blooms. "How can anyone *think* in the spring?" Dutra said one March day, as he swung in the hammock, which because we'd never taken it in was now frayed and gray as some scrap of net flung from the ocean. Of course what we welcomed as spring was a temperature just above freezing, and the filthy gray snow battlements turning slick on the top from the afternoon sun, and the little white snowdrops that bashfully hung down their heads, as if sorry that less demure flowers would soon hoist their skirts. Spring in that town was what most humans would have called winter, but where there is general agreement—to go without a hat, to sit at length outdoors, to even wear shorts with one's parka—there is seasonal change, even if just ahead of the weather. The Hallett-Brodeurs must have known this. I found out from a little note in my department mailbox, in Nicholas's strained, oddly juvenile hand, that they were hosting a party, to which Laurence and I, still honorary TAs, were invited.

"Thank god they are asking you both," Sahba said on an evening they cooked dinner for me, the weekend before the event. "So you will go with Laurence as his date, Regina, and let me stay home." Sahba accused Laurence's colleagues of looking down on her for her long-ago hobby of winning beauty contests, and her postexile fate representing the House of Chanel, though I was an exception, as was Nicholas.

"Oh, come on, Sahba," Laurence tried. "You do like Nicholas, and he adores you. Given Regina is invited in her own right, she's entitled to bring her own date. It's not fair to make her squire me."

"I don't have anyone I'd bring," I assured him, wanting to please Sahba, although I knew Casper would have enjoyed it.

"I do like Nicholas, but he will understand. I must stay home with Beb." The charge in question was asleep, it being past nine P.M., and the three of us were sitting outdoors, in thick sweaters and beneath heaps of blankets, on their deck, which jutted off the hillside and seemingly over the lake, as if we floated offshore on a ship. Like all the lakes in the region this one, while wide, was much longer, in the shape of a crooked cigar. Now the opposite bank was picked out distantly by a strand of dock lights spaced at long intervals, but the north and south terminus points might as well have plunged over the ends of the earth. It was a very deep lake, glacier-made Laurence had said, and even without the play of light on its surface I could feel its restless activity, and the ropes of its currents, as if it weren't a lake at all but a vast magisterial river.

"We can bring Bebi," Laurence persisted. "We can bed him down there. They have a baby now. They understand."

"Please, Laurence. The idea is giving me stress." This was said with such tranquil finality that even I knew the matter was settled. And so the following weekend it was only Laurence who pulled up outside in the Alfa Romeo, to drive me to dinner.

I told myself it had been distinctly-not-shy Sahba's aversion that made me so nervous. I'd found myself revising and revising my clothes, and in the end had been glad Dutra hadn't been home to observe the outcome, a resurrected come-hither costume of calfskin miniskirt with a zip up the side, patterned tights, lace-up boots, and a cropped chenille sweater that slid off one shoulder and was knit in a pattern of purple and gold. At least Laurence had also dressed up. Like me he was very different from his daytime self, in a black turtleneck and black slacks and black shiny wingtips instead of his accustomed double-pleat khakis with Top-Siders and Fair Isle sweater. His tonsured hair was glued flat and gleaming with some kind of gel. "Sahba dressed me," he acknowledged my compliment. "I tried at the last minute but she wouldn't be budged. She says our story is that Bebi caught a cold. But she insists you and I have a wonderful time, and we're supposed to remember everything Martha cooks so we can tell her about it. I don't know if you've heard what a phenomenal chef Martha is."

"Is she?"

"Astonishing. She's very serious. You know she once cooked professionally. It was while they were living in Berkeley. She was finishing up at UC but she was more serious apparently about cooking. She's very intrepid, Martha. She lived on Madagascar for a year for some reason, and learned to cook anything in a can. Truly—she can cook you a multicourse meal with no more than a fire and a large-size tin can. The first time I went to their house it was summer, and Martha had constructed a fire pit of stones in their backyard, and she'd set up a wrought-iron grill, and she served clams casino, wild-mushroom pizza, whole lobsters, a corn salad, and, I am earnest, a peach pie, all of which she produced from that fire without setting foot in her kitchen. You know Nicholas almost can't boil water. Sometimes he's successful and sometimes he isn't. And Sahba is a magnificent cook but even she isn't up for this macho survivalist thing Martha does. Sahba and I need a kitchen and a recipe book and the right kind of pan, and then we do very nice things. But Martha—! Sahba wants to know just what she makes, and whether she does it outside in a hole in the ground." And so Laurence rattled on as we climbed up the hill, managing somehow in the course of this epicurean tantalization to ruin my appetite, for I could feel he was nervous also, a condition in which I had never seen him, which made my nervousness even worse.

The driveway was already full. "Can we be late?" Laurence exclaimed as he shifted the Alfa Romeo forward and back in its difficult spot by the side of the road, alternating between his tires on their lawn, and his tires in the road, and displeased with both options. In every other respect we seemed early. No lights were on outside the house, and we had to grope our way to the solarium door and from there to the door to the kitchen— but within was abrupt light and heat and a noisy disorder. And Martha, amid a chaos of plastic bowls, plastic cups, plastic spoons, seltzer bottles, crumpled bags, takeout menus, dirty pots, and incompletely unpacked sacks of groceries occupying every inch of the yards and yards of deep counter space, and the central island, and even avalanching here and there onto the black and white tiles of the floor. Every leaded window was coated with steam. A dull roar shook the room that I realized must be a dishwasher but was more like an animal stuffed in a cage. Martha was dressed in unraveling jeans that the wash had turned white and the sort of limp, depleted tank top—unambiguously underwear, not outerwear— that the wash had turned gray. I felt a stab of panic—had we come the wrong night?—even as she said, "Hi, Laurence, Regina," remotely, and plucked the bottle of wine out of Laurence's hands. She shoved it into the mess beside her. "Everybody's in the dining room. Actually, take this with you," and she thrust the wine back.

In the dining room the temperature dropped perhaps twenty degrees. I noticed a window cranked open. The gargantuan slab of the table, despite being set for twelve, appeared desolate and institutional beneath its twelve matching white plates and twelve neutral-toned placemats and napkins and twelve sets of cutlery and twelve empty wineglasses. The insides of the glasses were coated with dust. A cloth covered the table but there was otherwise no festive embellishment, no centerpiece of dried flora or bowl of fruit, apart from a pair of tapers and a pair of candlesticks that had been taken to the far end of the table as if into protective custody by an ursine man in wool sweater and corduroy jacket and slacks who was struggling, with no tool apart from persistence, to fit the tapers, the bases of which were slightly too large, into the candlesticks, the tops of which were clogged with old wax. He was watched with disproportionate intensity by two younger men, as if he handled a bomb they all hoped he'd defuse.

"Ah!" he cried with too much relief when we came in. "Laurence, isn't it? Gareth Waggoner from the Hum Center, Regina, is it? Gareth Waggoner from the Hum Center, just visiting here for the year. I'm so sorry we haven't yet met, the year just began and it's practically ending—you have matches, don't you? Doesn't anyone smoke? I always have matches in all of my pockets, books and books of matches, and today I should decide to wear something that was just to the cleaners' and my pockets are empty. But a penknife is what we need first. I'm almost never without a penknife and now tonight when we need one—"

"*I* might have a penknife in my car!" exclaimed one of the two younger men.

"Good thought, Karim."

"I might even have matches—"

The two young men disappeared down the dim hall. The dining room's other adjacency, a vast parlor I had never been in, was in absolute darkness. A cold breeze was flowing from there, in current with the breeze from the dining room window. I could just make out the vast marshmallow forms of a modern-style living-room set, everywhere confusingly supplemented by other irregular spindly forms which must be the baby's equipment, but perhaps optional, for the silhouetted disorder, obscure as it was, gave the strong sense of a room not in use, like an attic or basement. Laurence had begun pouring wine, and put a glass in my hand as the doorbell, a ponderous clangor like the bells of a church, broke on us with the force of an earthquake. Laurence ran to get it. "They never use the front door," I could hear him apologizing. Karim and his friend reappeared empty-handed, but with a comp lit professor named Frank who produced a lighter. "Oh! Give it here!" Gareth said.

Soon all ten of the guests ringed the table, yet still no host, hostess, or food. With frantic high spirits we accosted our neighbors to the left and the right, as if we sat at the table, though we didn't dare sit, nor venture into the murk of the parlor, nor the blaze of the kitchen. Tendrils of steam from the kitchen slipped between the doorframe and the door, as if the kitchen housed the hellish boiler works of a coal-burning ship. I'd drawn Karim's fellow match seeker, a postdoc named Joe, when the influx of the rest of the guests left him trapped between me and the sideboard. What year were we? What were we studying? Who were we studying with?—the whole duet performed with flushed cheeks and raised voices, as if our lives hinged upon it. Even as I was speaking to Joe I had no idea what I was saying. I only knew I must not let Joe's eyes stray from mine or the threat in the room would become real and triumph; and Joe understood it also; so did everyone else. An ardent gratitude enlivened us all, that no one of us knew more than two or three others so that we could be a long time hollering our professional associations, departmental matriculations, academic specializations, permanent or temporary addresses, and opinions of the weather at each other before the fuel ran low; and at almost that moment, as if her entertaining instincts continued to serve her no matter how little she wanted them to, Martha abruptly appeared, with the terrifying air of a contemptuous waitress who has had almost all she can take of a table and is only continuing service in order to bring off a mass poisoning. She shouldered the kitchen door open and came clanging in with four more bottles of uncorked red wine, two per hand, to replace the four long since drained dry. She slammed them onto the table and went straight back out. Hardly had the door closed on her than these bottles were empty also.

All this time Nicholas never appeared. No one dared mention him. And then just as sufficient confidence, or perhaps drunkenness, had led the professor named Gareth to drop his weight into a chair, a high-pitched wail rose in the distance, like a siren approaching, and Nicholas materialized in the mouth of the dim corridor, perfectly blind to the roomful of guests and with a red, shrieking child in the crook of his arm.

"MARTHA!" he thundered.

"Nicholas! Oh! This must be Joachim! An angel . . . how lovely . . ." we were stupidly saying, tripping over each other with fear as if he'd caught us in the process of robbing his house. But this reaction of ours wasn't noticed any more than our presence had been.

Martha responded so quickly she might have been waiting just behind the kitchen door. She mowed us down from one end of the room to the other, snatched the screaming child from her husband, and disappeared up the stairs.

Nicholas disappeared also, without a word spoken to us. We were imploring each other: "So how do you know Nicholas and Martha? Oh, *where* do you stay in Provence? Oh my God, *what* did you think of her latest? Could you even get through it?" Laurence was still on the far side of the table from me, crimson from his pate to the part of his neck I could see just above his thick sweater. Now not just the one but every one of the windows had been opened in response to the furnacelike heat the trapped ten of us, in our fear, had produced. Even as I systematically elicited from Joe his detailed opinion of every Hitchcock film either of us could think of—*Strangers on a Train? The Thirty-nine Steps? Rope? Shadow of a Doubt?*—I couldn't take my eyes from those windows, and the unalloyed blackness of night they held just out of reach. Any stranger passing by would have thought that we ten were in heated conflict with one another, and maybe we were, underneath the barrages of small talk. Could no one, we raged wordlessly, have the courage to call this thing off, or at least venture into the kitchen to look for more drinks? And then something shifted; I was very drunk already; a moment passed between my perceiving the shift and perceiving its source. Nicholas had joined us. He wore a beautiful sky-blue dress shirt so new as to still be knife-creased, and into which he was calmly installing the cuff links as he stood in conversation with Gilles, a visiting Foucauldian from Paris, and an English professor named Larry Kornblatt, whose satirical book praising sloth as a virtue had met with surprising commercial success.

And then Martha was standing beside him, a peasant blouse thrown over her tank top, as if it were already summer. She had painted her mouth with a dark red lipstick in such a way that the delicate skin of her lips, parched from winter, seemed much more exposed. I could see their detailed scaliness, even the place where the lower lip's plumpness had split, like an arrow of blood.

Now Martha became yet more swift and determined. She still spoke to no one, but sliced back and forth through the double-hinged door. A tureen of extremely green soup was banged onto the table. Vivienne, a professor of French with her hair in a gleaming chignon and her sinuous body in a tight sweaterdress and thigh-high leather boots, trailed Martha into the kitchen and was apparently tolerated. Vivienne's departure left a hole beside Gilles the Foucauldian which was soon filled by Laurence. Slowly, I began to decode the guest list. Visiting Gilles from Paris would appreciate serpentine, French Vivienne, who wore no wedding ring, while Larry Kornblatt alone of the guests was accompanied by his spouse, a women's studies professor named Lois. Both of them were garrulous, hearty, and with drink increasingly profane, which endeared them to Gareth, the ursine visitor from Scotland, who was also, I realized, the sort of gay man whom to that time I'd never encountered: thick in the middle, unkempt, and plainly on the prowl for the young, groomed, and slender. Karim, an Americanist whose adviser was Martha, was for Gareth. My dull Joe, another Americanist whose adviser was Martha, was for Karim, to disguise Karim's function as bait. Karim and Joe, allied to Martha, balanced Laurence and me, allied to Nicholas, while the comp lit professor named Frank, who made ten, was a young, recent hire, unmarried, easygoing, good looking, always equipped with a lighter and smokes, the sort of high-value crowd-pleasing guest every party requires.

Careful logic had been brought to bear on this party, of the sort that is strictly female. Nicholas hadn't assembled these guests, hadn't thoughtfully balanced and tagged every chair. Martha had meant for this party to happen. But at some point, perhaps mere hours ago, her intention had changed.

We were still, in our increasingly louche drunkenness, cracking bad jokes about boy-girl seating, as there were half as many women as men, when Martha sliced in again and said impatiently, in her first utterance to the room, "Would you sit please? The soup's getting cold." We scrambled into nearest seats with beating hearts, as if spurred by the silence in musical chairs, and Martha returned from the kitchen again with a long baguette under her arm and went around the table twisting chunks off and actually flinging them one after the other, pitching roughly for each of our plates.

Shamefacedly we gathered our bread chunks, and passed the tureen.

The soup was strangely textured but good. It tasted of spring, the real, true spring that yet lay ahead—of little shoots and a nice sourness. "No, not fresh—I had favas in the freezer," Martha said over her shoulder to someone, leaving for the kitchen again, as if she would shortly return and relate something more, but she didn't return. Her words, which had seemed so mercifully mundane, as if she, herself, was the savior we'd all been awaiting, the one who would throw herself onto the rudder and steer us all back into harbor, hung for too long in the air, until they twisted and stretched and dissolved, like the ribbons of smoke issuing from the two candlesticks, upon which the two candles, so recently hopefully lit, had devoured themselves. More empty wine bottles than glasses were crowding the table. "That's a rich thing to say, considering the French in Algeria," Lois shouted at Gilles.

"Oh, so you excuse slavery? Everybody does it so I do it as well?"

"Good Christ, the Federation of Suffering Souls. Is there a single dark-skinned people on the planet for whom I might not take up arms? It would be so refreshing. Or perhaps I could do a subscription. Ten dollars a month and you, Gareth, Need Not Give a Shit. Wouldn't that be terrific?"

"That is an incredibly racist statement."

"Yours was the subscription to nonracist statements? Forgive me, I've got all the subscriptions fucked up."

"Do you have any *fucking* idea how many black men are locked up in this country—"

"I suppose you have seen the movie and as a result it has made you an expert. This is a miraculous movie, you only need to sit through it and you are better qualified to judge than the people themselves! I am waiting for someone to make such a movie about the Palestinians."

"I hear a lot of derision directed at *me* and not a lot of justification for what your government's doing—"

Laurence was missing. As soon as I noticed I felt myself perspiring from my scalp to the soles of my feet. I didn't think Laurence had left me but it seemed possible he'd been kidnapped or killed. I was drinking compulsively from my wineglass, and not tasting the wine. I heard *glog* and a patter of drops on the cloth as Joe tipped a fresh bottle to fill it—I had somehow wound up with Joe close by my left yet again, heard him distantly saying, "More like *Un Chien Andalou*." There was a case of wine torn open on the floor in a corner, which perhaps had just been carried in. The table bucked at me as if I had tripped. At its farthest end I saw Nicholas, with whom I'd exchanged not a word, blankly smiling as Vivienne spoke in his ear. Larry Kornblatt had changed Martha's congealed bowl of soup for his scraped one and set to work on it. Frank had inserted himself between Lois and Gareth and now was shouting at and being shouted at by both. Karim and Joe were missing also, the chair to my left was empty. And then two roast chickens appeared on the table, being not carved so much as torn up. Laurence caught my eye from his chair, which he had reclaimed though perhaps he had never vacated. When the chickens reached me they were stripped carcasses. I shoved back my chair and plunged into the darkness beyond the archway, and found myself in a maze of objects I kept pushing behind me as if climbing sideways through some sort of jungle, yet with the heightened coordination of extreme drunkenness I somehow upset nothing, and emerged in a part of the house that was dimly familiar. I found the powder room, locked myself in, and threw up.

Right away I felt sober, though it might have been only by contrast. I leaned on the sink until I had my breath back. On impulse I opened the undersink cabinet. Empty. No stack of clean towels anymore. Now, as I hadn't the first time I'd been there, I closely examined the miniature room. It was very tastefully, thoughtlessly done. Striped wallpaper, chrome and porcelain fixtures. In the tall oval mirror I saw a sprinkling of minute purple markings in the soft skin just under my eyes where I'd exploded blood vessels while retching, but I hadn't brought my bag and so couldn't use makeup to hide it. I washed my face and rinsed my mouth, and tried to govern my hair. Reassessing my face it occurred to me, for the first time, that I hadn't seen photographs anywhere in the house. Of Nicholas and Martha, singly or together; of their extended families; of their child. The absence of photographs was of a piece with a broader absence of personal objects of which I now took a sort of reverse inventory. There was nothing in the house that seemed chosen.

Outside the bathroom again, where I'd spoken with Martha that day, the tide of raucous voices splashed down just in earshot, but I couldn't discern individual words, only spikes here and there of dissent or derision. I was determined to make contact with Laurence without going back in the room. The open windows I'd faced from my side of the table were just behind Laurence's back, and surely I could get his attention through these without anyone else noticing. Too resolutely I rushed down the hall. Before I had seemed to myself like an arrow. Now my shoulder was bumping the wall. I thought with longing of Dutra. If I could just find a phone he would come rescue me. He would even enjoy it. He might enjoy it too much. Vividly I pictured him crashing the party, and throwing fuel on the various ideological fires. No, it was Laurence I must reach at once. The plush carpet yanked itself out from beneath me and the soles of my

boots came down loudly on flagstones; I'd arrived somehow in the solarium, which was pumped full of savory smoke. At the far end was the
door to the driveway, blocked by Martha and Joe and Karim, who were
smoking a joint.

"There you are," I said to Martha, and all three of them looked up at
me. My voice had struck a note of accusation no one had expected, including myself.

"Were you looking for me?" Martha said.

I hadn't been, yet it came to me now that in fact I'd been looking for
her the whole evening. In the startling disorder of her kitchen, on the
dining room's shrill battleground, it hadn't been possible or even conceiv-
able to take her remote rudeness personally. Now, I felt retroactively
stung. "Yes, I was," I replied, as if she ought to have known. My tone
seemed to tell Joe and Karim they'd intruded on Martha and me, and
not the other way around. Karim in haste accepted the joint from Martha and applied himself, gorging on smoke; as he did he held his other
arm outstretched, toward Joe, to keep him in wait or to send him a signal;
then the procedure was finished, he'd passed the joint to Joe, and together they'd slipped back inside, with an adequate air of apology, while
Martha and I, gazing curiously at each other, failed to note their departure.

"Were you going to say I should come back inside?" she asked after a
moment, but now that we were alone, an unruly sprite seemed to be leap-
ing about the solarium, which we both watched slantwise while pretending it didn't exist. I knew she no more meant to go back inside than I did.

"I was going to say this party has about run its course. It feels like
time to leave."

"I'll be sorry to see you go."

"I mean, it feels like time for both of us to leave. We could go somewhere else."

She considered the proposal gravely. "It's tempting, but my car is
blocked in."

"We could walk. It's a beautiful night."

"Also, though I probably shouldn't admit it, I'm the host of this party."

"All the more reason to leave," I said reasonably.

"You know, Miss Gottlieb—may I call you Miss Gottlieb?—you're interesting. I could almost think you're trying to corrupt me. After the day you were here grading papers, I realized I'd seen you before."

"At the farmers' market."

"Why didn't you remind me?"

"We didn't talk to each other that day at the market. There was nothing to remind you about."

"You and your boyfriend were drinking the coffee-iced coffee."

"Not my boyfriend," I corrected, more sharply than I had intended.

"Oh?"

"My housemate."

"But you're not involved?"

"No."

"The very lovely Miss Gottlieb and the more-than-adequately handsome Mr. X are . . . just friends? He *is* very good-looking," she persisted, as if doubting my truthfulness, or my judgment. Then I saw that half smile again, as she lifted one side of her beautiful mouth.

"I suppose," I said brusquely. All at once she annoyed me. Despite the sloshing of my innards, and the lightness of my head, and the alcohol fumes steaming out of my pores, and the neutered residue of panic—of my newly irrelevant need to find Laurence—now washing away through my veins, I understood something that Martha, like a coy child, seemed determined not to recognize. The very moment I admitted we were flirting, I lost patience for it. All women are powerfully affected by examples of beauty among their own kind. Those who claim they can't appraise another woman's allure because they're of the same sex are embarrassed, or lying. Like almost any woman I had extensive experience of idolatrous attraction to beautiful women, dating roughly from the tender age of six, but these love affairs were a form of fantastical self-transformation; they belonged to imagination, not the pragmatic realm of appetite. Appetite knows what it craves, without cerebral embellishment. It tends not to waste any time laying hold of its tools. That was the thing I had recognized here: appetite. I recognized it precisely because, in a context like this, it was so unfamiliar. It had forced me to rule out everything else. And there was a second reason for my recognition, which because unprecedented was not recognition at all, but astounding discovery: Martha's face told me. I saw appetite there, even more as she dithered, even more as she festooned our electrification with bunting and baffles and coy indirection like throwing so much laundry onto the line.

"You're not involved—but you're hoping you might be?" she asked, making a great solemn show of attempting to root out my meaning, for of course such an effort of deferral is its own exquisite pleasure, and the chance for it comes only once; it can't be re-created but only prolonged. Martha's own talent for putting off pleasure being very impaired, as in time I would learn, she now hoped for assistance from me, but she didn't receive it.

"Perhaps you're interested in him, but I'm not," I concluded, to whisk this irrelevancy from my path.

"And if you're not, I shouldn't be, either?"

"You can do what you want, I suppose!"

"What are *you* doing?" she said, through her uneven smile, for having had enough I'd closed the gap, and each of my toes now confronted its opposite number, and my kneecaps their sightless reflections, and the points of my hip bones collided with hers and the points of our breasts shocked together, hard as thumbs, through the unimpeding layers of our thin party clothes. It was cold in the solarium, the still-wintry air ceaselessly insinuating through the seams between the hundred panes of glass, and I could feel the fragile nimbus of heat baking out from her skin, before the drafts snatched it away. I was trembling violently, with surprise at myself and with counteracting furious resolve, and my teeth were chattering, and my fingertips were numb, but none of these impairments counseled anything but speed, as if the more I delayed, the more the impairments might be permanent.

"You know exactly what I'm doing," I said crossly, so irked by her tone that for a moment my fear was forgotten and sinking my hand in her heavy blond hair I took hold of the hot, perspiration-damp slope of the nape of her neck, and raised my chin slightly and drew her toward me, for she was the slightest bit, perhaps a finger's width, taller—I'd been right, she had known—the thought came to me but could not be completed as my tongue filled her mouth and we bloomed smoothly out of our skins as if some gorgeous fruit that aspires to devour itself. Her answering kiss was unstinting; it excavated me down to my bowels, and I uttered a long susurration, more vibration than sound. My hand that did not have her nape roughly seized a fistful of her blouse, and we fell back against the cold spine of the solarium's metal doorframe. She broke away and whispered urgently, "Shh!" but her legs scissored open just slightly and my upper thigh notched between them and felt the shuddering grip of her hotly drenched crotch through her jeans; like mine her breasts seemed to be linked, by conductive short wires, to the node of her sex that was hopelessly hidden from me in her clothes, so that when I slipped a palm under her blouse and brushed over one nipple she gasped, as I would, and pushed the breast hard against me, as I would, not to rush but to muddle the progress, to blur the high note and attenuate pleasure . . . all this while our mouths fed on each other, their sameness so shocking as to be somehow sweetly inevitable, and for all the urgent thunder the length of our veins I knew we stood there almost silently, gently entwined. Had it truly been spring in that chamber of glass a vine might have scaled our bodies and unfurled its pink trumpet-shaped blooms. Who knows what we looked like—but from Laurence's face I'd guess lovers, of more than five minutes' standing, gratefully closing our seams after long separation.

So shocked was Laurence's tact, or so tactful his shock, that I would never know how long it took him to gain our attention. He might have been there the whole time.

"Regina," he coughed at last, "time to go now. I've got your jacket and bag."

Hearing Laurence's voice was like stumbling while strolling along in a dream. I jerked with alarm and lost hold of Martha, who stepped quickly away, yet I felt when I turned my eyes toward her I'd gained her to a greater degree. She stood crimson-faced and extensively rumpled, as if she'd been rousted from bed, and my guts avalanched within me and I knew I adored her.

Laurence was crimson-faced also, for even if he'd been blind, the aroma of incipient sex assailed all our nostrils like the yeast-earthy blast from a hardworking bread oven. Somehow, Martha managed a smile. "Thank you, Laurence," she told him, and gave him a peck on the cheek.

"What are you thanking me for?" he managed, in feeble imitation of his chivalrous self. "It was lovely."

"Good night," Martha said, and went quickly inside before either of us could reply.

In the Alfa Romeo Laurence lay his forehead on the steering wheel a moment, as if in unutterable pain, before starting the engine. I was trembling again with even more energy than before; I was barely sustaining contact with my seat. My appalling carnal stench was so strong now penned into the car that only the moment's paralysis kept me from jumping back out. Then it came to me that the smell was roast chicken. The car reeked of it. We started descending the winding and secretive streets, past the stone walls and dense privacy hedges and wrought-iron gates. "Laurence," I croaked.

"Perhaps we won't talk much just now," Laurence said, sounding strangled like me.

"I've never done anything like that before," I burst out, for Laurence's horror had made me ashamed. "I've never kissed another woman, or one who was married, or in fact anyone who was married—"

"I really would rather not talk much just now."

It wasn't just the misery of shame, but of quashed exaltation, that bore down unendurably on me. For though Laurence's presence had made me feel mortification, its dull tar was shot through by threads of pure gold, and I was approaching a state of such euphoric excitement I thought I might shriek. And these went together, the shame and the glory, the self-horror and the blood-lusty triumph, so well that I might have been some kind of Viking whose pleasure in killing is only enhanced by the twinges of conscience. How awful it was and how good! I wanted to exult in my crime and also be excused for it, and who else could I speak to but Laurence? At the same time I wanted more Martha. I was starting to shiver and twitch from withdrawal. It was so absolutely unpleasant, so far from the ravishing pleasure in which I'd been lost only moments before, that I covered my face with my hands and heard myself cry, "I'm hungry! I'm so fucking hungry! Where the hell did you go for the chicken? Why wasn't there *more*?"

"Oh no, darling! Don't tell me you didn't get any?"

"There was only a back when it reached me. And pieces of skin."

"Oh, Regina! I didn't buy nearly enough. But they only had two and both very dried out, they were from Hobo Deli's rotisserie—"

"I didn't know they had a rotisserie—"

"It's brand new. And not bad. I took one home the other night when

Sahba was too tired to cook. They won't have started more at this hour but they'll surely have something."

"No, Laurence, please don't, you don't have to take me, you should go home to Sahba—"

"It's right on the way. I could use something also."

"You really don't have to—"

"But Regina, we're practically there—"

Speeding down the hill with new purpose I think we both truly believed that whatever had happened, whatever mad impulse I'd hotly pursued, was actually Laurence's fault, for failing to guard my interests, and thus leaving me hungry and weakened and vulnerable. If that were true, Laurence only need act like himself and it all would be mended. He only need find me a nice midnight snack and I wouldn't go on craving Martha; I wouldn't assist her in smashing her marriage with the unavowed bludgeon that swung from my hands. . . .

Hobo Deli was a landmark of town life, the only store of its kind open twenty-four hours, glowing blue with fluorescence by night on its skirt of asphalt at its puzzling location amid dilapidated Victorian houses in an otherwise entirely residential part of town. It less violated the usual rules of municipal organization than seemed attuned to a powerful node that municipal leaders had tried to ignore. Its parking lot was a changing tableau all night long, clattering with skateboards, hosting swing-shift meals of microwave burritos, but even by day it was more of a center of town than the "Commons," a failed urban renewal pedestrian plaza, or the mingy town park with Town Hall to one side and memorial plaques at the center. And Hobo Deli belonged utterly to the town, and not at all to the school, so that the nearer we drew, the farther away for the moment felt the realm of the Hallett-Brodeurs, and the more possible my reprieve. And who should happen to be there, when we came through the door, but Dutra, leaning against the back counter sharing a Tombstone pizza with his old friend Ross from community college, amid the microwave and coffeepots and ramen noodle tubs and the freezer chest of defrostable dinners.

"Aw, was the food at your swank dinner party that bad?" he razzed me, but the state of my face must have drawn him up short. "Head on home, man," he reassured Laurence.

Laurence didn't need to be persuaded to say good night then, nor did I. As he left I imagined my secret went with him. He was the soul of discretion, and what had happened with me and the wife of our host and shared friend was no more than a typical drunken night's damage. It would be neither repeated nor acknowledged, and might not have happened at all. By the end of that night I'd convinced myself of this, and, determined to shore up the conviction, when I got home with Dutra, after two chili dogs at the Hobo and a Saranac Ale in the car, I followed him into the room we'd once shared and slid my hands into his pants.

"Hel*lo*," he said.

I wonder how often the ravenousness of a lover, her uncharacteristic degree of abandon, is suspected by her partner of the moment for the fraud that it so often is. I fucked the stuffing out of Dutra that night, as he poetically said when at last we were done. He couldn't have known he'd been used to shore up my convictions. He succeeded so far that, though groundless, the convictions survived the entire sleepless night. They only expired, with a furious struggle, at dawn.

Even now, all these years later, I pause at the brink. Any telling seems sure to diminish, to transpose what was so overwhelming and painful into something absurd. And perhaps it was absurd, in its keening emotions and weakness for froth. At the time, I believed the least relevant factor of all was that we were both women. Of course this was the first fact that anyone saw, but for us it felt last. It failed to register, at least with me. My adoration of her was so unto itself it could not refer outward, to other affairs between women or even between human beings. It was its own totality, bottomless and consuming, a font of impossible pleasure that from the start also bore down on me like a drill until at last it accomplished a permanent perforation. And yet, irrelevant as I thought gender was to our sex, and to all the disasters it wrought, I now see that the form our love took was fundamentally girl-ish. The gender-blindness I sensed did apply to the content: I didn't love Martha for being a woman, and would have loved her no less had Shake-spearean whim turned her into a man. So much for the reasons for love, if such even exist. But the *way* that I loved, and the way she loved me . . . we might as well have been sylphs capering through the glade, crowned with daisy tiaras and trailing lace rags. We lay hours on end raptly strok-ing the other's smooth face, or disbelievingly tracing the wavelets of damp lip and brow; we wept a great deal and loudly; and endured our orgasms like shipwreck survivors with hoarse shrieks of actual fear.

That spring Nicholas was teaching his undergraduate Spenser survey on Tuesdays and Thursdays; his graduate seminar, close-reading *Areopagitica*, Wednesday afternoons; his office hours he held after Spenser lectures, or by appointment; he had no obligations on Monday. Having worked with him so closely, having come to know him so well, being in possession as I was of his schedule even now that I no longer TA'd for his class, had either heightened my conscience in favor of him, so that I might have hesitated at stealing his wife; or, less happily to upholders of morals, it might have given me such knowledge, as of the hours he was sure to be out, to assist in the theft. And so the fact that I phoned their house Monday seemed to suggest that my motives were pure, if "pure" can be meant to describe a compulsion forbidding the slightest resistance. I felt no malice. I meant no one harm. Saturday night I had kissed her. The wee hours of Sunday I'd willfully sullied my body with Dutra. In the hard light of dawn I had washed myself clean, yet the ardor for Martha remained, after torrents of water, immobile as bedrock. Realizing this was a sort of bereavement, and bearing it alone, for the rest of Sunday's daylight and darkness, had been almost intolerable. How could I wait until Tuesday to call her? Likely immediate consequences—Nicholas picking up his own phone—I disregarded with a rashness I mistook for courage.

But neither Nicholas nor Martha picked up. "Ah-lo," said a distracted Latin voice. "Hellett-Brawder rezidenze."

"Is Martha there, please," I exhaled.

"Whoze calling?"

". . . It's a student."

When she came on the line she said, quietly, as if assuming someone was eavesdropping, "Miss Gottlieb. I thought it might be you. You know I'm not teaching this term, and even if I was, I never give my home number to students."

"I was wondering," I began with new uncertainty, for she was so reduced and abstracted, and I couldn't watch her mouth for the telltale asymmetry, or scent the heady nectar creeping out from her clothes, or lay hold of any other encouragement, so that my wonder, like a shy tentacle finding nothing to grasp, began to shrink back on itself. "I was wondering if you'd meet me for lunch."

"I don't think that's a good idea," she said so kindly I thought she might pity me, and a sweat of righteous anger broke out on my scalp.

"Just coffee, then," I countered.

"Listen. The other night, everyone here had a little too much—"

"Just meet me in Memorial Park, by the flagpole. Just for a minute. We'll just take a walk."

"Regina—"

"You want to see me," I declared, for she'd spoken my name, and all at once I'd felt the telephone disclose her. I knew that if indifferent or bored or alarmed she would have promptly hung up without scruples. She wasn't a courteous woman. She didn't protract conversation in honor of form. She had thrown stale baguette at her guests in the hopes they would leave—and she was still on the line.

"Maybe we should have this conversation in person," she conceded. "Because you really can't call here again."

"I understand," I said, dismissing her injunction like tossing a hat in the air.

She ruled out both lunch and a walk, I knew without her stating it outright because both were too personal; the cup of coffee she accepted. She chose a downtown café highly favored by professors and students for off-campus meetings that was always crowded, that played at excess volume the three-chord anthems of frenetic social outrage favored by the melancholy pierced and dyed counter employees who were all the teenage dropouts and faculty brats of the town, and that was long and shallow with no secret crannies and located on a street corner, with two walls of full-height windows, that made of passersby an exhibit to the patrons, and of patrons no less to the passersby. Its tiled floors were permanently grimy, its pastries were stale, its coffee was rancid, and its bathrooms were effectively public and frequently used by denizens of a bar down the street which had delicate plumbing. Even the most dirty-minded of lovers would not choose this place for a tryst. And so I knew, from the trouble she went to, that the solarium was as vivid in her mind as mine.

I arrived more than an hour before the appointed time, and she was more than fifteen minutes late, so that I was able to secure a booth along the inner wall, with relative if scanty privacy. Most of the privacy there was provided by noise, and by the self-absorption of the other patrons. Before rushing out of the house I'd remembered to bring a notebook and a pile of paperbacks, and these sat on the table as camouflage. I even tried to absorb myself in them, so that she would come upon me in beguiling profile, bent scholastically over a tome, but I couldn't; I couldn't take my eyes from the windows, nor stop readjusting my clothes, over which I'd gone crazy before leaving the house, putting on and taking off until I ran out of time, so that I was dressed very strangely, in a gingham sheath dress that the weather was not ready for, and a thick cardigan, and scuffed, ugly black boots.

She turned out to be dressed strangely also, in a fancy and ugly silk blouse, matching slacks, and dark, chilly lipstick, as if to make the point of her superior age and position while also denying her beauty, but this final objective, which couldn't succeed, had confused the effect of the rest. As soon as I caught sight of her through the windows I erupted all over in mutinies. An idiot's grin split my face, even as I saw, in her face, a clear series of calculations; she seemed to toss out the script she'd prepared as, perhaps, too polite. "We're talking about your term paper," she said warningly as she sat. "Don't lean so far across the table. I shouldn't have come."

"You wanted to," I insisted, fearlessly combative now because so replete, not with particular joy or desire but whatever that common juice is that engorges the pump works of all the extremes of emotion. Now that she was here at arm's length, there was nothing inhibiting about the café. If not for her schoolmistress gaze keeping me in my place, I would have lunged over the table.

"I don't always act in my best interests," she agreed, "but I didn't come here to protract our," and my heart threatened to burst when she used the possessive pronoun, "misunderstanding," she finished.

"I don't think it was a misunderstanding."

"It was very much a misunderstanding."

"It didn't feel like one."

After a moment she said, carefully, "I hope I haven't hurt you."

"Do you think—" I gasped suddenly with unpleasant insight. "Do you think I'm just a student with a crush? Who's going to stalk you, and threaten suicide over you, and tell the dean you harassed me, to get my revenge?"

"I could argue you're stalking me now," she said, attempting levity but failing, for gravity had condensed at our table; she was leaning far forward now also, as if she hoped to trap my words under a dome.

"I'm not a student with a crush."

"Then what are you?"

"I'm in love with you!" I declared with exasperation, for she'd enraged me with this repeat of her coy question: *what are you doing?* And then I saw her blanch behind the stain of her mouth, and knew at least she was listening.

"Keep your voice down!" she said.

"And you," I went on, ignoring her. "You—"

"I cannot get involved with a student," she stated, all the color of her face, having ebbed out of sight for an instant, resurging now as if she'd been slapped. "Let alone a student of my husband's."

"We're already involved."

"That's absurd."

"It's true. You're the one in some kind of denial—because you think it's inappropriate, or because you feel guilt—"

"I'll thank you not to tell me how I feel or what I think," she exclaimed, now as livid as I; she'd equally forgotten where we were. "You're very young," she warned me. "I'd rather not say that I'm old but I'm older than you. I've been stupid and had stupid impulses, but I'm not ruled by them anymore. I don't know what you know about me. I haven't been an exemplary wife and I've caused my *husband*, your *mentor*, many serious problems and he's caused many problems for me but that's over, that chapter is closed. I'm married. That's what marriage is about: you work this crap out. Recommit. I have a child. In fact, I have to go now. I'm sorry we all drank and smoked far too much this past weekend. I hope you'll forget it." I sat stunned as she delivered this speech—so the script had not been irretrievable—and as I did, my mute astonishment grew its reflection on the silk of her blouse, for in the course of her words, her heart started to bleed. The stain spread as I watched, a dark drenching that more and more clung to reveal her breast and its hard, bumpy nipple. She must have noticed my gaze the same instant she felt it, and her hand went to cover the spot. "You see," she murmured, but her voice had sunk and its low roughness thrilled me. "You see, I have to go." She rose and threw a last glance at me which remained even after she turned and wove back through the tables, and past the bank of windows until out of sight. *You see*, the glance said, *my body tells the truth, if you think that I don't.* But I already knew this.

Once, when still heavy and tethered; and intimate and yet hard, like some tool of a doctor's, against which, with a sense of transgression, we could squash a hot cheek; when transmitting the sound of the other with that erstwhile fidelity that allowed us to feel they were with us in bed; the telephone, that old bludgeon-shape thing with the corkscrew-curl cord, was intensely romantic. We always wanted to seduce it from its central location to some lovers' nook, hearing the serpentine hiss of its cord as we dragged it the length of the hall. Success of connection was never assumed; the beloved's voice saying "Hello?" always felt like good fortune. The handset a seashell, enclosing the perfectly audible breath of far-off, inaccessible flesh; it was no wonder that Dutra had found me, asleep and entwined with the phone as if clutching a proxy, when he followed our household's cord under my closed bedroom door.

"Hello? Hello?" he barked into the handset, roughly uprooting the phone from my arms before slamming the handset back into the cradle. "Your boyfriend hung up," he said, pulling the phone back out into the hallway and kicking my door shut behind him.

I understood why he was furious with me. After persuasively ravishing him on the night of our relapse, not only didn't I touch him again, I could hardly speak to him. Either I stormed into his room without knocking, when the urge to confess what was happening with Martha was too much for me to resist—yet I always did resist, once I saw his outraged bafflement— or, instead of bursting through his door, I closed mine, with our shared telephone as my hostage. *"What?"* Dutra would shout when I opened his door and stared stricken at him and then turned and rushed back out again, "close the door, you premenstrual freak!" or, as the case might be, "OPEN THE DAMN DOOR. I NEED THE DAMN PHONE." For, the night of the day she forbade me to call her, Martha instead had called me.

"I didn't mean to flounce off," she mumbled, barely audible even by way of that outmoded, quality phone. "I'm sorry. I was embarrassed. I should've worn pads. For lactation, I mean. You don't even know what I'm talking about."

"You don't need to apologize," I said, in my trembling elation very consciously quiet and calm, to preserve the enchantment. I comprehended the fact of her voice, of her having called me. I blithely disregarded her words. Of course I didn't know what lactation was; nor did I wonder. "Where are you?" I said.

"I'm at home."

"I mean, where in your house?"

"Are you wondering whether Nicholas is here?"

"Yes."

"He's at a dinner. To which I was invited as well, but I pled overdeveloped maternal instincts." I laughed when she said this, again in response to her wry tone of voice, not her meaning, which brushed over me. I was intoxicated, by my hoard of her voice, which I clutched in my hands and against which I squashed my hot cheek, so much so I hardly know what I replied to her comments; I hardly know how we conversed. Yet we did, sleepily, as if the process of early acquaintance had been declared over, and the critical questions—who were we, and what would we do—long since answered, yet at the same time more profoundly unknown. But isn't this always the progress of love: circular, full of gaps and unlikely accumulations, and unevenly governed by sense.

". . . I always mean to read when the baby is sleeping, but then I just stare. I see textures vibrate. Like, the threads in the carpet. Because I'm so tired . . ."

"I'd like to read the same book that you're reading."

"That's sweet. But I've said I don't read anymore."

"I think bicycle thieves might be living next door. Under my window, in the little side yard you can't see from the street, there's all these dismembered bikes strewn everywhere."

"Have they spotted you up at your window? Be careful. They won't want a witness."

"If I disappear, you can avenge me. It's the house to the left, when you're facing my door."

"You say that as if I've been there."

"You could come here."

"Could I?"

"I wish you would."

"Why?"

"I miss you."

Her husky laughter. "You don't know me. But maybe that's why."

What did we talk about? Nothing. The night sounds. The incomprehensible show that her nanny/housekeeper, off the clock for the night, was watching down the hall in her room, on her tiny TV. The loud, angry music that Dutra was playing downstairs—but only the music, only the fact of there being upstairs and downstairs, and not Dutra, not anger, not anything close to my separate existence, or hers. We seemed to be dozy night watchmen, on some lofty tower beneath teeming stars, offhandedly trading remarks as we lay side by side with our greater attention cast far out to space, to some imminent wonder we both sensed was making its steady approach . . . the actual words that we spoke seemed inconsequential. Yet sometimes, for a moment, on the wing of some ambling irrelevance, again we'd dip gingerly into our selves and our strange situation. "I only wanted to say," she repeated, by way of another attempt to conclude the phone call, for every few minutes she began, yet did not reach the end, of an ending remark, "I was sorry I flounced out like that. I'm not angry at you."

"It's funny to hear you say 'flounce.' You're not flouncy at all. You're an opposite something."

"Like what?"

"Now you're asking to flirt."

"I didn't mean to. No flirting."

"Isn't that why you called me?"

"It's not."

"Then why did you?"

"I don't know. Just to talk for a while. Just to say I was sorry for flouncing."

"I'd like to see you."

"No," she said, a reflex—as if she, like me, hardly heard what we said to each other. For we spoke for the sluiceway of words we created, that bore us along; to discuss the direction might somehow inhibit the motion.

Sometimes she called me at eight, and sometimes at eleven; sometimes we spoke for two hours, and sometimes a few minutes; a week might have passed in this way, or just three or four days. The measure of time mattered less than of weight and momentum, and one night when these seemed to have crested a preordained mark, and as Dutra sat smoking his bong on the couch with the TV on mute and the turntable playing and the slabs of his textbooks in heaps around him adequate to protect him from me, I knew talk was no longer required for motion, and walked out the back door without waiting for Martha to call. I walked up the long hill to the campus, the steam from my body replacing a coat. It was still very cold but I smelled the wet earth, dark bare patches of which now exceeded in size the gray crusts of vestigial snow. Under moonlight I bisected the quad, my shadow sharp-edged and elongated on the flagstones. I passed the bright yellow squares of the library windows, behind which my erstwhile fellows were still toiling over their texts. My purpose seemed suddenly, thoroughly different from theirs, as if a point of divergence had long passed me by, and only now did I notice the change. I passed the ugly juridical hulk of the English department, its colonnade raised in the thirties as proof that the school was a serious place—but at night, under moonlight, in spring, all this moon-silvered kingdom of turrets and archways was plainly the same little state agricultural school it had been at the start. The field's furrows awaiting their seeds and the animals restlessly pawing their stalls. The landscape I crossed was abiding and elemental; I seemed to see through its various garments to what lay beneath. I left the region of campus, and sidewalks, and walked at the edge of the steep, curving roads, where the shadows of trees thickly barred the moonlight. Houses lay at the backs of deep lawns, and then disappeared behind masonry walls. The few times a car passed, sweeping me with its headlamps, I thought that the driver might call the police. I wasn't jogging in exercise clothes. I wasn't walking a dog on a leash. My reason to be there was clear to no one but myself—and Martha. Despite her consistent refusals to see me, I felt expected.

When I passed through their stone entry columns and walked up the drive, I could see a few lights on upstairs. I rounded the side of the house.

Through the double interference, of the solarium's glass and the kitchen's, shone the solitary light of the breakfast-nook lamp. I thought of Nicholas's cozy encampment, and wondered if that nook was his particular place. But the nights Martha called me, she was usually in the kitchen. I'd hear her filling a kettle for tea, stacking dishes in a cupboard, sliding drawers open and shut. Performing what struck me as pretexts, for lingering there by herself. It was dark close to their house on account of their numerous prospering trees, and already, in the course of my walk, I'd turned into a creature of shadows. It only briefly surprised me how easy it was to become a voyeur, and duck into the shrubs on tiptoe, the noisy uproar in my heart somehow only enhancing my stealth.

It was Martha in the breakfast nook's pool of light. An open magazine and a steaming mug sat on the table before her, untouched. Her hands lay out of sight beneath the table, perhaps in her lap. Her gaze was cast forward in thought. Past her I could see the telephone, mounted on the far wall. In love contrary impulses constantly war with each other. I wanted to feast on her image unseen, and I wanted to seize her attention, so that my hand flew up to tap on the glass even as my inner voice exclaimed angrily, *Wait!* It was too late; she'd seen me. Astonishment and anger froze her face, and then she scooted so quickly out of the snug nook she almost spilled her tea, and it seemed possible she'd shout for Nicholas, or phone the police. But she came out the kitchen door and through the solarium, stopping me at the threshold before I came in. "Nicholas is home!" she exclaimed in a sort of shrieked whisper. "What are you doing? He's up in his study." But she'd taken hold of my hands, or else I'd taken hers, and she was warming the gnarled, icy claws they'd become in the course of my walk, for despite all the heat beating out from my core, my hands and feet and lips and ears had gone numb. "You're wearing pajamas," she scolded, of my thin, inappropriate clothes. We were wringing and squeezing and clutching our four hands together as if we'd given them the task of communicating on behalf of the rest of our selves. I tried to pull her close to me and kiss her and she said, "No! Are you out of your mind?" Yet her hands kept their tight grip on mine; she pressed her forehead to mine so our mouths couldn't touch but our stern gazes locked, at such close range our eyelashes tangled.

"Let me come in a minute," I whispered.

"No! Nicholas is upstairs. Everyone is upstairs."

"I won't do anything. I'll just sit and warm up. I feel cold."

"How am I supposed to explain you, if Nicholas comes in the kitchen?"

"You can say that I came for a visit."

"At ten-thirty at night? In no jacket?"

"You can say I was taking a jog."

"You don't jog. You're not dressed for a jog."

"He won't see me. If we hear him, I'll run out the door. Besides, he's already in bed."

"What makes you say that?"

"Because he goes to sleep early, and you stay up late. When you call, he's already in bed." I wasn't sure if this was true. I only knew that, when she called, she was alone—whether Nicholas was out, or asleep, or for some other reason behind a closed door.

Her hot, bony forehead still pressed against mine. "Ten minutes," she finally said. "I brewed tea. You can have some and go. While sitting on opposite sides of the table."

We crept like thieves into the kitchen and gingerly I seated myself at the outermost end of the breakfast nook bench, on the side that was nearest the door. It was the same spot I'd sat in before, grading papers the previous fall, but some translucent reality membrane had been peeled away so that it no longer seemed the same place. I was shuddering and chattering with cold, and hugged myself, and clenched my jaw, to keep quiet, while Martha almost silently poured out my tea, and the silence of the house reasserted itself so that, at its deepest profundity, it yielded to me the faintest broken thread of a televised voice, that might have even been coming from some other house. Apart from this, nothing. I felt sure that, if Nicholas coughed, I would hear him and slide out the door long before he set foot on the stairs. But then Martha, once she'd set down my tea, instead of seating herself on the opposite bench, pulled a chair to the end of the table, so that we were seated diagonally, and only need lean the slightest bit forward to touch. The sledgehammer blows of my heart filled my ears, and my exquisite attention to audible clues was destroyed. I raised a hand and cupped her cheek, and inwardly swooned at its softness, and she, tipping forward, again tented her forehead on mine, and took my own cheek in her hand. "We must stop this," she whispered.

Lovestruck, almost moaning with shame, we caressed our reflections, my tea going cold. Science tells us that scent is retained by the brain for a longer duration than the evidence gathered by eyes, ears, or hands, but my experience differs. I can still feel with unparalleled vividness the strange vulnerability of Martha's face on my palm and the pads of my fingers, as if it were the first such, of some rare or taboo category, I'd ever dared trespass upon with a touch—a shy and sheltered buttock or breast, even a velveteen scrotum, hot and dry and just powdered with down, and not the dazzling aspect she most often turned to the world. And at the same time I knew that my face felt as strange and forbidden and tender to her, for we could not stop avidly stroking each other, as if we were a pair of Helen Kellers who had just linked the name with the flesh—caressing and heaving our guttering breaths, and passing from solemn surrender to dismayed embarrassment to embarrassed bemusement to solemnity again, as if all our foreignness to each other were encompassed in the ambit of a cheek.

"We must stop," she repeated at last, sitting back suddenly so that she broke all our points of contact. "I'm sorry. I need you to leave."

"Do you want me to leave?"

"Yes." Her face had gone bleary and distant and offered no purchase. Stunned, I believed her to the point of mute despair, yet disbelieved her to the point of almost laughing in her face, and for a moment it seemed possible that I really would laugh, and that she would laugh also, and clutching hands we'd run out her back door and keep running to some unknown place. At that age I'd only lived four different places, of which the town where we'd met was the fourth, and I truly believed that commencing a wholly new life was just a matter of changing location. But her face and her voice were so altered, that instead I stood blindly and went out her door, and back down that long, ludicrous hill that the glacier clawed out of the rock all those eons ago. At home in my bed, clutching blankets, I grieved at the loss.

At the same time I still disbelieved her, and kept one ear pricked for the phone.

Only Martha's omniscience, in which I believed by instinct and without reservation, enabled my fierce dignity in the following months. I avoided all groups, to be sure not to hear her name spoken. I kept my eyes sternly downcast, to prevent them from seeking her out down the halls, or in the throngs on the sidewalks, or among loungers sprawled in the strengthening sun on the quad. I stayed away from the department on the days I knew Nicholas taught. With equal prompt care I deleted each message from Laurence, all identically warm and upbeat and devoid of allusion to what had occurred at the party, and with luck and some diligence didn't run into him, either. I would not seem to put myself under her gaze—her omniscience got no help from me, hence retained my untroubled belief. She saw me. She saw me, near midnight, framed by my own lonely square of yellow library light. She saw me in silent attendance of each of my classes, at all moments purging her face from my thoughts, meantime grinding my molars to dust. She saw me at home, grimly watching my printer saw out the accordion pages of three end-of-term papers that were each, in distinctive ways, brilliant and overly long and excessively weighted with footnotes and for good measure handed in early, and destined to be skimmed and rewarded the cursory A. She saw me achieving ceasefire with Dutra, not by confession nor supplication, but the simple resumption of habits. She saw me sharing the bong with him nights, watching *Star Trek: The Next Generation*, and eating the stir-fry I made for us both out of all things not rotten dug out of our fridge. She saw me go to bed alone, and rise alone, and refrain, in my fierce dignity, even from masturbation; she even saw me refrain, when the term finally ended, from the distraction of a trip to New York. "You sure?" Dutra asked one last time, heaving his duffel bag into his Volvo. I knew he wanted very much for me to come. He wanted to show off his city to me, for, to his boundless amazement, despite my adequate wit and sophistication, which this past year had endeared me to him, I had never set foot in that place whose very image appeared in Webster's as the birthplace of both "sophistication" and "wit." "I'll show you a *fabulous* time," he cajoled. At least for the four-hour drive, he was afraid to be lonely.

"Another time." I refused him firmly, for Martha's eyes on me seemed to lend me her superior composure.

"But you've never been there! It's humanity's greatest creation! I want to be the first person who shows you the city. I want your Big Apple cherry."

"You'll get it," I made the error of promising. "Just not today."

Watching him go, waving his left arm wildly and sadly out the window, it occurred to me I might have botched my performance for Martha. Until now I'd shown no sign of weakness, but declining to go to New York could suggest I was pining for her. Equally it could suggest I was wholly content, in no need of distraction. I stood a long time on the porch after Dutra had gone. The term was over. I had done all my work, unnecessarily well. By every available measure I'd succeeded in not falling short, and no available measures remained. Her magical eye rested on me, goose-pimpling my arms, and I exhorted myself to appear unperturbed and even considered lying down in the hammock and inviting its taut knotted cords to bite into my limbs. When the phone rang, despite the fact that her days were still ruled by the same school calendar as Dutra's and mine, it seemed possible I had conjured the call with the sheer abject force of my longing. "He's gone," I heard Martha confess. "Nicholas has gone out of town. On his annual trip. Canoe trip. Georgian Bay. He'll be gone for three weeks." And then amid our breathless overlapping exclamations, I somehow managed to direct her to my house, for in our impatience she was going to come pick me up in her car.

"... the north side of Pin Creek," I was babbling. "It doesn't go through, you have to jog down to Elmwood and take the bridge there. The pizza guys never find it. They go to the south end of town—"

"I can find it," she promised. "Ten minutes." And with the spring on the timer thus wound a moan wrenched free of me, so unwilled I could have thought it had come from the couch cushions.

Only aircraft could have traveled from her house to mine in ten minutes. It took her more than twice as long, long enough that I mastered myself. Urgency and solemnity banished emotionalism. I could scarcely let go of the phone but once I did every separate grain of my condition, both inner and outer, seemed to present itself to my unsparing gaze. I showered again, and soaped the grooves between my legs with thoughtful fingers until they might have squeaked. The same scouring finger slipped into my anus as into the teardrop-shape gaps between each of my toes. My body seemed as neutered as a child's, as if it had never been used, at least never for pleasure. Toweled dry I had no odor at all. All warmth seemed to have left me. I pulled the comb through my hair and the deathly white furrows of scalp lay exposed to the light. The clothes I pulled on could have been for a latter-day monk; I was already dressing as she did without my realizing. Loose man's jeans that just clung to my hip bones over white cotton panties; a white cotton T-shirt; no bra; hoary Birkenstock sandals. Before you, everything is revealed, I seemed to concede in this sexless and dowdy attire. Any effort to consciously flatter myself, to be beautiful for her, seemed pointless. But she wouldn't set foot in my house, with its glacial formations of cassette tapes and bong parts and empty beer bottles; to await her I stood on the porch. If we'd been alone on the planet I would have waited there naked, not as provocation but as an admission. When she pulled up, in a black Saab wagon as glossy as a patent leather shoe, I descended the three wooden steps from the porch as if mounting a gangway, to a ship of the seas or the skies, and did not care if I ever again saw my house, or Dutra, or anyone else I had known this past year, or the halls along which I had learned, or the books I had read or the papers I'd written or any of the items of which I'd assumed that my life to that point must consist, and from then I would go on not caring for a very long time.

In the car she took hold of my hand, and turned toward me her stunned, windblown face, and we gazed at each other as if from the opposite sides of a chasm. Then she relinquished her hold to return to driving. The car might not have even halted before we were moving again, quickly, through the downtown streets with their shabby frame houses on handkerchief plots, and then, nose up, onto the hill. To all sides heaps of end-of-term moving detritus, disjointed floor lamps and dog-eared, dry-mounted Warhols and blackened, crumb-glutted toaster ovens and the doughy folds of exhausted futons obstructed the curbs, abandoned by the graduating seniors in the course of their ascension to postgraduate life. Goodbye, goodbye, tolled in my mind, not because I sympathized with the annual rite, the completion of toil and attainment of credentialed enlightenment; nor because I saw myself commencing, in the terms of the familiar metaphor, a new course of education. No conceit requiring my separate existence was tenable now. I yearningly bid it goodbye because I longed to be grappled against her and thoroughly used and subsumed; I couldn't start to imagine just what we would do, whether we would fuck with our mouths or our fists or an improvised suitcase of devilish tools, but I somehow felt very precisely the final result, and couldn't have gained it too quickly. I was singed in advance; though I sat very still in the car, my gaze fixed on her face I'd already so carefully mastered, on the slight bluish dent on one side of her nose, and the almost invisible down of her cheek, and the incipient spidery wear at the crease of her eye, when the car stopped, and I made to get out, my right knee popped with pain, for I'd been pressing so hard on an imagined gas pedal I'd ground up the delicate joint.

"Lucia's at the park with Joachim," she was saying as we fell out the doors of her car, but amid all the other exigencies passing between us that moment, these particular words were illegible.

We sliced through the rind of the house like two knives. Nothing now was of interest to me except her; that house I'd first come to because of Brodeur, my abruptly imploded polestar, was just so much waste to be shouldered behind. In a more circumspect frame of mind I might have admired the quality of the house's construction, as the door to her bed-room did not fly off its hinges when we came crashing through. Her bed, a fragrant welter of matelassé and ecru and other characteristics I was yet to be taught, was as she had recently left it, also perhaps as her husband had recently left it, as I might have assumed in a more circumspect frame of mind, but in a more circumspect frame of mind I might have allowed her to tell me that she and Nicholas hadn't shared the same bed since before Joachim had been born. This was too much to allow her to tell me, when her mouth at that moment was so crucial to my survival that I fell onto it as if drowning, and determined to drain her last breath, even if this consigned her to drowning as well—she might not have been able to handle me if my aggression had not been as frantic and disorganized as hers was efficient. Once again I was wringing the front of her shirt—my hands were abruptly afraid of her skin, so that I wanted to crush her to me without having to touch her; I would have liked a single rope to bind us together, with tightly stacked coils, so that we formed a sort of Siamese mummy within which our two bodies got mashed into one—and having fought me to half an arm's length so she could undo my jeans, and peel them off with a hard downward step of her deft pointed foot, she simply seized me by the armpits and heaved me away from her onto the bed, and as I struggled to regain her kiss pinned me flat with the heel of her hand so that she could, when I gave up the struggle, with a leisurely sigh sink her face in my cunt. I seemed to come right away, with a hard, popping effervescence, as if her mouth had raised blisters, or an uppermost froth; but beneath, magma still heaved and groaned and was yearning to fling itself into the air. Until now, my orgasms had been deep and ponderous things; slow to yield to excavation; self-annihilating when they finally did, so that in their wake I felt voided and calm, every yen neutralized, and gazed on whoever had managed the work with benign noninterest. Never had there been this tormenting, self-heightening pleasure, like a hail of hot stones, and yet she seemed to recognize just what had happened, so that before I had even stopped keening she bore down again. She made me come so many times that afternoon that had I been somewhat older, I might have dropped dead. Had I been a doll, she might have twisted off each of my limbs, and sucked the knobs until they glistened, and drilled her tongue into each of the holes. Certainly had the windows been open, as would have made sense on that sunny June day, my thundering cries, in the end, would have summoned the neighbors; for Martha, in dismantling me, dredged a voice out of me I did not know I owned; the devastation of my pleasure surged outward and outward again, like an ocean-floor tremor, while that voice I had never imagined was bellowing harshly Oh GOD, Oh GOD, OHGODOHGOD!—and it was then that Martha finally flung herself onto my shore, and through violent sobs kissed me, as if drenched in my juices as she had become, eyes glued shut, stringy-haired, fever-cheeked, parched and gasping for water and air, she'd been born out of *me* in those hours, bodied forth by titanic orgasm, and now she was helplessly, utterly mine for the rest of all time. Love is tutelage, after all; and ardor, such as we had laid hold of, that same tutelage greatly compressed—so that, knowing nothing but what she'd just taught me, I was somehow no longer afraid, and rearing up on the heels of my hands I threw open her spent, helpless body, already softened as if by a mallet from the hours of toil she'd expended on me, and plunged into her headlong with fingers and tongue not unlike, the thought burst in my mind, having leaped without forethought or parachute out of a plane. Yet, all the while I was plummeting down, I still wafted and roved, and was drawn along ropy cross-currents, and seemed at my leisure to swim in a lush element . . . until with a fearsome huge groan like the earth cracking open I found Martha suddenly near, rushing upward toward me. *"Oh,"* she wailed, with strange desolation, as if the nearer she came, the more receded her voice, *"Ahh . . . OH . . . ,"* and then came the sodden implosion of impact, and her bed elephantinely bounced up and down, and her cries filled my ears and we burst into tears from the shock.

Weeping we knotted our bodies together, caressing and hushing each other, until we both must have slept, to awake it seemed many hours later, and gaze at each other in mute wonderment.

"Fuck," she said, sitting up. "What the fuck time is it?"

Outside the closed windows the horizon-bound sunlight was guttering now through the limbs of the big handsome trees. With the labored strokes of a swimmer pulling dead weight to land Martha got within arm's reach of a tiny bedside alarm clock while I did everything to impede her, while I nuzzled her neck and her armpits and with fresh resolve nosed toward her crotch—"Oh, God," she realized. "It's already six-thirty. Okay," she said, more to herself than to me, as with adrenaline visibly coursing she leaped out of bed. "Okay. Okay. You'll have to stay here. Just stay here in my room." From some far-off realm of the house, I now realized, an irregular noise drifted steadily toward us, part percussive, part exhalative—as of water or wind—part obscurely verbal, and part high-pitched, parrotlike shriek. "I've got to take a quick shower. You'd better take one as well, look at you! Your hair looks like a nest—come on, hurry—"

I couldn't help but behave as if drugged in the shower. The sight of her body agleam with the coursing hot water seemed to muzzle the rational part of my brain. All the minor imperfections of her superior age made me insane with adoration as I one by one rooted them out of her smooth opalescence: the minute dark-purple varicose squiggle midway down her right thigh, as if a single gaudy thread had dropped there from an unraveling garment. The thin rippled furrows streaking out from each side of her pale flat belly, where snagging needles perhaps had been dragged down the silk of her skin—or where her pregnancy had stretched her, I realized only much later, for I was so young then that I had never seen those marks that become so mundane, like the first kinky, colorless hairs on one's head, just one decade later in life. Either I was poring over her skin with my tongue—"Stop. *Stop!*" she admonished—or slumped swooning against the wet tile as she soaped me with businesslike hands, but regardless I was no use to her and yet she had us in and out of the shower quickly, as she'd stated she would. Back in her bedroom I lurched and stumbled and fell over in my hapless effort to put on my jeans while she disappeared into a closet and reappeared a moment later in khaki shorts and a pale green tank top, her breasts shifting under the jersey fabric in a way that made me shudder with recognition—and pulling a tortoiseshell comb through her hair. "I've got to go down now," she said. "I have to nurse. Do the dinner thing. Stay here. Just stay here—" In her panic she rushed from the room.

The irregular noises from downstairs continued, very distant and hard to interpret. I swayed on my feet, the walls pitching around me as if I'd developed an inner-ear balance condition, but there was nowhere to sit in her room but the bed, and I disliked the bed without her. I felt the peculiar gratification of having been made a taxidermy of myself, disassembled and rebuilt with some sort of narcotic-soaked gauze densely stuffed in my cavities—I was that deeply satisfied, down to my marrow; all the bones in my pelvis seemed loosened and bobbling around. That tawdry skeletal dishevelment made me grin with remembrance. Martha's agitated precaution that I stay in the room never could have sunk in, I was so inundated with pleasure, and perhaps, looking back, there was also reluctance on her part to fully avow the requirement of secrecy, to embrace the adulterer's furtive procedures by declaring outright that my choices were hiding for hours in her bedroom, or inching my way down the outside drainpipe. Such behavior as is natural to criminals could not have been less natural to my feelings, which were most like uncontainable pride, so stratospherically levitating I hardly felt myself in that room in the first place, though for the moment I floated on the outermost fibers of her round bedroom carpet. I did notice, but very remotely, because such things as furniture seemed now so misguided, so many props for distracting the body from what it did best, how impersonal the room was, as was that downstairs powder room. No photos or knickknacks, not even a bookcase. Just a short pile of paperbacks set on the floor, a Penguin Classic of *The Last of the Mohicans* on top looking wholly untouched. The clothes she'd been wearing before we made love lay strewn about the floor in arrested positions of ecstasy, and descending from the altitude of giants I scooped them up and pressed them onto my face, and devoured her pungent aroma. I was ravenous; sexual satiation flipped over neatly and showed its reverse, which was wolfish hunger. And so it was that without any pang at ignoring her orders, without in fact remembering her orders at all, I left that room in which we'd remade each other, which now looked so diminished, and danced down the carpeted hallway and stairs to the part of the house that I already knew.

It was hot and moist in the kitchen, and redolent with human smells, steam fogging the mullioned windows where it had risen from the great maw of the gleaming dishwasher, its unhinged jaws bristling with fresh-boiled stemware and forks, and from a large saucepan, agitating its lid on the stove. The loud agitation was irregularly doubled, perhaps deliberately, perhaps just by coincidence, by a spoon being banged on the edge of a hard plastic bowl; and a mingled smell of heated starch and salty milk filled the air which swept me back to the sweaty pungency of Martha's crotch and the marsh we had made of her bed—but of course this scent, though it might share a few of the same molecules, was not like that odor at all. It was salt without sweat, and every glandular species of stink to which sweat can refer. And it was milk without flesh, like the milk I once squeezed from a green clover stem sitting in my backyard as a very small child; because of course it was child smell, though very little of the mixture came from him, but from his bottle and bowl and his one-piece striped suit, like a prisoner's outfit, and perhaps something recently stuffed in the trash.

He was seated atop an elaborate high chair and observing me with silent thoroughness, his gaze having found me the instant I stepped in the doorway. I only understood now, but with the force of retrospective revelation, those sounds I'd been hearing ever since I'd awoken in Martha's hot arms and drenched bed. Martha stood with her back to me, half bent over, facing the baby across the wide kitchen island and plunging her arms to the elbow, with excessive and dangerous vigor, in the depths of the dishwasher's cauldron. Arm's length from the baby and the other arm's length from the stove stood an older woman I had never seen before, with a creased, alert, orange-tinged face and a puff of orange hair, in a turquoise sweat suit. Unlike the baby, she made clear she had seen me by continuing to stare, not at me but at the baby, reaching awkwardly back to the stove, as if her eyes lacked the freedom to roll in their sockets. It must have been the peculiar appearance of their stares crossed like swords, firmly pointed in different directions, that made Martha, when she'd straightened her back and seen them, then glance over her shoulder toward me. The baby's hand holding the spoon resumed banging it hard on the bowl, as if the hand were asserting itself as an agent distinct from the eyes. Martha flushed, or perhaps she had already turned very red from the dishwasher's steam, and whipping back toward the baby emitted a sharp warning sound lest the force of the spoon on the rim of the bowl flip its wet contents into the air—"No, no, hey!"—which even in its brevity was truncated by the instant response of the orange-tinted, turquoise-clad woman.

"It don't move," the woman told Martha, still averting her gaze.

Her tone could not have been convicted of rudeness, but any conscious person would have tried to make the charge. The bowl on closer examination was a specialized one that adhered to the tray of the high chair by some sort of suction, but Martha's failure to remember this feature, or possibly her failure to have known it at all, seemed hardly an adequate motive for the woman's contempt. Nor could I believe, at least not yet, that her motive was me, however inexplicable and freshly showered my appearance. Rather the contempt seemed instinctive, as if it were the third thing, along with the saucepan and baby, that this woman consistently kept within reach.

"Either way he doesn't seem to be enjoying this much," declared Martha, making for the baby's other side as if to intercept an enemy combatant and attempting to unstick the bowl from the tray. Though she was still crimson to the roots of her hair she added as if as an afterthought, "This is Regina. She's one of Nick's students. I forgot to tell you she's doing some work for us. Research assistance. Regina, this is Joachim's nanny, Lucia."

"Hi," I heard myself say, so stung by this alibi—by the seeming ease with which, despite her blush, Martha had made it—that now I blushed also, and barely raised a greeting hand, though I saw that I could have said nothing, or stuck out my tongue, Lucia had so resolutely ignored Martha's introduction.

"He is crazy for his cereal today," Lucia contradicted. "This is third bowl I give him."

"Well, he's obviously done." Martha wouldn't return my gaze, hard as I sought hers, as if she'd joined Lucia's backward swordplay, in which the object was evading contact, and Lucia for her part did not dignify Martha's comment with an answer—unless the answer was the wrist-flick with which, pivoting, she abruptly extinguished the stove burner, seized the handle of the saucepan, and dumped the scalding contents, of short, pointy noodles, in a colander placed in the sink. She extracted a tub of black stuff from the fridge, scraped a blob of it into a bowl, then dumped the colander's noodles in the bowl as well, and went to work furiously with a spoon. Martha had set upon the baby as if he presented a door she could lock against me and Lucia. She looked at neither of us nor, in truth, at the baby, but was grimly uprooting him from the high chair and uprooting the spoon from his fist and then sitting down at the table with him and pulling up her tank top and pinning it with her chin, vainly seeking to screw his mouth onto her breast while he swiveled one way and the other, whatever he needed to do, to keep me within sight while he meanwhile hid Martha's bare breast. But I didn't begrudge him; if not for his loyal attention I might have thought I had ceased to exist.

"You bought pesto?" Martha said to Lucia. "Damn it, Joachim, settle down! What did you buy pesto for?"

"He is not hungry now," said Lucia with meaning. "It got so late I gave him his dinner. Now it's time for his bath."

"The garden's already got bushels of basil. I was going to make pesto fresh."

"I'll leave it out or I'll put it away."

"Leave it out. Regina and I will eat it. Are you hungry, Regina?"

So abruptly had I been reinstated that it took me a moment to speak. "I guess," I said, launching my own freight of furious meaning, but as mode of conveyance I'd chosen my eyes, and Martha still wouldn't look at me.

"Time for his bath," Lucia repeated. Never had I been so in favor of a baby's being bathed. I wondered if Martha would cling to her baby, gurgle at or fawn on him or worst of all hand him to me, but with hauteur she yanked her tank top back down and held him out to be taken. In transit his smooth round head turned back toward me on his neck's frail stem, so that I remained his sole object of study. He didn't attempt to regain Martha's arms. As Lucia bore him out of the kitchen the two of them made a Janus, Lucia's outraged gaze boring ahead, the baby's placid one emanating behind, until they'd finally rounded the doorframe and vanished from sight.

Alone at last we rushed at each other like dueling snakes. "What the fuck are you doing?" hissed Martha. "I said stay in my room!"

"For how long? I can't hide there all night."

"All *night*. You hid there for two *minutes*."

"I shouldn't have to be hiding at *all*."

"Regina, Lucia works for me and Nicholas, for fuck's sake. She's our nanny!"

"And I'm your 'research assistant,'" I said witheringly.

"You'd better hope she believed that," she said sharply, wheeling away.

"Or what?"

"Or you won't see me this way again." She'd commenced cutting the space of her kitchen to ribbons, returning again to the dishwasher to snatch bowls, forks, tumblers, a cheese grater, a corkscrew—"What the fuck is this doing in there?" she snapped at it—from its still-smoldering mouth. Objects accumulated on the wide slab of gleaming black stone that divided the room; a pale melon, unearthed from the densely packed chaos of her refrigerator, was trapped between the counter and her knife and butchered to perfectly uniform crescents; so vehement were her movements she'd not only deflected my touch but had beaten me back to the doorway again, until she abruptly commanded, "Come here," and thrust a white envelope in my hands. "Prosciutto," she said of the pink skin within. "Drape it over the melon. Or wrap it around. Or attach it with toothpicks." But there were only so many serving options with which she could ward me off, and I caught her wrist in my free hand and her mouth met mine roughly and then broke away. But something was dispelled, or deferred. "Let's eat," she murmured. "We're starving. We've lost our right minds."

"Let's go out," I begged. "I'd rather not see your nanny again."

"I can't do that," she said patiently. "I have a baby to say good night to. But if it isn't too cold we can eat in the pergola." She might have equally said we could eat in the bathtub; I didn't know what a pergola was. I did know that the longer the nanny and baby stayed out of the room, the more Martha returned and was mine. Our vehicle now, that would keep her with me, was the meal. I opened the white envelope with a fraudulent show of experience and the precocious sense that the bathing of the baby upstairs, and the meal preparation downstairs, were in direct competition for Martha's attention, and I must throw my energies onto the side of the meal if I wanted to win. It helped my cause that the turbulence left by Lucia had finally stopped agitating the room; Lucia even grew sufficiently absent for Martha to joke about her. "It's classic Lucia to buy grocery-store pesto when my garden is already choking on basil. She learns 'pesto' from me—she's Brazilian—and then to show off she buys it at Friel's in June, when it's half-price, because everyone makes their own pesto the whole summer long in this town. Look at this stuff. It's like kombu. That's Japanese seaweed. It's practically black." But this harangue was pro forma; it told me Lucia was no longer a threat. Not only Martha's speech but her movements had changed. They had slowed, and admitted the pleasure of usual tasks, and I could hardly complete my own task for the pleasure of watching. She brought out a green bottle of wine, a rough chunk of some stone—this was cheese!—a narrow box stamped with gold as of pricey cosmetics that turned out to be cookies. Now I couldn't stop catching at her when she passed near enough, or raining kisses on her when she leaned her face briefly near mine, so that my incompetent bunching of pink flaps of meat on the slippery spears of green melon proceeded so slowly she took it from me and like the rest of the meal prepared it herself, and crowding everything onto a tray, led me through the solarium—even tossing a sly smile over one shoulder—into the violet twilight. Down stone steps and along a stone pathway we passed verdant swells of luxurious lawn, to a little wood structure tucked just where the lawn began losing itself to one more of those striking abysses that with their unwarned-of drops past abutments of shale into sooty hemlocks made a rare kind of property line.

"Pergola," she confirmed, as she set the tray down on the built-in stone table in the tiny octagonal shelter. "Nicholas's folly. I think it's supposed to resurrect some cherished boyhood memory of hiking with his scout troop in the Alps." The lawn rising behind us concealed the house from our view, but despite this, or perhaps because of it, the house now felt somehow more present, and returned to the form in which I had first known it: his house. Her mention of him seemed to tell me she felt this as well. It was unlike the mention she'd made of Lucia and pesto. It didn't confirm a safe distance from someone who anyway lacked consequence. Though the wine was, perhaps, the best-quality wine I had ever yet tasted, so that I didn't perceive it as "very good wine" but, as her body had been though with many times less potency, as some entirely new category of pleasure; and though the food, Friel's pesto and all, dazzled me with its goodness and elegance, for I had never seen cheese that resembled quartz stone, nor a cookie from France with a boy's figure so neatly stamped in the chocolate that each of his coat buttons showed, nor a silken pink meat that was not boiled ham from the deli; and though we ate mutely, like wolves, as the light died around us, restoking our bodies of all they had spent; in truth we were not really tasting the food or the wine, and our muteness was swollen with words. Mine were all different forms of the same hungry question. Hers were likely retractions, and warnings. When she finally spoke, what she said was, "After I've gone up and dealt with bedtime, I can drive you back home." A warning, but veiled.

What I said was, "I don't want to go home." Hungry question, thinly veiled if at all.

"Regina," she said. After a moment she added, "You understand why I can't have Lucia getting curious about who you are."

I thought to say, facetiously, "I'm the research assistant," in the hopes she'd refute me. Then I longed to say, "Who am I—to you?" but was afraid she would laugh at the question. At last I steeled myself to demand, "What happens when *he* returns home?" but this I was afraid she would actually answer. After such long hesitation, my silence and hers became part of the dusk, in which I could no longer make out her face though she sat just beside me, and speaking, regardless of what the words were, seemed unnatural.

It had grown very cold. With the afterglow gone winter seemed to return despite the loud chirring of insects. I pressed her to me and felt her arms rough with gooseflesh and her thin tank top sodden in front. She winced at my touch. "Engorged," she murmured. "Ugh, you're all wet. I'm sorry. Because the kid wouldn't eat." Although her voice was calm she twitched away sharply when I peeled back the drenched cloth from her breast. "No," she said, but I'd already felt the breast's hardness and heat, as if changed by infection.

"No!" she repeated, and now I felt what she must have, overpowering me at the start of our day, when she shuddered and capsized, emanating a guttural, helpless, admonishing moan as I sucked on the nipple until with a shocking mechanical suddenness, like a shower head being turned on, her hot milk filled my mouth. It queasily tasted of vegetation, and of her, but mostly and sickeningly of itself, but I was so hungry for the taste it obscured, of her flesh, that I gulped it down just to get past it, and past it, and past it, until her soft breast moved and squelched, deflated, underneath the harsh probes of my tongue, and she'd groaned in relief and then grabbed my head literally by the ears, and forced the other hard breast in my mouth.

"You sick thing," she gasped when I was done.

"I love you," I told her gravely, but she brushed this off, nimble and devilish again.

Nothing could have better excused my failure to accompany Dutra on his trip to New York than my confession, upon his return, that I'd fallen in love with not only a woman but the same sanguine blonde he'd accosted that day at the market. Dutra verily hooted with glee. Of course, being Dutra, his response wasn't mere titillation. He was honestly thrilled I'd found love—though it was true he was thrilled all the more that my love was so racy. There was no man on earth for whom my ardor could have prompted an ardent desire on Dutra's part that they meet, but for the privilege of meeting Martha, Dutra launched an onslaught of persuasion not unlike an onslaught of threats. "Bring her over to have a beer with me! I'm like the *father* in this situation, I have to approve. Don't make me start following you. I got Injun skills, *sabe*? Me track you. Me not make a sound."

I was desperate to keep them apart, for every obvious reason. It wasn't only, or even mostly, that Dutra, with his elaborate bongs and his heaps of ska records and his juvenile know-it-all-ness, had been my most recent lover; had fucked me on his orange Dacron couch and on his cap-sized king mattress amid a squalor of coffee-damp Styrofoam cups; had been fellated by me while a rerun of *Star Trek* illumined our nude, writh-ing limbs; or had pleasured me in our shared shower amid pads of hair and fallen gobbets of toothpaste overseen by a giant ashtray in the shape of a crab keeping laden precarious balance on the tank of the toilet. Far worse was that my alliance with Dutra, whether carnal or not, hopelessly marked me as someone far younger than Martha. In the course of our first torrid week Martha and I had made love in the back of her Saab; in the armchair she kept in her office in the English department; in a stand of lilacs in the riverfront park, on the frigid and dew-sodden grass; each of these trysts taking place at some hour between bedtime and dawn, when she slipped from her house to meet me—but never once in my house, though the whole of that week it stood empty, as if tailor-made for our needs. The idea of bringing her there was unbearable to me, and to her must have been at least sufficiently strange that she never once asked me about it. Perhaps she could sense that the sight of my home would present a disjunction she'd rather not ponder. Yet in my desire to match her adulthood, I somehow failed to notice the logical lapse by which our madness of lust often drove us straight back through *her* doors—"No noise!" Martha would urge in a whisper as she opened my jeans with one hand and we sank to the checkerboard floor of the kitchen, where I would cringe from the recurring apparition of Lucia bursting in with a shriek of "DIOS!"—"Regina," Martha exclaimed, looking up smeary-faced, "what's the matter? I *need* you to *come*," much the way she might say to Lucia, "I *need* you to *clean up this mess.*"

In truth, the distance between our ages and stations of life, about which I at least had the sense to be worried when it came to the difference between our two homes, was much effaced in our first weeks together, but by Martha, not me. Nine or ten in the evening—whenever it was, I assumed, that the baby was sleeping and the nanny ensconced in her room with her late-night TV—she would call in low tones from the kitchen to say she was free. I'd rush into the night to meet her—in the same demimonde of our town I had learned beside Dutra. The High Life, the Pink Elephant, the Silver Dollar Saloon. They all crouched beneath guttering neon or behind penitentiary bars, along the farthest-flung, least well-lit, working-class streets most remote from the hem of the Hill. Here erstwhile comrades of Dutra's from the county community college might join ranks with an unchanging cast of geriatric alcoholics who held down their stools sixteen hours a day, but never university students, let alone the professors. Even I, who had never before had a female lover; much less one who was married; much less married to my own former mentor; much less a professor herself at the school at which I was a student—even I who, due to all this compounded inexperience, truly believed none of this posed a real obstacle—even I understood why she kept our affair to this realm. She might have left the country, so unlikely was she to cross paths with somebody she knew. But of course this was where she met Dutra, whether because he'd tracked me, Injun-style, or because such a meeting was inevitable.

The Pines was a relatively higher-quality establishment, because a car was required to get there; an old-fashioned roadhouse, it featured music on weekends and even served food. I'd ordered fries on a pretense of hunger, putting off the moment at which I'd join Martha on the little dance floor where the tables had been shoved aside. The band had taken a break, and Martha stood dancing with the jukebox while perusing its list, one hand flat on its top as if preventing it getting away. She wore black jeans, black motorcycle boots with silver buckles, a white Hanes undershirt the right size for a twelve-year-old boy beneath which her milk-heavy breasts were squashed flat. She'd begun pumping her milk for the baby with a frightful contraption she'd bought through the mail, and sometimes, halfway through our clandestine evening, we'd repair to the Saab to take care of this chore while I lay across the seat with my head on her lap staring up at the suction cup crushing her nipple. "Sexy, isn't it," she'd say wearily, her body briefly the captive of the pump's tubes and coils. I knew mine weren't the only eyes in the dimly lit bar watching her. I'd felt the room watching us—watching her, and me as her adjunct—ever since we'd arrived. And then a weight dropping into a nearby chair made me glance over, and there Dutra was, with a victorious grin on his face.

"So," he said. "Introduce me."

The trio accompanied him that since long before he and I met had established themselves as the owners of the other three seats in his car. Alyssa was a self-described Jewish-American Princess Gone Bad from Shaker Heights, Ohio, who had graduated the previous year with Dutra but stayed on, not enrolled, to continue her prodigal spending of her family's money on marijuana for herself and her friends. Zaftig and freckled and borne along on an elaborate rat's nest of gingery hair, Alyssa bore a remarkable physical and temperamental resemblance to Janis Joplin. She was always so high she was almost asleep, and radiated benign out-of-it-ness from beneath half-closed lids. She shared the backseat with Lucinda, one of the more wayward faculty townies, the bony, viper-tongued daughter of a well-known economics professor. Lucinda had been discharged from Dartmouth on a medical leave after overdosing and had never gone back. The front seat was reserved for Ross, Dutra's comrade from his days at community college, unless I was along, in which case the trio, with resentment, all squeezed into the back. I had never been comfortable with them, because whenever my relations with Dutra went back on the rise, his with them went back on the decline, but I was most horrified to see them for the reasons I've mentioned above. Now they all came to roost at my table, merrily studying me from behind their pint glasses, because Dutra of course had told them.

Martha came to stand beside my chair and passed her hand over my cheek to rest splayed on my collarbone, so that her fingertips just brushed the tops of my breasts. "What's all this?" she smiled. "Someone's taken my chair."

Dutra said, with a broad lying grin, "We thought Ginny was here all alone."

"Only a fool would leave this girl alone," Martha said, and from the grin she showed him in return, I could see she recalled precisely who he was.

The band had come back onstage and throwing her grin around to include all of them Martha seized my hand and led me onto the dance floor. In the privacy of our affair, in the secretive nests where we fed on each other, I was heedless and greedy, and had earned Martha's scolding for ripping a seam of her shirt in my hurry to separate her from her clothes—but now in the dim, seedy bar I discovered she could be brashly extroverted, while I was hamstrung by inhibition, despite the pride that I felt by her side. It was thrilled pride, but it was still shy, and it didn't stop me from being afraid—of the man who muttered "dykes" as we passed by his stool, but perhaps more of Martha herself, whose provocative smile seemed to challenge not the drunk, wary men staring at us, but me. "Can you?" her eyes asked, their penetration concealed from others by her lopsided smile. Can you follow me out in public, and not be afraid of what others will say? But this wasn't her public, I half-reflected, even as I emboldened myself to join her. She was insinuating trails through the smoke-heavy air, astraddle the beat of the music, and I pretended to share in her trancelike indifference and juked loosely beside her until Dutra and trio joined us, Dutra dancing alone in the pent-up, skilled way that marked him as a child of Manhattan, Alyssa and Lucinda tossing arms overhead and whipping hair side to side so they looked like two trees in a storm, and Ross sardonically doing the pogo to conceal his discomfort at having to dance, so that Martha and I were absorbed by the group, and I became grateful that Dutra was there.

"Smoke break," everyone agreed several songs later, and we shouldered our way back outside.

The backseat of Martha's gleaming black Saab was half taken up by a baby seat, a sort of wide plastic bucket lined with calico cloth and a strappy web harness that would apparently safeguard the baby from a violent impact. I had never paid the seat much attention, but I couldn't imagine it was hard to remove, and my first desire now was that Martha not see Dutra's car, ankle deep like our living room with Dutra's typical sediment of takeout boxes, fruit peels, sodden tea bags, stray rolling papers, unraveling cassette tapes, empty beer bottles, and cigarette butts. I rode in his car all the time with no thought of its filth but envisioning it now through Martha's eyes I was disgusted—it was possibly worse than the house. "We brought a car," I offered as we crossed the gravel lot, and was surprised when Martha sharply dissented.

"There's no room in the back," she reminded me.

"I could help take it out—"

"Where's your car?" she asked Dutra, decisively following him.

As always Dutra had parked in the lot's remotest, least-lit corner, the better to smoke pot or snort cocaine off the car key, and the better, at least, for me to conceal my mortification as Martha made herself comfortable in the front passenger seat amid heaps of refuse and pulled me down onto her lap. Of course Dutra sat at the wheel, and the trio in back. Alyssa's thick joint made the rounds. Martha sucked long and held even longer before slowly exhaling.

"Nice," Dutra said.

"Very," Martha said as she gave it to me. "Thanks, Alyssa."

"That's cool." Alyssa had stretched her legs over Lucinda and Ross, and lay against the car window enthroned on her nimbus of hair. "So you live in town, Martha?"

"Yeah."

"Where at?"

"Taughanock Heights."

"Oooh. Lucinda's old nabe. Very swanky."

"My parents' old nabe," Lucinda clarified testily.

"I might have cleaned out a pool up there once," reminisced Ross. "Or mulched someone's hedges with dog shit."

"You live with your folks up there, Martha?" Alyssa went on. Martha was leaning against the headrest with eyes closed and lips forming a very slight smile of bemusement, or contentment, or both.

"Nah," Martha said, eyes still closed. "I've got my own place up there."

This wonderment made Alyssa the most alert I'd ever seen her. "Wow!" she said. "That must be awesome!"

"It is," Martha said. I could see Dutra silently laughing, gazing out the windshield.

"Do you go to school here?" Alyssa asked almost shyly, aglow in the warmth of new friendship.

"Nah, I went to school on the West Coast," Martha drawled.

I'd been on the point of correcting Alyssa that Martha was no student, but a professor—but Martha's swift embrace of the imposture had left me speechless.

"Oh, that's *cool*. I've always thought that I shoulda gone west."

"It's not too late."

"Oh, man. I just feel like I've got roots here now."

"Alyssa's been here even longer than me," said the wise man Dutra. "You've been here like, what?"

"Fuckin' five years, man," Alyssa revealed.

Their banter was endless. "Wow," Martha said. "Holy shit," Dutra said. "I road-tripped out to Portland once," Ross announced, making his own bid for Martha's attention. "Shelton Circle—the brick and limestone one," Lucinda admitted under Martha's encouraging queries. My silence had evolved now into something that Martha, at least, couldn't ignore. She said to me, "Tired, huh, baby?" though it was she who more needed to leave. It was past two o'clock in the morning. I knew her breasts must be painfully swollen and I was even, in my growing hostility, purposely sagging my weight against her.

Driving away in the Saab she said, "That was just what the doctor ordered."

"Being mistaken for a college student by a dim-witted pothead who can barely see past her own hair?"

She rotated her head very slowly, to study me, even as the car raced down the dark lakeside road. She was letting me know that I hadn't hurt her, though I might have embarrassed myself. "Don't worry," she said. "I know I can't pass for nineteen anymore."

But the truth was she could. She was a changeling. In the bar, in the front seat of Dutra's Volvo, in her fading black jeans with her uncombed hair carelessly draping her face, that other putatively actual backdrop of professorship and husband and mansion and child made no sense—you understood her impatience with it. You might even see some of the habitual gestures of hers I had started to learn—the way she had of quickly straightening her shoulders; of roughly hooking her curtain of hair on her ears; of sweeping objects out of her way when she was ready to make love and they had made the mistake of falling into her path—as her repeated attempt to shrug all this stuff off and be rid of it once and for all.

"No," I conceded. "You can, actually." But it wasn't my disapproval of her fleeting charade that preoccupied her.

"I guess I'm entitled to my little escapes now and then," she was saying, whether speaking of this evening, or the whole of our affair, I couldn't tell.

"What do you have to escape from?"

"I think you've met my husband."

"He doesn't seem so awful as to call for escaping," I said, so surprised as to argue against my own interests—for not only was this the first time she'd disparaged him to me, it was the first time she had mentioned him at all, since the night in the pergola. Did I think he had vanished forever, or wish that he would? It was far worse than that. I still admired Nicholas, as much as anyone I'd ever known. My esteem for him was hopelessly mixed with my ardor for her. And at the same time, the two felt so confoundingly separate that Martha's speaking to me of her husband was somehow perverse.

"I suppose he just took you to bed a few times," she went on. "It's once you've been sleeping with him for a while that it's really soul killing."

"What?" I cried.

"The inattention," she said, misconstruing my question. "The remarkable absence. He's right there, but there's nobody there."

"I never slept with Nicholas! Never. Not even sort of. Never anything like that."

"For goodness' sake, don't freak out. Can't you see that I wouldn't have cared if you had? In fact—" She broke off. "Am I driving you home?"

"In fact, what?"

"Nothing. It's nothing to do with you. Am I driving you home?" But she couldn't withstand my silence. It was a power I was learning to use, in our voluble passion. "In fact, I would have been glad," she said finally. "If it had made him happy."

"You would have been *glad*," I repeated, incredulous.

"If he was glad. I would have liked him to be happy. I would have liked to be happy, myself."

"I don't understand."

She looked at me frankly, while bending the wheel toward my part of town. "I don't want you to understand," she said after a moment.

"Take me home with you," I suddenly insisted. "I'll hide in the morning. I'll hide the whole day. I'll climb down the drainpipe. Just let me sleep in your bed. I want to come, and make you come, and fall asleep and not have to put on smelly clothes and walk home in the dark." I couldn't know if her desire, or her guilt, from having made that admission to me, played the larger part in her consent—for her face in desire, and her face in the

unease of guilt, often looked much the same. When we came to the desolate light near the Hobo Deli, instead of crossing toward my neighborhood she took the left turn, toward hers.

"I didn't know you when I hoped you were his lover," she clarified, as
the car started climbing the hill. "You were the latest of his female TAs.
He tended to go to bed with them. Though never for long."

"So that stuff with the petition was true."

"That was bullshit," she said, with a surprising flare of loyalty. "The
so-called harassment? Neurotic virgins who were fixated on him. He
never touched an undergraduate. Never so much as looked at them—that
was their actual grievance. But with his TAs, the affairs were consensual.
And sanctioned, I guess you could say. We never made an explicit arrangement. I tried, once. Quite a long time ago. I suggested that we have an open
marriage."

"Might as well not have the marriage at all."

"God," she said. "You are young."

I winced as if she'd hit me. "Don't talk down to me."

"No, you're right. Your reaction might have nothing to do with your
age. Nicholas was also repulsed when I made that suggestion. He preferred to have poorly kept secrets."

I remembered her warning-off speech. *I haven't been an exemplary
wife but that's over, that chapter is closed.* At the time I had hoped she was
bluffing: in my selfish and shortsighted hunger I had hoped that exem-
plarity continued to elude her. Now I feared that it did. "So how many
affairs have you had before me?" I asked coldly. "Is this just your latest
'escape'?"

"Please don't," she said.

"Don't what?"

"Don't . . . drag us into the quagmire of what ought to be. Just let
it be."

"Oh, that's very Alyssa," I sneered.

"Alyssa isn't my type. Regina. Just let us be for a while."

"I love you!" I raged.

"I know," she said, which made me that much more shrill and combative.

"You *know*?"

"Come on, Regina. You 'love' me, you want to come set up house? You 'love' me, you want to be Joachim's other mommy? You want to pay half my mortgage? You want to bake little pies every day? What is this bullshit? What more do you want? You *have* me. Quit the *'gimme.'*"

"What *'gimme,'*" I whispered, my throat walls grown thick.

"Your 'I love you' is like *'gimme, gimme,'*" she said, pulling into her driveway. She turned off the engine and we listened to its *tick-tick* dying noise as if marking the hours before dawn. Then she seized my hand and at her touch I yanked her close, a tug-of-war stalemate across the gearshift of the Saab. "I want you here, too," she whispered. "I want you sleeping with me, in my bed. I want that even though it's insane, and my life goes to pieces if we get ourselves caught, I still *want* it. Can't that be enough?"

Love bestows such a dangerous sense of entitlement. That first morning, waking up beside Martha in her own fragrant bed, dense with pillows and finely spun fibers and waffled goose down and with Martha, her body unsheathed, hotly pressed against mine, did I marvel at such change of fortune? Did I store up delicious sensation, against a day it might only exist in remembrance? Did I recall all my mornings awaking alone, so this contrasting morning was all the more sweet? No. I exulted, I reveled, I buried her flesh beneath tireless kisses, but I also felt arrogant justification. I felt I was finally where I belonged.

And I felt this despite being told that I must be clandestine; despite Martha's leaving the room very early to wrest from Lucia her smug satisfaction at reaching the baby's crib first when he stirred; despite Martha's urgent reminders, which never relaxed, that I stay in the room until fetched; despite how she pulled the door shut as if wanting to bolt it; despite my confinement sometimes lasting hours, until the nanny transported the baby far enough from the house that I might make my tawdry escape—and not only despite all of this, but exactly because of it. Because the great risk was all Martha's, and all undertaken for me. What did I risk but squalor—for the injunction to silence forbade me from taking a shower—and boredom—for I was even reduced, while I waited for her, to reading that unloved copy of *The Last of the Mohicans* she'd chucked on the floor? The answer, my only real risk, was that hers would become unacceptable to her. But to this I was blind, even though it lay clearly before me, the same way I was blind to the bright little bottles and bowls and spoons of an infantile breakfast that lay in plain sight in the kitchen dish drainer, once Martha had freed me at last from the bedroom and was hurrying me out the door.

Only days could have passed in this way though they felt like luxurious weeks. One morning the quality of my awaking was so different I lay in momentary confusion, unsure where I was. The door to the bedroom stood open. A light draft I'd never felt in that room, where my body had shed so much vigorous sweat, slightly chilled me. Her bedside clock said twelve-thirty P.M. A note by the clock added: *Everyone's out for the rest of the day. Come down whenever you want.*

I pulled on a T-shirt and jeans and stepped into the hall. The house was perfectly quiet. I didn't feel that slight alertness of the air that can tell us, even through a deep silence, that some unseen person is sitting nearby. Five other doors lined the hallway, only two of which I could identify, for they were the two, side by side at the hall's farthest end, we slipped past late at night when we crept like thieves into the house: one the baby's, Joachim's, and the other the nanny's, Lucia's. Like the door at my back they stood open, emanating a calm emptiness. Irresistibly compelled, my swift footfalls silenced by carpet, I went and looked in. I'd never done this before. I'd always lacked opportunity, but it was true I'd also lacked curiosity. A riot of color in one, very clean but tight-packed. Tufted hot pink bedspread such as it was inconceivable Martha would buy, with many figural wildly colored pillows in a similar vein heaped on top, posters as from a travel agency hung on the walls, bedside table bristling with photographs of grinning toothy children in imitation-metal frames. The other room used such a different palette as to seem a different planet. Robin's-Egg Blue, Cappuccino, and Leaf would have been fitting names for the paint. Wood crib restrainedly flounced with a pattern of monkeys. Small colorful wood sculptures which perhaps were expensive playthings, placed haphazardly over the carpet. All these impressions in a single furtive glance. I turned to face the other three closed doors again. Martha's bedroom was opposite the head of the stairs, which suddenly seemed a strange place for her bedroom to be. Still the house lay in deep silence. Like Bluebeard's wife I walked the full length of the hall to the opposite end and pushed open a door.

An immense corner bedroom, with two walls of windows, framing fine views of trees. Floating at an angle, an enormous wood bed with tall headboard and footboard, a twist of quilts hanging off to one side as if someone had fled, gotten tangled, yanked free in great haste, and then left the quilts half on the floor. A chest, lamps, books, wastepaper basket with waste, chaise with a robe crumpled on it, door standing open to a large walk-in closet within which I could see a pale ranking of shirts, and below, a dark army of shoes. Unopened dry cleaning box on the floor. Here and there, something—a camisole, a pair of leather flats—I knew was Martha's. Not much. She'd taken her most needed stuff when she moved down the hall. In one corner, a club chair with a small shelf beside it containing perhaps fifty palm-size books bound in crumbling red leather with their nearly illegible titles stamped in flaking gold onto the spines: *All's ell at nds Well lfth N ght Th ercha t of enice e Me y Wi es f Wi ds r O hel o*

I stepped back and closed the door noiselessly. Two doors remained, both of them closed. Behind one was his study. I didn't need to open the door to know just what it looked like.

I showered and dressed, and when I went down the stairs she was there, in the breakfast nook, reading. I didn't know why I felt angered, and somehow deceived, that she'd been sleeping with me in her guest room. Perhaps I felt foolish for not having realized it sooner. She tented her book on the table when I slid in beside her. Those upstairs rooms into which I had trespassed had followed me down, bearing witness in silence, so that it did not feel surprising when Martha said, "Joachim's with Nicholas. Lucia's taken him over."

"Over where?" Though I knew we were alone, our voices sounded too loud.

"At the moment, the Holiday Inn." She studied me for reaction to this and despite not receiving a protest went on, "You must have realized his canoe trip was over."

"I hadn't been thinking about it," I claimed, which was narrowly true. I'd been making a furious effort to not think about it.

"Did you lose track of time? I would have liked to but it's something I can't seem to do anymore." She stared across the table and through the far wall as if her lost capacity to lose track of time lay there, just out of reach. "I don't know when that ended. It was after my marriage, but long before having the baby. I started to always know what time it was, practically to the minute. I stopped wearing a watch and I've never been late." Again she looked in my face as if expecting I'd argue with her, and I remembered the day we'd met in the coffee shop, and her lateness, which she was telling me had been deliberate. As if her thoughts mirrored mine she added, "At least, not because I've lost track of the time. While Nicholas never has the remotest conception of what time it is. I called up the ranger last week, on the day he was due to come into the lodge, to leave a message for him to call me. He was amazed I remembered his schedule—he could barely remember himself. I asked him to put off coming home. A short-term separation." Perhaps she'd been afraid I would crudely exult at this sudden announcement, because she added, harshly, "It's not because of you."

"Is that a reassurance or a warning?"

"Neither," she said. "Just a fact."

We were sitting with shoulders and thighs pressed together in the snug little space, but less like lovers than like accidental seatmates on a train. "Either way it's a cruel thing to say," I said, meaning to sound very calm and, I thought, succeeding. "If it's not because of me then why is it?"

"Regina, I don't have problems in my marriage because of you. I have you because of problems in my marriage."

"*That's* sophomoric."

"I think you might have meant sophistic. Even if you didn't, you're hardly old enough to call me sophomoric. I might have to ask for identification." But there was nothing joking in her tone, and I lost what composure I'd had.

"Why not say what you were too much of a coward to tell me before? I'm your *escape*, just like acting eighteen at a roadhouse and smoking a joint. When you're all done with me you'll just flick what's left into an ashtray—"

"Can this really be true? I've told my lover we have more time together, and all she does is scream and cry and complain."

"Because you're at such pains to tell me that it's not because of me! 'We're gonna have more time, babe, but it's not because I wanted time with *you*.'"

"I *did not fucking say that*, Regina. I said that I've asked Nicholas to give me some time, to sort out what the fuck's going on with our marriage, and that's about *us*, that's about myself and Nicholas, not you."

"What the fuck is the difference?"

"I need time apart from my husband; I want time with you; but these two things aren't caused by each other. They're not connected!"

"How the fuck can they not be connected?" I screamed, shoving her breakfast-nook table behind me. For love had bestowed such a dangerous sense of entitlement I thought nothing of storming my way from the house into which I had tiptoed just hours before. Just hours before, when we'd whispered our blunt urgencies, and suffocated our climaxing shouts in her pillows. Now that we had privacy I was shrieking and throwing her kitchen door wide on its hinges. Down the length of her drive and the prosperous lane with its tasteful stone walls and its fake hitching posts I went wailing without inhibition, and when the Saab pulled up just beside me I was so overtaken with woe I did not even realize at first who it was.

"Get in the car," she urged me. "You cannot put this show on in front of my neighbors!"

"Why should *I* care what your neighbors are thinking?" I snarled. But I got in the car, and for once she had no quick response, and we drove down the hill in silence.

We continued the silence a long time in front of my house, gazing out her windshield, again like uneasy travelers who are no longer sure what direction they're going. At last I said, "Did you tell him you're seeing me?" and with too little hesitation she said,

"No."

"Because—the fact that you'd rather not see him has nothing to do with the fact that you'd rather see me."

"Yes," she said after a moment, remotely. "That's right."

I turned my head slightly, allowing her into my sights. I was only trying not to shed more tears, but she seemed to feel my gaze as a further chastisement. "I don't think you can understand—" she began, in the worldly-wise, weary voice that I most would have liked to despise, if I could have despised any part of her.

"Please don't," I said, getting out of the car, "add insult to the injury."

"Nicely put."

"I've always been bright for my age," I said, slamming the Saab's door as hard as I could.

I sobbed myself to sleep at the height of the day and that evening awoke through a fug of trapped heat to an awareness of weight at the end of my bed. My lamp was off and my door almost closed, but a needle of light crossed the floor from the hall. The TV was nattering faintly downstairs. "You and Dutra really do live like pigs," mused her voice in the darkness, and then she stretched out beside me and I gasped in the vise of her arms.

"That prick let you in," I protested.

"He was happy to see me. He said, from one prick to another, that I'd better shape up or be sorry."

"I love you," I said, with my face hotly pressed to her neck.

"We need to get out of here," she was deciding. "We're going away."

Any amount of time later I'd far better understand what at that time I barely understood at all, though Martha might have approved of my incorrect, seafaring view of our progress: sometimes against the wind, sometimes with it, but always forward. She might have approved, in her maritime way, but she would have been equally wrong. We weren't zigzagging forward but wildly seesawing, the ups ever higher, the downs ever lower, our fulcrum nailed smartly in place. Martha's flights of hedonism—Martha's brooding resolutions and remorse. Martha's desire—Martha's duty. I'd like to say I defied gravity just as often as feeling its snare, but my efforts were more likely spent clinging on with white knuckles to not be dislodged. Still, that was my heroism—my tenacious fidelity to her, though it was based on a grave misperception. I thought desire *was* duty. No trial could not be endured nor impediment smashed in desire's holy service, or so I believed, with naïve righteousness. I didn't grasp that desire and duty could rival each other, least of all that they most often do.

Since the start of their marital troubles, which at least I had rightly perceived had begun very far in advance of my entrance, Nicholas and Martha had been in the habit of borrowing homes—always on the pretext that they lived in the middle of nowhere. They knew many accomplished people, principally New Yorkers, who were always decamping for Paris or Oxford or Stuttgart or Rome for a month or semester or year, to accept invitations to research or teach or complete overdue manuscripts. Nicholas and Martha would ask for the keys, so they need not reserve a hotel when they came into town for their opera subscription—but there was no opera subscription, and their travels together had long ago ceased. Tacitly alternating, one would go for a weekend or week to New York, then the other, and though both liked New York very much they went less to be there than away from each other.

This routine, once the baby arrived, had become both more halting and more necessary. At Christmas, a Manhattan professor they knew relocated to Los Angeles for the semester, and Nicholas, in response to insistent suggestions from Martha, became able to spend frequent weekends away. In May, the professor decided to remain in L.A. until August. And so it was that when Martha asked Nicholas not to come home right away from his three-week canoe trip, she knew her request would be, if not easy, at least possible for him to grant, and that in fact the Manhattan apartment was already fairly well stocked with his clothes.

That was where he had been since he'd left the Ontario woods, with the exception of the day he had driven five hours to spend a wretched less-than-two with his eight-month-old child at a Holiday Inn. At the time I didn't ponder this insult to Nicholas's parenthood. Far less did I dream Martha might have, or that she'd set out to redress the imbalance, if only to safeguard her interests. When she explained to me that she and Nicholas were switching places for a week, I didn't number the innumerable grains of need, and counter need, of hurt and counter hurt, of expectation shortfall and unhappiness surfeit that might, all bagged up, have the heft of a faltering marriage. I didn't see the circumstance as having much to do with marriage at all. Some forgiveness is owed me: Martha meant my perspective to suffer strict limits. Perhaps she wanted to impose them on herself. Her husband would enjoy the freedom and mastery of his own home and the company of his own child for the first time in over a month; but what she said to me was, *We need to get out of here, baby. We're going to New York!* Could I have blamed her, had I realized how many enmeshed purposes she was serving by each of her actions? In fact I might have loved her more, for the exhausting intricacy of her achievement, but this was the last thing she wanted.

We were going to New York—that was all I need worry about, and in the days leading to our departure I indulged that concern every way that I could. I bought new clothes of the sort I naïvely imagined would make me appear a New Yorker. I had my hair cut and my toenails done. I fretted, in the campus bookstore, over which was exactly the right sort of casually intellectual, urbane novel to read in New York in whatever spare moments I had. André Gide? Djuna Barnes? The morning that we were to leave I awoke by myself in her bed, morning light streaming through the tall windows. This time she'd left no note for me. It was already nine-thirty, the house very quiet as it always was this time of day, for Joachim and Lucia would have departed by now on their unknown, by me un-thought-of, rounds. Martha must be downstairs waiting. My eager efficiency in the shower was blunted somewhat, as if encountering headwind, by the enveloping recollection of the shower we'd taken the previous night, when we'd come in by stealth at some hour past one in the morning. We liked to make love very clean and go to sleep very dirty, sweat-enmatted and pungently syrup-adhered. Now back in the shower my attempts to self-cleanse became counterproductive, as my hand dropped the soap while one cheek squashed against the cool tile, and I muffled a groan that emerged like a gurgle and, though standing, almost drowned myself. Even with all this digression it was just ten of ten when, in a brand-new short skirt and short-sleeved leotard and new wedge-heeled sandals, I hurried downstairs to make coffee for Martha and instead almost stepped on Lucia. She knelt before the open refrigerator, silently accusing its disordered contents with a dripping rag poised in one hand. A cloud of bleach fumes scorched my face, originating logically from a bucket that sat on the floor but more persuasively from her contemptuous, unsurprised gaze as she slowly revolved it from the open appliance to me.

"*Ree-search assistant*," she satirically addressed me. "You don't have your own home?"

"I didn't realize you were here." In my shock at encountering her, my words sounded brusque, even rude. I hadn't faced her since the first time I'd met her, though we'd logged scores of hours beneath the same roof. Now I wondered in a cascade of panic if she could have been conscious of me all that time.

"You don't realize much," she agreed, returning eyes forward again. "You are young but you supposed to be smart. One of *his* favorite students." In another speaker, or in another speech, the emphasis might have meant snideness toward Nicholas but here I understood it meant snideness toward me. I was all the more contemptible, for failing to live up to the esteem of such an admirable man.

"I'm not so young," I snapped, for she couldn't have chosen a better way to rouse my indignation.

"Then you worse," she said. "Better young and stupid than old enough you should know better."

"Know better than what?" I demanded.

"You got kids?" she demanded in turn.

Lucia was, as I knew via Martha, a great-grandmother at the age of fifty-eight. Bullet-shaped, orange-skinned and -haired, partial to fuchsia and orange tones as well for her eye shadow, rouge, blouses, and elasticized slacks, Lucia was, I would recognize later, as thorough a manifestation of uncompromised will as I've ever encountered. Marooned in the northeasternmost corner of the opposite America from that which she preferred, she had responded to a seven-month snow season, a twelve degrees median wintertime temperature, an average of two hundred and eighty-nine overcast days every year, with a personal palette of tropical colors that would brook no dilution; and the unwavering glare that she cast with her wardrobe was well matched in strength by her judgments of people and things. Lucia subscribed to notions of honor and blood loyalty with which no amount of enlightened employer-employee behavior on the part of Martha could ever compete. Martha might pay Lucia a staggeringly generous wage; procure her health insurance and a retirement account; attempt chatty, confiding analysis with her of Joachim's abilities and temperament; and it would never offset Martha's fundamental crime: that she was not, by her nature, maternal. Martha left the lion's share of decisions regarding Joachim's diet, sleep schedule, quotidian amusements, and even, as he grew a bit bigger, his discipline to Lucia, under the hopeful assumption that such obvious respect for Lucia's judgment would inspire Lucia to have respect for Martha's judgment, in return. Of course the opposite happened. The less Martha bossed Lucia, the larger and louder grew Lucia's contempt. Lucia now resorted to almost flamboyant sedition, as if she hoped, perhaps with the last shred of respect she retained for Martha, to instigate from Martha the sort of brute retaliation that would restore Lucia's regard to the exact extent it put her in her place. Instead Martha continued to give Lucia yet more reasons to disrespect her, of which I was merely the latest.

But all this insight was yet to be mine—it lay years in the future—for it was contingent on the very condition she'd sarcastically asked me about. At that time she knew better than I did how far children were from me, not just chronologically but mentally.

"Of course not," I shot back, as if she'd given offense.

"Why 'of course'? Your age, I had two kids already. Now five. Fifteen grandbaby. Last year, first great-grandbaby." She still squatted where she had been but she had turned her whole body toward me, hunkered on her haunches like a toad about to spring, both extremities of temperature skewering out from her eyes, the overtaxed refrigerator, its door propped wide by her muscular rump, raising the pitch of its whine as its compressor went into high gear. As if to show me that I would not, by my malignant presence, cause her to neglect that appliance no matter how I might try, she seized a tub of sour cream out of its depths, pitched this into the trash, and then with some obvious pain straightened up to her full height and smacked the door shut. "I give them everything," she concluded, pushing her eyebrows at me as if to dare me to doubt it.

"I'm sure you're a wonderful mother," I said unkindly.

"*Everything.* I have nothing. Still they have everything. For my girls always beautiful clothes. For my boys always bikes, they get soccer, they get good shoes no one wore them before. Then they get big, they go, I come here so I do for them better. All my grandbabies, my great-grandbaby, I want I am giving to them. Always giving! Not taking!"

"Why are you yelling at me?" I yelled at her. "Where's Martha?"

"With *him*," she condescended to my utter stupidity, and then as I gaped in mute astonishment, realized she was still giving me too much credit. "The *baby*," she clarified in exasperation.

Even had I guessed on my own I would still have felt somehow deceived. "The baby? Where are they? Where did they go?"

"How do I know? He's her baby. I guess she can take him somewhere." After a beat she appended, as if to herself, but without at all changing her volume, "That the way she do it. Don't give nothing. Don't give nothing. Then give a little. Then leave. Now he'll be all week asking for her." Her face enlivened with satisfied mischief as she completed this speech. It was bald sedition: if I didn't dispute her I implicitly agreed.

"You shouldn't talk that way about someone you work for," I said prudishly. The insult to Martha outraged me, yet strong inhibition, the accurate sense I was out of my league, held me back.

"I don't work for her," Lucia surprisingly dismissed me. "I work for him."

"Professor Brodeur?"

"Joachim." She compressed her lips smugly at me. She pronounced the baby's name the Spanish way, a tender *"wah-KEEM."* By contrast Martha used the British style of willful mispronunciation—"JOE-a-keem"—a decision I acknowledged, if deep within, as pretentious and somehow remote. Even in this, Lucia staked her claim to the natural order of things.

"Of course you work for him, in a way, but you're not *employed* by him."

"I work for him," she persisted. "He's the boss. If you were smart, he'd be the boss of you too."

"What is that supposed to mean?"

"You'd leave her alone. You'd stop taking like stealing from him."

"How on earth am I *stealing* from him?" I exclaimed. Then we both heard the car crunching into the drive, and a door thumping shut.

Lucia was on the far side of the big kitchen island from me, so she leaned over it, with deliberate theatricality, though in her squat stature she did not reach far. "You selfish like her," she said, smiling to show she did not feel rushed. "So you make her be worse." Again came the expression of satisfied mischief. She didn't fear I might tell; she was goading me to. She might be crestfallen if I did not.

A gay, perhaps overly gay, babble of singsong and nonsense now came up the walk, and grew louder passing through the solarium. Then Martha shouldered open the door, Joachim on her hip, and saw us. That she registered the unprecedented conjunction of Lucia and me, my red-faced combativeness, Lucia's malevolent gleam, was unmistakably betrayed by her behaving as if nothing was strange. "So we had a fabulous romp in the park," Martha informed Lucia, as if I weren't there. Martha set Joachim in his high chair, with much mugging and tickling of him on his belly to which he responded with gales of laughter which redoubled in resonance and helplessness each time he managed to squawk new breath into his lungs. His fluff-crested, jug-handled head, very slightly wider than tall on his soft little neck, like a small pumpkin or a cartoon child drawn to endear, a Charlie Brown or a Dennis the Menace, kept rearing back so he could better square her in his sights, fill his gaze with more of her; and each time he did his laughter died back a bit and he gave out a noise of pure surfeit and adoration. "Heh," he sighed at her. "Heh . . ." It struck me first as a disorientation for which I then had to locate the source that he looked very different from when I'd last seen him, some five weeks ago. No one feature had changed; the gestalt was transformed. He seemed far more *there* than he had in the past. At the same time his eerie watchfulness of me, which had formed such a large part of my first impression of him, had now vanished—but perhaps he was taking his cues from Martha, who could not seem to look at me. With great effort his eyes left her face for Lucia's, which had more and more intruded on his peripheral vision. "Chee!" he finally cried, with an imperious gesture, and Lucia fairly glowed with her summons.

"He needs new diaper," she tutted at Martha, undoing the elaborate high chair safety harness Martha had only just finished engaging. "And wash hands before eat."

"He needs those playground germs for his immune system," Martha mock-argued.

"So he wants to be sitting in poop for nice skin," Lucia countered, hefting Joachim into her arms while Martha kept up her clowning claim on him, goofing with her eyes and tongue until he'd chuckled and *heh*'d himself into a mild state of hiccups.

"It's not poopy—"

"Full enough."

"You change his diaper twice as often as I do. Those go in landfills, Lucia. They're made to take a lot more and you waste them. It just makes more garbage to strangle the earth." But this was still in the key of indulgent teasing, of a listing of foibles.

"Baby's butt more important than earth," Lucia huffed as she bore Joachim from the kitchen—but she was teasing Martha too, in her way, and Martha laughed as she left.

Throughout this diaper badinage I had been standing there as mild and inconspicuous as Joan of Arc with the flaming sword raised in one hand, yet Martha, like deliberate Lucia, had all but ignored me—how triumphant were Lucia's footsteps up the stairs! How exultant her banter with the baby! Martha yanked open that mute witness, the refrigerator, and said in low tones, "Now you're shooting the breeze with my nanny?"

"I beg your pardon? I came downstairs and practically stepped on her. She *ambushed* me, then she *insulted* me—"

"What were you doing downstairs?"

"Martha, you were gone when I woke up! What was I supposed to do, shiver like a kitten in your room until you brought a bowl of milk—"

"You know the drill for sleeping over."

"You were gone. You did not leave a note."

"I can't fucking *leave a note* every fucking occasion! I'm leaving my house and my child for a *week*, I have, possibly, a couple of things on my mind, can't you use your common sense—"

"My common sense told me to make myself breakfast. It didn't tell me my lover had left me alone in her house with the person she least wants me 'shooting the breeze' with, who happened to insult me, and *you*, not that you'd ever care!"

"All you needed to have done was stay upstairs—"

"Why? Why, exactly, do I need to hide upstairs like Anne Frank when you've asked your husband for a separation, and there's nobody here but your baby and nanny, who, by the way, has not an ounce of respect for you—*why* am I hiding from her? Why, Martha? Why won't you tell her who I actually am?"

All through our escalating argument, which we conducted in stage whispers, not for risk of being heard but because, perhaps, hissing is second only to shrieking for the gratification of heated emotions, Martha had been concocting herself a breakfast of yogurt and granola and dried "mirabelle" plums she and Nicholas had brought home, I for some reason knew, from their last trip to Paris a lifetime before, first hurling yogurt bowlward by the spoonful, then reducing the plums to a mince with impossibly rapid-fire blows of the huge butcher's knife, then beating in the granola until the result was appropriate for mortaring bricks. Preparation complete, she leaned on the kitchen island and ate standing up, at a steam shovel's rate, at the same time as launching and dodging our argument's barbs. But I, motionless and foodless, had the better of her. However thin she constitutionally was, however many debauched evenings she'd passed with me dining on nothing but Jim Beam and ice cubes and Marlboro Lights, Martha was particular about food. She hated eating food that wasn't worth it, and hated eating if she couldn't commune with her meal in peace. She wouldn't have stooped to granola and yogurt without the "mirabelle" plums. And she didn't bother with breakfast at all if it wasn't sun-drenched and serene, conducted, ideally, in the breakfast nook with her lover tucked close beside her and the *New York Times* paving the table. For some moments she kept up the act, as if she liked eating glop standing up, but I won: I spoiled her meal past her tolerance point.

"Why won't I tell her?" she repeated, throwing her swiftly scraped bowl in the sink. "Are you truly naïve? You don't seem to notice that this is my life."

"And it isn't mine?"

"No! That Nicholas should know all about it, that Lucia should know all about it—that's *my* life. I'm not asking you to tell *your* husband, tell *your* nanny, tell the father of *your* child—"

"I haven't got such people."

"Exactly."

"Does that make me less deserving?" I cried. "My existence is less complicated and so less important . . ." but I trailed off, having somehow proved the very point I had meant to rebut.

"I don't know what you mean by 'deserving,' but no. It doesn't make you less anything." And yet we both knew, standing there, that I was somehow less; I could have walked to the Greyhound bus station and boarded a bus anywhere and it wouldn't have touched any life but my own. To be less entangled felt shameful and trivializing. Oh, youth!—that hopeless condition that marked me as different from her.

"I don't want to hide upstairs!" I was saying, like a petulant child. "I don't want you to say I'm the 'research assistant' . . ."

"I know, babe, I know. Give it time . . . can't you please give it time . . . I don't know what I'm doing. . . ."

Thankfully no transit of Lucia's and Joachim's through that house

could have ever been stealthy. Now we heard them returning, her resolute stomp on the stairs, and his voluble babble, and her attentive, I had
to admit admirable, responses, as if he were Horace relating the Odes.
"No!" came her shock. "Oh?" she realized. "Oh *my*," she marveled anew.
As Joachim had, I drew back from Martha the better to see her, and my
heart burst again.

"I love you," I said ardently. She was right; it was always my trump
card. *You don't know what you're doing? I do.*

But—"I love you," she echoed—at last! "Let's just get to New York,
okay, babe? Bear with me . . ." And her overwhelmed eyes spilled their
tears: joyful tears like my own, I was sure, though the tears of exhaustion,
concession, and bafflement are reportedly equally salty and wet.

Still, my tears were joyful enough upon hearing her speak those three
words. Exhilarated I shouldered past Lucia and the baby as they made
their return to the kitchen, and upstairs, before zipping my suitcase, I
flung myself back into bed, and scooped the damp, redolent bedclothes in
a heap to my face, and inhaled them and kissed them and clutched them.
Outside I waited for her in the Saab, enthroned on its palm of black
leather, and no more than ten minutes later she'd heaved her bag into the
trunk and climbed in beside me. "You never ate!" she fussed. "We'll pick
up bagels. Nicholas said he would be here by one."

We sprang into flight like the arrow released from the bow. Racing
down the two-lane state road between humped Ice Age hills and the little
red barns and the round silver silos, music fugging the rush of the car
with a sideways vibrato—it was the summer of Beck's first, irresistible
single, with its twanging bass line. My bagel vanished unheeded by me,
was devoured for fuel, for I hadn't yet fully absorbed Martha's lessons of
living, and then a ball of brown sack and wax paper distracted my hands.
"Just chuck it in back," Martha yelled, wanting both my hands free to
clasp hers, and so I did chuck it, and it surely bounced off Joachim's
Swedish-made child restraint, already obscured under coffee cups, sun
hats, Martha's summer-weight silk cardigan . . . so that only a full hour
later, at the junction with the interstate highway, did Martha realize it
was there.

"Fuck!" she screamed, in a sudden access of such frustrated rage as I'd
never yet witnessed. "Fuck! Fuck! Fuck! Fuck! Fuck!"

"It's okay," I soothed. "We'll get there, we'll get there, we'll get there . . ."

Then the full hour back to the start, for if Nicholas wanted to drive Joachim in his car, there was no second seat. Almost all the way Martha screamed "Fuck!" and her tears of frustration recorded their paths down her face, but I kept up the mantra *We'll get there* and *Look! Our vacation's already begun* and I kissed her all over her face and her neck and her gear-shifting arm. We trailed a dust plume through her yard and she yanked out the car seat and hurled it in the solarium. Then we retraced the road a third time and at long last climbed onto the interstate highway with New York just another four hours down the road.

"What did you mean, that Lucia insulted you?" Martha realized, as the noise of our speed settled safely around us, like silence.

"It was nothing," I said, kissing her. It had shrunk to a speck.

How had I lived with my perfidy up until now?

The question was put to me quietly. Not by the glittering reach of the Hudson alongside the car. Nor by the somber limestone edifice, facing a riverfront park, through whose shadowy door we came pulling our bags. Nor by the mute uniformed man with a Mayan's fierce warrior face and a robot's impervious arm, cranking the wheel of the Victorian oak elevator with the brocade-trimmed, velvet-topped bench. No, these dazzlements were too grand and too distant from me to slip the admonition, like a feather's quill end, in the coil of my ear. It was not until we were inside, and Martha rooting through the kitchen for something to drink, and myself helplessly in the bedroom with the idea of unpacking my bag, that I heard it. I had opened the obvious drawer, the top drawer of the room's only dresser, and found myself gazing into a masculine cache of compressed, crumpled things. Wash-worn Brooks Brothers white cotton shorts now a pale shade of gray. Snake-tangled, unpaired argyle socks, all in bright Easter colors like clover and mauve which still showed fairly crisp near the tops, but down toward the heels were marred by thread pills and snags, and at the toes by the outright abjection of holes. To see laid bare in their entirety those socks, of which I'd heretofore glimpsed only brief merry stripes, when a pant cuff rose up from the rim of a shoe, was like seeing the man himself fully exposed to me—naked. Of course I would know whose these were, even without the additional scatter of items strewn over the top or sifted down into the gaps: a geode, a whale tooth carved into some sort of large rodent or bear with long ears, a clothbound copy of *Areopagitica*, a handful of spare change and tokens, and a photograph of Martha in a plain wooden frame. The photo showed so little of her face that only someone who well knew her body and carriage, the way she held herself standing or sitting, would have instantly recognized her as I did. She sat, facing mostly away from the camera, on a sort of steep hillside or bluff, dressed in a T-back jog tank top, loose pants, and heavy boots, with a windbreaker tied at her waist. A baseball cap covered her head, her long hair carelessly pulled through the vent. She had glanced slightly over her shoulder, as if just realizing there was someone behind her, so that some of the left side of her face could be seen, but her attention was still clearly cast forward, toward whatever the view.

I glanced over my own shoulder, hearing Martha in the living room now, one room closer to me, calling out titles of records. "Handel," she called out, "Haydn, Haydn, more Haydn." "Anything!" I called back. Now I noticed the low bedside table, entirely bare except for a cheap radio alarm clock. I knew that Nicholas had cleared off that table, probably at the last moment, perhaps after he'd already gone half out the door— rushing back to sweep the loose coins and little totems and portable shrine to the adored wayward wife off the surface in one hasty motion and so into his underwear drawer. He would have done so not to protect these items from her but to offer her the uncluttered table, get them out of her way.

How had I lived with my perfidy up until now?

The apartment, elegant and small, was still very much the apartment of the professor acquaintance who was spending his summer in California. As I took the further measure of the bedroom, I understood even more the effort Nicholas had expended erasing his presence, for there had been very little room here for him to start out. The other two drawers of the three-drawer chest were so full of clothing I could not fully open them; clearly the resident professor had overstuffed them to offer one drawer to his guest. It was the same in the closet, a mashed upright bale of drab-colored, unfashionable men's clothes to one side, and at the other, a mere handful of hangers, half of them bare, the other half double-hung with handsome shirts I recognized. Double-hanging meant trouble for the sleeves of the shirts underneath, besides being a pain, but I knew why he'd done it. For her. Had there been a cubic inch in the other two drawers of the chest he likely would have mashed his things in there to give her the whole upper drawer, but this was physically impossible.

I closed the chest of drawers and the closet doors also and was leaving the room when an impulse drew me back. I found myself reopening the top drawer and reburying the photograph of Martha, at the very bottom and back where she could not ever happen across it, as I had. I didn't do this because I feared that the sight of it would melt her heart toward him. I did it for the opposite reason, to shield him from her scorn. I owed that much to him.

In the living room Martha had filled two glasses with greenish wine. "I don't have any idea how old this is, but I know it was cheap to start out," she said. "For a man of his supposed refinement Nicholas is an amazing ignoramus about spirits and wine. Left to himself he'd drink Jameson's for every cocktail and sticky grocery-store red every meal."

"I know you haven't told him, but if you were to tell him, what do you think his reaction would be?" I wondered abruptly.

"I don't see the point of speculating, nor do I see the point of revisiting this conversation. Regina, look around. We're here in this apartment in Manhattan, all by ourselves. I want to enjoy that. Don't you?"

But it didn't feel like we were there by ourselves. Somehow in his paltry exile, his dispossession he'd even seen fit to erase, Nicholas felt more present to me than he did in his home. He felt more present than he had in that well-furnished, book-lined master bedroom wherein sat his abandoned dry cleaning, awaiting his doubtful return. The trouser-pocketful of spare change scattered over his shorts, the double-hung shirts, the framed photo might have all had his eyes. When Martha persuaded me onto the sofa and began with one hand to tease open my blouse, I was stiff as a corpse. But this remoteness of mine, which was rare, seemed to deepen her amorousness. She put her wineglass on the table and metaphorically rolled up her sleeves.

"Am I the first woman you've been with?" I now wanted to know.

"I'm afraid not," she said, not elaborating because too intent on her work, like a mariner leaving the dock. There was uncleating and unfurling and hoisting, and all to be done with quick, deft forcefulness.

"Why did you marry Nicholas?"

It must have been the optimism of lust on the scent of its gratification that allowed her to lightly endure such an onslaught of questions. "He was not the first man in my life, certainly," she remarked, in refutation of some logic I couldn't follow, but then she firmly disregarded further queries and I stopped making them. For all my history of love, which coincided with my history with her, an exquisitely porous membrane lay between the mundane and the deeply ecstatic. She'd only needed to caress me, even send me a glance down the length of a room, and pure ardor bloomed. The transit from reading the paper or taking a shoe off or draining a glass to the howl of titanic passion was no transit at all. Now for the first time I experienced delayed, obstructed passion as it stubbornly burned its way toward me through a lacquer of fear. What was I afraid of? Losing her. What alone quelled that fear? Having her. So the woe and its cure locked their horns, each gaining what inches the other gave up, until finally cure muscled forth and I wailed and shook in her arms. But afterward as we languorously dressed the forewarning stayed with me.

Yet we thrived in New York, that first night the germ of the week, that one week, afterward, the beau ideal of our whole time together. Heat, the day's and our own, had built up in those rooms. Passing back out the doors of the building into indigo twilight a temperature differential submerged us, like going into cool water. The doorman—a new man now, pale-skinned and black-haired and transfixed by a tiny TV he'd set up on an overturned bucket—glanced without surprise at our linked-fingered egress, made with one of his own hands a careless salute, and in a flash I perceived the lifeblood of that city, its particular meaning, paradoxically mapped at the cross point of the greatest breadth of possibility with the highest expectation. You could be anyone that you wanted, yet you had to be *someone*. I was wearing her clothes—she had vetoed every item I'd brought—but I felt less diminished than transposed into my more ordained form. At the corner of Broadway the subway was two blocks away, but she hailed a cab and directed the driver to almost the opposite end of the island. "We might be in this cab for an hour," she predicted with satisfaction. Our driver turned his attention to traffic and we turned ours to each other, and the endless innovations of fingers and tongues.

In the deep velvet booth of a crepuscular velvet-rope club she gave me my first gin martinis. At the white marble bar of a clamorous French brasserie she fed me my first oysters. Everywhere we went we attracted approving attention, the more so the drunker and more flamboyantly demonstrative we grew. At the brasserie when we surfaced from necking, the shells of the oysters denuded and strewn on the ice, the bartender, middle-aged and avuncular in a white Oxford shirt with sleeve gaiters, stood grinning at us with arms crossed. "What are you grinning about?" Martha said, but flirtatiously—the more she groped me in public, the more flirtatious with others she grew, but the less, I now found, that I cared.

"I find your friend very attractive," the bartender said.

"She's my lover, you dolt," Martha smiled.

"That's disappointing. Maybe you'd like to go out sometime?"

"I'm *her* lover."

"Oh, twist the knife," the bartender admonished.

And yet there were times in that endlessly dilating week—for every day's newness made days within days, so that the week seemed to magically lengthen, the more it diminished—when Martha and I, having drunk our way past drunkenness to a gritty sobriety; having eaten ourselves hungry again; most rare having fucked ourselves calm, so that sex relinquished its hold for a while on our minds; would sit across from each other in that professor's apartment, or in a white-doily coffeehouse run by Greek Orthodox nuns, or in a bleach-washed linoleum Chinatown diner with scum-covered lobsters in tanks by the door, simply pouring ourselves out to each other in talk, as we somehow had not done before. "I married Nicholas because I didn't know him or understand him, and that gave him mystique," she said with regret one late night, as we ate salt-baked shrimps from a bed of limp lettuce, and carefully stacked up the shells to keep count. "There was something so impenetrable about him, he had this surface that was so alluring but everything just bounced off, he was always charming, you never saw him upset or confiding or out of control, and I thought—I think I thought—that getting past that, being on the inside, must be extraordinary. To be the One he was intimate with. But he isn't—there's no intimacy. There's no *inside*, inside."

"There's something so intimate and disarming about his casual manner, just the first time you meet him," I recalled.

"There *is*! But that's as deep as it goes. You get there right away, but then—" She mimed with her hands a blade striking a wall. "You don't get any further."

"Having the baby with him must have gotten you further," I said, as I might have said to a friend—not to a lover. Instantly I wished I had not.

"That's why I did it," she replied, looking sharply at me—a challenge, to see if I judged her. I didn't. But I also doubted it had been so simple, the baby as a tool to pry Nicholas open. For at other times Martha spoke with real wistfulness of just the sort of thing she claimed Nicholas lacked: his element of surprise, of disclosing aspects of himself both unexpected and unknown to observers in general. In Berkeley, where they had met, he'd had much the same public persona as now, if an occasional Far East/West Coast trend to his clothes. He was not above wearing, and with perfect success, a Nehru jacket, leather thong flip-flops, and pajama-loose striped linen slacks. He could have looked like a mincing bohemian or he could have looked like a soldier of empire gone native (and indeed the wrong idea that he was British clung stubbornly to him, on account of his superlative charm and his scholarly specialization). If the latter, still Martha's surprise was complete when, to woo her, he took her on a grueling backcountry canoe trip in Yosemite Park and turned out to know what he was doing. He'd been as deft as an Algonquin portaging their boat, perhaps a Canadian national trait but for that no less sexy.

Growing up in Maine Martha had been the sort of statuesque girl who is a natural athlete, but Martha's particular athleticism, though versatile, was severe. Exceedingly competitive and self-contained, she did poorly on teams. She was a fine horseback rider but disliked the culture. There was a period of skiing, and, my personal favorite for its apt symbolism, of archery, but what suited her best was to sail. All that cleating and tacking and furling—these were really the earliest habits ingrained in her limbs. And so she and Nicholas had that in common, she said smiling wryly, disparaging such a slight bond. But it was more, at that time of her life, than she'd found herself sharing with anyone else. Both very smart, she and Nicholas had wound up professional scholars, in a milieu where climbing stairs was considered exertion and driving a nail a rare physical skill. Yet they were both, unbeknownst to their colleagues, outdoorspeople partial to small wooden boats.

That discovery made, their alliance was rapidly sluiced down the obvious channels. They took sea kayaks up from Fort Bragg along the so-called Lost Coast, with the migrating whales. They sailed among the Channel Islands, and south to Baja. That each possessed a slightly different expertise gave them much—at the start—to discuss. But from the beginning there was a strange discontinuity between their modes of interaction. Certain types of togetherness seemed to mesh them as snugly as beings can mesh. They did wonderfully on boats, all the more if there were challenging conditions. Their steps easily synced on remote hiking paths. They never struggled with shared physical tasks. And though they seemed their best in wilderness, it was not mandatory—they had terrific abstruse arguments about some books and films (not all: Nicholas, unlike Martha, was indifferent to popular culture, not snobbish so much as uncomprehending and bored, so that she could not even keep him awake through *Pulp Fiction*, let alone make him argue about it). Yet much of the rest of the time a space of unfamiliarity, even abashed awkwardness, seemed to open between them. It happened very regularly at the table, when their talk was as halting and random as that on an ailing first date. It happened on walks in Berkeley, where the sublime wilderness wasn't there as a shared interlocutor. It happened while socializing with their colleagues, when Martha—always animated by desirous attention to a height of brash, husky-voiced, devil-may-care posturing—would feel herself turned into their mascot, while Nicholas, smiling much like a parent, withdrew into silence. But it happened most often in bed, most particularly after foreplay. While a master of coy and withholding techniques of arousal, Nicholas always seemed to conclude at some point that his dues had been paid, diving into her body with as much savoir faire as a twelve-year-old boy diving into a pond. He wasn't restrained or inhibited—he'd once abraded her tailbone bloody with his furious thrusts, and he screwed his whole face up, and yelped like a dog being pulled by its tail. But neither did he seem aware of her. She had the uneasy sense, when he fucked her, of spying on him while he got himself off—of intruding on a private and unguarded moment to which she lacked any claim.

Once she'd grown aware of this sense of aloneness, which weighed down at precisely the moments she ought to feel closest to him, the moments of untroubled intimacy also took an odd tinge. She wondered if he felt so porous and attuned to her when they mended a sail or pitched a tent less because she was his lover than a sort of fellow scout. Nicholas had a boyishness to him, a shy, watchful sweetness that joined to his romantic appearance and his mercurial clothes was a significant source of his sexual cult, of the countless women and men of all sorts slavering in his wake. But the boyishness, reframed by their affair, proved incompatible with sexual feeling. After sex Martha found herself watching his back as he mopped with a Kleenex and slid into his robe and from there a hot shower. They rarely lingered in bed after sex, nosing over each other, carefully nursing depleted limp flesh back to life. They never showered or bathed together. Martha, who had never given a thought to nudity, began using a robe as he did. Martha had pursued her carnal interests since the age of thirteen, with no small number of women and large numbers of men. Always, in her lengthy experience, sex had been the key to a door behind which lay a realm of shared secrets. Sexual love was conspiracy, the blood pact with the partner in crime—you didn't spend the evening with that person wondering if conditions would tend toward a fuck. You didn't find yourself, some twelve years and twenty lovers after losing your virginity, wondering if you were "good" at sex as had wondered those overpainted, knobble-kneed girls you grew up with, aggressively fellating their boyfriends as if swallowed spunk would improve the complexion. But if sexual insecurity had been foreign to Martha before now, so had certain types of esteem. Nicholas neither marveled over nor competed with her professional accomplishments. He expected them, as he expected and desired her enormous intelligence. For her part, she had never been involved with a man she knew to be her intellectual equal. This might have had to do with her previous habit of favoring, for example, the sexual attentions of a cocaine-addicted motorcycle enthusiast and bar owner who lived on her street over those of her departmental colleagues, but no matter. Her partnership with Nicholas gratified needs her previous lovers had not even suspected. This was enough, for a while, to distract from the niggling distance she felt.

A vague futurity settled on them like fog. Within it, keeping busy as if keeping ahead of too much circumspection, they did what they did best, executing elaborate plans. Martha must defend her dissertation. Nicholas must publish again. Both must throw their charismatic weight around on the scholarly job market. Two appropriate jobs in one appropriate place was a pay dirt that most academic couples did not dare expect in the early part of their careers, but Nicholas and Martha achieved it, perhaps because, being so striking, they seemed more than the sum of their parts. There was a touch, Martha said in a tone of admission, of a prom royalty atmosphere. Nicholas and Martha were dazzling where dazzle was rare. Had they met as professional windsurfers, perhaps; as 1940s Hollywood contract players; as vacant-eyed fashion models somewhere in Milan; had they simply not seemed so remarkable, to others and so to themselves, none of it might have happened—the earnest boat trips, the uncomfortable fucking, the marriage.

Yet marriage has its own momentum. This was a truth she was forever impressing on me, and that I was forever disputing. Like any inexperienced fool, I believed that one need only follow the heart.

Our time together in New York had granted me the sense of partnership I'd so badly wanted. I was no longer just Martha's lover, but her equal and most trusted adviser. Strangely, yet perhaps not so strangely, this was owing to Nicholas, who'd so obligingly surrendered his shade, that we might theorize, anatomize, regret, and deplore him for hours of the day, days on end. Nicholas had gone everywhere with us, our ghostly third wheel, not an intrusion but the basis of a bond. His prominent role in our conversation was the proof of our intimacy. I believed then—perhaps I still believe—that such complete confidence is exclusive, or at least, it should be. In sharing his secrets with me, she'd replaced him with me—or should have. But then we returned and acquired a different third wheel, with very different, even opposite, effects.

Martha and Dutra had developed a mania for bar pool. I couldn't play pool at all, and found myself, in their company, less and less able to learn, so that from the beginning their fondness for pool left me sitting alone with my drink. But soon they'd debuted as a team. It was inevitable that this should have happened—on any given evening Martha and Dutra could play against each other only so long before another player, or several, signed up on the dusty blackboard with the nub of gray chalk for the privilege of playing the winner. Then the only way both could stay on the table was to suggest a contest between teams. But it wasn't inevitable, or to me unobjectionable, that they should do quite so well—that they should win quite so often, and, worse, start to practice their game in the daytime with grave self-importance.

Their preferred venue was the half-derelict poolroom of the town bowling alley, a windowless concrete-block tomb that was open for business from ten in the morning. This made it ideal for Martha—no sooner had baby and nanny embarked for the playground than Martha and I hurried off to meet Dutra, so that they could play pool for an hour free of all competition, and equally free of what threats to intense concentration are posed by a bowling ball knocking down pins. Not even the most purposeless in our town bowled or shot pool at ten in the morning, though like me a few of them drank. I tried to drink only for show, from a glass of Budweiser I hoped to make last the whole length of the visit, and pretending to read while my lover and housemate crept around the worn felt taking aim with their cues like game hunters surprising an elephant. I could find this amusing just up to a point. One day when the stroke of noon found them still playing, I demanded of Martha, "Can I have the keys?" interrupting their lazy trash talk. I'd driven us home late at night many times in the Saab, though of course she had always been there in the passenger seat. "I'm hungry," I added brusquely. I was daring her to refuse me, in a similar way, I now felt, she'd been daring me to complain I was bored.

"You are, babe? There's food here," she said, bent from the waist in a perfectly right-angled, upside-down L as she lined up her shot. Dutra, one long leg triangled in front of the other, one elbow stuck out as he planted his cue just in front of his crotch, watched her with a motionless concentration he very rarely achieved. It was his way to be twitchy, impatient— but pool brought out a physical kinship between them. With their long-limbed and meticulous predation they seemed, perhaps, less like armed hunters than elegant herons beak-skewering fish.

"Those hot dogs have been riding the wheel since June. I'll go to Jade Dragon. I'll bring you back something."

"Moo shu pork and egg rolls," Dutra said without looking at me. "Aw, fuck you, Hallett," as Martha sank two in a row.

"Lend her the Volvo if you're asking for food."

"Am I actually standing here begging for keys?"

"You're not begging," Martha said, straightening.

"Gottlieb can't handle the clutch in the Volvo. It's too specialized."

"Fuck you, Dutra."

"Fuck me? I'm on your side!"

"There's not sides," Martha said with annoyance, excavating her keys from her pocket and tossing them to me.

"Do you want anything?"

"Just a Pepsi."

"They sell Pepsi here."

"They sell food here too, but you're leaving."

"I'm not going to Jade Dragon for *hot dogs.*"

"It's soooo sad when the honeymoon ends," Dutra said with a sigh.

"Shut the fuck up and take your shot, Dutra," said Martha, as if I had already left.

Outside I slammed myself into the Saab and squealed out of the lot and bounced over the freight railway tracks and took the wide turn onto State Road 15, among the strip malls of which lay Jade Dragon, putting Jade Dragon half a mile in my wake before I realized I'd passed it. Jade Dragon was another of Dutra's esoteric bequeathals, a linoleum temple to peppers and grease situated as far from the flagged walks and greenswards of campus as a person could go without crossing the town line in the general direction of Canada. Of course Martha had not known of it before meeting Dutra, despite the fact that the town's most inexpensive supermarket, Mighty Buy, was also located here at the back of a vast lake of asphalt. Now I had to turn into the Mighty Buy lot, to reverse direction and go back to Jade Dragon. That parking lot was always a confusion of mud-spattered four-door pickup trucks and professorial Volvos and other commingled town/gown/John Deere vehicles among whom there was no right-of-way consensus. I was a long time getting back to Jade Dragon and by the time I arrived I was no longer angry. I just wanted Martha. Had it not been for Dutra's moo shu and egg rolls I would have blown off Jade Dragon and gone straight back to her with the claim I had eaten the food in the car. It was strange to be there in her car, so surrounded by her, yet alone. There was Joachim's Swedish car seat, a sliding pile of Xeroxes—she'd started research on a book—dumped in its cradle of cushions. Here was her stainless-steel travel mug, with its fitted rubber lid and its mountaineer's clip, suitable for attachment to backpacks. A vestige of wholesome Berkeley. Here, on the black leather seat, lay a pale orphaned hair. Human movements in the parking lot woke me again— other car doors being opened and closed. Again I remembered my errand. I wanted to go back to her; and I wanted to protract this strange moment alone in her sanctum; and I had to go order the moo shu and rolls to achieve a reunion at all. With a sense of sacrifice I got out of the car and found Nicholas there, his face alive with combating emotions, as if he'd both meant to surprise me, and been shocked by me at the same time.

"No good ever comes of spying," he said. The sun beat down onto our heads and back up from the asphalt, despite which squirms of cold raked the goose pimples out of my skin. "I thought I'd find the owner of this car if I followed behind. I saw you in the lot at Mighty Buy. Not you—the car. You know the windows are tinted." I might have affirmed that I knew this, or conceded never noticing before, or made a sound of surprise or acknowledgment, or perhaps only chattered my teeth in the motionless heat and stared at him, because I understood now that despite all I'd said to Martha, the demands I had made for acknowledgment, I was a coward. I had tried to pretend Nicholas didn't really exist, and now I felt all the defenseless secret history of his I had come to possess like ill-gotten loot bulging my pockets. If only I could have returned it, just emptied my thief's sack and run.

"I wonder why you have Martha's car," he went on steadily. "I wonder where she is."

"I was just—picking up lunch for her."

"It's thoughtful of you, Regina. Martha's kept so busy. Our nanny informed me she's hardly at home anymore."

"And you—you took a trip?" I attempted, as if we were making small talk.

"I did. My canoe trip. It was generous of Martha to let me go this year, despite the baby. I did have a wonderful time. But the trip's lasted longer than I had expected. Strangely it's still going on. Don't you need to go order your food?"

"No," I murmured, or perhaps I only shook my head mutely at him.

"Martha won't be expecting you back?" This consideration of his verged on unkind and he realized; he didn't persist. "In that case I'd like to waylay you a few minutes more. I'd like to talk. Somewhere out of the sun. It's lucky I happen to live just a short way away. Did you know that? Did you know that I have a new home?" My face must have told him I didn't. All this time he'd kept me pinned beneath his merciless, pale-eyed gaze, yet in my wordless reaction to his disclosure he saw me anew. He actually tilted his face very slightly to alter his angle of gaze, as if he might, in that way, see beneath the mute mask that I wore. He should have seemed masked to me also, because so transformed, but the transformation further revealed him. The canoe trip had painted a rose-tinted brown on his usual scholarly pallor. His face seemed both harder and younger, the same shape as his anger, which was not at all veiled by his mock-courtesy. Recognizable as he was he also seemed a very different person from the one I'd known before, and despite the suffocation of the moment I recalled Martha saying of him, "There's no *inside*, inside," and wondered if she could have said this if she'd ever seen him angry at her— truly and maximally angry, as he now was at me.

He released me for the moment from his gaze, like letting a lid slam back down. "Follow me," he said, turning away. Though I could have sped off in another direction, could have ignored his high-handed directive, or even laughed at it, such defiance of him at that moment was unthinkable to me. It was more unthinkable than clutching the slippery thighs of his wife through the arduous thunder of dual orgasm; it was more unthinkable than gazing on the perforated toes of his socks and the flaccid waistbands of his boxers. It was somehow most unthinkable of all. Could he have believed I respected him more, since I'd fallen in love with his wife? Could he have believed that in fact I loved him, with a comrade's compassionate, sorrowing love? Perhaps he, of all people, could have, though I wouldn't have dared make my case. Dumbly I got back in her car, to follow.

Halfway up the hill he turned on one of the transverse streets and into a small parking lot behind a building I wouldn't have noticed. Left in the lot side by side, perhaps the two cars would discuss everything that their owners could not. A few paces behind Nicholas I passed down corridors without noticing them, but through the door he unlocked I stopped short. Blinding masses of light filled a vast, almost unfurnished space. "Do you like it," his voice startled me, but it wasn't a question. The cheap lock had imprisoned his keys, which he wrenched loose and impatiently hurled on a counter in the galley-style kitchen just inside the door. Past the kitchen the ceiling height doubled, and then after a time the room ended, on a distant horizon, in gigantic windows. "An old munitions factory. It's unfurnishable. Apparently unheatable also. My friend Walter Debrango—history department, revolutionary France—moved here when he got his divorce. He calls it the Home for Scorned Husbands. Walter says that because it's so hard to get comfortable here, there are always available units. I'm pouring a drink if you want one. I only have gin. I'm not well set up to play host." The kitchen appeared to be empty, except for lonely glasses in the cupboard, and ice cubes in the freezer, and a two-thirds-empty bottle of gin. The emptied box that had held the glasses, a set of eight from Woolworth's, sat with torn-open flaps on the floor. "In the living room you'll find an armchair. Please take it. I'll sit on the floor."

"I'll sit on the floor!" I implored.

"I insist that you sit in the chair. It's my prerogative as host." If he'd intended to allude to my transgressions, in the past, as his guest, he couldn't have chosen a better means of enforcing my compliance. I sat down in the chair, among other dwarfed objects. There was a spindly floor lamp and a spindly potted ficus that had shed a few leaves, a small stereo system set directly on the floor, and several short piles, new growth, making tentative claim to the vast territory—a little pile of scholarly hardcover books, a little pile of compact discs, a pile (shortest of all) of trade paperback novels, and a slim pile of folded, seemingly never-opened copies of the *Times Literary Supplement*, perhaps five weeks' worth. Each pile was perfectly squared. Altogether the armchair and stereo and printed matter and ficus made no impression whatsoever on the sense of stark emptiness. I drank from the glass he'd thrust at me and my mouth filled with protesting saliva but I managed to swallow. Nicholas seated himself on the floor with his back to the opposite wall. It put him far from me, which was worse than if he had been near: I'd have to speak up, to respond to his questions. Then he did not even start with a question, but an accurate statement.

"You didn't know I'd moved out of my house," he observed.

"No—but why would I have known?" I'd been wrong—silence so filled that cavernous room I could whisper to him and be heard.

"I would have thought Martha would tell you. Lucia said you accompanied her, the week that she spent in New York. The week that she spent in New York to be out of my way, so that I could move out, as she'd asked me to do."

"She said you were coming to see the baby," I said after a moment.

"Of course. Joachim was my primary interest. Hers was that I should get out, and be gone by the time she was back. I'm surprised that she didn't tell you," he repeated.

"Why?" Now my voice rang out harshly. "Why should she have told me?"

"Wasn't it for your sake that she asked me to leave?"

So he knew. Yet I'd learned something, too. She hadn't told me she'd asked him to leave, precisely because it was not for my sake. She had told me this plainly herself, but I wouldn't believe her. "I don't think so."

"What makes you say that?"

"She would have told me. And she didn't."

"Maybe she wasn't yet ready."

"I don't think so. It doesn't have to do with me," I said wretchedly, quoting her, but he thought I was trying to dodge his suspicions.

"It doesn't have to do with you?" he exclaimed. "You should know that I have a reliable source. It's you who've shown me how reliable she is. I've done Lucia a great disservice. Until I found you at the wheel of Martha's Saab I assumed she was mistaken, or lying. Lucia has always played a game with us I didn't enjoy. She's always tried to tattle on Martha, to me. Martha doesn't nurse often enough, she doesn't sing Joachim songs, she doesn't dress him in warm-enough clothes. It's annoyed me. If Lucia hadn't otherwise done her job so impeccably I might have tried to dismiss her a long time ago. But this felt like the limit, this gleeful new slander. Regardless that it wasn't even true—in fact, to me it was much worse for being clearly untrue. Martha sneaking out of her own house at night like a teenage delinquent? Martha returning at dawn with a young female lover, and moans and groans heard through the walls? You can see how even someone without my vested interest would find such a story far-fetched. Yet it seems I've done wrong by Lucia. Or have I? Is Lucia a liar? Perhaps the victim of her own imagination?" He had spoken a long time, and beautifully; he'd suffused his tan even more deeply with blood so his flush climbed up into his hairline, and descended his collar; he'd drained his glass, and averted his gaze from my face so that now I could dare to return it.

"Lucia's not lying," I said, and my flush rivaled his. Between the two of us we might have outperformed a furnace in that very large, very cold room. All my physical points of connection set up an unbearable hum as if a cyclone had punctured the room and was trying to suck me apart— my knuckles were white on the soft leather arms of the chair and I was grinding my molars. The sun-bleached crest of Nicholas's hair seemed to stand slightly farther away from his scalp.

"Regina, are you in love with Martha?" he asked quietly.

"Yes," I said, and I was so sorry, and so relieved, to tell him that to my shame and relief I erupted in tears, and once started, could only gain strength, so that, clapping my hands on my face, I sobbed with gusto and drenched my shirtfront in my effort to spare his armchair being stained.

He let me cry for what felt like a very long time. When I had reclaimed some small part of composure he also looked more composed, as if my outpouring had washed away grime and restored his calm, handsome outlines. He disappeared from the room for a moment, and returning refilled our two glasses, and set a toilet-paper roll on the arm of the chair. I pulled off a streamer and mopped at my face while he resettled himself with his drink on the floor. "Having ascertained the facts, I suppose I ought to throw you out," he said thoughtfully.

"I'm so sorry, Nicholas," I said into my wad of stained tissue. By this I truly meant, without arrogance, I was sorry she no longer loved him.

"I'm sorry also. I'm not sure how to say this without seeming to belittle your feelings, which I don't mean to do. My and Martha's history— comprises many chapters and in fact many people. I'm very sorry you're now one of them. I wish you weren't."

"I understand," I said, to make clear to him the past held nothing to surprise or frighten me.

At that moment, I think we each genuinely believed ourselves to be the protagonist, and the other a naïve and pardonable walk-on whose role might even have a tragic end. Still, it was good to trade compassion in that large and chilly room, regardless if one of us, or perhaps both of us, would turn out to be mistaken.

"Thank you for defending Lucia's veracity," he said after a while. "I'm glad to know I hadn't trusted my child with someone prone to malicious falsehoods. But she had to go. It isn't what she said—the truth or false-hood of it. It's the way that she said it. The pleasure she took in disparag-ing Martha. But none of that means I enjoyed firing her."

This was the "disservice" of which he had spoken. I must have looked as amazed as I felt. Lucia gone? She seemed as permanent a part of their lives as the baby himself, and for an unreasoning moment I imagined the baby was gone, banished alongside his loyal factotum, the two of them perched on a box of his arty wood toys and her garish bedspreads by the side of the road. But no, they had been separated.

"I couldn't let her spend another hour with my son. A child shouldn't grow up in the care of a person who is constantly calling his mother vile names."

"Such as what?"

"Careful, Regina," he warned, "my concern is for *him*. It's *his* dignity and self-love I am talking about. There was something of that bile he understood. I'm not defending Martha's honor, or yours." Standing abruptly, he tossed his spent ice cubes into the ficus. "I must get back to Joachim."

"Where is—Joachim?" It was the first time I'd spoken his name. Until now I had called him "the baby."

"At the moment, with Laurence and Sahba. Laurence did me the favor of picking him up, using Bebi's car seat, because I didn't have our one for Joachim. I had to take Lucia to the Greyhound bus station. Then I was going to Mighty Buy to get something for Joachim's dinner when I happened to notice the car I'd been looking for all over town. Martha told Lucia she would be in her office, but that wasn't the case. You never did tell me where Martha is." He came to take my empty glass and stood a moment regarding the top of my head as I stared at my lap, the two glass-fuls of barely iced gin eating holes in the pit of my stomach. Nicholas's regard correspondingly drilled on my scalp. I couldn't return it. It wasn't because I had wronged him, but because the idea that I'd wronged him now seemed so inadequate, self-regarding even.

Back outside I stood out of his way as he struggled to remove the Swedish child restraint from its complex installation in the rear of the Saab, but Martha's papers impeded him, and I finally ventured to open the other rear door and go to work fitting them into an empty seltzer box. For some moments we hunched together in wordless labor like spouses whose entire involvement has worn down to the sharing of such dowdy tasks. Martha had complained to me that Nicholas was never proactive in household affairs. She claimed he contributed nothing, took the initiative in nothing, and yet seemed unsurprised that they should have, for example, a large house which she had shopped for and purchased—Nicholas passively contributing his share of their funds—and furnished and, with increasing distaste and resentment, maintained. She charged him with being unsurprised that they should have a spectacular garden which she had laid out and planted, not with distaste and resentment this time—imprisoned inland since they'd moved to this town, now her garden served much the same purpose her sailboat once had—yet still with the desire, which could not be so strange, that he take notice of the scope of her efforts every once in a while. She would say it was the same with their admittedly infrequent entertainments; with the contents of their refrigerator and liquor cabinet and wine cellar; with their subscriptions and their museum memberships and the expensive, unique, tasteful gifts they bestowed upon friends when occasions arose, and the same with their glasses and flatware and linens and with their house cleaner, lawn boy, and nanny—he didn't know whence any of it arose nor what was required to keep and pay for it. He was like a child, she said, accustomed to having his whole world outfitted for him.

Yet today he had fired Lucia. Either Martha underestimated him, or he had made an extraordinary departure. One might think the latter, if judging by his rapport with the child restraint. Finally, in exasperation, he yielded to my offer to give it a try. I knelt on the floor of the car and peered into the crack where the backrest and seat came together, meanwhile following straps where they descended and crisscrossed each other. I remembered the suction-cup bowl, and Lucia's reflexive insolence, that Martha had not been aware that it stuck to the tray. Certainly Lucia had been a maestro when it came to the child restraint. If you can do it I can, you old bitch, I encouraged myself. My hand squeezed a cold metal bar and all the plastic and padding and straps came away in one piece.

Nicholas seemed almost blind to the cumbersome thing as he took it from me. He pushed it in the back of his Jetta and slammed the door shut. Laurence would have to install it, but of course Laurence would, the right way. Equally senseless as my vision of Joachim and Lucia hitchhiking, the idea flashed through me that Joachim would be staying a long time with Laurence and Sahba, as if he'd been orphaned. I pictured Lucia at the Greyhound bus station, throttling the pay phone receiver and stuffing the slot with coins raked from the depths of her purse while cataracts of mascara asphalted her face and she poured out her tale of woe to her outraged and voluble clan banging skulls to get close to the earpiece in a crowded little house in São Paulo. Perhaps I should have raced to the station myself, just in time to grab Lucia as her wide, stubby feet in their puffy white sneakers clumped disconsolately up the rubberized stairs of her city-bound bus. Perhaps I was starting to realize she'd been my ally— she'd enabled my lover to lavish attention on me. Nicholas climbed in his Jetta and started the engine, then glanced at me out his window. "Regina," he said, and I stepped close to hear him. "Martha will be very angry Lucia is gone. Just because you and I spoke about it, it isn't your job to defend what I've done."

"I understand," I said, just as I'd said it before. But I already knew I'd defend him.

Something crossed his face, a pure motion like wind over water—I couldn't have guessed what emotion it was. "I'll miss you," he said. "Your friendship."

"Is it gone?" I wondered, but with luck he hadn't heard my foolish question as, gesturing me to step back, he drove off.

Lucia's disappearance struck the house as might a natural disaster, an earthquake or flood. Electric power still emerged from the outlets and potable water from all of the taps, but you would hardly have known it for the chaos entailed by an oatmeal breakfast. Martha's inherent capability, which allowed her to build outdoor ovens of rocks, or patch sails, or cultivate asparagus with such unprecedented ease for an amateur that a professor of the Agricultural College had produced a monograph on her methods, seemed not to drop off in certain arenas so much as simply to vanish in a massive perforation, a scissor-hole in her brain around "bathing a child" and "spoon-feeding a child" and "soothing to sleep an overtired, distressed child" where some continuity, some carryover from other realms of exceptional competence, might have been expected. One potentially soluble problem she could not seem to solve was that she did not know where anything was that pertained to her child. She could not find the child-size towels, the specially short-handled bright plastic spoons, the wipe cloths or replacement crib sheets or, worst of all, favorite toys for which Joachim wailed in a repetitive, surely translatable argot to which Martha did not have the key. To her credit the uncomfortable parallel, between Nicholas's uselessness as deplored by Martha, and Martha's own that had now been revealed, was not lost on her. Here was the difference she saw: Nicholas did not prize Martha for all Martha did, while Martha *had* prized Lucia, as they say, above rubies. "I knew what she was worth!" Martha said, almost weeping. "I don't *care* if she called me a dyke or if she thought I was going to hell. She did a great job. She did everything and she asked me for nothing and now just to spite me she's gone."

"Who wanted to spite you? Not her."

"Of course not. Nicholas! Don't believe that bullshit about safeguarding Joachim's dignity. Joachim adored her. Look at him. How must this feel, having her disappear? A lot worse than hearing his mama called Satan's handmaid. As if he can grasp what that means. He can grasp that she's gone."

Just as Nicholas had predicted and tried to forestall, I did find myself taking his side. "You might think that she did a great job, but Nicholas thinks that respect for you is part of her job. And frankly, he's right. The way she talked about you—how could you tolerate that?"

"Easily! Who cares if she didn't respect me? She respected my child. She *loved* him. Nicholas had no right to send her away. And don't you understand why he did this? To get back at me. Shorten my leash. Leave us less time together. Who replaces Lucia? I do. You of all people ought to complain!"

But in fact both of them replaced her. Nicholas relieved Martha on alternate days, and when he did, when Martha had a full day to herself, during which she might do anything that she chose—during which she might research her book, or perfect her pool game, or perhaps even sprawl in the bath while her devoted young lover test-drove on her body the ingenious sex toys that, in happier days, had been jointly selected and ordered by mail—her mood, and our relations, grew worse. Lucia's departure posed such a crisis, so thoroughly gripped Martha's mind and reduced to inconsequence other concerns, that days passed before she acknowledged, much less discussed, those connected developments that, to my mind, were of equal interest: that Nicholas had moved out of the house, and that Nicholas knew I'd become Martha's lover. "It has to be an au pair," Martha ranted as she hurled items into the dishwasher. "Someone who'll live in and knows how to drive. That's Lucia's one failing: she would not learn to drive. Though it wouldn't have mattered if Nicholas hadn't rented a place on the far side of campus. Fricking Walter Debrango and his Home for Scorned Husbands. They don't just share a building, they share the same jokes."

"You didn't tell me you'd asked Nicholas to move out," I said, not for the first time.

"Can you please hand me those plates from our lunch?" she demanded. "Of course I told you he'd moved out."

"You didn't tell me that you'd *asked* him to move out. Nor did you tell me he *had*."

"Of course I did. You *know*, don't you?"

"I know it from *him*!"

"What difference does it make?"

"You didn't tell me: why? You didn't want me to know? You said he was going to come spend a week with the baby, not that you'd given him that week to move out."

"And this is some crime against you? That having possibly a few fucking things on my mind, I failed to keep you apprised of my husband's movements?"

"That's not the point. The point is you came to a major decision about your marriage and you *didn't tell me*."

"Because it's my marriage, not yours," she said, slamming the dishwasher shut.

"So you admit it?"

"What am I, on trial?"

"You wouldn't be on trial if you weren't so evasive!"

"So *you* admit that you've put me on trial!" While we bickered Joachim, on the floor on his stomach with his head slightly raised, had been shoving the floor with the heels of his hands, so that, though he had his eyes fixed on a goal well ahead—Martha's feet—he never moved forward but backward, and now had wedged himself under the legs of a chair.

"You didn't tell me you were asking him to leave for the same reason you didn't tell him we're lovers," I theorized furiously as Joachim unleashed a wail of frustration.

"I *did* tell you I was asking him to leave. Are you out of your mind?"

"You did not!"

"And there's a tradition, perhaps you don't know, of refraining from telling one's husband all about the adultery one is committing," she said as, bisecting the room, she snatched the baby out by his tiny armpits, which rescue only further outraged him, so his wails became screams.

"So much better to let the news come from the nanny."

"Why don't you call Nicholas and commiserate then. Poor wronged lover and husband!" But our screams were no match for the baby's, and that argument, like all arguments, as well as all peaceable conversations, and all meals, and all sex, was cut short.

To a depth no lecture of Lucia's could have ever achieved I'd begun to understand Joachim's disproportionate power. His very inability to walk, talk, obtain food, obtain toys, change his own elevation, control his own waste, added up to such efficient tyranny no five minutes elapsed that was not interrupted. No activity wasn't derailed. No coherence attempted to harden its edges that wasn't immediately smashed. And somehow, Martha's stubborn attempts to control her existence just deepened the chaos around us, so that I, who'd idolized her independence, and her unfettered intelligence, and her many achievements, now wished she'd concede her defeat and tie on a babushka and do some housecleaning. Martha was grimly determined to write her book, and the heaps of her research appeared everywhere, well-intentioned haystacks beside the high chair or in sight of the doorway bounce swing or wherever she thought she might steal a few moments for reading, so that in addition to misplacing Joachim's things, she was always misplacing the page where she'd had to leave off, and would ransack the house in a rage, grabbing up and discarding. Nights when Joachim was tranquil in his crib, and we might have made love, or at the very least slept, Martha's books would form jagged deposits all over the bed, and Martha herself would sit up with her face barricaded behind her bifocals, and the breast pocket of her old Oxford shirt bristling dangerously with black razor-tip pens. If I managed to doze underneath the hot glare of her lamp, I would often wake up with a sharp-cornered library binding impaling my gut. Yet I never went home, nor to some other room of her house where the light wasn't on. I would still rather lie with my cheek pressed against her bare thigh and the *Norton Anthology* splayed by my head. For some nights, when she finally clicked off her lamp to reveal the dawn starting to texture the room, as if freed by our shared tiredness, like composites of darkness our bodies would merge. Without words or struggle a fluid of pleasure would seal us in its cocoon, and final outcries would be quakes without sound, as if taking place on the floor of the ocean. For the night's short remainder, we slept blissfully, and whatever it was that we shared would seem inviolate.

If only she would tell me what it meant that Nicholas had moved out, that he knew we were lovers—if only she would tell me the one thing I wanted to know, which was what sort of future together we had. And yet the future arrived every day, until half of August was gone. Then questions of my own separate future, as a student and scholar, grew hard to ignore. Though I tried, for a while.

One morning when it was Nicholas's day to spend with Joachim he called to say he was sick. An au pair had been hired, but had not yet arrived. Nicholas had aches, a high fever, was sweating and chilled, and had vomited twice in the night. I heard Martha repeating his symptoms back to him as if she were expecting something more. Their conversation was brief, and when Martha set down the receiver she was pale with anger. "I suppose that you think he was faking," I said, nastily.

"Go ahead and side with him again."

"Side with him! Do you really believe he's not sick?"

"Of course he's sick. He could barely make sense. But I have just *ten days* until I'm back in the classroom. Ten days left to research and write, and now this day is shot." For some time, scarcely seeming to see me, she continued to scold me, as if I'd suggested she give up her career. Just a half hour later the phone rang again, and answering Martha turned not pale but red with unease.

"Oh, Laurence! How nice . . .

"Yes, he's sick. Oh, he called you. Then why—

"Lunch?—No, I had no idea.

"A '*play date*'? Oh, I see.

"Can I phone you back later? Of course I'd love seeing you too . . .

"A '*play date*'!" Martha cried when she got off the phone. Today Laurence and Bebi, it turned out, had expected Nicholas and Joachim to come over for lunch and the activity Laurence called a "play date." Having heard from Nicholas he was sick with the flu, Laurence had called Martha to urge her to accept the invitation in her estranged husband's stead. Joachim's absence, and hers, would be a great disappointment; Bebi had been awaiting his playmate's arrival for days.

I hadn't seen Laurence in months, since the night of the dinner, and Sahba and Beb in even longer than that. For a moment the dense interval, of my time with Martha, disappeared, and I was plunged into a prehistoric world, and felt I hardly knew who I was anymore. "Laurence loathes me," Martha was saying. "This is some kind of divine punishment! Not only denied my workday, but now I have to have lunch with my ex-husband's friend who loathes me, so the babies can have a *play date*."

"He doesn't loathe you," I reproved her, although I was more lost in thought about whether or not Laurence might now loathe me, so that for a moment I didn't realize what she meant when she said, with a gasp of insight,

"You should go—you and Laurence are friends."

"*I* go?"

"I'll leave you the car."

"No!" I cried, understanding she meant it. "I haven't seen Laurence in ages—I don't think we're friends anymore. Just call him and say they should have their date some other time." But I knew it was hardly the play date that Martha most wanted.

"Please, babe," she said, sliding onto my lap. "I have so much to do and so few days to do it. I won't ever get these days back. I've never asked you for a favor," and before I could halfway discern if this statement was true, she plunged her hot tongue in my mouth and I groaned when I'd meant to be silent, and slid my legs open and crushed her to me, and for the first time in weeks, in the daylight and conscious, we set ruthlessly after each other. But after some moments I pushed her away.

"You want me to take him to lunch and what else?"

Rosily disheveled, she leaned her head on one elbow and thought. "Could you look after him until six?"

It was eleven in the morning. "Martha," I exclaimed. "That's seven hours."

"Until five? No, how about this: you tell me how long."

"You're asking me to babysit."

"I trust you! You're far more trustworthy than me," she attempted to joke. But this wasn't my objection, and she knew it. That she so frankly hoped to use me coursed through me like a charge, and I felt I understood, perhaps for the first time, the warlike accounting of love: the storing up of credits and debits like a forging of shackles.

I made her wait until she should have grown uncomfortable before I said, with some refrigeration in my voice, "I'll watch him because I love you, and I'm happy to help you. Not because I haven't got something better to do." She'd gone too far, and yet, I was perversely glad she'd done so, which might mean I had gone too far, also.

"Of course. Thank you. I'm truly grateful, babe. I hope you realize how much."

Our ardor of moments before had evaporated, and it only felt foolish to be lying, as we had somehow wound up, on her dining-room floor. We stood and Martha straightened her clothing and then, with tenderness but not heat, gathered me in her arms. "I know you've noticed," she said in my ear, "that I'm a much more inventive lover when I've gotten work done."

"Then by all means go do it. I'll expect to enjoy the rewards."

"You will," she said, kissing me deeply again, but briefly, as if she feared that the longer she lingered the greater the risk I'd renege. After much energetic ransacking of rooms she located her most needed papers, and with a shout of "love you!" tossed back over one shoulder, she rushed from the house.

All this time Joachim had been taking his late-morning nap. Had he been awake the discussion could never have happened, let alone the outcome. He was more skilled at retaining her presence than I. His absence had enabled her departure, and now, as he continued to heedlessly sleep, it forced me to reflect on my own situation despite how unpleasant would be the conclusions. I was alone in Martha's house and in charge of her child, yet I felt not like her trusted ally but a child myself. I would have liked to think it was because I hadn't babysat since the age of thirteen, but I knew this wasn't true, just as Martha's belief that I could have refused her was somehow untrue. She wouldn't think she'd overstepped. She had asked, I'd consented; then why did I feel like a child? Martha liked to pretend her adult obligations, her parenthood and her professorship and mortgage and the rest of the dread weighty things, added up to a prison forged only for her, but in fact it was armor. Thusly clad she could make every other claim yield, for what *did* I have better to do? Not a thing, as she knew even better than me. I had my summer reading list, off of which I had crossed not one title. I had my fall classes to choose: Cross-Dressing and Cultural Contestation? (M)Other Tongue(s)? How would I ever decide? And right then, though I loved studenthood, perhaps loved it too much, I was finished. I was finished with all forms of life that resembled a child's. At my age, twenty-one, my own mother had been already married and pregnant and entrapping new clients in my father's little office like the spider traps flies; twenty-one wasn't inherently inconsequential. And though I could have decided, in my angry resolve, to kidnap the baby and hold him for ransom, I meant to pursue consequence along dignified paths. No longer would I be the student, to Martha's professor. No longer denizen of a house full of empty beer bottles, to her mansion owner. And while she'd fled Laurence and in fact her own child, I would calmly attend to them both.

I went upstairs and crept down the hall to his nursery door. As usual it was ajar; after a moment's hesitation I inched it just open enough to squeeze through. My heart was beating so loudly I thought it might wake him—I really had no idea what I was doing. In all my career babysitting I'd never cared for a child so young. I saw only the crib, its monkey-patterned bumper sufficiently high that the baby, asleep, was obscured. I knew this and yet still grew convinced he'd somehow disappeared. I was alone; no one could judge me; I dropped to all fours, and with the caution of a predator—or prey?—noiselessly crawled toward the crib, the heels of my hands and my knees sinking into the carpet. I didn't have to get all the way there to come in range of the sound of his breathing. Once I heard it, so faint yet so steady, the quintessence of self-containment—here he'd been all this time—I was compelled to make sure it was him breathing there and not something else, like a raccoon. I raised my head just far enough to peer over the bumper. He'd bundled himself in a corner, limbs tucked under his body, face turned toward me. Because his eyes were closed I felt I had no idea what he looked like. I might never have seen him before. And then his breath snagged in his throat and he let out a strange, high-pitched whinny and shrugged himself more tightly into a ball and with wild haste, as if fleeing gunfire, hunched over I ran out the door, and closed it to a finger's width behind me, afraid of the noise of the latch.

The nearest phone was in the bedroom, where my clothes and Martha's seemed to have been raining down from great heights for a great length of time. With a pang I discovered I still knew Laurence's number by heart. And then hearing his chipper "Hello-oh?" I almost hung up but would not let myself.

"Hi, Laurence."

"Martha!" with a great gust of mustered delight. "Are you able to come?"

"It's Regina," I said, trailing into the uncertain silence that followed. "Martha asked me to call you. Something came up and she can't come to lunch."

"Regina!" poor Laurence managed. "My God, I'm sorry. You sounded just like—hello there, how are you?"

"I'm babysitting Joachim today, and I'd be happy to bring him to lunch. I heard Beb was excited to see him."

"Well—wonderful! That's terrific! We'll be thrilled to see you."

Martha was right—it was truly exhausting, adult artifice. Standing there beside the unmade, hard-used bed, Martha's phone in my hand, Martha's unlaundered panties and cut-offs and wife-beater T-shirts ankle-deep at my feet, and Laurence's voice in my ear, I was two places at once, or perhaps more exact, two times: before Martha, and after. Laurence didn't know who I'd become and was not sure he wanted to ask. "Come on, Laurence," I said, my voice seeming to drop a full octave. "That's not necessary."

"Certainly it is!" But as always, Laurence was betrayed by his honesty. "Sahba might be uncomfortable," he admitted, "but she's not here. She's gone down to New York for a girls' weekend with an old school friend. That was why, when Nicholas fell ill, I thought I would ask Martha over. She and I could break the ice, and Bebi wouldn't have to be disappointed. He loves other children, and there are simply no children out here where we live."

"Now you'll have to break the ice with me."

"I hope there's no ice to be broken," he gaily protested, but Laurence was Laurence. He'd known me too well to pretend he might not, at this point, know me less. Still he kept his tone light when he said, "We can just keep it simple: it's a play date, for your charge and mine."

For me at least it was more, which I realized before we arrived. My nervousness at driving with the baby—somehow heightened instead of allayed by the Swedish restraint, with its Space Shuttle catastrophe straps, as if Joachim would be shot into orbit—at first made me drive very slowly. Then my growing eagerness to see Laurence again made me speed. I'd so badly missed Laurence. His friendship, it seemed to me now, had coincided with a sense of pure rightness, a time of being just who I was without needing to try. Herky-jerky, going too fast and then going too slow, Joachim and I struggled toward Laurence's house. Waking Joachim from his nap so that we could set out I had found myself declaiming, in an improvised mixture of self-consciousness and lack of inhibition, while he sat staring at me from the crib, "Mommy has gone to her office. To work on her book. So I, Regina, am going to stay with you. What do you think? Is that okay with you? Mommy asked me to stay. So I'm going to pick you up now. Then we'll have a new diaper. Then we'll get in the car. Then we'll drive to see Laurence and Beb. What do you think, Joachim? Does that all seem okay?" I tried not to bellow as if he were deaf, yet I couldn't stop recalling that parrotlike volubility he had shown with Lucia, those musical babbles and shattering squawks. Now he was silent. Was it the silence of protest? Not necessarily, I felt. It might be the silence of deliberation. All the way down the hill, and through town, and out the other side along the two-lane state highway through farmland to Laurence's house, when I was not accelerating or braking I was stealing quick glances at Joachim in the rearview. He would be gazing either into the deep distance or right into the mirror, at me. "Here's the new road where we turn! There's a barn falling down! There's a birdie up there on the wire!" I thundered inanely, imagining his silence alternately as assent, or disagreement. But when we turned into Laurence's driveway—"Here we are! Here is Laurence's house! Which is also Beb's house! Where they LIVE!"—all at once a fluty noise of acknowledgment rose from his throat, and he kicked up his feet. Laurence was already crossing the lawn with a long-legged, sooty-eyed boy in his arms— the baby Beb, metamorphosed. Perhaps to lessen my shock at the passage of time Laurence was dressed as always, which meant overdressed for the weather, in his uniform khakis and button-down shirt underneath a light blazer, and braided belt, and Top-Siders.

"He seems to recognize your house," I said, sparing Laurence the question of whether to kiss me in greeting or not by submerging my entire upper half in the car, in order to free Joachim from his seat. But when I got out again, holding the baby, Laurence bestowed his chaste brotherly kiss.

"You're looking wonderful. Come on in. I've got lunch all laid out, baby things and some less mushy items for us."

I'd never seen Laurence's house in its full summer glory. The back deck was ringed around with flowerboxes and urns of eggplant and peppers and staked cherry tomatoes. A picnic table with an umbrella in its center was set for four, with high chairs before two of the places, one that clamped to the edge of the table and one of the usual kind. "This is Beb's travel high chair," Laurence said, taking Joachim from me, "and so also his guest chair when he entertains. Will you fit in it, darling?" he asked Joachim. "Yes, you'll fit very nicely. Let me get them installed and I'll get us some vinho verde. Just small glasses. I won't let you overindulge." The table recapitulated the abundance and variety of the deck, spread as it was with little bowls of olives and cashews and exotic-looking crackers, as well as halved grapes and halved clementine sections and halved cherry tomatoes and pale pink rubber erasers which I belatedly realized were pieces of hot dog and which gave me the key to the feast, the items intended for babies, and intended for us, although all were presented with care. Even tantalizing were the colored purees, in pale green and pale gold and pure white and a deep indigo. "Not that we're barred from partaking of mushy," Laurence assured me, returning and setting a wineglass in front of my place. "The mushy is all rather good. That's a fresh pea puree. That's fresh corn with a bit of yogurt, that's just yogurt, that's wild blueberries Beb and I picked today, again mixed with yogurt—"

"You *made* these?"

"I love the summer. And now that Beb's almost two we can try him on all sorts of things. Last night he had asparagus spears and wild mushrooms. I don't read anymore, I just play with the blender."

Outside our oasis of shade, blinding platinum sunshine ignited the lake. All we heard was a motorboat dragging its zipper of froth. Laurence and I ate, fed, wiped, shifted items within or beyond the babies' reach depending on what could be gauged of their changing intentions. At one point Beb upset his squat plastic cup, and Laurence said, "Shall we clean it up, darling? You take one napkin and I'll take another," and it seemed then, as it had seemed the whole meal, that there was nothing so special involved in the care of young children. In fact, it was the simplest thing in the world. It was as simple as cooking five kinds of puree, and cultivating produce and flowers, and keeping a home clean and ordered, and ironing button-up shirts. Moderation in drinking seemed equally simple, because Laurence accompanied me. We had both only sipped at our thimbles of vinho verde. Everything had slowed down. No one was crying and nothing was lost.

When they had eaten their fill Laurence spread a blanket in the sun and anchored its corners with baskets of toys, setting Joachim in the middle, while ambulatory Beb roved back and forth, presenting various of the toys to his guest and demonstrating their functions. They seemed not to need us, and it was now that Laurence finally broached a subject not having to do with the children, the weather, the garden, the food, or the lake. "Do you know what you're taking this term?"

"Only a leave of absence," I said, "but I might not even make it a leave. I might just withdraw."

"I'm sorry to hear that. Do you feel like telling me why?"

"Don't be sorry. I just don't want to do it anymore. Papers, and classes—I've been in school since I was four. I want to be in the world." It sounded childish even as I said it.

"What would you do instead?"

"Maybe get a job. It's a novel idea, isn't it?"

"But this is training for a job. A very good job at which I think you would be brilliant."

"*You* will be brilliant. Me? I just can't see it anymore. Two years of course work, then exams, then a dissertation, then the job market? I want to do something *now*."

"Fair enough. But what?"

"That's what I don't know," I admitted.

We directed our gaze at the children, though they still were contentedly playing and still didn't need us. In a sudden movement of resolve Laurence topped off our glasses. "I want to apologize to you for something. I told you on the phone that Sahba would have been uncomfortable to see you. I was an ass to say that. Sahba cares for you a great deal."

"But she's never cared for Martha," I said. "It seems more likely you were being honest the first time you spoke. It's all right, Laurence. I'm a big girl. I know you might not like me either."

"I like you very much, and Sahba does also. Her liking you so much is what makes her uncomfortable. Uncomfortable because unwilling to speak her mind to you, unwilling to speak her mind to you because she doesn't want to hurt you. That pains her."

"She can speak her mind to me. Why couldn't she?"

"Oh, no, Daddy," Beb despaired, for Joachim had begun flinging toys, and one had gone over the edge of the deck.

"Look at that pitching arm. It's all right, darling. It's on the grass there. I'll go down in a moment and fetch it back up. Regina, I don't want you to feel patronized, and I'm afraid that you will, but there's no other clear way of saying it. Sahba and I both, and Nicholas—yes—we all feel concerned about Martha's relationship with you. That your expectations and hers may not match."

"What expectations? Of a miserable faculty marriage and a big gloomy house? Those are the *last* things I want," I exclaimed caustically, just as if I were fending off Martha. For Martha accused me of wanting from her what I couldn't define and she couldn't provide—an accusation that enraged me in proportion to how accurate it was.

Laurence said, "Please don't be angry. If you are you'll prove Sahba right and me wrong, which will cause no surprise. Sahba insisted we couldn't be so blunt with you. She was afraid we would injure your feelings, and make you turn a deaf ear to our worries."

"I'm not a child, Laurence."

"It's because you're not a child that I felt I could speak to you frankly. You're not a child, but your life situation is very much different from hers."

"Because I haven't got a Ph.D., or a job, or a baby? Why do I feel as though I'm always being penalized for not having these things?"

"I'm talking about whether two people can honor each other the way that they should. It's not about matching possessions or matching credentials. I can't claim to have any idea what Martha requires in her life. I only know it will be complicated because we're all complicated. I am. You are. These little boys, even. Complex beyond imagining, the things that we need. And now she has *you*, Regina, and what do you have?"

"Everything," I said with bravado. Whether or not it was true, I knew the declaration made me sound like a fool.

After a moment Laurence said, gently, "I'm the greatest fan of love there is."

I smiled on the droplets of moisture still lining my glass, while adding a few of my own. Love's ecstasy felt like sorrow. "I'm glad you don't hate me," I said.

"Don't be absurd."

"I'm sure Nicholas hates me."

"I'm even less qualified to speak for him than for Sahba, but still, I don't think so. I don't think he blames his suffering on you. I don't think he would try to relieve it in hatred of you."

"But he's suffering," I said, as if I hadn't seen this clearly myself. Like any craven guilty party, I longed for absolution. For the first and only time that afternoon I caught sight of the nonsaintly Laurence, who could judge when required, and scorn when deserved. Now he let slip his impatience with me.

"Of course he's suffering," Laurence said curtly.

On the drive back, Joachim fell asleep. Little by little his face had grown jowly and skeptical, cheeks and lids drooping down while the translucent eyebrows struggled upward in failed counteraction. The thread snipped while my eyes were turned back to the road. The next time I looked the dark fringe of his lashes, like wee Spanish fans, had been spread. One cheek was flat on the edge of his Swedish restraint, squashing the small rosebud mouth slightly open, so that a thread of clear drool, like an icicle, hung from one corner. Asleep and inert, his face flickered with alien life, as if first Martha's ghost, then Nicholas's, chased each other across it. Hardly seeing where I went I passed by Hobo Deli and took the homeward turn onto my street, pulling into my driveway for the first time in weeks. I killed the Saab's engine and turned all the way around in the seat. Joachim stayed asleep. Once again, as that morning, I was surprised by his breath, how regular and audible it was, even immersed in the rattle-snake chorus of summer insects. After a moment a door slammed behind me. Turning back toward the windshield I saw Dutra come out on the porch. I got out of the car with a finger bisecting my lips.

"He's sleeping," I said as Dutra bobbed and squinted, looking past me. When he finally saw Joachim he raised his own eyebrows slightly, that were so dark and emphatic, unlike the baby's faint ones, little brush-strokes with water that would vanish as soon as they dried. When did people grow eyebrows? Or maybe some, like Dutra, had them in the womb.

"Now you're the nanny?" he said.

"Just today." His mockery annoyed me. "Put your head in the car and you'll hear that he's breathing."

"Where's Hallett?" His adoption of this bunkhouse familiarity was also annoying.

"Working on her book. It was Nicholas's day, but he's sick."

"And she couldn't quit work for one day to take care of her kid?"

"Jesus, Dutra. I'm not dangerously incompetent."

"No one said you were. I just think it's ballsy, using the girlfriend for free babysitting. Have a little pride, Ginny."

"Fuck yourself, Dutra."

"No other options. Are you coming in? It's been starting to feel like I'm living alone."

We didn't go inside but sat out on the porch, where I could still see the baby, slumberous in his seat, through the Saab's open window. The reflections of overhead trees weirdly framed him, oak leaves pulsing and glittering out of the glossy black depths of the Saab as if off the face of an undisturbed pond. I realized it had been a whole year since I'd first seen this house, walking here from the bus stop with a scrap of paper in my hand and being greeted by avid Dutra, with his long Roman nose and his tireless, percolating attention. It could have happened a decade ago. This summer, my time in this house had been simplified to intervals of sleep and then simplified further, to the occasional retrieval of some item. I lived with Martha entirely now. I wore her clothes and ate her food and read her books and even brushed with her toothbrush and washed with her soap, I left my drained coffee cups in her car and my shed hairs and sweat in her sheets. If I already knew that this couldn't go on, I equally knew that I couldn't move back in with Dutra. The house behind me felt as separate from me as it had on the day I'd first mounted the steps. And Dutra felt separate too, in an opposite way. I felt a reaching toward him like an ache. What I'd missed most was precisely this mode, this purposeless sitting together with beers while his mind paced and rummaged and ceaselessly tossed scraps of putative knowledge at me. The human mammal, for example, was not meant to metabolize wheat, hence beer made us sleepy; and yet this was the nature of civilization, these determined pursuits of the unnatural. Beer had been discovered when the stored wheat got wet and fermented, but what made man start storing wheat? What had made him start farming, stop hunting, forget who he was—

"I've decided to rent my own place," I cut in.

For a moment Dutra, halted midlecture, tipped his beer bottle and gazed down the street. "Have you found something?"

"Not yet."

"I've got the *Journal* inside. Take a look at the ads and if there's anything good I can drive you to see it. The way to do it is line up a bunch and I can drive you to see all of them at one time. That's the biggest pain about apartment hunting, all the time you spend seeing them." The more officiously he offered his help, the more I knew I'd hurt him. We were both staring forward but in my peripheral vision I could see his bottle being raised to his lips with a quicker tempo, as if he'd remembered he had to be somewhere and wanted to drain it.

"It's not anything personal, Dutra. I just want my own space."

"Sure you do. We all do. If it wasn't for money I'd live here alone. But I've loved living here with you, Ginny. Even when you've been crazy."

Perhaps only Dutra could use the word "love" as if setting out two separate, even opposite meanings, for the listener to choose from, at no risk to Dutra himself. I've "loved" living with you as a cheerleader loves, with indiscriminate, bouncy fatuity that in fact isn't love, because it privileges nothing, which means living with you has meant nothing to me. Or: I've loved living with you—words I've not said to anyone else. I knew the second meaning was his true one, from his calling me crazy.

"Wanting the shower curtain pulled shut isn't crazy, you asshole," I said, looking at him so that he had to look back. "Otherwise it gets moldy."

"Wanting the toothpaste tube cap on the toothpaste isn't crazy, either. Otherwise gobs of toothpaste get stuck on the sink."

"Much worse than the toilet seat always left up."

"*Much* worse."

"I've loved living with you, too. I'll miss you."

"It's been like you already left," he said after a moment. "Sure you need your own place? You're pretty much living with her."

"I want my own place. Besides, the au pair's moving in."

"The oh what?"

"The au pair. A live-in babysitter. It's like an exchange student, except she takes care of your kid."

"So she's going to be young?"

"About my age. A year out of college."

Now he was feeling better. A wolf grin split his face. "Oh, baby," he said. "*Now's* when you're going to move out? And let the au pair grab your spot in the bed?"

If I hadn't been feeling so tenderly toward him I might have broken my beer bottle over his head. "If all Martha wanted was a woman my age she wouldn't need an au pair. Women my age are pretty thick on the ground around here."

"But this one will be living in her house. Taking care of her kid," jerking his head toward Joachim, still oblivious in the backseat. "Might start to remind her of a very special person."

"Fuck you, Dutra." I shoved my chair back and stood up. "It's late. I should go."

"Aw, c'mon. I'm just teasing."

"I know you're teasing and I don't give a shit, but I do have to go."

He followed me back to the Saab, and stood a moment peering in the backseat. Joachim had shifted his head, exposing one flushed, dented, drool-varnished cheek. I found a clean cloth in his diaper bag and dabbed the cheek dry before getting into the car. "You seem good at this," Dutra said through the window.

"I used to babysit when I was thirteen. It's all come back to me."

"I really was just teasing about the oh-whatsit chick, but—don't turn your back, Gin. If you know what I mean."

"I don't. I have no idea what you're talking about."

"I just mean, when your lover leaves someone, for you—or is cheating on someone, with you—those kinds of betrayals are maybe a habit. I'm just speaking on principles."

"She didn't leave Nicholas for me. Their marriage was over a long time before it was over."

"Still. Hallett seems like a leaver. Just take care, okay, Ginny?"

I started the engine, perhaps more emphatically than was required, and as an afterthought glanced into the backseat. Still asleep. Joachim's capacity to sleep, at age ten months, through every kind of disturbance, would lead me to believe, incorrectly, that imperviousness was a component of his personality, and not just a transient feature typical of this developmental stage. "I know you like to believe that I need your protection," I told Dutra, "but I'm actually fine. Really. You can relax," and within I shored up this proud self-diagnosis by smugly reflecting that here was a man who required a six-pack, a packed bong, and both the TV and stereo on before his mind calmed enough to allow him to study. At least until I'd turned the corner he lingered in the driveway watching after the car. I turned slightly too sharply, as if shaking him off.

It had taken them a long time to choose the au pair, weeks of manila file folders passing back and forth between their departmental mailboxes bearing densely written Post-its by which each, with scrupulous courtesy, expressed grave doubts about the first choice of the other. The autobiographical essays, CVs, testimonials, and head shots of contending au pairs papered Martha's table, crackled in her bedsheets, slid underfoot when one climbed into the car. Wherever I looked, female faces looked back. They had an unpleasant effect on me. I too now needed a job. I too seemed to possess as my principal qualifications only youth and a uselessly broad liberal-arts education. Unwillingness to work as an au pair might set me apart, but then again it might not. The au pair applicants seemed to fall into three major types: the cheerleader/camp-counselor type, the premature-matron type, and a last miscellaneous type whose only trait in common seemed to be an unstated, but to me perfectly palpable, unwillingness to work as an au pair. It was written all over their faces, and loudly crammed between the lines of their overlong, self-regarding essays on their interests and goals. Perhaps inevitably it was one of this third type that Nicholas and Martha finally chose. She was a German named Anya, and I hypothesized that her pompous essay about studying Goethe had let them feel they were not hiring a substitute parent, but accepting a protégée.

When I'd told Martha I'd decided to drop out of school, her reaction had been so enthusiastic I'd started to wonder, in my mounting annoyance, if I'd hoped she would talk me out of it. "Baby, I'm so proud of you!" she enthused, sitting up from the postcoital snarl of bedsheets within which for some reason I'd thought to attempt serious conversation. "Graduate study of literature is the catchall for smart, rudderless people who can't think what to do with themselves—that's how *I* ended up here. I wish I'd had your guts. Honestly, babe, you're so lucky to be at the front of your life and not stuck halfway into the mire. I always want to say it to my most brilliant students: Get out! Go do something real! But I'm their professor: ironically the most qualified to tell them to get out of this field, and the least able to do so. I'm supposed to make clones of myself—" On and on she went like this, extolling my boldness and vision, until I could no longer quash my suspicions.

"You're awfully relieved I dropped out. Were you afraid that I couldn't have hacked it?"

"Couldn't have taught the great works to a room of stoned children? Are you joking? I think you could have—I think you *can*—do almost anything else."

This mollified me, for the moment. "The problem is, I can't figure out what the anything will be."

"You don't have to. You're twenty-one! Do you know what I'd give to be that age again?"

"Do you know what I'd give if you'd stop saying that?"

"I know what you should do: travel. It's what I should have done." With lusty vicariousness she began to plot out my itinerary. "London, Paris, and Rome," she began, "just to get those three out of the way. Then you keep heading east. Istanbul—"

"Now you sound like my mother. 'Europe's Crown Jewels.' 'Gateway to the Ottoman Empire.' I haven't got money to travel."

"Money? You need a backpack and train pass. In fact, I think you've got to buy the train pass while you're still twenty-one. When's your birthday?"

"November twenty-eighth."

"That gives you three months!"

"But you're teaching this term."

I might have finally irked her as much as she had irked me. "Regina," she warned. "Look around at my life here. I can't travel with you."

"And I don't even want to! I'm not interested in travel, I'm interested in you. And you seem interested in waving me off from some dock."

"I'm interested in what's best for you," she shot back, swinging out of bed. "I thought you wanted to be free."

"Not of you."

"Why does everything turn melodramatic?" she cried. But she returned to the bed and threw her unshowered body on mine.

The au pair finally arrived the first day of fall term, on the regional flight from New York that was always an unannounced interval late. Nicholas was teaching all morning, and after waiting several hours Martha had to rush down to campus to teach her own class, leaving me for a last time in charge of the baby. Just a few minutes later a taxi pulled into the drive. The au pair, Anya, looked just as she had in her picture, but larger. I imagined her ancestress swinging a scythe with her hair in a kerchief. Anya, however, was generations separated from outdoor occupations. Although August was ending she was as pale as if she'd spent the whole summer inside. She wore a long black tube skirt and an oversize black cardigan with large buttons and librarians' pockets, which costume should have been modest but somehow was haughty, as if by it she meant to imply that anyone who dressed better than she must be trying too hard. The quantity of her things was surprising. She stood by in calm idleness as the driver, the sort of sunburned, grizzled, eye-creased, twitchily feral white man I always assumed, seeing his doppelgängers lining the bar at the Pink Elephant, must be a Vietnam vet, with begrudged effort emptied the trunk. Things piled up on the grass: two large, soft, fat suitcases, a shoulder bag, a tote bag, sundry plastic shopping bags, and four small boxes which might have been packed full of lead from the way the man staggered with effort. "Which door?" she asked me, meaning I ought to direct him.

"I'll help you carry your stuff. He's a cab driver." She raised her eyebrows very slightly at this, then let her gaze fall on the baby, who'd been watching the process with interest.

"So you are Joachim," she said matter-of-factly, as if checking him off a list. She didn't offer to take him, so that I had to struggle, hitching him up with one arm, to get Martha's envelope open and pay the cab driver. I overtipped him for her presumption that he was her servant, somewhat hoping that as a result he would servantlike carry her heaped things indoors out of gratitude to me. He got back in his cab and drove off.

"Let's go in," I told her. "We can put Joachim in his playpen and then carry your things in together." But she was already making her way to the house, taking off her cardigan as she went.

"This is a nice house," she said over her shoulder. "Larger than it looked in the pictures."

"You saw pictures?"

"Of course. Of the kitchen and yard and my room. I could not have chosen to come if I didn't know what I would find."

"I thought it's more like they chose you."

"We chose each other. Otherwise there can be bad surprises. Sometimes there are, anyway." She'd led me through the solarium and now her gaze flicked appraisingly around the vast kitchen. "I would love to drink some coffee, if possible."

Everything in the kitchen interested her—the marble mortar and pestle, the heavy glass blender, the cast-iron Japanese teapot, the elaborate French press coffeemaker like a piece of equipment from chemistry lab, the dishwasher with its drenched racks of freshly bathed mugs, the double-door refrigerator stuffed with fresh berries, heavy cream, bundled members of the onion family dangling gobbets of dirt from the bountiful garden. This was going to be her coffee cup, that her vase for fresh flowers. I could have thought she was casing the room like a professional thief had she not been just the opposite of furtive. She was plump with self-regard and entitlement, and she asked me for a butter knife, a small plate, a teaspoon, and some sort of fruit jam as if I were working for her.

"What sorts of bad surprises?" I asked in spite of myself. She'd continued to pay no attention to Joachim whatsoever and I'd finally installed him in his high chair with a pile of board books and a bowl of cut grapes which he was throwing alternately to the floor, first a book, then a grape, then a book.

"Don't," she interrupted as I stooped to retrieve his projectiles. "You're only teaching him to throw it again. I can tell you about my bad surprises if you're interested, but then you must do the same thing for me. Tell me what I need to know about them. What time do they get here?"

I realized she assumed I was a fellow babysitter: who else would I be?

"Noon," I said. "He'll go down for a nap before then."

"Are you a student at the school here?"

"Until recently."

"I miss my student life. With little kids there's never any peace. You saw all my books in the boxes outside. When I was in school, almost each day I read a new book. Now, since I'm doing this work, it's a book in a month, reading little by little, so my thinking is all broken up. When I get to the end I've forgotten the start. It makes everything pointless."

With this preamble she related the list of her bad surprises, which was much the same thing as her résumé. She'd had two prior jobs in the States, the first in Los Angeles, the second in New York. The Los Angeles family had been a television writer (the father), a talent agent (the mother), and three children ages three, eight, and ten. The father drank and had affairs. The mother shopped and disappeared to desert spas. Worst of all were the children, so insecure that they required almost constant attention and misbehaved almost all of the time. The parents provided no values and no discipline, and it being Anya's job to uphold such a structure, not create it herself, she quit after a year and moved on to New York, where she encountered a contrasting problem. In New York she worked for a hedge-fund manager (the father) and a textile designer (the mother) with two children, seven and five. These children were so venerated by both of the parents their every utterance and whim was celebrated. If the boy mentioned rockets he was taken to NASA and given a professional-size telescope. If the girl mentioned flute or piano she received flute and flute lessons, a piano and piano lessons, trying everything, sticking with nothing. The children had French instructors and cooking instructors and soccer and ballet and juggling instructors and only God knew what other kinds of instructors. If they wanted to mold clay then fresh clay must be found. If they wanted to repaint their rooms, paint must be acquired and assistance provided and plastic sheets over all of their things. "These parents worshipped their children, but it's just the same thing. There's no structure at all. It was very bizarre." This time Anya was fired, for not being "the right fit," her employers had said. Nevertheless they'd written her a glowing referral, practically an encomium. "Guilt," she concluded, confirming her assumption of our sisterhood by this final disclosure, for not even the agency knew she'd been fired.

"And what about them?" she now asked. "I've been interested to meet them. Professor Brodeur, I ordered his book. Of course I had no time to read it, but it looked very good."

"They're great. Of course you know they're separated. But they've been great about it. It's for everyone's good."

"So their relationship is amiable?"

She was probably thinking of "amicable" but her choice was far better: more sun-splashed and bouncy, without the trace of discord that "amicable," in its exclusion of discord, retains. "Very much so."

"It is a shame, though. When a child is so young. I wonder what's made them do a divorce?"

She was determined to root out a scandal, but if the scandal itself blocked her way, she would never succeed. "They just grew apart," I said tersely. "It's time for his nap." Perhaps now she might notice the sticky-bibbed, slump-lidded child in his seat. "If you bring him upstairs I can show you his bedroom and stuff."

"I hate her," I greeted Martha in the driveway a few minutes later.

"Good thing her job isn't to take care of you! Joachim go to sleep?"

"After I fed him and washed him and changed him while the brand-new au pair helped herself to your bookshelves."

"If the job opens again shall I tell you?"

"Fuck you, Hallett," I said to her back, for she was already striding inside. But as always the very rare times I was rough and profane, because really furious with her, she turned magically soft and coquettish.

Returning she gave me her deep, searching kiss, as a promise or bribe, if these aren't the same thing. Either way I accepted.

My new apartment was the second floor of a blue wood-frame house with a steeply pitched roof that sat just against, was in fact almost part of, the base of the hill. Climbing University Ave. one could actually pass, at foot level, the house's rear-facing second-floor windows. This was how I had found it, spotting the small FOR RENT sign almost obscured behind the veil of roadside goldenrod and fleabane. The sign was repeated again in the front, where the little house sat blue against the green of the hill at its back, behind a wall of hydrangea whose blooms were blue against the green of their leaves. I didn't yet know the name for hydrangea; this would be a late bequeathal of Martha's, along with the name of the tree whose boughs scraped on the second-floor window: redbud. But even without this botanical knowledge I felt proprietary. I knew I'd live in that house before stepping inside.

There were two free apartments, the top rear, with its view of the steep wall of weeds, and the top front, with its view of the redbud. I took the front although its monthly rent was eighty dollars more than the back. So far I had one very part-time and poorly paid job, doing research for a leprechaun-like retired professor of English named Angus McCann who had a rosy chapped face and abundant white hair. He was completing a treatise on longing. "Bring me all sorts of quotes about *longing*," he'd exhorted me, with such energy he was practically pogoing out of his chair. "All those folks who are *craving* and *hankerin' after* and suffer from *yens.*" Whether he would pay me by the quote or the hour had not been made clear. "And I'll be getting some writing assignments," I supplementarily lied to the taciturn landlord, who stood impassively in a mud-stiffened Carhartt barn jacket and mud-spattered boots, holding the signed lease and awaiting my check. When I handed it over he quartered them together as he might have a grocery list and shoved them into a pocket.

The landlord's name was Tim and he lived not in the house but somewhere outside town. This was all that I would ever learn about him. But he was clearly no absentee landlord; he kept the house freshly painted, the hydrangea beds weeded, the redbud boughs pruned, the porch floorboards nailed down, and the gutters devoid of dead leaves. He was tall, with a wedge-shaped upper body and big, callused hands, and the sort of rough-hewn, brooding face that does well in the movies—perhaps a movie about a solitary rancher with an unknown tragic past who elicits gasps, onscreen and in the audience alike, when some twist of narration requires him to shave, trim his hair, and put on a tuxedo. Something about Tim kept ringing a bell for me, as he almost wordlessly led me on a perfunctory tour of the building, showing me, as if he already ascribed to me the Martha-like sophisticated expertise I expected this home to bestow, not only the fixtures within the apartment but the hot water heater and circuit breakers in the basement. The basement also held untold years' worth of items abandoned, presumably by previous, prodigal tenants, all stacked in an orderly way by someone, presumably Tim, who could not abide waste and hoped to see it all returned to use. He noticed me looking and nodded. "Up for grabs. Anything you can use, feel free." I realized then who it was Tim reminded me of. He was the double of every other terse and wounded and good-looking and rarely washed man of a particular mold, after whom I had *hankered*, for whom I had suffered a *yen*, whom I'd *craved*, starting with Han Solo when I was ten. Was a time, and not long before, when this mumbled exchange in the basement, witnessed only by the noiselessly revolving electric and gas meters, might have gone in a different direction, and ended with my mouth and the upper insides of my thighs stained raw red from protracted abrasion. Now I only looked on Tim with remote curiosity, as if at a photo of some dead ancestor. I understood that we shared a connection but no part of me felt it.

"There's a whole box of stuff to go with that," he spoke up, when after choosing a rattling futon frame and gray lumpy futon, and a rust-pimpled chrome-legged table and chairs, and a threadbare armchair with scratched carved wooden things at the ends of the armrests like knuckles, I paused with frivolous greed at an empty fish tank, slightly clouded with limey deposit but otherwise clean. I'd always hankered after a fish tank the way some have a yen for, or crave, a fireplace. It seemed to me that with fishes to gaze on, I'd be safe and serene. Tim went on, "It's all stuff that's been used but I boiled it in bleach. The filters and air pump and heat element, even some of the gravel. It would save you a fortune."

"I'll take a look," I agreed with pretended reluctance. "Are you sure you don't need it?"

"You can see it's just sitting here taking up space."

Without the bed, everything I was bringing from Dutra's could be moved in one trip in the Volvo. "There's a futon already," I told him as we packed up the car. "I'll leave my bed here for Ross." Ross, who had fallen in love with a waitress from Thailand he'd met at a Japanese restaurant, had given up his room in a group house to move in with her, which arrangement had ended when her husband returned from a tour in the army. "I scored so much nice stuff in this house. Everything I need, I got out of the basement. Even a fish tank."

"No shit? How many gallons?"

"I have no idea."

"Well, how big is it, Ginny?"

"I don't know. Big." I framed air with my hands. "Like this. Taller than wide."

"Pretty, but less practical." I should have known Dutra would claim expertise about fish tanks. "What kind of tank are you going to set up?" he demanded. "Freshwater or salt?"

"What's the difference?"

"What's the difference! Freshwater: our lakes, ponds, and rivers. Saltwater: the ocean. Jesus, Ginny."

"I didn't mean, what's the difference between fresh- and saltwater! I meant what's the difference in terms of a tank."

"I'm having second thoughts about letting you live on your own. I'm not sure you're ready."

"Shut the fuck up, Dutra."

"Has anyone shown you the pilot light yet? It's supposed to stay on."

"Shut up, Dutra."

"Don't stick your finger in sockets. Do you know about sockets? Where you plug in the lamp?"

"Shut up, Dutra."

"And saltwater's not good for drinking. Make ouchie in tummy."

"Just fucking shut up."

Our landlocked northern hamlet turned out to be served by two tropical fish stores, as far apart from each other, one southward, one north, as if a noncompete pact had dictated the sites. Back and forth Dutra drove me, first to one, then the other, always in search of some new crucial thing, as we puzzled out nitrogen levels and argued about the decor, Dutra so bent on a hinged treasure chest that it might have been his fish tank we were outfitting. Dutra now highlighting passages from my *Saltwater Tank Manual*, a joint pinched in his lips; myself now mislaying the water-test tablets amid the tofu and rice for our dinner, and ransacking my three little rooms in despair—for a couple of days we could almost believe we still lived with each other. I knew that Dutra was apprehensive about Ross moving in, as Ross had no money, and was unlikely to ever pay rent. But more than that, Ross presumed a certain Dutra to be the sole Dutra, just as easily as he'd presumed, when he'd learned I was leaving, that Dutra would be eager for him to move in. Almost no one who orbited Dutra—neither Ross nor Lucinda nor Alyssa, nor any other of the town's becalmed flotsam, Birkenstocked and fogged in by pot smoke, with whom Dutra sedated himself—would have ever suspected that Dutra was dead serious. He was even more serious than the standard correction for standard underestimation of him would suggest. He'd done absurdly well in his classes, and had been singled out for the most prestigious of the second-year fellowships; he was now broadly viewed in the world of his school as the person to beat. But he kept that world carefully far from the world of his friends. Among his friends, Dutra's smart-ass posturing was a typical symptom of having no prospects. It allowed him to hide in plain sight his true secrets—his brilliance, and his equally outsize ambition, and the certainty, almost like doom, that he'd be a success. But I knew, and he knew that I did, and that meant something to him.

I kept putting off Martha's first viewing of my apartment, until without having meant to I'd provoked her real curiosity and equal frustration. Then I kept tweaking her to buy time, because the apartment kept falling so far short of what I'd envisioned. "Is it on the hill or off?" she might wonder. "A little of both." "In a house or a building?" "A house *is* a building." "No more sophistic bullshit. Housemates or alone?" "Wouldn't you like to know." "Now I'll have to assume it's a commune devoted to orgies." "Aren't you petulant!" "In fact, I'm annoyed, Regina, that you won't show it to me—" "All I said is I wanted to clean it. You're the one having sinister thoughts." The apartment was far from the Shangri-la that inflamed expectation had made it. My first poststudent, adult apartment, it was, to the very last detail, a student apartment. It was uncomfortable and homely and bare. It was furnished with cast-offs and a half-dead houseplant and a shimmering cube of saltwater enclosing one fish half the size of my thumb. I was almost flat broke; I had paid a month's rent and discovered no pithy expressions of longing. There were only my own, like an ocean tide forcing its way up my channels and rills, swelling me into regions of rash exaltation; and then washing out all at once. Subsidence and collapse. *Longing.* "It's just an apartment," I told Martha crossly when I called her, my line newly set up, on my cheap plastic phone from Woolworth's. It would only, I knew, collect fingertip grime and require yearly cleanings with Windex. It disclosed only absences: absence of money and absence of taste.

"I'm coming over," she said. "I'll have Dutra with me. He can give me directions."

When they arrived, an hour later, they were almost as long coming in: with an antique brass floor lamp with a clear blue glass marble on top that screwed down the lampshade; an old crazy quilt I'd admired countless times where I'd seen it tossed over her downstairs armchair; three framed paintings in radiant, lush sunset colors, all bosomy with afterglow clouds and ripe fruit trees and avalanches of velvet and languid or serenely dead sylphs; and two loud boxes of mismatched kitchenware, more kinds of pots, pans, and skillets than I'd realized were made; and towels and pillows and sheets in a motley of patterns, all pleasantly washpaled and exceedingly soft; and penultimately a glazed pot full of green glossy leaves and very small, very white star-shaped flowers exuding a honey-rich scent like a swoon; and finally, Martha and Dutra each hefting an end, a massive rug rolled in a tube and secured with duct tape. My painstaking, awkward furniture arrangement, the futon-couch at an angle on one side, my armchair and half-dead houseplant marooned opposite in unsuccessful colloquy, was quickly erased. The rug—a boxcutter emerging from Martha's back pocket—was sliced out of its bindings and unfurled into the room. It was an Oriental rug, in a palette related to that in the pictures, but more darkly saturated: bloodred and apricot orange. I stood to one side with the jasmine, for that's what the plant was, in my hands, rooted there by my pleasure and shame which were trying to strangle each other. In the end pleasure might have prevailed, but her toga was stained, and her eyes blurred a little with tears.

"Is it all right I helped warm your house?" Martha whispered to me nuzzlingly, when Dutra, inaugurating my bathroom, briefly left us alone.

Was it? Now the apartment looked just as I'd hoped that it would, when I'd hoped to impress her. In fact, apart from the fish tank, it now looked like it ought to be Martha's apartment.

"Of course it is," I murmured. "Thank you."

"It's a sweet place," she said. "I love it."

"I hoped that you would." I fell speechless, an inexplicable lump in my throat. I'd copied my door key for her, imagining it would make a significant gift. Childishly I'd envisioned the act of bestowal: like sliding a ring on her finger I'd lay the key onto her palm. And as fairy-tale keys tend to do, it would open far more than a mere wooden door. But it now seemed superfluous. Everything beguiling in these rooms she had brought in herself. The key stayed in my pocket.

Dutra returned and a hammer and nails and a bottle of Glenlivet ("*The* Glenlivet," mugged Dutra, impressed) emerged from one of the two kitchen boxes. While Dutra poured, Martha hung the three Maxfield Parrish reproductions (for that's what they were), shifted my furniture to her satisfaction, and removed the jasmine from my hands to the front windowsill where she thought it might get enough light. Along with all these things of hers into my rooms had come a smell, encyclopedic and subtle, like a threadbare tapestry on some epic subject: her former lovers and gardens and meals and travels and sails and wounds and orgasms and perhaps even failures, a dusty and vegetal, floral and heat-baked and cool-moist and unnameable smell. The smell of her past, her past self, here where my self was seeking its future.

"I can't hang out," Dutra declared in a voice that would not brook dispute, throwing his scotch back and raising a hand in goodbye.

I didn't object, but Martha said, "Oh, come on. I haven't met the fish yet."

"The fish is right there. Ginny can make introductions."

"Martha, Country Joe. Country Joe, Martha."

" '*Country Joe*'?" Martha said.

"Dutra named him."

"Jesus, Dutra. I forget what a hippie you are."

Provoked, Dutra forgot he was leaving. "Here's a case where you don't understand the big picture. Country Joe is the pioneer fish. To establish the right chemical balance in a saltwater tank you have to start with one tough little fish. He eats, he pisses, he shits, the levels seesaw like crazy until the nitrogen cycle gets going and the tank's safe for fish. Get it? Country Joe isn't really a fish! He survives where most others would die, and by his very existence creates an environment healthy for fish. So after this preliminary stage, it'll be *Country Joe and the Fish*."

"You really are a fucking hippie," said Martha.

We sat, Martha and I on the futon-frame couch, Dutra at an angle to us in the armchair, all of us framed by the rug's boundary as if riding a raft. We passed the bottle of scotch back and forth. We watched Country Joe flutter up, and drift down, and flutter upward again in his luminous cube. There was no other light in the room. How had she done it? She had bound the room deftly together, as if tucking the ceiling and walls into the carpet which served as their bed. Now all was snug. It was graceful and spare but not bare. I was growing drunk, and her scent, which had flooded my rooms, and uprooted my frail little seedlings of self, now drugged and aroused me. I wondered if style such as Martha possessed was inherent, or learned. Learned, I decided; give me ten years and I'd have it as well. God, give me ten years, but right now! What was the future with Martha that crowded my dreams? What bright shapes bodied out of the clouds? Much of the time my desire was so humble it didn't reach past the next day: if only she'd lavish me with her assurance. She was a generous, ravenous, unrestrained lover, yet this she withheld. If only she'd tell me she never intended to leave. Other times, covertly ambitious, I ventured to install her in the very same domestic fantasia I'd nursed since girlhood, which in fact required little renovation to replace gruff Han Solo or gloomy Lord Byron with lithe, sly-mouthed Martha—still we lived in some sun-drenched abode and reared flawless offspring and made love every day years on end. Very often, and sometimes unkindly, Martha posed me the challenge of describing to her any future at all we could share, as if I were the water-bound fish, and she the versatile frog, in one of Joachim's sad picture books. She implied there was simply no world for us. Yet I saw it clearly—too clearly to dare share with her.

The tank steadily burbled and hummed. Dutra and Martha were talking about the Great Barrier Reef, their low voices sheltered in vastness. "I feel like we're outside," I said suddenly. "Camping."

"I would love to go camping," said Dutra.

"Then we should," Martha said.

"In the woods," I agreed. "In the woods, with that smell . . ."

Martha got up to go to the bathroom, but the sense of entrancement remained. When she returned she slipped behind me on the couch, scissoring her long legs around me and holding me close, as if we were sharing a horse. I sank into her, closing my eyes, and felt her hands, with their rough finger pads, steal under my shirt. She gardened without gloves, too impatient for them, and her long narrow fingers had become stained with dirt in the needle's-width creases, like esoteric tattoos, and her fingertips were shaggy and dry and undid me far more than when they had been creamy and smooth. I heard her quick breath, and my own, and then my mind seemed to yaw between hunger and the dim recollection of Dutra, still in the armchair. Struggling upstream against pleasure I looked and saw him, his own eyes remote as he watched us. Martha craned over me, catching my mouth on her own, and when I arched back to kiss her more deeply her hands closed on my nipples and assailed them with torments, tender shapings and whispery teasings and sudden hard pinches and twists, and I let out a groan, no longer caring who heard or saw what, and her mouth broke away.

"Did you used to touch her like this?" I heard her wonder to Dutra, her voice thick and bemused. "It's amazing. She's so sensitive. You have every inch of her nerves in the palm of one hand."

"You're a psychopath," Dutra remarked. It might have been in that way that he had of giving two opposed meanings from which one might choose—but the words, though I heard them along with the rubbery squeak of the scotch bottle's cork thumbed back into the bottle, and along with his loud angry tread on the stairs, couldn't pierce the dense fug of my lust. I would not allow them. If I did, it was only to think, with superior pity, *Poor Dutra.* I did not even know if he'd closed my front door, as I clawed off her clothes and devoured her body, sprawling over her hand-me-down rug, as if I could force not just tongue breasts and hands but each knuckle and toe joint, each shoulder and kneecap, the whole rib-cage and skull, somehow into myself. Sucking here, shoving there. When all else failed swallowing whole. Then I really could keep her.

Because school had resumed without me—because there wasn't even Dutra running late to his class, spanking his alarm clock on the far side of the wall; because my Professor of Longing operated on a rarefied emeritus calendar which placed our next meeting somewhere between Christmas and Easter; because, for more money, I'd begun writing movie reviews for the local free weekly, at a fee of thirty dollars per review out of which I must pay for the ticket, so that to make any money at all I spent hours on end by myself in the dark watching all the worst films of 1993—it was weeks before I realized what it meant, that school had resumed without me. It meant that Martha had resumed her conspicuous life on the campus, without me. Already, on the pretext of Anya's Teutonic se-verity, Martha had managed to shift our affair entirely from her house to mine, so that I no longer stepped through her doorway, let alone slept in her bed. Now I equally didn't walk with her the length of the Quad, my arm brashly snaking her waist, regardless of how many times I'd imag-ined just such a perambulation. She and I, sitting shoulder to shoulder at some visitor's lecture, weren't stared at or whispered about. My name wasn't comprised in a fresh, titillating graffito. Admiration, notoriety, envy—I didn't need any of this, but I wanted acknowledgment. I was so proud that she loved me—did nobody know? Her separation from Nicho-las, her love affair with me must have been the first-ever installments of the tale of the Hallett-Brodeurs that hadn't been broadcast all over the campus. Yet when I said as much to her she gaped back, amazed and of-fended. "I suppose that you want me to publish the banns," she exclaimed.

"I didn't say that. I just asked why it seems to suit you, that I'm never on campus, now that I'm working and not taking classes."

"It doesn't suit me. I miss you all day. Can't you tell, when it's night?" It was night now, and she lay on my bed, in between her old sheets, and, to make her point further, slid one thigh between mine and reached under me, seizing my ass. But, though gripping her greedily back, I pur-sued my subject.

"If you miss me all day, let's have lunch. At the Movable Feast." Movable Feast was the student café in the English department's basement, where professors and students held meetings while dining on sandwiches named, to cite just one example, *Absalami, Absalami!* Movable Feast was the English department's piazza, its most heavily used public space.

"I don't have lunch on days that I teach. I don't ever have time. And if I did, I would sooner eat dirt than at Movable Feast."

"Then take me as your date to the dinner for Slavoj Žižek."

"Have you been reading my mail?"

"You left the card on my table, Martha. Tell me why you won't take me."

"I'm not *not* taking you—I'm not going myself. That man subsists entirely on Diet Coke. Why would I go to a dinner for *him*?"

"Then take me someplace you *are* going."

"I don't go anywhere! Regina, when I go out at night, I see *you*."

"And you only ever see me at night. Here. In my apartment. Ever since I moved here, you treat me like your mistress."

"I'd much prefer being treated like a mistress to being treated like a wife. Lots more fun."

"We're talking about my preferences, not yours."

"Oh!—would you prefer *this*," she renewed her assault, deftly reversing herself so her redolent cunt squashed my face, ". . . or would you prefer *this*?"

Small as our town was, even when I did make the hike up to campus my move had put me on completely different paths from before, and this was how I ran into Casper, my friend of the first weeks of school. Even before I'd dropped out Casper had drifted into a world of postmodern cereal boxes and abstruse applications of Freud to broadcast television, and I'd hardly seen him. Now we were thrilled to discover we'd moved to apartments just a couple of blocks from each other. "What are you taking?" Casper asked as we mounted the crumbling shale steps of the steep creekside trail. "I haven't run into you anywhere."

"I took the term off, but I probably won't reenroll. I've been working. Long, tedious hours at very poor pay. It might be a career."

"Really!" Casper cried, his admiration more pleasing than Martha's. "God, I wish I'd thought of that. I have two papers overdue from the spring and one from last fall. Every day in the morning I think, Today's the day that I'll start work on them. And by lunchtime I think, Why do today what can wait till tomorrow?"

"Where are you going now?"

"Happy hour at Hot Jalapeños. Haven't you been? It's the best happy hour on the hill. Two-for-one margaritas and three-for-one shots, and if you're able to eat a whole one of this really hot pepper without having water for five minutes after, they take half off your whole evening's bill."

"Wow. That sounds really tawdry."

"It is, absolutely, downscale. A frat-boy-type place. Shalom Kreutzberg"—an art historian and shopping-mall theorist—"turned me on to it last semester. It's the so-bad-that-it's-good place to go."

"Irony can be a health hazard. Who do you owe papers?"

"Oh, God. And not even a margarita yet safely in hand. Kreutzberg, of course. Luc Botelli, that Hum Center visiting scholar."

" 'Aesthetic/Prosthetic'?"

"The same. But he's gone back to Venice, so it's hard to get motivated. And Hartmann for Baudrillard and Ballard last fall."

"You must have something around you can hand in for that."

"That's the problem. Why bother at all? If I've already said everything, all by myself, then how trite must it be?"

My true self felt so far from this conversation that, paradoxically, I homed in ever closer, fascinated, my true self trailing my physical self just offshore of, perhaps, my left shoulder. Casper was Casper but I was a perfect impostor; every cell that composed me had remade itself; I was not the same person he'd known. Aesthetic/Prosthetic and Ballard; I'd never care a fig about these things again. Only love mattered to me: the singularity of it, the damnable difficulty of it, the certain solution I knew must lie just out of reach. We emerged at the top of the trail, streaming sweat from the effort just the same as before I'd met Martha, but my sweat was invisibly different; its scent must have changed. All the chemical soup of my body had changed. I thought of Country Joe, creating his environment, excreting the waste that would then feed the wee organisms that would then feed the algae to feed Country Joe—if that was even what happened; Dutra had so patiently labored to teach me the nitrogen cycle on which all the life in my tank would rely but my brain was too scrambled by love to absorb anything—and then I thought of Martha, her elusive life force, swimming in, swimming through, firing chemical changes and cycles. And at the same time I was laughing with Casper, and now weaving a little as I shifted from shoulder to shoulder the lead weight of a bagful of library books I'd been skimming for pithy expressions of longing and was now on my way to return. A car crossed the sidewalk in front of us, exiting out of a faculty lot, and without breaking conversation or stride we diverted around its back end and as if God had cut the sky's string I was smote on the top of my skull and sent flying, like the ball by the star slugger's bat, with a shattering *CRACK!* and pain yanked the blinds on my eyes and I hit the asphalt.

"Jesus! Oh my God! Regina!" I could hear Casper shouting. My vision slid around like grains of sand. Whatever image it last held had been smashed to the smallest component. The dead weight of my head, lightning-struck, dangled down from my neck. Its pain arrowed out in a ceaselessly flowering starburst as if strewing wide all the shards of my skull that were actually crunching around in my scalp. This is how a broken neck feels, I thought wonderingly, except that somehow I had heaved up my torso, I was no longer sprawled on my face. Casper had me beneath the armpits and pulled me onto the sidewalk, well clear of the subtle driveway. Bit by bit I blinked together a smeared panorama, my library books strewn in an arc.

"My books," I mumbled. My tongue was still there. I dragged it over my teeth. They were still there as well. I had a pink and white skid mark the length of my forearm, where I must have thrown the arm up to shelter my head as I fell, but somehow nothing was broken. The throb in my skull now retracted and grew more intense, as if defining its outlines, but even my skull was somehow in one piece. "Ow," I added. "Ow ow ow! What hit me?"

"That parking-lot barricade thing," Casper said, indicating. "It was raised up for that car and we walked under it, and it came down right on top of your head."

"Ow!" I cried again, belatedly frightened.

"No shit." Casper's teeth were chattering in the heat; he was almost more frightened than me. "It sounded like, some sort of—"

"Like a two-by-four hitting a huge ball of bone." Pushing away Casper's effort to help I struggled onto my feet. Anger and embarrassment had quickly outstripped fear. I had the idea that the sooner we moved from the site of the mishap, the less likely that it could inflict any permanent damage. In my impatience I reeled on my feet and Casper caught at my arm.

"Are you sure that you're okay to walk?"

"Of course I'm okay to walk! But I have a headache."

"Of course you fucking have a headache! And your arm is scraped up."

"It's okay. Stings a little."

"I feel absolutely horrible, Regina," Casper burst out, stricken. "I should have noticed that thing!"

"It's not your job to notice the things I walk under. Don't feel guilty. You'll make my headache hurt more."

"If my guilt gives you headaches, you're in for a very uncomfortable future."

After Casper had picked up my books and insisted on carrying them we resumed on our way, both of us darting glances side to side as we proceeded up the sidewalk like soldiers afraid of an ambush. My head's throbbing deepened another half-octave, seemed to tuck in its elbows and knees and settle in for a permanent stay. "I can really use that margarita now," I remarked when at last we had reached the library and surrendered my books to the heap of Returns.

"You still feel up for it?"

"More than before. Lead the way."

"Here's to Numbing the Pain," Casper said.

Hot Jalapeños was on the Collegetown Strip, just outside University Gate, so that Casper and I were now headed back downhill again for the first time since we'd started to walk. Adding that to the loss of my library books, I felt buoyant. Tonight Martha was coming with me to the movies; the theater showing the film that I had to review wasn't close to the campus, but it was an art house, which made it a campus appendage. There was a strong chance we'd see someone she knew. My eagerness for this to occur was counterweight to her unstated, but to me clear and vexing, reluctance for it to occur, and I was eager to refute that reluctance, to lay hold of the proof that it didn't exist. When we ran into her eminent colleague while buying our popcorn, her arm would hook my waist and her voice state my name as she made the unhesitant introduction—it was this pleasingly natural scene, vividly enacted in the playhouse of my mind, that so buoyed me as Casper and I strode toward margaritas. But the scene also blotted out others. What if the person we saw was some friend of my own—like that erstwhile friend of my own who was also her husband? Theorists of passion often term it "all-consuming" but I found it excluding instead; there were vast realms of life it refused to consume, but boxed up out of sight. I charged Martha with happily keeping me separate from campus, with its many ogling eyes and wagging tongues, but there were times I suspected myself just as glad, and that my bravado in quitting my program was disguised cowardice. I brazenly wanted the shock and the envy, but I shrank from the possible condemnation. Perhaps just like her I was selfish in love, and not brave. And so I hectored her to meet me at Movable Feast, to accompany me to the movies, while all the while I kept Nicholas, and friends and partisans of Nicholas, and the very concept of Nicholas, boxed out of sight—his last intrusion, on that day I had seen his apartment, not complicating but assisting the effort. For I had seen him consigned to a separate if parallel realm. It consisted of those bright and cold rooms with the scant furniture and the ficus; perhaps the parking lot at Mighty Buy; and perhaps a few more strange locations neither Martha nor I could have found even if we had tried.

Ducking into the Wawa I bought a bottle of aspirin and then Casper and I, bouncing with restored merriment, entered Hot Jalapeños. The gaudy teal and yellow dining room was eerily empty but a racket of music and voices reached us from somewhere in the back. "Will you be joining us for Happy Hour on the patio?" inquired a ponytailed hostess, in a hot-pepper-monogrammed golf shirt and khaki short-shorts. "All the tables are taken, but there's standing room at the Cocktail Palapa."

The patio was as raucous and crowded as the inside dining room had been silent and empty, but I still spotted him right away. So did Casper. "Introduce me," Casper implored as I froze in my tracks, for of course Casper knew I had served as the Chaucer TA, and had no idea my role, in relation to Chaucer's professor, had changed.

"No, Casper—"

"I'll be so well behaved!"

"It's not that, you don't understand—" Yet for all the density of obstacles, of drunken young men in backward baseball caps and drunken young women in ponytails and short-shorts all packed shoulder-to-shoulder between oversize white plastic tables impaled with umbrellas exclaiming ¡Sauza!, the unwanted encounter came rolling toward me as if it were Nicholas parting the crowd, and not, somehow, myself, leading Casper, in helpless acquiescence to Nicholas's own helpless wave. Sitting on the far side of the patio framed by two other men, on a bench with its back to the trellised rear wall, he was as trapped by my startling appearance as I was by his. It was the secrecy of our relation that trapped us, in preventing our rushing away from each other. But it peculiarly freed us as well, by enforcing fatuity. "I see you've made wise preparations," he yelled when we reached him, with necessary loudness and superfluous cheer, and indicating my bottle of aspirin. "Regina brilliantly taught Chaucer with me last semester," he announced to his companions, who were Harrison Franklin, the often condemned Southern Gentleman writer, and a scowling and dead-white-complected young man with copious and in some strange way lewd, as if both simian and pubic, long and tangled black hair pouring out of his face and his scalp. "Working with me has taught her the true value of aspirin, as you can observe. Andrew Malarkey of Trinity College Dublin, and our esteemed visitor this semester; and Harrison Franklin, professor and author, whom I think you may already know; meet my dear friend Regina Gottlieb, and her friend, I'm afraid—"

"Casper Rosen," managed Casper, now all head-bobs and gulped syllables. "Second year, English department—"

"Of course I recognize you. You're one of the young prodigies who understands Shalom Kreutzberg."

"I'd hardly say I understand!" Casper cried with delight.

"Caspar happens to be my favorite name," Nicholas revealed, as if his own discomfort fed the flame of his charm. His hair was drenched at the scalp, and his cheeks burned with color. Like an octopus his companions had reached out from the table, Franklin this way, Malarkey that, and somehow captured two chairs, into which Casper and I were assimilated. "Even Regina might not have known that," Nicholas went on, grazing me with his voice as if he'd touched my knee under the table. It was a furtive signal—we knew what they didn't, and could keep it that way. "But she can no doubt guess why."

"The painter," I offered, accepting my cue.

"I was hoping to name my son Caspar," Nicholas abruptly added, as if, just when he'd pledged discretion, impulse had him veer the other way. Now he'd made mention of Martha inevitable. With a flash I understood— as if, soused in the bosom of Hot Jalapeños, such understanding was some sort of insight—that serious drinking was happening here. All three men were already drunk, not in the way of the undergraduate students tumbling like puppies from table to table, whose drunkenness was more than half mob behavior, a raucous effusion that burned as much alcohol, in the heat, as they were likely consuming. By contrast the drunkenness of Nicholas and Malarkey and Franklin was packed in the marrow, disproportionately dense for its volume. It might blow up without any warning and God knew what would happen.

But then Casper, unknowingly snuffing the fuse, said, "I'm afraid mine's the Friendly Ghost spelling."

A waitress had appeared. "Four margaritas," we urged her. "Two— plus the two that are free."

"All at once?"

"All at once," I affirmed. I had learned from Laurence.

"Quite right," said Malarkey. "Casper the Ghost is American, and you're an American. I don't understand this poncey trend of foreign names for American children. Bloody American children named 'Kwame' and 'Dante' and 'Krishna' instead of just normal American names."

"What's a normal American name, Andy?" asked Nicholas kindly.

"Well, 'Andy' does very nicely, doesn't it? Just as nicely for you as for us."

"Very neutral and Christian."

"Matthew, Mark, Luke, and John do quite nicely as well. But no, we must have *Joachim*."

Back in danger again; yet attention had drifted. "Open that aspirin, Regina," Franklin badgered me. "Your bottle says two hundred tablets. That's forty for each of us here."

"Are we doing a suicide pact, or averting hangover?"

"Suicide is a form of hangover aversion."

"Andy, you bring out the camp counselor in me when you say things like that. I'm going to take you canoeing this weekend. That will clear out the cobwebs. It keeps me alive."

"Regina doesn't hold your faith in boats, Nick. She's aspirining up."

I wondered if these three men had confessed to each other their reasons for anguish, or if, far more likely, they hewed to an unspoken code to say little, ask nothing, and drink all they could. Franklin's sadness was proud, almost savage, as if he dared you to take it away. Malarkey's sadness was distracted and sullen; of the three he seemed least to enjoy his companions, as if somewhere, his solitary teenager's room was still waiting for him, with its Sex Pistols posters and refrigerator-size stereo speakers and a scuffed patch of wall where he propped up his feet, and he longed to get back to that refuge as soon as he could. Nicholas's sadness was apologetic. He seemed to hope it would bother no one, even me. I realized the secret we shared was far more intimate than the knowledge of who was, or wasn't, whose lover. The unspoken code was mine also. I must stop noticing Nicholas's sadness; his steady gaze told me to leave him his pride.

"Actually I'm recovering from an assault," I declared to the party, swallowing two of the aspirin with the rest of the first of my two margaritas. "I was hit on the head with a two-by-four not long ago. I'm getting a goose egg," I added, massaging it where I'd just noticed it starting to grow at the crown of my head.

Now they all grew absorbed and excited.

"My God!"

"Were you mugged?"

"She's not kidding. I can feel the bump."

Casper and I alternated and overlapped, telling the story. "Relating this event has taken almost one hundred twenty times the length the event itself took," I observed through their oaths of amazement and horror.

Casper was repeating, "My masculinity is the real victim here. Did I avert the catastrophe? No. I may never recover."

"Regina," Nicholas was saying to me with solemn persistence, as I received my third and fourth margaritas. "Regina, darling, look at me."

He'd broken his own rule. It was the same compulsion he'd already shown—mentioning Joachim as a pathway to Martha. Hesitating, I looked at him. A bell jar might have dropped over us. He reached for my innermost gaze and took that, and in doing so, surrendered his own. It seemed a fragile, darting thing, momentarily stilled in my care. His eyes were that color that people call "hazel," that is actually green, gold, and brown, each thin petal distinct in its hue, as if laid on by a brush. The skin of his face had developed a slack, tender look. If I'd pressed a finger against it, I imagined a dimple would linger a moment, recalling the touch. He had aged. And yet his beauty, being male, seemed more potent on account of the wear. We wanted women to be smooth like children, and men just the opposite way. Was this true? The fraudulence of such ideals abruptly amazed me. I adored Martha's subtly rough imperfection. And feeling her body as I always did, against mine and within it, I realized I was seeing him now as she did, and a boundlessly receding horizon dropped out of the back of that intimate gaze, like an empty keyhole at the centermost part of the pupil. Pursue me this far and you lose me, it warned, though the dazzle continues—the featureless fields of gold all around. But the landmarks are gone.

"Your pupils don't seem abnormally dilated," he concluded, leaning back, "but it depends on the size that they normally are. Are they usually large?"

"I have no idea," I said, blinking at him.

"Do one more thing for me. Stand up, like this—" he stood awkwardly, where he was on the bench with his knees partly under the table—"and spread your arms wide like this." I obeyed, and we faced each other over the table like matching scarecrows.

"What's this now?" Andy demanded. "May I play along?"

It conveys the atmosphere of Happy Hour, which had continued, around and behind us, to grow more and more crowded and loud, that Nicholas and I in our cruciform pose attracted no general attention at all. Only our own tablemates were attentive to what we were doing. "Now bring the tips of both index fingers very quickly to the tip of your nose, just like this." I complied. "Again." Like repeating a strange calisthenics we outstretched our arms, pointed our fingers, swung them fast on the fulcrum of elbows to land on our noses; a few times, going fast, I was off by an inch. "Not bad," Nicholas said. By now Andy had joined us and the three of us shifted around to not bump our wingspans.

"Warming up?" asked our waitress.

"Just cranking the hollow leg open," said Andy. "Another round, please. Let's try strawberry now, everyone. Are the strawberry ones really lovely? All frothy and pink?"

"All right," Nicholas concluded at last. "If I were Coach Clive, that infallible sage of my youth, I'd pronounce you All Right to go back on the ice. No concussion, Regina. You may lace up your skates."

"Is that really a test for concussion?"

"Coach Clive said it was, and Coach Clive was a leader of men. I always felt safe, trusting him."

"If it's a test for sobriety I've flunked," Franklin said. "Just watching you has made me nauseous."

"I agree," Casper said. "I'm exhausted."

"Five frozen strawberry margaritas!" our waitress sang out as she banged down the frost-furry mugs.

Afterward I couldn't be sure if it was at the time, or only in retrospect, that my awareness of my transit to the women's bathroom disappeared. I found myself alone there in a stall and had the sense I had been there too long. The women's bathroom at Hot Jalapeños was on the far side from the patio entrance of the main dining room, very near the street entrance where Casper and I had come in; these geographical facts were disclosed to me as if for the first time once I'd put my clothes in order and gotten through the bathroom door, as if pulling myself, with both arms, vertically through a hatch in the ceiling. A festive roar told me which way to go to get back to my table, but I struggled as if sunk to the waist in that invisible gelatinous impediment of dreams. Like a sailboat fighting the wind I tacked with painful slowness leaning to my port side, then switched to my starboard, avoiding a table; the dining room seemed entirely empty, abandoned even by the ponytailed hostess, though in the distance I heard a door swinging, and young voices calling out things like, "Six frozen, one rocks, no salt, eighty-six the jalapeño cheese poppers!" Then all at once I'd dropped through the trap door and was out in the sun, the gelatinous impediment was gone, with new determination and power my legs pumped beneath me as my table, land ho! eked up over the distant horizon. I could see Nicholas, seeing me, the frothy crest of his dirty blond hair standing up on his scalp in alarm. "Whoa!" someone shouted, as I plunged full length over a table that had rotated into my path. Heavy glassware crashed down and a wave of wet drenched my shirt front. I neither expected nor sensed any laughter, only paralyzed awe and alarm, as if a resurrected prehistoric monster had brought down its huge foot on the crowd, smashing tables and chairs into kindling as the nimble young drunks all dove out of the way. I saw fear on their faces, and empathy, the beast, talons out, apparently just at my back; saving arms and hands seized hold of me and with pooled strength tossed me like a doll to my table. I landed in a tangle of my limbs and Andy's and Franklin's and Casper's and Nicholas's and with the force of the impact threw up, arcing fountains of pink, and at the same time was suddenly lofted in Nicholas's arms—I felt myself rushing up as my spatters of vomit were still audibly raining down.

"Check, please!" Nicholas cried as he bore me away.

Then we were in his car, speeding like a torrent downhill. "Stop," I gasped and with a shriek of brakes he pulled over and I pushed the door open and vomited onto the curb. It seemed to happen again and again as if the drive, Zeno's-paradox-like, by fractions was being stretched out to infinity. In a parking lot somewhere Nicholas said to me roughly, "Wake up!" and dropped a shopping bag from Hobo Deli full of lumpy cold stuff on my lap. "Drink that Gatorade in there, Regina. Now. Drink. All of it. No, don't doze off Regina KEEP DRINKING." Then we were driving again. "Stop," I gasped and with a shriek of brakes he pulled over and I pushed the door open and vomited onto the curb. . . .

"Is this it?" he was saying. "This one?" Hands—large, tense, rough finger pads, square-cut nails, a row of calluses dangling skin-shreds marking off like sentries the frontier of the palm—took hold of my face and pried open my lids.

"Stand up now. Walk with me." Like a marionette's my feet paddled the sidewalk as I looked down on them from a distance. "Is it this one, Regina?

"Is it this one?

"Are your keys in your pocket? Are your keys in your bag?

"Is it this door, Regina?

"Drink the Gatorade. All of it. That's the way. . . ."

Then a column of pale, bluish light had unfurled like a banner, but from the top down, and the bottom up, at the same time. Perhaps it was better described as a mouth yawning open. Jaws of faint light stretched apart from each other. The aperture they made was a doorway, submerged. Drowning light filtered in from above. A skin layer peeled itself free but then lingered there, twisting and shifting its shape. Now it ebbed and withheld its movements. The pale light died away. Exhausted, I sank away also, and as if to reward me for setting it free the luminosity disclosed itself again, but by the slightest indication possible, a faint pulse in the darkness. It grew steadily closer without growing brighter, homed in on my helplessness now, and to mark its progress drove a needle of pain through my skull.

There were two things, which perhaps I took years to unbraid and discern. The dying light in my bedroom window, where my gauze curtain rippled a bit in the breeze; and the telephone, ringing. The ringing noise wasn't the light, which was bleeding away. And the ringing noise wasn't arriving from somewhere far off, but was in the next room.

I staggered toward the sound, dragging blankets behind me, and upsetting a glass of red juice of some kind. My hand reached for the phone and a fear-cataract paralyzed me in place with my hand still outstretched, my heart beating my ribs like a club, for Nicholas, in my penumbral room, only lit by the tank's chill fluorescence, had spectrally risen, as if from the floor—where in fact he had been, on his knees, to one side of my armchair.

"Answer it," he whispered. "I thought I'd unplugged it but I had the wrong cord." He could have said to me, "Step out the window." Was I dreaming? Of course! Staring at him, hypnotized, I picked up the phone. "Hello?" I asked thickly, through parched, rubber lips. Nicholas remained in his spot just beside and behind the armchair, an awkward space no one would use but a ghost. I realized I was wearing only panties and one of the old cotton T-shirts I slept in, though not the one I'd been sleeping in lately. I passed a hand through my hair and got stuck; my hair was stiff at the ends with dried vomit. My gut heaved and I would have thrown up again had there been anything left to expel.

"When did you get home?" I heard Martha ask, her voice biting each word.

"I don't know." I stared at Nicholas, staring at me. He must hear her voice also, the room was so hushed. "Are you still coming over?" I whispered.

"Gee, sure! I guess waiting twenty-five hours for a date doesn't count as being stood up. There's no reason I should be angry."

"What do you mean? What time is it?"

"Ten past nine."

"Weren't you coming at eight?"

"I was coming at eight *yesterday*, Regina. If you're trying to be funny, or cagey and sexy, please stop."

I had never felt less funny, cagey, or sexy. I implored, "I don't know what the fuck's going on!"

"Jesus, are you play-acting?" I heard Martha wonder. "Is this some kind of game? I've got to check in with Anya and then I'm coming over. Do try to be home." On her end she slammed down the handset and I winced at the snip into silence as if I'd been slapped.

"What are you doing here?" I asked Nicholas in a whisper. The effort to whisper was almost too much. A powerful wave of disorientation, physical as an ocean swell tipping the deck, rose through me from the floorboards straight up through my painfully pulsating head and I thought I would faint. I flailed with one hand and seized hold of the back of the armchair.

He appeared to be equally broken. With a visible effort he came around from the side of the armchair and pressed me down into it by my shoulders. Then he let himself drop on the couch. "I brought you home from the bar," he rasped, interrupting himself with an unwholesome cough. "I kept myself up the whole night. Then some time this morning I couldn't hang on anymore. I had very much too much to drink yesterday. And I've had very poor sleep the past month. I passed out, like you. Inexcusable. I woke up just now when the phone began ringing again. I was here on the couch," he appended.

He'd spoken at too great a length for my quivering brain. The phone fell with a startling noise to the floor; I'd still had it clutched in my hand. Very far behind him I managed, "You stayed here all night? Why?"

"To check on you. I woke you up every hour to make sure that you didn't go into a coma."

"Is that a joke?"

"No. I should have taken you to hospital immediately."

"I'm glad you didn't."

"I should have. Clearly, you've had a concussion. But then, my judgment was not operating as well as it should have. I got foolishly scared out of going. I'm ashamed. Thank God you woke up and came out of your bedroom. Thank God."

"You're frightening me," I objected, feeling so baffled I was nearly in tears.

"I mean to. Your life is what matters. Please make me a promise you'll go to a doctor first thing in the morning."

I grew more fully conscious of being half nude. He must have undressed me, changed my vomit-drenched clothes for these sleep things and perhaps even sponged off my skin. Whether the logic of those actions dictated an image, or whether I actually now recollected, I felt his tense arm at my shoulders, and caught a glimpse of the length of myself wet and naked and seemingly dead in the tub. I dragged the welter of blankets I'd brought from the bedroom more thoroughly over my lap. Country Joe, still alive, raised and lowered his orange and white flag. When was the last time I'd fed him? I'd fallen overboard from time and it was steaming away, its vast blind bulk indifferent to me, yet there was so much transpiring onboard I could not comprehend. My message machine was on the point of exploding, its light pulsing a frantic red blur like a hummingbird's heart. It came to me that this was what the light did when the tape had run out, and that the tape running out would explain why the phone had been endlessly ringing. I pressed the rewind button on the machine and its little toy wheels hurried backward through time to the start of the story. Nicholas stood suddenly. "I should go. Promise me that you'll go to the doctor."

It took me a beat to realize that the volume was all the way down. ". . . just about eight. Are you splashing around in the shower? Oh, here you come, a gazelle trailing droplets across the wood floor. Pull the blinds, please. Okay, you are not picking up. Listen, I got held up but I'm on my way now and I'll be there in less than ten minutes. I'm sorry we're missing the movie, but I'm bringing some pasta I made and a bottle of wine so don't worry your head about dinner."

"Gottlieb, eight twenty-five. I'm using the Hobo's pay phone. Why aren't you home?"

"Regina, I'm over at Dutra's. He hasn't seen you all day. It's *nine*, we said eight. Please call Dutra the instant you hear this."

"Regina, I've just been back by your apartment. Your downstairs neighbor guy says he heard you come in more than three hours ago and never heard you go out, so I'd like you to pick up the phone, please, and kindly stop fucking with me."

"PICK. UP. THE. PHONE."

"I've come home now and had the pasta and wine by myself. I hope you realize your only good excuse has you bleeding and dead in a ditch and if that's the case I'm going to feel like an asshole for being so angry, so either I'm an asshole, or I'm legitimately angry, and either way it is fucking unpleasant."

"Regina, it is seven o'clock in the morning. Wake the fuck up and answer your phone."

"Nine-forty A.M. I'm going to class now where I will be the queen bitch to my innocent students. No news reports of you bleeding and dead in a ditch."

"All right, Gottlieb. It's noon. You've woken up now, wherever you are, and found your panties and shoes and tiptoed past your sleeping new friend—"

Nicholas brought down his finger on STOP. "Why not enjoy the rest of these in private."

"She was *here*," I realized with horror.

"Yes, she was. Quite a number of times. And I, in my drunk foolishness, didn't answer the door to her knock, and ask her, as someone who was hopefully sober, to drive you to the hospital. Regina." He'd taken the crown of my head in his hands. "I'm going, before Martha arrives here again. Look at me and say you will go to the doctor."

But I didn't care about doctors or health. I didn't care about my brain, perhaps suffocating in the dented and tight-fitting vault of my skull. Perhaps it was the swelling of my brain that prevented my caring about it—I only cared about her, and what she might think of me, and how quickly and permanently such dark groundless thoughts might dampen love.

That was enough to swell with fear my foolish heart, and send it running around my ribcage like the proverbial chicken relieved of its head. "Where did you park?" I demanded. "Are you parked out in front? Did she notice your car?"

He withdrew his hand now and perhaps also reeled in something else that was less tangible. "In fact I'm parked three blocks from here," he said after a moment, "because you had trouble explaining to me where you live. Worry about your head, Regina. If for no one else do it for me. I feel responsible. I was too deep in my cups." And then before I could go to my window, to make sure Martha wasn't at that very moment arriving outside, he'd shut my door behind him and was descending the stairs. I heard the downstairs door as I reached my front window, in time to see him passing the trunk of the redbud and crossing the street.

His sudden absence was as strange as his presence had been. Dropping my toga of blankets, I made my way gingerly to my tiny efficiency kitchen, holding on to the walls. In the fridge were two liter bottles of red Gatorade, one half empty, and a jumble of moderately decent and fresh edibles: an orange, a banana, a yogurt, and a loaf of white bread. All of this had come from Hobo Deli and Nicholas; apart from Smucker's jam and Tabasco my fridge had been bare. My hands were trembling: hunger, I hoped, though I felt I had no appetite. I made myself peel and eat the banana, and then looked in the bathroom. My clothes had been rinsed out, though not entirely cured of pink stains, and hung over the rod. A towel lay like a rug on the floor, and was damp. On the closed toilet lid, on the far side of the sink from the tub, lay a very small book, blue cloth-bound, almost looking, from a few feet away, like a pack of Gauloises cigarettes. I picked it up and saw, faintly stamped on the front, *Shakespeare's Sonnets.* He must have had it in his back pocket when he started to bathe me, and then removed it to the relative dryness of the closed toilet lid. He must have also had pink vomit stains on his own shirt, though in the twilight in which I'd just seen him, I hadn't discerned them.

I lost time again as I sat on the closed toilet lid with the book in my hands. Its cloth binding was very fine, but very dry, and in some way alive, strangely warm. Perhaps silk. It felt disproportionately heavy in my hands, as if every wrong I had done to its owner was closed in its covers.

I could almost think that I'd ruined this also, dropped it into the toilet already. But for the moment the book was still dry. The necessity of keeping it so didn't soften my sense of deceit as I hid the book on a high shelf, at the same time as I heard Martha's car pulling up.

If Martha's fury was titanic when she thought I was standing her up, even more titanic was the countervailing flood of her remorse. It agonized her that she had banged, shouted, worst of all darkly concluded while all the while I lay helplessly—alone—in my apartment in the grip of a head injury. "I should have broken down that door!" she declared. I knew that some of her distress was concern for herself and not me. It was the lesser part, but potent—she intensely disliked that she'd lost her composure, that she'd betrayed an insecure and anxious need, and what was worse with Dutra, and my downstairs neighbor, for onlookers. And so perhaps I was able to feel I was sheltering her with my lies and omissions, and not just accepting emotional tribute I didn't deserve. The little blue book of sonnets lay gathering dust in the darkness. The key I'd made for her— with which, when I failed to answer her knock, she might have let herself in to discover her estranged husband vomit-spattered and drunk on my couch—was lost in a jumble of junk in my desk drawer. In my story, it was Casper who'd gotten me home. "Why did he leave?" she demanded. "He should have stayed with you." "He didn't know, Martha. He didn't know I was hurt. *I* didn't know I was hurt." I basked in her fussing attention while a part of me grieved. I didn't think that I'd ever grow used to this fact that pure-feeling emotion comprised every possible taint, dishonesty and excess self-love being only a start. Of course I did grow used to it, but not soon enough.

Nevertheless I devoured her repentance. After weeks of having used every pretext to confine our affair to my apartment, she swept me back into her house. I was made to sleep late every morning, awaking to jars of fresh flowers she placed by the bed. To prevent dehydration she harassed me all day to drink mineral water, pouring me glasses herself out of blue-tinted bottles. She cooked me cream-drowned wild mushrooms and sweet pea risottos and vibrant red ratatouille, all the life-giving foods of late summer. Murmuring jokes and admonishing lust, she insisted we must be restrained making love, "so as not to burst any blood vessels," though always, in the end, the first pebble bounced down the hill and the avalanche followed, and we found ourselves heaving for breath in a nest of stained bedsheets and uprooted hairs.

One morning the clock ticked past ten and we, strangely unhurried, remained standing entwined in the kitchen. A noise of thick soles and pram wheels over gravel forewarned us, and yet Martha did not rush me out of the room. Anya entered, with Joachim in his stroller, to encounter the person she assumed her professional predecessor.

"Anya, this is my Girlfriend, Regina," said Martha, her arm looping my waist and her hand nuzzled in my front pocket, lest her meaning be misunderstood.

"We've met," Anya said, rousing herself from an onset of amazement visible as a rash, despite the fact her stolid features had not even twitched. I could hear her future recitation of this résumé item—*then there were the two college professors with the one little boy. Beautiful house, with an excellent kitchen, and they were both so good-looking—but they divorced. You know why? The wife was a lesbian. Total rug-muncher. And the girl she was doing it with was the old babysitter!*

It wasn't quite the introduction to an eminent colleague I'd already scripted and staged in my rosy-hued mind—but Martha made clear it was merely a start. By increments, adding less and less water to cocktails, and more and more vigor to sex, we brought my convalescence to an end. One night, as we sat in her bed with a bottle of Glenlivet ("*The* Glenlivet") in the pillows and an old Hitchcock movie on pause, she remarked, "The department is giving a big bash for Ernie O'Rourke. It might be a can't-miss. Should we go?" Ernie O'Rourke was the crown jewel of the English department, an octogenarian poet who, having already racked up every national honor, in the last year had received the Nobel Prize for Literature. Any party for him would be lavish with high-quality free food and booze, but I knew, as she meant me to know, that the caliber of the event wasn't why she had now brought it up.

"Should *we* go?" I asked, peering at her.

"There's not anyone else in the room."

"I don't need to be introduced as your 'research assistant,'" I said. "I've already got all the research work that I can stand."

"I'd introduce you as my Girlfriend," she said. "To those guests so poorly brought-up that 'Regina Gottlieb' won't suffice."

We'd slid sideways into the sheets and lay facing each other, the movie forgotten. "Are you sure?" I asked seriously. "Everyone in the world will be there."

She reached for my hair, as she liked to do sometimes, and toyed with the coarse, bristly ends. "Yes," she said. "Why am I hiding you? Nicholas knows."

I didn't say, with a satisfied pounce, "So you *were* hiding me." Some moments are free of all taint. I kissed her, and she drew me against her, though first we removed the scotch bottle and TV remote from the bed— to give love a clear field, or clean slate.

"I have to say, for someone who's supposedly fully recovered from head trauma, your short-term memory's really alarming," complained Dutra as we drove to the mall to ostensibly shop for a piscine companion for Joe. My real agenda was makeup and shoes for the party for Ernie O'Rourke, for I was so elated and agitated, and impatient for and frightened by, the prospect of what felt increasingly like my debut, or my public deflowering, or both, that my mind skittered and spazzed when it functioned at all, and Dutra, whose characteristic agitation rather took the form of tenacity, was finding me close to intolerable. "For niTRATES you want no more than twenty parts per million," he persisted, "for niTRITES you want zero. Null. Zilch. Nitrites kill. Now say again, what were your readings—"

"Have you ever been inside the Scroll and Compass?" I interrupted. The Scroll and Compass was the fancy private club that due to its un-apologetic exclusivity was somehow both outside university bounds and most deeply embedded within them, the secret wheelhouse. It was there that the party would be.

"Once, when I was an undergrad. We broke into the tunnels that con-nect the quad buildings, where all the plumbing and heating and cooling stuff is, and from there we got into the Scroll. Only as far as the basement before somebody tripped an alarm."

"What was it like?"

"It was like a basement," Dutra said impatiently. "With big heaps of white aprons, I guess for the lackeys who serve at the dinners. Ginny.

Focus. You had pH above eight-point-oh, right? But below eight-point-five. Ammonia should be *zero*, nitrites should be *zero*."

"I can't tell nitrites and nitrates apart."

"This is just what I'm saying about short-term memory loss."

"But I never could tell them apart. Who can tell them apart?"

"Ni*trite* has the *i*, like in *kill*. Ni*trate* has the *a*, that's *'okay'*—"

"Is this the way that you ace all your classes?"

"Mnemonics are one piece of it."

"Nemonicks? What on earth are nemonicks?"

"You see? You were a literature grad student, Ginny. You used to know what 'mnemonic' meant! I told Hallett I thought you should see a neurologist but she's such a fucking WASP about doctors."

"You called Martha? Why? How are WASPs about doctors?"

"They don't need them because they're immortal. I would have called Hallett because I hadn't seen you in days but then she called me first."

"About what?"

"About *you*, Dopey. Jesus! Your brain's like Swiss cheese. She called to tell me about your concussion because you hadn't bothered."

"I'd had a concussion, Dutra. I wasn't in my right mind."

"*And* she called me to ask my advice, but of course didn't take it."

"What was your advice?"

"Did I not say two seconds ago that I told her you should see a neurologist? You have zero retention! Who am I? Where are we going and why?"

"Kidnapping!" I called out the car window, my voice snatched by the wind as we sped down the road. "Help! A strange man is taking me I-don't-know-where!" At last I saw Dutra suppressing a smile.

Since the boozy night of my apartment's "housewarming," Dutra's manner when I spoke about Martha had been palpably different: constrained, and at moments of lapsed self-control even irritable, as if, though he wasn't aware that he showed it, he'd had his fill of her. From the start of my romance with Martha I'd suspected that Dutra, despite being, according to self-diagnosis, unusually highly evolved, was unable to take us as seriously as he would have had Martha been male. We were pleasingly racy, and pleasingly decorative; being third wheel to us meant a ringside seat to a diversion, not exclusion from something profound that did not involve him. He teased us as he might have a pair of kid sisters—and not until that night in my apartment had he started to doubt that he still had the prominent role.

Now, as I pretended to share his absorption with browsing fish tanks—"I can't picture the fish that goes with Country Joe, but I know we'll know it when we see it," he said frowningly—I was aware of how lonely Dutra must be. He hadn't had a lover since me. He hadn't had an actual, publicly at-his-side girlfriend since the unnamed, foresworn girlfriend of his drug-dealing days. I knew Dutra got laid—among other ephemeral ties he had slept with Lucinda—but as for nourishing intimacy with a person who knew what he truly was like; a person who knew he was stupid with hubris and unstintingly, joyfully kind; a person who knew that if given his bong, *Donahue, London Calling*, an everything bagel with scallion cream cheese, and a coffee-iced coffee, sitting on his sofa he could master any subject and retain it indefinitely—in other words, as for being known, which is the best part of love—by whom was he known, even chastely, apart from myself?

Meanwhile the shape of my future with Martha had finally begun to emerge, like the earth's familiar face from those maps of the old blobby continents bumping around. It was a miracle yet inevitable, the only outcome I'd been willing to foresee. If attending the party for Ernie O'Rourke as a couple was going to shock, it would shock all the more for how clear it would be that we weren't just a transient fling. *They've been together in secret for months* all the gossips would murmur, with grudging respect. I knew Dutra must feel the tectonic plates shifting him off to one side, the more keenly the more Martha and I kept him part of our life. Urging someone to make himself feel at home only serves to remind him the house isn't his; nor the saltwater tank, for that matter, though I practically let him think so, from the kindly remorse I was feeling toward him, that Martha and I in the end would be forced to—indeed were already beginning to—leave him behind.

"The blue chromis," Dutra announced, directing me to a wafer-thin, silvery-pale little fish with no blotches or stripes or dorsal banners or quill-like extrusions at all.

"Why?" I objected. I'd been pondering a choice between the bristling lionfish and the Picasso triggerfish, as gorgeous and weird as an African mask. "The blue chromis is totally plain."

"And you're a total amateur who needs an amateur fish. The trigger-fish is high-needs and high-risk and it costs twenty bucks. It'll die, guarantee you. Blue chromis is the friend that Joe needs."

"I'm not an amateur. And it isn't Joe's tank or even your tank, believe it or not." But of course I would let Dutra win.

Abstracted from the dazzling bazaar of the tropical fish store, the simple blue chromis did ignite with its own luminosity, so that the penny-candy brightness of Joe's orange and white stripes was offset by a cool lunar glow. But the glitter that far more entranced me, once Dutra had taken a set of tank readings and reluctantly left me alone, was that of the dangly new earrings I'd bought; with careful hands I juxtaposed them to a fragrant new lip gloss, and a new pair of high-heeled Mary Jane shoes. The clothes I would wear to the party had begun to consume me with equal parts pleasure and anguish. I longed to remake myself into an image I could scarcely intuit, let alone put in words; my mind groped toward sinuous forms and aloof, careless gestures. I suppose I wanted Martha's effortless perfection by the opposite means. If she could sweep her face distractedly with rouge while yelling over her shoulder to Anya to take Joachim out of the bath—then I could pore over department-store displays of rouge brushes, of the broom-flared and the fat as a pom-pom, the cheap bristly and the shockingly pricey like the cut tail-stump of some silk-pelted beast, for the one that would touch me with feverish magic and make me like her. If she could retrieve a silk shift off the back of a chair it had limply embellished for months, and in pulling this sweat-fragrant, never-once-dry-cleaned tube over her head emerge creamy and cool as the young Princess Grace—then I could spend secret days muscling through packed racks of clothes at Filene's of the Glacial Lakes Mall, and straining my neck as I stared at my ass in all sorts of encasements, from all possible angles, and then plying my cheap Woolworth's iron on an ironing board made by shrouding my desk with a towel. If Martha could, the afternoon of the party itself, call to tell me she and Dutra were going to get in a few games of pool at The Pines before she swung by her place to get dressed and then picked me up around six—I could spend the whole day, almost since waking up, in unsystematic, fastidious preparation. I styled my hair before showering, showered, and ruined, and redid my hair. I made up my face before donning my dress, put the dress on, dredged the neck on foundation and rouge and had to take off, spot-wash, and re-iron the dress and re-make-up my face. I brushed my teeth and in jittery dizziness ate a banana and brushed them again. I poured myself a double scotch for courage, and brushed my teeth again, and then poured scotch again and then brushed a third time. I threw over my whole painstaking ensemble for a completely different outfit and different hairstyle and wondered if it was too late to buy different shoes, but it was now five P.M.; in agitation and despair I drew the blinds and lay flat on my back on the sofa and tried to freshen myself with a nap, without moving a muscle, all my weight on two thumbprint-size spots on the back of my skull and the top of my rump, so as not to wrinkle my dress or disorder my hair.

I hadn't slept well the previous night. Until now I had never had problems with sleeping, but since my concussion, and especially nights I was staying at Martha's, I'd often found myself awake at two or three in the morning, sleep snatched from me so abruptly that no drowsiness softened the onslaught of fretful alertness. I would wonder, made anxious by Dutra, if this was some tardy response of my body, defending me, after the danger, from succumbing to coma. I suspect that what really awoke me was surfeit—of the elation of having won Martha, and the terror of it; of satiation, my mouth webbed with sap and my tongue paralyzed with fatigue; and for some reason grief, as if I already knew I could never possess her enough. All in surfeit, beyond what I'd ever contain or endure, as I lay close to her in the dark. Her thin flank in slumber, hitched up, sometimes pinioned my hips. Her breast hung as if tucked in the fold of her arm, and subsiding from there to the curve of the other. Sometimes she looked older when she slept. Then the horror of her mortality, as if it were an unjust curse on her and me alone, would demolish my pride and restraint, and with a convulsion as unwilled as willed I would jostle her roughly so that she woke up. Sometimes, as if we'd arranged it that way, we would lavishly fuck. Sometimes, with a groan, she would tell me to get up and read, or to finish the joint on her dresser. One time we fought—"You are *so fucking selfish!*" she snarled. But the risk of that wound was offset by the prospect of love. By one side of her mouth rising up in the way that she had of attributing great wicked slyness to me, as she roughly unzipped me and spilled out my fear so that sleep could return.

Other nights, I never woke her at all but slipped silently out of her bed.

Then her home would seem alien to me, its own elaborate nitrogen cycle. Those six doors on the second-floor hall: her own; the former master bedroom that now served as her study; the former study of Nicholas's that was now a guest bedroom; the former "library" which was dedicated now to the transient, to boxes being packed or unpacked; and past the stairwell at the opposite end, the corner rooms belonging to Anya and to Joachim. And an entire "stand up" attic above, and then the slovenly grandeur below, the vast kitchen and breakfast nook, the only rooms on that floor that seemed wanted and used; and then the formal dining room and living room and den and the entry foyer with their dust-pale refugee camps of side chairs and armchairs and side tables and end tables and sideboards and "consoles" and other words that would sometimes scud past that I had never yet linked to an object. At that time of my life I had no understanding at all of such houses as these, of the process by which they come mushrooming all on their own from the compost of cohabitation. I had no experience of adult sediment, no experience of that chemistry of domesticity by which x, which is love or its likeness, becomes y, which is not quite the same, becomes z, which is more different yet, to the point that sustains, or that smothers and kills. The twelve years she had over me, thirty-three to my wise twenty-one, meant no more to me than the one year Joachim had just recently notched on his belt. Had those twelve years separated us later in life—my thirty-seven from her forty-nine; my forty from her fifty-two— this blindness, which was really the thoughtless belief in our sameness, might have been apt. But it was treacherous now, so much so that despite my complete ignorance of how little I knew, I intuited somehow my weakness. I knew her house was strange water to me, when I bobbed there alone.

The phone startled me awake where I'd lain so conscientiously motionless that even as my heart broke out into a gallop my arms and legs blundered, benumbed. For a moment, catching sight of my glittering skirt and my hard glossy shoes throwing back the aquarium light, I did not know who I was, let alone where and why. The red numerals on my alarm clock spelled 6:23. "Are you looking outside?" said her voice. Clutching the phone I lurched to the window, somehow expecting to see her though there wasn't a telephone booth on my block. The window framed noiseless snowfall, like a rain of ashes. The redbud's bare limbs sprouted fluff as I watched.

"Where are you?" My voice strangely vibrated my ears. My apartment was so plunged in silence I might have been underwater along with my fish, except for the dense little windstorm of noise coming out of the phone. A faraway clamor of music and voices through which I could barely hear her though she seemed to be shouting.

". . . walked outside and my car had been *buried* in snow."

"Where are you? It doesn't look so bad—"

"It doesn't look so bad! It must have just started falling in town. Here we're getting socked in."

"*Here?* Where are you? It's six twenty-five."

"I told you, we came out to The Pines to shoot pool. Now the roads are fucked up—"

"Martha, it's six twenty-five!"

"Would you please stop obsessing on time? That's why I'm calling. I'm running a little bit late."

"A little? You're still in Trumansburg!"

"That's my *point*, Regina, and the roads are fucked up, so I'm running—"

"But it's almost six-thirty."

"We don't have to be there *at* six-thirty. That's just when the cocktail hour starts, little food things on trays, I doubt people'll start sitting down before eight—"

"We're not getting there until eight?" I exclaimed. *I stopped wearing a watch and I've never been late*, I remembered her bragging. *At least, not because I've lost track of the time* . . . My whole body came back to me now, I was thrumming with monster adrenaline as if on the legs of a giant I could cover the distance between us, crush houses and cars, the fresh powdery snow jumping up in alarm. I would rip the roof off of The Pines and seize her in my fist.

". . . getting there as soon as we can. This fucking snow is not just happening to *you*, everyone'll be late . . ."

But it was just happening to me. Her phone call at six forty-five, to sketch the merry mayhem of trying to dig out her car. Her phone call at seven-fifteen, less a call than a broadcast, as if, after dropping her quarter and dialing, she'd dropped the receiver and wandered away, though the mufflement of sound must have been her own palm closing over the mouthpiece like closing a door in my face. Then the connection reopened and I heard Dutra's voice strike a note in the background, his words tumbled and lost, leaving only the coy, needling tone.

". . . wait for the plow . . ." I seized on the shred of her voice as if catching a glimpse of her face through a crowd. Then the curtain of noise closed again.

"Martha!" I shouted. "Martha!"

Outside my window an orphan flake made its way down like a feather, tossed this way and that by the wind. The snowfall had ended. Perhaps a fluffy inch lay on my sill, mostly air; press a palm flat on it, as I did, and it melted away. Below me a passing car painted black stripes on the street. Certain snowfall reminds you that snow is just fancier rain. A plow out in this would be raising its blade up and heading back to the garage. The air was wetter than cold where it streamed in my part-open window and painted my guts, tarred them thickly in dread. But The Pines lay on Trumansburg Road on the opposite side of the lake; I stood mumbling this to myself like a simpleton chanting a memorized prayer. Sometimes a tornado will drill down one side of a street while the opposite side goes untouched. Surely the same thing must happen quite often with blizzards. Surely Martha would not lie to me—and not even lie plausibly, but with brazen conspicuousness, declaring herself in the grip of a blizzard that hadn't occurred. The front of my slippery dress had gone damp from the air. And my feet, crushed like fleshy dead stumps in the punishing cones of my high-heeled shoes, and the rims of my eyes gummed around with black clots of mascara, and my gnarled hands, cross-hatched with blood at the knuckles where the damp frigid draft, like an acid bath, ate them away. Stand as still as you can and the beast never finds you. Don't run. It'll just catch your scent. Stand as still as you can and your body's death slips out of hiding: you can hear its faint faraway noise like a river that runs underground. In possession of that, how can any harm ever befall you? Martha loved me. She had chosen tonight to announce to the world that she did. Martha did not make elaborate plans—plans best suited, perhaps, to please somebody else—and just chuck them. She did not invite people to dine in her home, and decide, at the hour, not to cook. She did not tell her lover to put on a beautiful dress, and decide not to show. The next instant would bring her if only the unending now could be butchered and done with. Years before, all of four years before, when I'd been seventeen, I'd taken acid with a man I had known just a little and liked just a little bit more. The horizon had constricted and constricted around us, all past time, every possible future, had withered away, reality outside his window was swallowed by void, his doors opened onto a nothing, if there had been a supermarket, a neighboring house, a police station near where he lived I would not have known "supermarket" or "neighbor" or "police officer," I would not have known "hot dog" or "handcuff." The man had tied me, wrists and ankles, to his bed using shirts from his closet, the ones with long sleeves, and had fucked me in a mad thrashing panic, as if he'd lost something he hoped to spade out of my guts, and then like a madman he'd lurched half-dressed out his front door and had ceased to exist. I worked first my friction-burned right hand and wrist from its noose, then my left, then left ankle and right. Once I'd accomplished this task time attacked me like furies. I was helplessly trapped on the far side of hours with a mind scorched and bare, agonized by its own emptiness. Being conscious was torture. A clock hung on the wall framing me with its motionless hands. Push them forward and live. Kill the minutes and live. I found a box, turned it on and made pictures. Found another, turned it on and made noise. I found a slippery heap, cleaved it open and words leaped at me and were lost, little motes in the great molten lake; my consciousness burned viciously, the more stuff I threw on it, the hotter it grew. I was watching *Donahue* and reading Marx and listening to Tchaikovsky and doing the crossword and memorizing the phone book and counting the yarns in the carpet all at the same time, and none of it snuffed out my stark naked dreadful awareness, I still didn't know who I was and time still didn't pass, it was still seven-twenty, seven-fifty, eight-ten, eight-sixteen, and at some point I stood up and took myself into the bathroom and scoured my face and reapplied all my makeup with a white-knuckled half-steady hand and then going back to my post by the window smashed the handset of the phone against the cradle with such force that both were destroyed, and the mute metal discs and the uprooted wires and the phone's other guts scattered over the floor. Then there was nothing but Martha, the dusty indigo thumbprints that sometimes appeared on the frail skin under her eyes, the slight shine of the bump on her nose, the hairsbreadth chink of light between her upper front teeth, the tart taste of her cunt, and the river was dry in its bed and no boat slipped its mooring and no one departed and Martha was coming to get me because she was mine.

At a quarter past nine in the morning an engine roared up to the curb underneath the redbud and the Volvo's door slammed like a detonation. Then I heard Dutra's heavy boots pounding the boards of the porch and his heavy fist pounding my door.

"Ginny!" he bellowed. The bright cube of saltwater lurched in its box. Country Joe and the chromis stood perfectly still in the storm as if hanging from strings. The door strained in its frame. I remembered shopping with Dutra at the tropical fish store as if it were some rare, squandered moment of heedless existence from childhood, my hand in my father's while climbing a stairs, my mother seated on the edge of my bed radiating her tenderness on me like heat, all my stuff like that suctioned away, all the worse to have ever occurred. Better to have been pitched in the woods like a football at birth. The lock wasn't much, not a bolt, just the cheap little wedge kind that springs in and out. At some point in that night I had drunk my whole bottle of scotch and I couldn't sit upright; I couldn't even raise an arm; creased at the waist by hot pain I inched to the door and raised my arm as if ripping out stitches and did up the door chain and fell heavily back on the floor. I heaved over my knees but again, as with all but the first time, no vomit came out. Now Dutra had heard me. He paused in his pounding and shouting and we both heaved for breath raggedly on our opposite sides of the thin wooden door. And then the whole weight of what seemed like far more than just Dutra flew onto the door as if having been dropped there from miles above. The door stove in, splitting from the doorframe, but the chain caught and held. Dutra's bulging, chapped eye, branched with blood, stared at me through the crack.

That downstairs neighbor of mine, who must have by now had his fill of my door being banged on and screamed at, was a heavyset, unhappy poet named Donald. I heard him open his door and say something. Dutra's eye disappeared.

"Get the fuck out of here!" Dutra barked. After a pause, the door slammed.

"You get out," I whispered to the bloodshot eye, when it reappeared.
"Please just listen to me."

"YOU get out."

"Ginny, I beg of you, listen to me."

"Did she say it was you all along that she wanted? She noticed you all the way back on that day with the coffee-iced coffee."

"Ginny, please listen—"

"You want me to *listen* to you!"

"It's like, imagine I was drinking all night. Getting more and more high and fucked up." His voice squeezed out of him like a paste, stiff and thick with emotion. "And it's like, imagine that I came home, I'm blind drunk coming home, I don't know who I am, I don't know what I am, but you're there, Ginny, you're still living with me, just imagine, and now I come home, and you're upstairs, asleep in your bed," he was weeping, "asleep in your bed, just imagine, and I come home so drunk, I don't know who I am, I don't know what I'm doing, and I'm *hungry*, like an animal, hungry, no thoughts, and I grab your fish out of their tank and I fry them and *eat* them." He paused, heaving for breath. "And I don't mean to! I don't want to do it! They're not fish to eat! They don't even taste good but I DO it, I EAT them, and now they're gone and I can't bring them back, I can't fucking undo it!" The bloodshot eye glistered and streamed, alien and repulsive. Of course it was far worse for him than it might be for me. Worse for him, with his strict codes of honor in which he took such inadvisable pride. Now in betraying me he'd betrayed them, and he'd never have quite the same vigorous faith in himself. Time stood still. I stood up, I could not fathom how, soul-sick and exhausted and drunk as I was in my slick tawdry dress, and went so near the broken door Dutra's hot breath dirtied me through the gap, and then, as he had, rammed my shoulder so hard that I slammed the door back in its splintery frame, and perhaps broke his nose, though if so, he did not make a sound. And all my furies burst out of my chest like the fireball out of a bomb, with their thousands of fists and their thousands of tongues, so that even I didn't know all the things that I said, all the ways that I shamed him and smote him, except that the violent migration had vacuumed me clean so I realized in fact I'd said nothing, and might never say something again.

Not even when she came, hours later, though I opened the door. I had sat in my living room, propped on my sofa, tightly wound in a blanket, unable to sleep or wake up. The wretched deathless consciousness: this was why people murdered themselves. Morning might have changed to day and day begun to fade though I can only assume. Yet at the noise of her engine arriving outside I stood up, in a trance, and I undid the chain on the door and sat back down again. In my own shock I must have been shocking, as if it were all physical, entry wounds and soft clots of brain matter strewn into the folds of my limp party dress. Smeared makeup and snarled, de-coiffed hair and unused fancy shoes—I saw her, seeing me, give up on whatever she'd thought she would say. I say I saw her, but she was metamorphosed, the violence she'd done to me making its ricochet back. She was diminished and hardened, as if her restless appetites were a prison that had overnight whittled her down. Her skin gray, her hair heavy and dark with its oils, two fine lines I had never seen scoring her face linking nostrils, mouth corners, and jaw. Dressed in her sour-smelling pool-playing jeans and unraveling sweater and cracked bomber jacket as if she'd been out not all night but for months, on the streets, with the snot-crusted runaway teens on the methadone line. And seeing her so besmirched and exposed I felt choked with fresh love and hatred for her, that she'd so thoroughly ruined herself in my heart, by design and beyond all repair.

"I'm sorry, babe," she said, her voice pitched too high, her eyes redly damp, her jaw clenched. "I couldn't do it. I couldn't walk into that party with you.

"Every hour all night I kept thinking, It isn't too late. But I already knew when I left to play pool that I'd never get there.

"I couldn't let you believe we'd keep going, when we'd already lasted too long.

"I don't suppose you'd come out for a drink. Talk a little about it."

Into the silence came a rattling noise I realized was my teeth chattering. My window was still standing open. I did not feel the cold.

"No. I didn't think so," she finally answered for me.

Perhaps she thought my silence was strength, and not a helpless condition, as if she had pulled out my tongue.

"I kept trying to tell you I couldn't give you what you wanted. I don't think you ever understood—could have understood—how different my life is from yours. You're *twenty-one*, Regina," as if it were a self-indulgence, a foible. "I'm almost thirty-four."

But in the absence of ready assent with her thoughtful self-justifications, in the presence of ongoing silence, she swiftly lost patience. "At least with Dutra, we already realize we need different things. That didn't take long. In fact, at risk of betraying to you that you weren't my first choice, I can tell you he won't have a drink with me, either." A ticlike tremor, of regret or self-pity, for a moment distorted her face. "You should have seen him bolt awake and come running to you to confess. Then he came back and said, 'Get the fuck out.' Just like you. Though you're saying so in not so many words.

"Go ahead. Tell me what a cunt I am.

"Go ahead! Oh, poor fucking you! So fucking wounded you can't even speak!"

Yes, I was. Though as she wept and raged at me—for I'd cornered her into it, hadn't I, and I loved her too needily, didn't I, and would always want more from her, wouldn't I—my desire to speak, if it had even still been there, pilot light for the flame of my voice, softly snuffed itself out. The thread of smoke melted away. No, I would not speak again. Such a promise of peace.

At last, solitary and wronged, she turned her back on me. "I get it," she shot over her shoulder as she went out the door. "No one drinks with the bitch. The bitch drinks by herself."

That winter, I destroyed what was left of Casper's struggling career as a scholar. Grief made me coarse, a perverse predator. I snared Casper as sidekick in part with my lurid confessions of passion, but more with the sheer force that madness exerts on the sane. The raving bereaved have an awful charisma, to which such an amiable soul as Casper—long on compassion, short on self-serving ambition—was destined to be vulnerable. Soon Casper and I were consuming a liter of bourbon a day.

Work began around noon, at a vile pizzeria where we'd meet for a hangover pitcher of beer and cheese slices for Casper. I might gnaw on his discarded crusts for the taste of damp starch, but I rarely could eat. My unwashed jeans hung from my hip bones as if I might shed like a snake. That year's birthday gift from my mother was a turquoise-and-silver bracelet, sent air mail from the Navajo country, which fell off my skeletal hand and was lost the first evening I wore it.

Down the block from the vile pizzeria was a bar called the Red Rooster Inn in which Dutra, one late night the previous summer, had gravely offended a volatile man in a misunderstanding that seemed to have stemmed from a pile of quarters. Their disagreement rising quickly to threats, Martha and I, who'd been with him, had run with him breathlessly out the back door, collapsing once safety was reached in a gale of laughter. But while Dutra had been smirking and facetious in combat, afterward he'd grown as outraged as his enemy had been, and told Martha and me the Red Rooster would never be graced with his presence again. So far as I knew, he had kept to his vow. Now it was the one downtown bar I would drink in, for my vow was to never see Dutra again—never grace him, as he'd said of the Red Rooster Inn, with my presence. I would not even grant him a place in my thoughts. I had rubberized him: the rare times he entered my mind he went hurtling back out to the most inhospitable reaches of space, and sometimes I drank in the Red Rooster Inn all night long without even recalling the reason it held such a privileged position with me.

From the pizzeria Casper and I strode to the Red Rooster with great purpose, for all the world like two regular people who could only spare limited time from our wonderful lives for a quick game of pool. But no regular people lined up at that bar at that hour of the day, and our pretense would fade with the sun. Night would steal over the slotlike irrelevant windows, unnoticed by us. Perhaps we might leave and come back with hot dogs from the Hobo, for I sometimes could eat while blind drunk, and our bartender, that eminent, fatherly, featureless man who was Eddie or Jackie or Joey or John, who was cozy to me as a bed, whom I knew best of all men in the world, whom I wouldn't have recognized out on the street, would reserve our stools for us with two brimming doubles, and dole out paper plates for us when we returned, and with a three-point wrist-flick toss us two bags of chips free of charge from the wire carousel. Every fourth drink was free. If I played "Captain Jack" on the jukebox all lustily sang. Even Casper was embraced as a regular here, his urbane bespectacled feyness his required and ennobling impairment—like Big Tom's milky sightless left eye, or Little Tim's cortisone overdose that squeezed yellow crumbles of pus from his skin; or like my presumably erstwhile, presumably cured lesbianism. I could only assume they remembered me well, from when Martha and I, arrogant aliens, had brashly groped and gasped over each other in the jukebox's nimbus of light. Those ghosts never left me, as if some molecular error had splintered me off from my life; as if Martha and I still continued to gloat along gaily without me; some mornings I bolted awake almost trembling with joy, for I'd dreamed of her love, heard her voice chuckling intimately in my ear. Sometimes, at the height or the trough of a marathon evening, I briefly passed out of myself. A black shutter dropped. For an increment, consciousness died, there was only the surface of objects spread under my gaze, and the feeble drowned lights. I would forget. That she had left me. Even that there was me, separate and alone. And then, as if as a chastisement, the fact I was no longer wanted would rear up again with redoubled and terrible force, and I whimpered out loud from the physical pain of remembering.

"Gottlieb," came the chastising voice, but this night when I turned toward the sound she was actually there.

I felt Casper, on my other side, pass between solid and vaporous states, awaiting my signal of how to behave, but I was too helpless to signal. Hot tears flooded my eyes and a fist of incipient vomit indented my guts. From the well of my throat rose a powerful, noiseless vibration; its note might have shattered the bottles and glasses that walled the back side of the bar, but I didn't allow it to sound. A harsh desperation for her that was almost instinctive, like the homely abject little amputee hermit crab finally locating its shell. But this was all, this disabling interior storm. I didn't seize her taut milky neck in my hands. I didn't suction my lampreylike mouth to her breast. I didn't smash the butt of my lowball glass into her face. Because I still loved her: I could have stopped my own heart with my mind if it meant she'd come back.

"Come outside," she said. Helplessly I slid off my stool and hooked my jacket off its seat and followed her out the door.

It was deep winter now, the season when suicides rained down like apples from the limbs of the gorge-spanning bridges; when it was so cold it no longer snowed, and so cold that people stopped wearing their coats because coats didn't make any difference. Students from the community college roamed the streets in their T-shirts, their bare forearms marbled with blue, their sneakers slipping on the laminated ice. I was wearing my autumn-weight jacket, Martha her cracked leather bomber; neither of us zipped up and the cold struck my flesh through my sweater as if I were naked. We walked quickly, the searing cold synchronizing us like lovers, if lovers enraged beyond words. Wordlessly we passed into the street where bare patches more often stood out of the ice and allowed us to walk even faster. Down two blocks and she threw open the door of the fluorescent-lit late-night salad-bar place, with its crocks of lentil soup filmed by wrinkly soup skin and its stainless-steel tubs of gray, matted alfalfa sprouts. Inside she loaded a Styrofoam plate with vegetarian lasagna, macaroni and cheese, mashed potatoes, and rice pudding, every species of comfort glop in evidence, paid the stupefied teenage cashier, and led me upstairs, her violent footfalls making the whole structure quake, to a squalid mezzanine region of tables and chairs.

"Sit," she said, and when I did, she dropped the plate of grown-up baby food onto the table in front of me and herself into the chair opposite. "Eat."

I gazed at her, at the violet stains under her eyes, each with its reddened, slightly swollen canthus; and at her bloodless, chapped lips. Love me, I willed her. Just admit that you love me and rescue us both.

"You've got to eat, Gottlieb," she said.

"Fuck you."

"Look at you. You look like a skeleton. Your jeans that used to be tight are about to fall off."

"You look like shit too."

"Just fucking eat."

We were alone in the livid fluorescence of almost-closing time, sticky plastic trays and fork-dented Styrofoam plates smeared with half-eaten food crowding most of the tables. I swiped the full plate off our table and it sailed several feet, its load spiraling off in fine spatters and chunkier globs. "You're a fucking child," Martha said, shoving back from the table and descending the stairs, so swiftly I almost had to run to stay with her, down the stairs and back out the front door.

"You're the child!" I cried. We were rushing again down the sidewalk, back toward the Red Rooster where I had left Casper, skittering so quickly on the shoe-polished patches of filth-colored ice we were practically skating. "You're always lording your age over me, so why can't you be an adult? You don't make decisions, you just make a mess! You got tired of me so you fucked the *one* person we shared as a friend. You got tired of your husband and so you fucked me. Why can't you just say what you're doing? Why can't you be honest?"

"Oh, listen to the saint! Every time I was honest with you, you would cover your ears."

"Bullshit! That's a lie. Even this is a lie. Why are you here, anyway? Why are you trying to make me eat dinner?"

"To keep you from starving to death."

"To congratulate yourself on how caring you are. Everything that you do, it's to make you feel better. All those meals you cooked me and flowers you picked me—"

"Even when I was kind I committed a crime? How the fuck could I ever win with you? I always cared deeply about you. I hoped to keep you as my friend—"

"I was *never* your friend."

"Gottlieb—"

"Stop calling me Gottlieb!" I shrieked. "Stop acting as if we were pals! I *loved* you. I *love* you."

"Always the trump card! You love me, that entitles you to something? You *love* me, so we move in together, adopt a crack baby—"

We were standing so near to each other that when I threw my weight into her chest, shoving hard with my palms, she almost took me down as her boots pedaled out and she fell backward hard on the ice. But I wind-milled and stayed on my feet, my blood roaring and thrown a notch higher and roaring yet more as the admonitory whoop of a siren immobilized us and a police car materialized out of nowhere and pulled to the curb. Its near window rolled down. "You," the cop said to me, "step over here." His door swung open and by instinct I took a step closer to Martha, still gingerly getting herself to her feet, her bloodless chapped hands finger-splayed on the ice for support. "Step away from her," the cop barked, each of his words like a stick breaking.

"I think we can handle this," Martha said, upright again.

"I didn't ask what you thought. You, last chance. Step to the car. Don't look at her." When I had obeyed and stood numbly before him he said, "You want to be booked for assault?" He was young, his face stone-eyed and thin-lipped and pale with distaste beneath his dark uniform hat and above his dark uniform bomber and perforated gloves and billy club and sidearm and side-striped slacks and laced leather boots. I could feel the parching heat pouring out of the cruiser's dashboard, its leading edge lapping me like a blanket. As if to deny me that comfort the officer stretched and stood out of the car, his gaze pinioning me, and slammed the door shut behind him, at the same time as his partner, his double, got out on his side and slammed his own door and came around the nose of the car. At the edge of my vision I sensed a loose ring of spectators. "I said, you want to be booked for assault?" the officer said again, his tone pitching the slightest bit higher.

"No," I scraped out, just audible enough to escape his reproof.

"ID?" As I struggled with spasming fingers to dig out my wallet he added, over my shoulder to Martha, "Please stay where you are, Miss," his inflection just noticeably altered for her, as if she were a meddling bystander, in danger of hurting herself. To me he said, in another, now lower, very cold and yet intimate tone, "You intoxicated?"

"No."

"You're not drunk? Had a couple too many? Got a little too high?" He handed my university-issue ID to his partner, who disappeared with it into the car.

"No."

"You think it's okay to attack people?"

"No."

"I didn't hear that."

"No."

" 'No,' what? No, you don't think it's okay?"

"I don't think it's okay."

His partner signaled from inside the car and he turned his back on me, leaning into the reopened door. Across the car's roof I saw Casper, watching from the middle of a small knot of patrons in the Red Rooster's propped-open door. The cop rose up before me again, obscuring Casper, holding out my ID. I closed my fist around it and the blunt plastic edge seamed my palm. Lifting his chin at Martha, inviting her now to approach, the cop said, "You want to press charges?"

"Of course not," she said, to which he responded by staring at her as if she hadn't yet spoken. "No," she said after a moment.

"My advice is, you girls go home. Don't let me come across you again." He and his partner got back in their car and as it drove off our audience, smirking or cold, drifted off except Casper, now alone, with a cigarette lit, in the Red Rooster doorway. When neither I nor Martha moved, he dropped the cigarette, ground it out, and went in. My humiliation felt like a gag in my throat. I couldn't look at her. My tears couldn't fall. My numb hands couldn't crawl in my pockets. She'd even denied me the solace of being her victim.

"Lucky girl," she said quietly. "You don't know how lucky you are. How much you love me, how painful your pain. You don't know. Maybe someday you will. I hope not."

"I don't know what you're talking about," I said, pressing my face on my fists, for my body had started to shake with such violence I almost bit off my own tongue.

"I don't feel the way you do. I don't mean I don't share your emotions. That when you feel happy I'm sad. I mean something more basic. Not type but degree. Whatever I feel, I don't *feel* it the *way* that you do. Not for you. Not for Nicholas. Not for my son. And it's not that I'm cold, or abnormal. It's just that the way that you love never lasts, Regina. That's why people in your time of life and in mine just can't manage together."

"I don't believe that," I said, but it came out in disjointed shards, as if the jouncing cartload of my words had flipped over and scattered its load.

"Go back to your friend," she said, walking away.

Then they must have heard my sobs even through the Red Rooster's brick walls. Casper came back out and led me inside.

That winter, I misplaced myself.

I was not even lost, a condition which still retains something intended. There can be vigor in "lost." I only slid down, in near silence, from whatever had carried me forward. I slid down like a scrap from some pile on a cart. I slid down, into dusty unregarded margins, and was left behind and forgotten by the flesh part of me, which went on. But the flesh part did little apart from go on. Waking in the morning I was conscious I had woken, a pain so intense that it solved its own problem. It gouged like the edge of a spoon scraping flesh from a pelt, and destroyed what could feel it. Misplacement and void. I must have urinated and sometimes changed clothes. I no more recall these quotidian things than the arias I sometimes mustered, when drunk, such as putting a chair through my downstairs neighbor Donald's front window one night when I came home and found a neat box of my clothes sitting out on the porch. Or, again fenestrating, one night dancing with such fierce abandon at an unknown host's party as to hurl myself into a window and decorate it with a sunburst of cracks. Perhaps the darkness in my soul thus sought light. At the time it more seemed that glass always stepped into my path. I drank, however and whatever I could, and the more I succeeded the more panes of glass boxed me in.

The distinction between sociable and suicidally alcoholic had always been fine in our town, and to cross it was not to attract any fresh attention. That winter comprised a long train of dimly lit, underheated, overcrowded, and overloud rooms in which opposing teams pressed themselves toward or away from a flooded countertop bristling with bottles of booze. Handle jugs of cheap vodka and bourbon and gin, those guests who'd brought their own liters of Jack Daniel's or Gordon's without embarrassment hoarding them under an arm. Casper remained, more than I, in the know about parties, and like one ragged tramp leaving signs for another where a dry bed or a meal could be found he made it his business to keep me informed. One night we'd ascended dark sidewalks in silence, our feet keeping time, and scuffed over some region of gravel and through oversize, institution-like doors and were homing toward noise down a lint-colored hallway before I grew thickly aware I had been there before.

"This is Brodeur's building," I told Casper.

He turned back to me, where I'd stopped short. "I don't think it's his party."

"Still." But like a swollen hand, groping, my mind could not quite make the shape of its worry, although it could feel it.

"Do you want to leave?" Casper said, his voice rising slightly with ill-concealed pique, for he was by now as alcoholic as I, with less money. We still drank in bars every night, but if part of his night was supplied by a party he'd accomplished a savings.

"No," I demurred, though anxiety dogged me the rest of the way—never quite making contact, because as I've mentioned my self had gone dead in my gut, but bothering me all the same.

The party was not at Brodeur's but directly next door, if I wasn't mistaken—although the old factory building, with its vast, windowless, cryptlike halls, duplicated itself every way that I looked. Still I felt sure I was looking at his door, 1F. An annex to the party, a slumped group of comp lit and art history mingled, had unrolled like a tongue outside the door to 1G. "Greetings!" cried Casper in his expansive and fraudulently jovial way.

"It's unbelievably hot in there," one of them said as they lifted their legs up to let us pass by. "Apparently the windows in this place don't open."

"Good news for you," Casper said to me as we went in.

I could no longer enter a crowd without seeing Martha. Her pale cheek's semaphore flashing at me from an opposite wall. The indigo well of her eye as it vanished behind an obtruding shoulder. Now her husband's ghost joined hers to tease me as well, luring me from one hot, crowded room to the next. There was his dirty-blond rooster's tail cresting above better-groomed, blander heads. There the patrician nose swift as the bow of a schooner. The more elusive he was the more doggedly I pursued him through the high-ceilinged tomb-dark apartment as if along the bottom of a canyon already poured full of a refugee column. I couldn't move a step without someone else shouldering into my path. I had come separated from Casper just inside the front door. Reaching the foot of a stairs I went up. Here was a sleeping loft, with a mattress and box spring afloat at the center of an oatmeal wall-to-wall carpet. Hunching, I crept to the parapet and looked over while keeping pressed close to the wall, although without a light on in the loft no one could have seen me. Below writhed the restless congregation of shoulders and heads, but though I'd gained the God's-eye perspective the crowd had grown dim and generic and I could not make out Casper. As oversubscribed as the party was, I was alone. No illicit pair groaned on the bed. No one was locked in the master bathroom. All this upstairs region had been overlooked. Beside the door to the bath was one other, closed door. Opening it I felt for the light switch and locked myself in.

The study. Like the rest of the mezzanine level, low ceilinged, and lacking windows. I sat down in the desk chair and substituted a hunched gooseneck lamp on the desktop for the overhead light. Entering the party I'd taken two bottled beers off the trashed countertop in the kitchen, and then in the crush had not even been able to drink them. Now I did, rapidly and without relish, one after the other. My purse flask was empty and I hadn't seen bourbon to fill it. Books lined the walls corner to corner, and impressed themselves on my attention despite my noninterest. Many repetitions of the words *citizen* and *Bastille*. The apartment must belong to Walter Debrango, the French historian. The noise of the party reached me in the form of an urgent vibration, as if just a few yards away from my underground tomb an enormous drill bit were implacably chewing through bedrock. My tears, always there at the ready, had started to fall. Obeying a strong intuition I yanked open Walter Debrango's bottom-right drawer and in answer a heavy weight rolled away from me with the same noise a bowling ball makes, struck the rear of the drawer, and rolled back. It was a two-thirds-full bottle of Islay. No less weeping I hiccuped with laughter. Sometimes, when I drank, I seemed to dance a quadrille with the world, as if Martha had not in fact killed me but released me to some higher order of grace. I plucked the bottle out of the drawer by its neck. It might sink out of sight if I didn't act quickly. There was a lowball glass pushed to the back of the desk, near the base of the bulletin board, with a rich amber skin of dried scotch painted onto its bottom. I squeaked the snug cork out and drank straight from the bottle. Above the glass, push-pinned onto the bulletin board, a typed index card read IN CASE OF EMERGENCY and then listed several suggestions, the first NICK BRODEUR (NEXT-DOOR NEIGHBOR).

The phone was there. I pulled it toward me and dialed while tipping the scotch bottle into my mouth. "This is Nicholas," came his remote, courtly voice, though he too seemed muzzed over, as if I had woken him up and he lay with his face half submerged in a pillow.

"It's Regina," I whispered. Saliva had flooded my mouth in response to the scotch, and tears streamed down my face.

In the same somnolent, unsurprised voice he murmured, "Where are you?"

"Next door. At the party."

"I hear it better through my walls than through the phone."

"I'm upstairs. In his study."

"Are you alone?"

"Yes."

"Better come over." With a muffling and rustling he seemed to sit up. "I'll unlock the door."

Going downstairs again the noise and darkness of the party closed over my head as if I'd passed belowdecks into the engine room of some enormous ship plowing black waters to no one knew where. I pressed for the door and was suddenly out, and faced a different, more numerous gauntlet blocking both of the doors, to 1F and 1G.

"And the bar comes to us!" someone said.

"Regina Gottlieb. Long time," someone else had begun, as head down, as if this might conceal me, I picked and dodged my swift way from one door to the other and reached for the knob, which anticipatorily opened on Nicholas, dressed in a half-buttoned white Oxford shirt and near-whitened blue jeans with large holes at the knees, his hair looking as though he had filled it with glue, a pale stubble like beach sand contouring his face. His feet were bare, his face calm and exhausted. He looked so like her, my erstwhile lover—in no simple, features-and-coloring way, but in that far more essential, intangible, soul-matter way—that I stood gazing wordlessly at him, scoured by revelation, as if we had not met before.

In perfect silence he stepped back and I followed him in, and the door swung behind me. Just as the latch clicked, the spell broke, and outside the comments erupted like mushrooms.

"Do you think it's a work-study job?"

"I never saw that one listed."

"That's a job I would pay for. For fifty percent more tuition, you can sleep with them both—"

Then we had passed down his alternate-universe corridor, the mirror of the other, but empty. Here all was still if not silent. The party beat through his walls like a massive irregular heart, and his darkened, austere living room seemed to amplify it. From the sleeping loft above a frail light sifted down, but downstairs his lamps were all off. I still had the neck of the bottle of Islay gripped tight in one fist. I hadn't intended to bring it. Nicholas appeared beside me from the cave of his kitchen with two glasses of ice, and filled them from the bottle.

"From Walter's desk drawer, isn't it. I'll repay him in kind."

He had a sofa now, floating like a life raft in the middle of the floor. He guided me to it and I sank down at one end and he, carefully, at the other. It faced the enormous and uncurtained windows which framed the black night. I looked there, afraid to look at him, and felt his gaze resting alongside mine, seeking the same void, as if he feared equally looking at me. "I woke you," I said.

"Not at all."

"All your lights are turned off."

"Because I was sitting in darkness. I was enjoying the party that way. With the lights on it was too obvious I was here all alone." His words, and mine, came at long intervals, between long silences that were not tense so much as replete, with the urgent drumbeat of the party, and our shared distance from and yet nearness to it. And whatever we said seemed like so many reeds we were linking together, to probe the dark air and confirm that the other was there.

"I thought you would be there," I said.

"I'm not much for parties. I tend to stand in a corner with a fixed smile on, as if I was mildly retarded."

"I don't believe that," I said, though I did.

"It's very true." He paused, and I understood that he would have said, "You should ask Martha," if I had been anyone else. Instead he said, "I might have gone over if Walter had been there."

"I thought Walter was there."

"He's on leave. He's sublet to a visiting Hum Center fellow."

"Not Gareth."

"Not Gareth. Another one equally Dionysian."

"Gareth was last year."

"That's right. And that dinner was meant in his honor." But now, and by such small degrees, having each equally led the other, we'd arrived where we hadn't intended—but of course we had meant to arrive there.

Standing before me, he refilled my glass. I was crying again, but without violence now, and with barely a consciousness of my own tears, as if they were streaming because of cold wind. Leaning over, he palmed my face dry and retained my cheek cupped in his hand, analyzing it closely. His palm as always was chapped, sharp with stiff bits of skin, like the deceptively smooth-looking bark of a birch, and I thought of him glovelessly paddling the unsettled North like a Jesuit.

"My beautiful girl, you are starving yourself," he said quietly.

He made me a strange meal, all out of boxes and cans on a single stove burner, as if we were camping: spaghetti boiled, and then a can of tomatoes, and then an odoriferous can of mackerel, all stirred and mashed together with a fork. "I'm not the cook," he said, factually, as he set it before me, but something in the unapologetic, utilitarian crudeness of the meal unlocked something in me. Sitting hunched at his unadorned table, at a single place setting, and under his watch, I devoured it. It was possible I'd eaten nothing in two or three days. He had poured us both glasses of wine while I ate and when that bottle was finished he opened another. In the course of it something was shifting between us. The food entered my bloodstream, and my brain and my chest throbbed with power; I felt sobered and even strengthened at the same time as I thirstily swallowed the wine. While Nicholas swiftly grew drunk. So it was that on balance I rose toward him while he sank toward me, until we locked gazes at last, recklessly energized. He was smiling in quiet recognition, as if he'd reached into my mind and were riffling its pages as he did those of books he'd long since memorized. "What?" I objected.

"I wasn't thinking anything at all. Only that the blood has come back in your cheeks."

"I was thinking the same thing, almost."

"I'm unusually gratified. I'm rarely of help when a guest arrives hungry."

"I didn't realize I was hungry." And then: "You're thinking again of the party. For Gareth."

"For Gareth among other things. That poor party was meant to serve so many ends. It's no wonder that it collapsed."

He might have had a fingertip in the soft of my stomach, and I in his, both of us gently yet steadily pushing: who would mention her first? And then, who would feel anger? Who shame? Who the groan of release?

". . . such as."

"Such as." We were back on the couch, with the bottle of Islay and empty wineglasses. Now clean glasses, ice cubes, were forgotten. He poured the scotch into the wine-damp wineglasses, splashingly, for us both. A sort of ruminative growl embristled his words. "Such as, demonstrating our marital ease with each other." He had as much as named her. I stiffened with mournful outrage—that his claim to her was eternal while mine was so slight he could sit here beside me and feel no outrage in return.

"You said so many ends."

"Yes. And all so enmeshed even when quite opposed. A party to show we were happy as parents, and to show parenthood hadn't changed us at all. A party to give a grand send-off to Gareth, whom none of us liked, and to conceal how much we disliked him, and at the same time to make him feel small, by demonstrating our great generosity to him."

I offered, "A party to show off your beautiful home, and also show people that neither of you cared about it, not enough to hang pictures, or even to clean." Then I saw that hot glow emanating from him, of confirmation no less than surprise, that I remembered from when he had first taken notice of me.

"Yes," he agreed, almost pleased by my indictment. We regarded each other another long moment.

"Yet more ends?" I asked.

"Only one more of major importance."

"To get rid of the fava beans crowding the freezer."

"To bring someone near me." When I didn't respond he went on, "In eyes other than mine, as a sop, or reward. But, no sooner to bring her near me, than to take her away."

"So many cross-purposes." My voice faintly scraped from my throat, for my mouth had gone dry.

"Some marriages are entirely constituted of cross-purposes. They make a plentiful if unstable building material."

The bottle of Islay was empty. When I stood up the floor seemed to pitch and I used its momentum to carry me into the kitchen. I filled my glass from the tap and drained it. I filled it again and drained it, and filled it a third time, the cuffs of my sweater sodden where I'd fumbled them into the downpour. I had every intention of leaving. The prim sentence unfurled in my mind: I have every intention . . . I'd finish my water and leave. I could stalk past that gauntlet of gossip, I didn't give a damn what those people might think. The water's noise was so loud I didn't hear him come in behind me but turned, alerted by another sense, to find him just next to me, leaning onto the counter. I turned the water off and drained the third glass, staring into the watery eye at its bottom. Now he stood between me and the door. I could smell the sweetly pungent forest-rot of the scotch cooked together with damp flesh and salt as it came sweating out of his skin. "I never meant to suggest," he said hoarsely, "that she pursued you to spite me. That would have been the job of an evening, not half a year. She adored you. I'm sure she still does."

"Whose feelings are you trying to spare?" I said. "Mine or yours?"

"Mine?" he said with a bitten-off laugh. "Would you be standing here in your—in your stocking feet, if I'd meant to spare mine?"

Involuntarily I looked at my feet. Indeed shoeless. Now I had to look for my shoes. I had no recollection of taking them off. When I looked up again his mouth caught mine and with a sense of breakage, of hinges decoupled, I yawned open for him and seemed to take half his skull in my mouth. A hot, stinging rawness spread over my lips and my cheeks with unexpected instantaneity where his bristles dredged over my skin, as if having loved only Martha I'd lost some basic callus required for men. The more painfully raw my flesh felt the more I crushed him to me. My very submission was violent, self-hating and vengeful and blaming but most of all perfectly matched to his own, for he seemed to both attack me and throw himself onto my mercy, to bear down on me with a furious gaze and to swoon beneath me with eyes closed. My legs looped his waist. My scrabbling hands sought some point of access through the back of his shirt. My short wool skirt, stretched taut from thigh to upper thigh, gave way with a brief ripping sound and slid to bunch around my waist and he slotted himself tight against me, so that I felt his constrained erection through his lumpy blue jeans at the same time as he found my nipples through my challenging strata of midwinter clothes—brassiere and leotard and not one but two sweaters—and artfully twisting them wrenched out of me a harsh moan of shocked pleasure, for he seemed to have borrowed her hands.

"Here?" he gasped, somewhere between stovetop and sink. But I shook my head, for I did still have limits, though they were growing very difficult to find. We stumbled upstairs, tripping over and grappling against and barely able to look at each other.

There, in his barely furnished, abject, wifeless sleeping loft, almost the double of Walter Debrango's, with its futon adrift on the floor amid a flotsam of books and strewn boxers and a tableless table lamp trailing its cord, our hunger forsook us. It departed so quickly, we'd never know what sort of hunger, whether for Martha, or vengeance, or even each other, it was. Still we dutifully shed all our layers of cotton and wool until, trembling and naked and neutered, we lay down together and tried to make love. I seemed to watch him from miles below and for hours as in peculiar solitude he plumbed my body; and again and again sadness welled up in me, and when it did I groaned and sighed as if transported, or gripped his buttocks, or arched my back and pressed my face into the nearly hairless, alabaster smoothness of his chest—but these efforts, like struggling in water, only drifted us further apart. Again I thought of him paddling alone through a vast wilderness. He grew smaller and smaller, and at long length, on the distant horizon, a cry left his throat and across the wide waters came echoing back, and his body left mine and he sifted back onto the sheets. I wrapped myself in a blanket, an arm's length from him, and only then did he feel real again.

"I'm sorry," he murmured.

"Why?" I said tenderly, as if both the word, and the tone, had appeared on a prompter before me. I felt exalted by a new, exotic sadness, as if some rite of passage were complete. It was my first experience with the strange honesty of that particular deception we offered each other. He fell asleep then, and so must have I, though later when I woke I had the bed to myself—he had moved to the sofa.

Every one of those uncounted, indistinguishable days we lived together like fugitives—eating from his bachelor's pantry, drinking from his cheap cases of wine that sat torn open on the floor, full bottles departing and drained ones returning until the whole box lightly rattled and stank with a faint rancidness—I told myself I would leave, and then at the end of the day I would find that I still hadn't left. I would tell myself, First thing tomorrow, I'll leave. I always expected to. Yet something kept feeling unfinished, some obscurity out of my hands. Sometimes we drove in his car for an hour to some other town, to eat burgers, or sit through a movie, or browse the musty inventory of some graveyard of valueless books in an unheated barn. But those were rare excursions; perhaps there was just one of each. If he needed to work he closed the door of his study on me. Other times, he went out and left me alone, and then I understood he must be seeing Joachim. He would return with fresh fruits and vegetables, fresh bread, other atypically wholesome foods, as if I were the child, or as if some belated impulse to nurture had pricked him. But we never discussed this, as we never discussed many things it would seem that we should have, with the exception of that first night together, when he'd brought up the dinner party. And the very mutual and thorough avoidance of all of those subjects seemed to me to denote profound kin-ship. The vapor of a mingled consciousness, filling whatever the vessel we shared.

Our lovemaking never improved. We might lie tightly braided to-gether and hungrily kissing for hours while our hands trembled just at the edge of a final abyss—but inevitably, once the threshold was crossed, the warm wax burned away and we bumbled and bruised at each other while attempting to socket our ungainly limbs. Often he couldn't stay hard in his efforts to fuck me. Often my flesh went so dry we would squeak like a rubber shoe-sole on linoleum tile. Only formality restored dignity and desire; he owned a pair of beautiful, snow-white robes with some sort of monarchical crest stitched in gold on one breast, to lie over the heart; it was many years before experience taught me he'd pilfered them from a hotel. We would put on those robes and return to each other. Then he was my golden, remote god again of the cheekbones and nose, the dirty-blond rooster's crest of his hair like some sort of Victorian coach ornament. Cleanly I'd lie in his arms like the blade in its sheath. I would feel the hard heat of his body translated to me through the rough terrycloth, straining for any contact with my innocent hand. To escape from my teasing per-sistence at last he'd recite in his ragged-edged actorly voice, equally mar-bled with ego and self-deprecation; on and on I would spur him, the stanzas accreting like bricks, the hard heat and the innocent hand ever more roughly grinding against one another, his voice booming now from a resonant dungeon containing the hissing pump-works of his lungs— until, still reciting, he'd seize me and in some way confusingly brutish and brief masturbate himself using the whole of my body, although never entering me, biting off his own words at the point he let go with a terrible bark, like a primitive soldier absorbing a spear in the guts.

So many things never discussed—yet while we were together, except during lovemaking's arduous toil, he never stopped talking. Later it hardly seemed possible to me, that he could have confided as much as he did, and with such eager and eloquent trust, as if he had never before found a person to listen. And with no tale touching on Martha, either as subject or implied prior listener, though of course, I reminded myself, he must have told her his stories in their first days of love. I couldn't have been the first woman to listen to this beautiful, strange man of forty, though his gift was to nevertheless make me feel that I was. His handsome, unaffectionate parents, whose closed-off adult life he had thrilled to, from his exiled little-boy's bed. His gold, naked childhood calves above knobbly wool socks. His speech impediments and the impatience and disgust they provoked in his mother, and his unconfessed terror of, yet utter resignation to, the unredeemable life of a half-wit. His grief-stricken love for his brother, the family's true mental case, who even as Nicholas spoke of him was determinedly pursuing the existence of a menace idiot-savant on the campus of the University of British Columbia, where he lived on the streets despite all interventions, and attended, up to eight times a day, undergraduate and graduate lectures on such subjects as particle physics, which he often interrupted with belligerent questions or sinister hallucinations which had led him to be hospitalized. The thousands of acres of small interlinked glacial lakes, like a gilt filigree, Nicholas had paddled alone, which he spoke of as if he were scissoring open their surfaces just at that moment. The Swiss housewife, his hostess when as a sixteen-year-old exchange student he was living in Zurich, who seduced him his very first night in her home, and became his first female lover, at a time when he'd still been accustomed to hand jobs and blow jobs with his boarding-school mates—and when he spoke of his sexual past he seemed both hypervivid and freshly obscured by mystique, and I would remember him as I'd first known him, and feel a brief jolt of that erstwhile ignorant lust, so delicious and rare now because ignorance was required.

I never climaxed with him, never even came close. Yet in some way I continued to want him. He alone knew my deformity. I less felt I'd lost part of myself than endured some disabling intrusion, which by my own inexplicable logic only Nicholas, like a loverly midwife, could ever remove. But of course he could not.

One winter afternoon he went out while I remained on his couch under blankets and reading a book. But soon after he'd left I heard movement outside his front door, followed right away by violent pounding, as if an interval of civil knocking, ignored, had already elapsed.

"Nicholas!" Martha shouted, while pounding. And then, "Regina!"

Her ferocity paralyzed me. I who daily longed to hear her voice, even shouting denunciations; I who would have risked arrest for one more chance to fling her down on the sidewalk, and pin her beneath me, and keep her with me that much longer; I who had bolted awake, more than once, in the bed of her former husband, certain that some microscopic pair of orphaned molecules, ghost of a ghost of her scent, had precipitated into my nostrils from the sheet I slept on, which had once clad their marital bed—I who had nothing to lose to her, and nothing to want but her, was too frankly terrified of her to open the door. And yet her outrage outraged me, for how obtusely mistaken it was. That she could imagine herself wronged by *us*—a pair of invalids who'd taken to tending each other? The longer she shouted and banged, the more the inaptness of her self-righteous fury felt like a demon's idea of a joke. When my rage weighed the same as my fear I threw off the blanket intending to open the door— she and I would now murder each other—and realized she had ceased her onslaught and departed, as abruptly as she had begun. Perhaps someone else in the building had come out to say they would call the police.

By the time Nicholas returned courage had left me and I was huddled again on the couch underneath the blanket. "She was here," I said when he knelt by me, and as soon as I said it felt the first outside air intrude into our hothouse, as if someone had cut a small slit in the membrane—not enough to collapse it. Not yet. Perhaps this was all she'd intended to do. "I didn't answer the door," I added.

"I'm sorry, darling," he said, as if I were the blameless young love of his postdivorce days, the intruder some she-hag I'd not even met.

"I'm sorry," I echoed him, by which I might have meant, I'm sorry that merely by saying "I'm sorry" I desecrate our secret code, that merely by acknowledging our code I desecrate it yet further.

"I was going to make supper," he said. "Should I?"

"Yes," I said, but after we'd eaten I put on my coat, standing a long time struggling over the toggles, as if it were a new coat I had never worn before.

"I'll drive you," he said, and at the curb in front of my house, he leaned across and lightly kissed me with thin, dry, chapped lips.

My fish were dead. They had been so tiny, their dead bodies scarcely made corpses. I had to search hard for them, my tear-gummed gaze clumsily probing that cube of cold light. The jasmine had died long ago. I had pitched its pot into the trash.

Nicholas and I didn't finish just then, but we did not in the same way continue. Our bed-sharing became almost chaste, though some nights when we drank we did stumble by chance on desire. Then we handled each other roughly, he twisting and biting my nipples, and bringing me as close as I ever would get, and my pinning him down and mechanically bringing him off while the heel of my hand mashed contemptuously on his face. But that sort of thing less and less often. We took care of my housekeeping—or house-losing—errands. I knew it was time to leave now, and not just his apartment, nor mine. He drove me, back and forth, back and forth, to the Salvation Army with loads of furniture and books and pots and pans until finally all was erased but the little I knew I should not do without. If he recognized the few things of beauty and worth, the lamp and rug and framed pictures, as Martha's cast-offs, exiled long ago from his marital basement or attic, he did not say so. I almost did not recognize them myself. That homely and mismatched apartment, the first place I had lived on my own, and for which I had harbored what now seemed such laughable hopes. Spring had come, and the redbud was blooming. The day I left town, I did not look twice at it. We packed my rented car together, a ten-minute job. I locked the doors and tossed the key through the mail slot for Tim and drove in Nicholas's wake back to his apartment, leaving only, I would much later realize, that little cloth-bound *Shakespeare's Sonnets* of his, that I'd hidden so well even I never saw it again.

An indoor setting seemed required for our formal goodbye, but once back through his door I didn't know where to stand, lurching from sofa to bathroom to kitchen until he pulled me with him onto the staircase, where we had never had reason to sit, but just then it seemed the right choice in its in-between-ness, a perch for neither staying nor going.

He passed his arms around my waist and held me tightly, either to retain me or to gird me to leave, I couldn't decide. I was starting to cry but I'd always cried freely with him; in whatever we'd shared it was one of my primary faces.

"What happened?" I said.

He somehow understood the question exactly. "I think we fell a little in love," he said after a moment.

"Just a little?"

"And then we decided. That it was enough."

I had wanted him to contradict this truth. Without some sort of lie I had nothing. "I don't want to go," I sobbed.

"You're going to be wonderful," he said into my hair. Then we both walked outside.

Often that first summer I would call him, and we always spoke in murmurs, for hours, like lovers, and very often I wept. But, though I longed for him to with such force that it must have translated to him through the phone, he never asked me to come back and visit. Once I even said, "I was thinking of taking the bus up this weekend," and he said, after just a slight pause,

"I don't think this weekend,"

with a sort of hollowness at each end of the sentence I understood later was mine to fill in.

Sometimes he wrote me, single or twinned sentences on the backs of austere picture postcards, almost always of Inuit art from the collection of the University of British Columbia, where I assumed he had just seen his brother. These messages were so impersonal I can't even recall them, except for one, his delighted response to my first publication.

A firm push, on smooth waters. After I'd traveled the distance, I saw what he'd done.

2007

"... and I figure you'll want to invite me to dinner now that I'm *married* and all," he signed off in his needling way.

"I'm sorry, what did he say?" I asked Myrna, who was helping me unload the groceries. Of course she would have no idea who he was, and would even find having to speak of my incoming calls a distasteful infringement.

"Oh yes," Myrna said with reluctance. "This caller. You'll have to back it up further. That's only the end of his most recent message. This caller first rang in the morning, while Lion was taking his ten o'clock nap. I had to lower the volume because I thought he'd wake Lion with speaking so loud."

"First rang?"

"You'll see there's four messages new. I believe they're the same caller, four different times. I'm not certain. I kept the volume turned down." Myrna often found evidence of my defects of character in locations quite separate from me, and her comments now regretted my vulgarity, in having such strange, loudmouthed callers as Dutra, and broadcasting the fact with an audible message machine. But she never was rude: saying she'd turned down the volume to help Lion sleep was a kindness of hers to my pride. Obviously I should have my machine's volume down all the time, but I just didn't know any better. For this failure, as for so many others, she supplied her own cure. One of Myrna's ironclad idiosyncrasies was that she wouldn't put Lion's soiled clothes in the hamper, because the hamper was kept in the master bedroom. When Myrna arrived in the morning, if the door to our bedroom was not already shut, she would shut it herself, pointedly. Then, as the hours elapsed, and little Onesies and elastic-waist short-shorts and overall sets grew besmirched in their varied quotidian ways, she would drape items over the bedroom doorknob, one on top of the other. I'd seen her get to the height of six items of clothing. The instant I came home they collapsed to the floor for nobody but me to pick up—but God save Myrna from crossing that threshold and putting the clothes in the hamper herself! It wasn't decent for her to set foot in our bedroom. She knew if we didn't.

"If this guy that called really is married, there must be alien abductors involved," I said now, because it was one of my ironclad idiosyncrasies to be nervously provoked by Myrna toward just the sort of jokey oversharing for which she had the least use. Of course, Myrna did not take this bait. She only blinked, as if to say, Does this pertain to the physical, mental, or emotional health and well-being of the little boy sleeping now in the next room?

No. In that case, is this something I ought to discuss with my pastor?

No again. Satisfied by the results of her silent inquiry, Myrna pretended she hadn't heard me. "There's leftover pasta with carrots and peas in the icebox," she said in conclusion. "He made one poop this morning. At the playground he played very nicely with Noah." She shouldered her purse.

"Thank you, Myrna," I said humbly. I never felt more like my own impostor than when speaking with her, but she was the best sitter, by many orders of magnitude, we had ever employed, and Matthew—who of course had less than nothing to do with our sitters, having laid eyes on each one of them no more than twice, first to hire, then, until Myrna, to fire—insisted on her. I'd indulged in my youthful experimentation, had my fun—the aspiring-jazz-singer sitter, for example, who diapered Lion backward, and was never less than forty minutes late—and now it was time for an "actual, competent sitter," to quote Matthew's passionate speech. A sitter who knew what her job was and did it, in order—so I felt went the unspoken subtext—that I might recall what my job was, and do it as well.

I never looked in on Lion while Myrna was still in the house. For all my alleged lapses in guarding my own privacy, I couldn't bear her to realize how eager I was to see him. I would potter around in the kitchen. Unload bags. Coolly glance at my mail. Never once would I ask how he'd been, as if I hardly realized he was there. Then as soon as she left I'd go into his room and kneel next to his miniature bed, where he lay in the throes of his delicious, sweat-dampened, enviable postlunch nap. Today he lay on his side, his legs scissored apart as if he'd been trying to outrun his slumber. His plump cheek squashed against the pillow had pushed his lips apart, deepening the arrowed indentation of the upper. His loose curls lay in a spray around his head. Carefully, fearing I'd wake him, I lowered nose and mouth into the cleft where his neck met his jaw, into that hot crease of cleanly odorous flesh, and there, eyes closed, inhaled and inhaled with hunger—if I could devour it, I thought, and so keep it forever, that hot, honeyed, clean scent of unfallen flesh—

From downstairs, the base of the building, I heard the muffled boom of the massive Victorian oak double doors: Myrna hitting the street. She was off to her other job, a pair of children she picked up from school and stayed with until someone got home. Beyond that I knew nothing of them, due to Myrna's discretion, which didn't mean I did not sometimes find myself thinking *Poor children*, no more shocked than amused by my smugness, as if, like a vice, it gave equal parts pleasure and shame. *Poor children*, to not have their mommy with them in the late afternoon, the best part of the day, when the languorous city belonged to the carefree alone. No one striding tight-lipped to the subway. Outside it was finally spring. When Lion woke up, we would go to the park and count tulips.

That an undeserved fluke, a strange coincidence of passable effort with outsize enthusiasm, was the reason I no longer needed a job, didn't hamper my feeling of moral supremacy over mothers with actual jobs, that I could spend so much more time with my child than they could with theirs. Nor did the feeling of moral supremacy hamper my awareness of being a fake, a do-nothing, unfairly lounging in leisure unearned. The two feelings were two sides of one weave, though it's hard to say which was the "good" side and which the reverse. More than a decade before, after losing my first job in New York as the assistant of an agent of extremely lowbrow fiction who had fired me for being "an incorrigible snob," I had written what I'd hoped was an extremely lowbrow book as a sort of revenge. "Call me a snob? I'll show you!" I had thought, though in truth I had not meant to show it to anyone. But my young-girl-in-the-city rehash, like a Frankenstein monster, had thrown off her bonds and gone lumbering into the world, and to this day had not ceased her surprisingly lucrative rampage. She'd got herself translated into sixteen foreign languages, and adapted for premium cable; she'd even gotten me, early on, to produce her a sequel. But that was all she would get, I had vowed. Since the second turn of the millennium, as I thought of it, in September of 2001, I had set her aside and expected that everyone else would as well, but strangely, they had not. In general, multiple overloud messages on my machine would have been from my agent, a crass, brassy, hyperactive, come-to-think-of-it-not-so-un-Dutra-like man-boy hustler, who possessed the additional interesting feature of being a colleague of Matthew's, though I'd met Matthew second, through him. My agent was the agency's cash cow; Matthew was their nonfiction cap-feather, their pride, all the more prized for his anomalousness, his wholly un-agent-like professorial solemnity, his Pulitzer Prize–winning projects about genocide and the coming oil crisis. It was a matter of enormous satisfaction to the agency's heads that Matthew seemed there by mistake, and that he'd married *me*, four years after we'd met at an agency party, was fondly considered by his colleagues the stuff of great screwball.

As quickly as I'd swooned into Lion's soft neck, I stood again and slipped out of his room. He had not even stirred.

Dutra had indeed involved himself with my machine. He really had called four separate times, and talked a total of almost twenty minutes, touching on the subject of his marriage exactly once, *gotcha!*-style, in the course of the sign-off I'd already heard. "I figure you'll want to invite me to dinner now that I'm *married* and all."

"Prick," I remarked without heat as I picked up the phone. It was a peculiarity of my relationship with Dutra that I neither possessed, nor even knew if existed, home phone or mobile phone numbers for him. For years he had virtually lived at the hospital, in and out of surgery, periodically placing calls to me, at random hours, from what I imagined to be an atmosphere of unremitting somber urgency affronted, if not outright maddened, by his breezy wisecracking. There he must sit, the bludgeon-heavy handset of a bright-red phone prominently labeled FOR EMERGENCY ONLY pinched between jaw and shoulder, his long legs propped up on some erstwhile sanitized surface, spinning a pen on one thumb and yakking to his tolerant friend about the fantastical idiocies of his most recent cabbie while scrubs-clad and blood-spattered nurses rushed past him with lifesaving tools in their hands. Or so I imagined the scene, which was why I never called him unless he called me. "Dr. Dutra, please—Regina Gottlieb returning his call," I ventured to the woman who answered. "I'll put you through," she murmured pliantly— it was a very famous and well-endowed hospital at which Dutra had landed, and always surprised me anew with its telephone manner of a fancy hotel.

"Hel-*lo*. Looks like I got your attention."

"What is that supposed to mean?"

"Such a fast callback. That must be a record."

"I always call you back."

"Eventually. Anyway, don't you think congratulations are in order? Aren't you so happy for me?"

"Are you seriously married?"

"I would never get unseriously married. Yes, I'm seriously married."

"Wow! Okay. Congratulations. And who did you marry?"

"I married Nikki." Here he paused, as if expecting recognition, but I knew he was smirking—I could practically feel his smirk through the phone.

"Have I ever met Nikki?"

"I don't know, *have* you? Her last name is Chevalier. Nicole Chevalier. She's thirty-nine years old," he declared, as if this were a primary characteristic, although the fact that he was thirty-nine himself was a matter of total indifference to him. "Family's originally from Montreal. Very big-deal people. They own a couple hundred of the Thousand Islands." Now I could feel he was grinning, his face-splitting, earlobe-to-earlobe, clown/wolf-with-the-upper-hand grin. "Don't you know her, Ginny? She knows you. She's a fan of your book."

"Jesus, Dutra. You're calling me out of the blue with the news that you're married to some woman you've never introduced me to, and now you're faulting *me* I don't know her?"

Oh, the delight! Oh, the satisfaction! Dutra verily burbled with glee—who needs a bride when one has an old friend to make fun of? "Of course you've never met her!" he crowed. "I've only known her for thirty-five days!"

Nicole Chevalier's elderly father had been operated upon by Dutra, it went without saying brilliantly and successfully, some two and a half years before. After the father's recovery, she'd gone home to San Diego, and dropped cleanly from Dutra's awareness, but as it turned out, he had not dropped from hers. Some six months ago she had written to him and included a photo. They'd shifted to e-mail, and then to the phone. Another man might have suggested a weekend in Vegas or Cancún to test the waters—but Dutra didn't have the leisure of other men or the patience for half-measures. He introduced a bit of drag to the momentum, made her twist in the wind a few months, then invited her to spend his vacation with him in New York. The day she arrived, he proposed. The next day, he took her shopping for apartments. The next week they were at City Hall. The rest of the month they had spent honeymooning in Tunis.

By the end of the conversation he'd extracted what it seemed he wanted even more than my shock: a dinner invitation. "How about next Thursday?" I'd suggested, feigning eagerness proportionate to his.

"Thursday," he repeated. "Gee. Are you sure? Don't you already have hot *Thursday* plans?"

"Thursday's the new Friday."

"'Hey, guess what? I got married!'" Dutra dialogically reminisced. "'No shit? How fantastic! Let's have a big celebration—on *Thursday.*'"

"Dutra's coming to dinner this Saturday," I told Matthew that night, by which I meant, in our marital shorthand, Start thinking about what you'll cook.

"Could you have told me sooner?"

"I just found out myself."

"Involuntary hospitality?"

"Sort of. But, you'll like this: he's bringing his *wife.*"

"He married Alicia?"

"No no *no.* Come on, he and Alicia split two years ago. He's married a woman he barely knew—I'm sorry. I'm guilty again of a misleading adverb. 'Barely' is not only needless but actually wrong. He's married a woman he *didn't* know—"

"Is this about to become a long story?" Matthew interrupted me, his pen poised in midair above the usual split ream of paper, the first draft of part twelve of *The Rising Fundamentalist Tide* or some such embryonic best-seller. "Because I need to finish reading this tonight."

"Why don't you just let me know when it's the time for easygoing marital chit-chat? Maybe we can put a little light above your head that turns green for, like, five minutes right before you pass out."

Matthew had already relowered his head to the page. "I'm sure it's an interesting story. I'll look forward to hearing it." He had a great talent for squeezing his mind's telescope to the width of a straw. Was a time, I reflected, and not so long ago, when *I* was that split ream of manuscript pages, spread beneath that most smoldering beam of attention—but this complaint seemed both childish and vain, and I took perhaps vain pride in not making it.

After I'd published my book, a certain kind of person from my past—the girl I'd passed notes with in seventh grade typing, the other waiter from the "health food" café where I'd worked for a summer in college—would tend to reappear for a while in my life, establishing contact with a phone call or letter, maintaining it briefly, then fading away. It was this category to which Matthew assumed Dutra belonged. The basis for the misprision was twofold, in addition to the fact that I didn't correct it. First, Dutra's reappearance coincided with most of the others, although I never thought it was my book that prompted him to call, nor did he use it as a pretext. Perhaps he'd reasoned that my having acquired a public profile, however minor and silly it was, meant his chances with me were improved. I might grant him the same graciousness I would grant to a stranger. Second, from Matthew's perspective Dutra was just as miscellaneous as the others—he formed no part of the contemporary pattern. He was a random odd fragment. The arbitrary groupings of childhood and young adult life, when our social contacts aren't yet fully aligned with our preferences, would account for him best—maybe Dutra and I, long ago, shared a second-grade classroom, or scooped side by side in the same ice cream shop.

What Matthew couldn't understand was why Dutra stayed on, and what I couldn't understand was why I didn't just tell Matthew who Dutra was. I had my reasons, or perhaps my excuses. Matthew had never been one to pore over the past, to fetishize my baby pictures, to play the voyeur to my lurid depictions of previous carnal milestones. Love for him was not a ritual of disclosing, confessing, or unearthing, but a resolute march to the future, well planned and equipped and unhindered by doubt. Our first weeks of love, when we managed to get out of bed, we hadn't spent telling our stories, or showing our scrapbooks and photos, or playing our most favorite records, or reciting our most favorite poems. We had bought me a helmet and flashing reflector, so when I cycled with him he felt sure of my safety, and we'd marked up the real estate section in search of a place we could live in a good school zone, so that when we had children, whenever that was, we would not have to move. I had never had a lover so unafraid of a future with me—and not just unafraid, but determined on it. The past didn't matter to Matthew because in the past, we had not been together—and this was a belief, like some religious beliefs, I suspected might benefit me if I shared it. And so I pretended I did, and readmitted Dutra to my life as a random odd fragment. It was an attitude to which Dutra, by instinct, gave his unspoken cooperation. Dutra and I never spoke of our earlier chapter of friendship, and this felt not artificial but natural, as if there were no past to speak of at all.

On the day he ambushed me with news of his marriage I hadn't seen Dutra in more than three months, but three months for us was a short interval, and Dutra tended to stay just the same a lot more than he tended to change. He still lived in the same five-hundred-square-foot bachelor pad off the Bowery he'd found when he first had returned to New York, although now he could have afforded the same apartment at its current market price, which was saying a lot, plus a few more just like it, exactly how many I couldn't determine given the corresponding absence of clear income cues and the continuing presence of not just the little apartment, but the rest of the time-honored Dutra attire. Dutra still had his hair cut by the Astor Place barbers, still wore the same bomber jacket he'd bought with his savings on Eighth Street at the age of sixteen. He still wore Vasque hiking boots in the winter with wool socks from Campmor (very likely the very same socks!—for he frequently bragged that, like all of the personal items he chose with such care, they were unparalleled for their comfort, endurance, and cheapness) and that same pair of Vasque hiking boots in the summer, but with white cotton socks now from Sears. He still "dressed up" for a glamorous evening in khaki trousers topped off with a black roll-neck sweater—the roll-neck his allusion to style—though five years ago, squinting at him through the crepuscular light of his favorite downtown restaurant, I'd been shocked by my sudden suspicion the sweater was newly cashmere, as if, even as our bodies had been replacing themselves cell by new, yet age-appropriate, cell, the sweater, too, had by fibers unknit and reraveled itself. Perhaps as a final, secret act of vanity it had traded its tag from J.Crew to Armani, or now even had no tag at all. Going to the ladies' room I'd tried for a look down the back of his neck, but the roll had been doing its job, rising up to just touch with its lip the shorn hair at his nape.

That night, the single time Matthew and Dutra and I ever dined together, had been to mark the occasion of Matthew's and my engagement. Dutra, on hearing our news, had awkwardly and needlessly and, it must be said, persistently in the face of Matthew's steady noninterest, insisted on taking us out. "What about Casper?" Dutra asked when I returned to the table, toiling, because we were with Matthew, to bring us to shared conversational ground, despite the ground being almost too small for us all to stand on. Dutra had barely known Casper when we were in school, and now did not know him at all. But Matthew, at least, had met me at the same time as I had rediscovered Casper in New York, and the two of them were better friends now than were Casper and I.

"He's been writing for this magazine called *Ultra*," said Matthew. "I think the third issue is just coming out. Apparently the business plan is, you can't buy it on the newsstand, and you can't subscribe to it, but if your net income is over six hundred thousand a year they send it to you for free without asking you whether you want it." Matthew and I had been dining out on the premise of *Ultra* ever since Casper, perpetually overtalented and un- or underemployed, had through friends of ours been hired to do *Ultra*'s art coverage, which took the form of a quick-shopping guide to works of art available for acquisition to millionaire collectors with unformed or catholic taste. Everyone with whom we talked about *Ultra* deplored it or laughed at it or distilled from it some sort of vile cultural essence, but so far no one had said, as Dutra did that night, dredging his mackerel sashimi through soy sauce:

"So *that's* what that is. I wish I'd known Casper was in it. I threw it away."

"Seriously," I said to Matthew later that evening, as we were riding back home in a cab, "how much do you think Dutra earns?"

"Now we know more than six hundred thousand."

"I thought *Ultra* went to people who made more than five hundred thousand."

"That's just half a mil. And, the less predictable number's a marketing trend. *Thirty-eight* ways to lose weight this winter. The season's *fifty-two* hottest looks. *Six hundred thousand* or more."

"Six hundred's just a hundred more than five hundred," I complained pointlessly.

"You've got to draw the line somewhere," said Matthew.

The next time we'd seen Dutra had been at our wedding, where of course we'd hardly seen him at all. The next time after that had been four months or so after Lion was born, though Dutra had conceived of the visit, and very likely had experienced it, as a visit to a newborn—to that distressingly remote and enigmatic extraterrestrial that had long since passed out of existence, what to me felt like two or three epochs ago. Since then had been the miraculous Smiling and Seeing Us baby, the terrifying, suicidal-thoughts-provoking Not Sleeping for Thirty Hours baby, the baby whose head must be held in one's palm lest it fall off his neck—such a boggling contrast to the baby who, at four months, could be plopped in a front-facing backpack without injury, and who then would dangle and bounce, smiling and babbling at charmed passersby. This was a baby who was practically ready for college—such was the depth and breadth of my experience as a mother by the time Dutra came to see us that I accepted his haphazardly wrapped offerings with a sense of anachronism—Lion had grown far too old for this gifts-of-the-Magi routine. Dutra wouldn't have noticed. As with that dinner he'd bought me and Matthew when we were engaged, the presentation of gifts to a newborn was the sort of gesture Dutra executed with equal parts anxiety and impatience, to get it done with and show he knew how, though I increasingly suspected he didn't. With Lion stuffed in the Snugli front pack I'd met Dutra on the Promenade in Brooklyn Heights, where we'd sat on a bench while I opened his gifts—a piece of stiff, multicolor-striped cloth with a white paint stain marring one end, and three crude wooden puzzles, of an elephant, hippo, and giraffe, made up of slightly splinter-edged, slightly warped pieces that had to be forced for assembly and forced even harder to break them apart. Dutra had in his spare time been flying abroad to donate surgery in various unswept corners of the third world where his patients would likely have died without him, but the more I tried to elicit the details of his actual work, the less enlightening he was, though he could talk endlessly, with his old near-insufferable swagger, about unhinged, untrained alcoholic helicopter pilots in the bush with whom he flew and even sometimes crash-landed, or about the squalid little saloons serving home-distilled rotgut from jagged cups made from the bottoms of Poland Spring bottles, or about the astronomically stupid white people with whom he, Dutra, had to contend. He discoursed for some time on the gifts. The piece of cloth was the exact ritual piece of cloth that the tribe with whom he'd grown so familiar would have presented to its next newborn child if Dutra had not come to alter the piece of cloth's fate; the puzzles were by local artists working with tools they had also handcrafted; with his usual bombastic pedantry Dutra established the gifts' peerless uniqueness yet aptness, and with his usual careless impatience he then shoved them back in their bag, which he proceeded to carry, as I had a diaper bag and handbag already. I made a mental note to double-seal the cloth's unknown allergens and the puzzles' likely lead-based paint in Ziplocs and store them in the basement until Dutra's next visit. We walked, over the Brooklyn Bridge into Manhattan, something we'd last done September 12 of a few years before, when all of downtown had been coated in ash and Dutra, utterly expressionless, had with his right arm held high in the air snapped one photograph after another with a series of disposable cameras he had stuffed in his pockets, *snap snap* every couple of steps, never looking where the camera was pointed, and never looking through the little viewfinder, as if to do so would be to lower himself to the level of the thousands of people who were also there gawking like us, if through tears, and with far less restraint. We hadn't talked about it since and didn't talk about it now. We fell easily into tandem, his unhurried gait matching my fast one. I had always walked swiftly with him because his legs were so long, and because he would not tend to notice me falling behind. One stranger after another graced me with a smile, often a positively luminous *beam*; I'd grown so accustomed to this since acquiring a baby I would hardly have noticed had Dutra not said, as another wave of approbation broke on us, "People think it's my kid. They assume you and I are together."

It was pointless to rebut this. He would have taken rebuttal as evidence of discomfort, which he as usual would have enjoyed. And besides, he was right. No one ever saw a man, woman, and child and thought, *Oh, he must be her exasperating friend, permanent as a sibling.* Instead I said, "Would you ever want children?"

I might have asked, "Is the sun in the sky?" Dutra pshawed noisily that I'd had any doubt. *Of course* he was going to have children. "Look at the things that I've done in my life," he instructed. "Sex, I've done every kind of fucking I ever dreamed of and a lot that I never imagined. Drugs, I was a heroin addict. Money, I was poor. Now I make so much money I can't even keep track of it. I cut people and get paid to do it—I cut a fucking maharani last month. I've traveled everywhere I ever wanted to go and I never want to travel again. The whole world's exactly the same. That's my biggest disappointment in life, that the whole world's the same. I've got to have kids. If I didn't have kids I would fucking implode out of boredom. It's the only way left I can challenge myself."

Flop-limbed in his harness, strapped snug to my chest, Lion absorbed this harangue in a state of entrancement, and when it concluded let out an empathic shriek, flinging all four limbs wide, as if Dutra's excess emphasis took the form of electrical charge. "That's not exactly what they're for," I said. "They're not some toy for relieving your boredom. They're for themselves."

"They're for the species, if you want to split hairs. Anyway, you can't tell me you have no selfish motives for having a kid."

"Well, sure, I *wanted* a kid—"

"The way you want all the trophies in just the right order. Book, boyfriend, fame, apartment, husband, baby—"

"Jesus, Dutra, I'm hardly famous."

"You're famous for what you do among the people who do it, the same as I am. You're the same as me in a lot of ways, Ginny, you just hate to admit it."

"You've got the big bucks, and I've got the baby, but otherwise, game tied," I humored him, weary of it.

Back then Dutra was still with Alicia, the girlfriend he'd been dating, and then living with, almost the whole time he'd been back in New York. Alicia was vastly younger than Dutra—when they'd first met, with Dutra already a resident and Alicia some kind of uncategorizable laboratory scullery maid, their age difference of roughly a decade had struck me as downright immoral. Through murky connections Alicia, who'd never finished high school, had been given a job maintaining experimental equipment—she literally washed tubes, and mopped floors—in one of the city's most prestigious medical research institutes. She had a security clearance, and was regarded by some of the bench scientists as a valued apprentice, despite the fact that she had never been to college and was by my guess about nineteen years old. Given that everything I knew about Alicia had been told me, with typically self-regarding bombast, by Dutra, every worst instinct of mine had been excited long before she and I met, but when we finally did, I'd been impressed. Striking, though hardly pretty. Her body that of a thin, bookish boy, her eyes those of a very old woman placed into the face of a very young girl. Unmarred flesh and a weather-worn soul; I couldn't decide if she was a frigid virgin or a retired child prostitute, and the information that she had lived for a time with her unmarried anthropologist mother on a seagoing yacht between the microscopic South Pacific islands did nothing to tend my conclusions one way or the other, although it helped explain the recognition I'd felt upon watching her sit next to Dutra at dinner. Through his noise and her silence, his tics and her stillness, I'd perceived their sameness: their unfitness for social relations, combined with their fierce competence. She was a hermit, and knew it; Dutra was also, but didn't. Henceforth I had blessed their alliance and been barely required to see her again.

That day we walked to the midpoint of the bridge and stood awhile suspended between the two boroughs before walking back to the waterfront park on the Brooklyn side, where we lay on the grass with Lion stretched on his stomach between us. I noticed that, unlike other child-less men I knew, Dutra felt no obligation to incessantly pull faces at or nonsensically speak to or otherwise signal his fearless enthusiasm for the baby. In fact he seemed more relaxed around Lion than he frequently did around other adults. Perhaps because he was a doctor, and Lion a non-speaking, hale little body whose physical needs Dutra understood better than me. "Alicia wants to get married," he said. Without forethought I expressed my delight, as if conventional sentiments, conventionally phrased, ever made it past Dutra.

"What makes you think it's so great?"

"Oh, God, Dutra, I'm just trying to congratulate you. I'm not looking for a long drawn-out dissection of the benefits of marriage."

"Uh-oh! A little defensive."

"A little not-stoned. Can you ever just converse like normal people? Marriage is great, Alicia is great, Alicia wants to get married, that's great."

"That's not how I remember you talking before you were married. Remember? Before you and Matthew got married you were superambiva-lent. 'I don't believe in marriage.' 'It's the path of least resistance.' That time we went out in my 'hood, you told me you were *terrified* he was going to ask you to marry him, because you'd *have* to say 'yes,' and then you'd *have* to get married, and then you'd *be* married, and you felt locked into it, like it wasn't your choice. Don't you remember? We were sitting at that crappy little place down on Orchard, with the fluorescent-lit bar—"

Of course I remembered. "Of course I remember," I snapped. "I was drunk and freaked out. Change is scary. Don't read me the transcript."

"Now you're married and marriage is great."

"Because as it turns out, it *is* great."

"Really? Are you sure it isn't because, once you're locked in, you have a greater vested interest in *thinking* it's great?"

It was just like Dutra to undermine all my hard-won maturity and wise acceptance of the inherent costs of marriage with a single remark. "Marriage as Stockholm syndrome?" I snapped irritably. "God, Dutra, you're right! Only you had the insight to realize!" But Dutra had already traded mockery for doe-eyed solicitude, as if at the flip of a switch.

"Aw, Ginny," he said, "I'm just kidding. I know that you're happy." My little malformed happiness, kindly noticed by him, might sprout leaves and grow tall after all.

It was Alicia's happiness he was worried about. Alicia was demanding they marry, but for all the wrong reasons. What Alicia really needed, what she desperately wanted, was a stay of execution for her mother. Her mother was dying, very rapidly and unpleasantly, of cancer, and Alicia could not come to terms. And so she berated Dutra or abandoned him, disappearing for days at a time to her mother's small farm in Bucks County. She always seemed to be slamming a taxicab's door in his face, her parting words choked and generic: "I'm sorry—" "I can't—." Dutra refused to propose until Alicia acknowledged the root of their problems.

"Which is what, that she's upset that her mother is dying? Jesus, Dutra, do you even want to marry Alicia?"

"Of course I want to fucking marry her."

"Then propose and don't be such a know-it-all. She's scared out of her mind, she wants love and security, she doesn't need you to act like her analyst. Are you being supportive?"

"Of course I'm supportive!"

"Not like a genius surgeon, like a boyfriend. Sometimes you need to can it with the relentless emotional honesty, Dutra. You should be hugging her and saying her mother won't die."

"I should lie to her? No fucking way. Her mom's untreatable too-far-gone *dying* and in a couple of months she'll be dead." He'd been right about this, as he had probably been right about the causes of Alicia's behavior—but not, if he'd meant to keep her, about how he should act. The next time I'd seen him, the following spring, Alicia's mother was dead and Alicia was married, to somebody else. Just after our day at the park, Dutra and Alicia had agreed to a separation Dutra somehow imagined would return Alicia to him as she'd been, as they'd been, at the start. Alicia began seeing someone with sufficient free time, unlike Dutra, to be willing to frequently visit her mother; arriving one midwinter late afternoon they'd found her mother propped up on her pillows in bed, a hole blown through the back of her skull by the handgun still hooked to her thumb. A funeral and a wedding had followed, in barely that order. "*That* person walked in that house with her that day—not me," Dutra said, without rancor but with a terseness that forbade any further discussion. And so his girlfriend of close to a decade, the only girlfriend he'd had in the whole time I'd known him, was never mentioned between us again. Since then he'd been single, or so I assumed, though busily enthralled as I was by my life as a mother, I'd rarely seen him. Just an annual glimpse through the crush of our holiday party, at which he invariably made a few fans and a few enemies, and perhaps even flirted. But so far as I'd ever observed, at the ends of those evenings he went home alone.

In the course of married life, the perilous transition I most often endured was the preliminary moment of hosting a dinner. The blundering scrum at the door; the salutation of Matthew, immured and in fact downright stony amid pots and pans in the kitchen; the dispatching of jackets and bags; the exclaiming in grateful protest over stuffed toys for Lion and bottles of wine; and all the while the secret, panicky struggle to surmount the great hurdle and serve a first round. At that point, the page turned. Knowing this I kept my head down like a sheepdog until I'd propelled everyone to their places. Once Dutra and Nikki were on the living room sofa with sloshing wineglasses and Lion was tearing the wrap from his gifts, I could analyze her at my leisure. I'd thought I had no expectations, yet I found myself very surprised. Perhaps "Chevalier" had brought me in mind of "chignon" or some other species of smooth elegance. But, "Regina!" she had squealed at the door, in the voice of a helium addict or a cartoon chipmunk. Even Lion, with his lifetime of experience with my mother's ear-rupturing voice, was momentarily stunned. The impression of a living doll, or a humanized version of some beloved cartoon, was so strong that he quickly recovered himself, and with the unerring instincts of the toddler seized her firmly by the hand and made to lead her to his room for an introduction to the rest of his toys. Her nonchignoned hair was a mess, not in spite but because of the effort she'd made, the front locks pinned unevenly back from her face by a jeweled barrette that might have sooner been worn, and perhaps even made, by a grade-school child. Her eyes were large and startled, like a doe's, and made up to look even larger by thick fronds of mascara which either failed to conceal, or created, a downturned effect, so that her whole expression, even while she was smiling, was droopily wistful. Her frame was very small, and lost beneath a witchy ensemble of black lace and black silken tassels and a black crocheted shawl of connected rosettes. In short, she spoke like a child, and dressed like a granny. I would have given her, if pressed further, a family of cats with whom she shared a secret language; a canopy bed; and at least forty-five years of life. "She's thirty-nine years old," I recalled Dutra stating, though he hadn't been asked, the sameness of their ages made even more doubtful by the fact that beside his new bride he looked many years younger than that.

"Does having a baby take up lots of room?" Nikki was asking me wonderingly, as Lion, having perfunctorily inspected the embarrassment of high-priced new toys he'd released from their wrappings, industriously distributed gift box cardboard and paper so that ankle-deep garbage now covered the floor. "Because Danny's place is so tiny, but every time we come back there from seeing apartments we just love it more. It's so him. It's where we've always known each other."

"It's not babies that take up the space, it's their stuff," I offered, as if not just the union of Dutra and Nikki, but their future offspring, were the oft-sounded themes of our long years of friendly discourse. "All they really need is someplace to sleep."

"But you'd want all those things," Nikki said dreamily.

"Ginny hasn't even seen my apartment in, what, almost four years?"

"You haven't invited us."

"Oh, bullshit. You know you're always welcome to drop by my place. Anyway, Ginny doesn't know all the stuff I've done there."

"Danny has such gorgeous taste," Nikki cried.

"Does he now?" I teased, but this went disregarded.

"She hasn't seen my place in ages," he repeated, as if to explain my extreme ignorance. "I did it all down to the inch in Italian modern. Down to the *inch*. Where I couldn't find the perfect thing I got it custom. Down to the inch. That apartment's only five hundred square feet. When I finished it looked like a loft. Only thing was, I designed it for me."

The surprise of hearing Dutra, for the first time, talk about spending his money was hardly noticeable amid all the other surprises. "We couldn't have a family there," Nikki said with regret of the customized loftlike apartment.

"We couldn't even have a meal. No functional kitchen. When I did the pavlova I had to work on the floor."

"When you did the what?" I said.

"Okay, this was insane." Dutra was laughing. "I had to buy an electric mixer—"

"He hasn't told you about the pavlova?" Nikki's hands flew together at her breast. "It was the *most* romantic thing."

"Nikki's favorite dessert is pavlova—"

"And my favorite ballerina is Pavlova!"

"You know pavlova's meringue with whipped cream. So I'd had our rings made, and I got the idea I'd conceal them inside a pavlova."

How much better it was to stop pretending their story was something expected, and instead give full expression to my incredulity. By so doing I gratified Nikki, who discerned in me no skepticism, only apt astonishment at her good luck. Dutra had, in fact, had their rings made—before he'd even met her, or secured her consent to their marriage, let alone measured her finger. The rings—hewn with their interlocked initials, thick and heavy as signets—were undeniably unique and beautiful. They'd been the devils themselves to suspend in meringue, and Dutra had almost gone mad from the effort, presuming he'd started out sane. The morning that Nikki arrived, on the red-eye from San Diego, neither of them had slept in more than two days, from in his case pavlova and in both cases nerves. Dutra had driven her straight from the airport to Montauk, a takeout picnic brunch from Russ and Daughters, and the pavlova on the rental car's backseat. On the winter-lonely beach he'd watched his guest break meringue with the edge of her spoon until, unable to wait any longer, he'd smashed up the pavlova with his hands and found for her the gob of crusted egg whites, and gold.

Lion was an easy child to put to bed, yet once I'd had him say good night and excused us, and brushed his teeth and tucked him under his covers, I lingered on the floor beside his elf's bed, in the undersea glow of his LED nightlights. Having weathered the night's cooking crisis, I heard Matthew emerge from the kitchen. I could see without actually seeing the hospitable face he would now have put on. He would refill their glasses and gather to him all the loose conversational strands. The compact of marriage: an intricate code of reliance. One always on if the other is off.

One up if the other is down. They would never know how little he'd wanted them here, nor how much I now wished they would leave. I heard their voices, burbling on without impediment, caught in the current of warm fellow-feeling and booze. It was possible I could stay in Lion's room for almost half an hour and not be suspected of anything strange. Only Matthew would wonder, and at the same time assume that a rare freak of Lion's had kept me. A twitch of the threadlike antennae. I was pregnant; a fact so recently established I refused to give it credence. "It's possible," I had told Matthew a few days before, "that in about seven weeks, I'll be about twelve weeks' pregnant. But it's equally possible that I will not." "Equally possible? Exactly the same odds apply?" "Also possible," I'd amended. And that had been that; tell Matthew that a fact was not a fact until further established, and he no more brooded on it than on something he'd never been told.

But Lion; Lion scented a change. The night before, at bedtime, as I was rising from kissing his cheek, he'd seized my hand with such unprecedented strength I had gasped in surprise. "I want to keep you forever," he'd whispered, still squeezing my hand like a vise, and my rush of adoration had been streaked with fear, as if he'd slammed a cage door in my face. "I'll always be your mommy," I'd whispered, already trying to draw my hand free. "No!" he'd said, his other small hand shooting out from his covers to buttress the first. I'd been half an hour extracting myself, my gratification alternating with rising impatience. Since emerging from changeable infancy Lion had been notably self-contained, sitting alone and absorbed with a toy or a book, toddling far away at the playground without so much as a glance at me over his shoulder, and I'd sometimes wondered how much of my enthusiasm for parenthood rested on this foundation. Now, though, with Dutra and Nikki effusing at my dining table, I longed for him to cling and detain me. He settled himself on his pillow, his face turned to the ceiling, hooked one arm around his bear, and closed his eyes. Tonight it was I who kept hold of his hand, and it lay in mine limply relaxed, as soft and slight as the fallen magnolia petals that for the past week had littered the streets. From the living room the voices rose and fell. How long had I been hiding here—five minutes? As many as ten?

"Mommy?" Lion murmured, eyes still smoothly closed.

"Yes, sweetheart?"

"Why you still here?"

"Just making sure you're okay."

"I'm okay."

"Okay, sweetness. Should I go?"

"Okay," he exhaled, dropping off.

Now I was unambiguously truant. A perfect solitude enfolded me, defined by Lion's slow, even breaths. *Coup de foudre.* That was what it was called. Mad love like a bolt from the blue. As different from compatible, practical, let's-live-together-for-four-years-to-make-sure love as an abruptly erupting volcano from a sixty-watt lightbulb. I was jealous of them, I realized, as I was jealous, always, of odd pairs. The fat girl, her upper thighs squashing and squeaking together with each awkward step, and the slender boy tenderly holding her hand. Or the deformed boy, with a withered right arm, and the beautiful blonde twined around his good side. Something foreign to logic cleaved such pairs together: pure ardor. A sheer force of love. Matthew and I were a pair of quite similar envelopes. Close in age, close enough in background, genetically lucky with our looks and our minds. Inclined, for all our supposed hairsbreadth "differences," toward all the same places, people, and things. One might wonder, if feeling unsteady, how deep a deficit of ardor such a list of matched traits could conceal.

It was a dangerous thought and it propelled me from Lion's bedside, back into the convivial glare.

Dutra and Nikki had followed Matthew to the kitchen, where, timers having gone off, the potential for crisis was resurrected. "Can you please set the table?" Matthew muttered at me through his teeth. So I had been gone slightly, or a great deal, too long.

"I had another nightmare getting Lion to bed," I lied, as I sometimes found I could, when the only other witness, not yet having turned three, wasn't likely to give me away.

"Should I go in to him?"

"No, he's asleep finally."

"You've almost missed the whole story of how I almost left Nikki a widow after two weeks of marriage." Dutra barged between us, dumping wine in my glass. "So what happened was, we're in Sousse, on the coast, in this place that's supposed to be famous for seafood, and I order lobster, I fucking love lobster. But Nikki goes, *'Ehhh,'*" Dutra made a moue, "'I'm just not in the mood for seafood,' and she orders, like, pizza! I'm really pressuring her to get lobster. Come on, we should both have the lobster. No no, I'm just not in the mood. I'm frustrated, fuck it, I'll just get the lobster myself."

"He always wants us to do things together," Nikki glowingly clarified.

"So our food comes. Her pizza is—"

"So funny! Like a cake with tomato sauce on it—"

"It's disgusting, completely disgusting, and my lobster is gorgeous. It's this fucking magnificent lobster. And I'm so into it, I'm getting ready, I'm putting my bib on, I've laid out my tools, I get my claw meat out first—"

"Danny always saves the tail for last."

"You know? The meat's less delicate and delicious than the stuff in the claws and the legs, but it's a *steak*. It's a fat, chewy, ocean-grub *steak* and I want to devour the whole thing at once and then relax and doze off like a pig, so I do the fine surgery first. Claws and legs."

"Legs!" Matthew said, for now we were all taking chairs at the table, the roast laid before us, the trough left behind yet again as the four of us rose yet again on a wave. "I should have figured a surgeon could deal with the legs."

"You don't eat the legs?"

"I can never get anything out of there."

"Are you serious? Aren't you from Boston? Matthew, man, we have to go out for lobster some night. I'll school you. Let the girls go out for a girls' night and eat pasta or something, we'll go out for a man's night and eat us some lobster. You will never again leave a lobster a shred of its flesh."

"Where's the part of this story where you almost die?" I cut in.

"It's right here! We've reached it! So I'm happily eating my lobster and," Dutra threw himself out of his chair and collapsed on the floor. *Ech! ech! ech!* came the sounds of his flailing and gasping, obscured from my view by the table.

"It was *unbelievable,*" Nikki took up, her eyes huge. "I was next to him, trying to help him, and all the waiters were just walking by with their noses in the air, saying things like, 'I guess someone's had too much sun!' Finally another tourist couple from France helped me carry him to our hotel. And he was all gray and convulsing and gasping and I couldn't get out of my mind what he'd said—"

"I forgot to tell what I had said," Dutra said, climbing back in his chair. "I knew I was going down. A split second before I went down, I knew I was going. I felt it. Remember, I've been a heroin addict. I've OD'd. I knew my systems were all shutting down, bam-bam-bam. I wasn't sure if they'd ever come back up again. And right before I fell out of my chair, I looked at Nikki and said—"

" *'I'm so sorry,'* " she wailed along with him. " *'I'm so sorry I married you!'* "

Over the neglected roast we gaped at each other, astonished.

"He felt so bad that he'd made me his wife, for just seventeen days, and now he was going to die and abandon me," Nikki explained. "But I wouldn't have been abandoned, because I would have died, too."

After a dumbstruck moment I managed to say to Dutra, "Will you ever eat lobster again?"

"Fuck, are you kidding? I ate lobster the very next day."

"He's *amazing*," Nikki said, beaming.

"*She's* amazing," Dutra corrected. "You know how we found out what happened? She had a BlackBerry with her, you know what that is? She starts going *tap tap*, the next thing you know she has it all figured out: *toxic lobster syndrome*. Certain lobsters, their flesh carries this toxin, you never know if you'll get one or not. People who've eaten it all of their lives, they get one of these, boom, they're dead."

"So you'll still eat it?" I exclaimed in exasperation.

"Sure, won't you? It could happen to any of us."

"If that's true, I don't think that I will!"

"That," Dutra said, "is the difference between us, Virginia."

A great deal, perhaps the whole final hour, of the dinner conversation was given over to plans that we four would embark on as soon as we could—trips to Vietnam and rented houses in Nice, at the very least brunch at their place on the first Sunday that Matthew and Lion and I were at leisure, all proposed by Dutra and Nikki with fervid insistence, as we sat over wrecked roast and glasses of bourbon. At last they were gone, and

Matthew and I spent what seemed an eternity loading the dishwasher before I broke the silence. "Do you think she meant she would have killed herself?"

"What?" Matthew said with terse noncuriosity. "When?"

"When she said that if Dutra had died, then she would have died, too."

"I took it more as a romantic sentiment than a suicide threat."

"I didn't say *threat*. I'm just asking, do you think she meant she would have killed herself?"

"I think I just said no."

Our silence reinstated itself, perhaps the silence of equal exhaustion, a form of union. Or perhaps it was the silence of inward-turned brooding, of taking our measure as a couple against that of our giddy and tireless guests, and finding it short. That task, however much shared, still must count as division. There was a danger in the room that I knew I would have to evade but I wasn't sure how.

"What did you think of her?" I asked at last, and I must have done the trick with my tone, because I felt Matthew actually pause and consider.

"I just don't know," he said at last. "I couldn't get a read on her at all. The only thing I wound up feeling sure of was that she's had more than one thirty-ninth birthday."

"Really?" I cried with delight.

"Oh, yeah. I might have said she's in her mid-forties, but something made me think she's even older than she looks. How girlishly she dresses. And acts."

"So what is *up* with her? Is she after his money?"

"I have no idea. I more wonder what Dutra's after. How long did you say he'd known her? Forty days?"

"As of *today* he's known her forty days. And all forty are since he proposed! But maybe no one's 'after' anything," I allowed. "Maybe it's love." It was easy to be generous now, Matthew's comment having made the possibility seem so remote. Yet in the following days my shame grew at how eager I'd been to discredit them. Who more than Dutra deserved adoration, after so much time spent on his own? *Coup de foudre*; perhaps it was real. One went from believing, when twenty, that it was the one kind of love that was real, to believing, once closer to forty, that it was not only fragile but false—the inferior, infantile, doomed love of twenty-year-olds. Somewhere between, the norms of one culture of love were discarded, and those of the other assumed. When did it happen, at midnight of one's thirty-first birthday? On the variable day that, while browsing a grocery-store aisle with a man, the repeating refrain of the rest of one's life for the first time resounds in one's ear?

Despite all the plans they'd proposed, all the nations they'd felt we should visit and all the brunches they'd promised to serve, in the days, then weeks, after the dinner we heard nothing from Dutra and Nikki, not even a phone call of thanks. It was all of a piece, I concluded, with their passion for each other, which swept up everything within reach, but temporarily and blindly; the accretions fell away again unmissed. After a while of musing and brooding, they fell away from me, too. I did continue to tell the tale of Dutra's toxic lobster syndrome, most often at the playground, to casual acquaintances, when the fitting occasion arose.

After Lion was born, I had gone temporarily crazy. The terror he'd unleashed in me—that he would cease to breathe and stiffen in the night and be blue and ice-cold in the morning; that cars would leap the curb and crush his tiny body as I passed with the stroller; that fever would incinerate him, or the volatile chemicals in the fresh coat of paint on his nursery walls give him brain damage, or that I myself would poison him through some bad thing I ate and passed into my milk—seemed inadequately accounted for by such a simpering phrase as "maternal instinct." "Mother love." "Mama bear, fiercely guarding her cubs." The knowing condescension of my female friends, who had gone before me and now had ancient one- and two-year-olds, and even—this hardly counted anymore—children who went to grade school, left me disgusted and alienated. None of them remotely understood the threats ranged against Lion, or me. For the first time in my life I sincerely contemplated suicide. I wanted to know what foolproof method to use if I lost him. I was aware that losing children had once been routine, and that even now it still happened, and people went on. Such people to me were heroic, and very abstract. Their resilience would never be mine. It was outside my limits.

And yet, at the same time as being engulfed by this postpartum paranoia, I'd been crazily happy. Doom dogged my steps, death displayed all its faces—I had become a compendium of freak deaths, I could find the fatal instrument in the most padded playroom—and life, like the sun's blazing hair in a solar eclipse, only dazzled the more. Each extreme was the back of the other. They couldn't be pried apart, watered down. I'd wondered if anything ever had felt the same way, and of course thought of Martha. But the resemblance was superficial. It only arose from the phrases and words that so poorly described the emotions. The emotions themselves, from one case to the other, had nothing in common. Why then all these overlapped words? *Love. Adoration. Ardor.* All, previously used, now felt a bit grimy to me, not to mention deficient, in the way of *maternal instinct.* There was no language of love that pertained to my child. Perhaps this was why I couldn't bear to lose sight of him—because there weren't symbols to translate him to me, to capture his essence and keep it preserved.

"I'm not sure if I can stand to have another one," I'd said to Matthew, "and I'm not sure if I can stand not to." Matthew, in his infinite wisdom, had said, "Let's discuss it on Lion's second birthday, and until then not discuss it at all." It was essentially what we had done. The very night of Lion's second-birthday party, the bright-colored paper plates heaped in the trash, I'd entered our bedroom with drama, while Matthew was reading, and lowered the lights.

"Is this the discussion?" he murmured, as I tugged off his boxers and, burrowing, even peeled off his socks. "I object . . ." Matthew's muffled voice said, "to this demeaning treatment . . ." But the rest of the subject was examined without use of words.

I'd always known Matthew wanted more children; it was me we had wondered about. Me and my stated historical lack of ambition to ever have children; my remote and beneficent attitude toward them; my nice-place-to-visit-but-don't-ever-need-to-live-there. Once Lion was born I could not fathom how such ideas had ever been mine. What had made me imagine that children were optional for me? Again I thought of Martha, and her very imperfect example of motherhood. And, though I might have expected to judge her more harshly, I found myself forgiving her instead, for those countless superiorities of hers, by which I'd felt crushed, which she turned out to have never possessed. She had not been infallible. The realization was melancholy instead of triumphant, and I remembered my confusion, a few years before, when I'd found myself having lunch in Manhattan at the same restaurant where amid untold glamour she'd treated me to my first oysters. The intervening decade alone could not have accounted for how small and out of style and even shabby it had somehow become.

One hot May morning I awoke three months' pregnant, by the clock I'd set seven weeks back. Matthew's head lay dented in his kingly pile of pillows like a bust made of lead, his breathing magically silent, testimony to the power of the strange nasal tape he applied without fail every night. "Wake up, Tiger," I said, climbing on him. "Awful news. Lion's getting a teammate."

"Another one?" Matthew cried sleepily. "God, no. We'll die in the poorhouse."

Dutra was the crimp in my elation: I realized seven weeks was the same span of time since we'd had him and Nikki to dinner. Had they spent it in bed? As always I called him at his hospital, despite the change in his domestic conditions, despite the fact that he now had an actual wife who might be sitting at that moment on his Italian Modern chaise, blissfully fielding his incoming calls. As always the mellifluous switchboard attendant put me straight through to his office, and as always he answered—"When do you do your lifesaving surgery, anyway?" I demanded as greeting, because the rare times I remembered it was a pleasure to inflict on him the sort of verbal ambush he routinely doled out.

"All the fucking time, Ginny, except I do still allow myself lunch, and you might have noticed that your biannual phone calls to me are always at the lunch hour, because you can't bring yourself to call me unless you're also making a sandwich, so you don't have to feel like you're wasting your time."

The son of a bitch: I *was* making a sandwich. I stopped mid-scrape of the knife over bread out of fear he would hear it. "For Pete's sake, Dutra, it's you who owes me a phone call. I haven't spoken to you since we had you and Nikki to dinner. Ever heard of 'thank you'?"

"You didn't get Nikki's note?"

"Nikki's what?"

"Forget it. It's probably still in her purse. Or she put it in the mail without a stamp. Or she never remembered to write it at all. Sorry. I should've just called but she was all into writing a note. I should have known that she wouldn't."

"How are you guys?" I asked after a moment.

"Divorcing. And you?"

It seemed so certain Dutra must have been aware of my skepticism about his marriage that my first reaction was tainted by guilt. For a moment I could not even lay hold of empathy, so self-regardingly worried was I to sound sufficiently shocked. Yet I was shocked—no less for not being surprised that the marriage had failed. I just hadn't imagined the failure would have the same speed as the marriage itself. "Oh, shoot, Dutra," I exclaimed. I realized I'd been able to put Dutra out of my mind not despite, but because of his marriage—because his marriage had let me believe, as one always longs to believe of that worrisome parent or sibling or friend, that against all the odds, a lifetime of increasingly lonely cantankerousness had by some miracle been avoided. "I'm so sorry. What happened?"

"Have lunch with me. I don't want to talk on the phone."

"Of course," I said, now falling all over myself to accommodate him. "Do you want me to meet you near work?"

"I'll come to you. I can't eat around here."

Such was his brusque urgency that I agreed to meet him the very next day, at the nicest restaurant in my neighborhood I could think of—"Whatever," he'd said when I asked him his preferences, "something decent. With wine." At ten-thirty that morning my phone rang. It was Dutra, barely audible amid an atmospheric howl as if he stood on the deck of a ship. "I'm coming now," he said.

"What?" I said.

"Now," he was repeating, almost barking, perhaps only to cleave through the interference, ". . . need to see you now," and half an hour later we'd converged at the restaurant, an hour earlier than we had planned. It had only just opened for business. The white light of midmorning drenched the farmhouse-quaint room, with its varnished plank floorboards and bare wooden tables and nude brick and undraped windows which amplified and ricocheted the slightest noise, but despite this Dutra's voice didn't scale itself down—when had it ever? "You choose, I could give a shit," he said with echoing clarity of the tables, all equally unoccupied, which the flustered waitress indicated to us with a sweep of her arm while retreating, her apron not yet tied, to the shelter of a cappuccino station. "Bring us a wine list," Dutra called peremptorily after her as I led him to a table beside the front window.

"How about 'please,'" I suggested, as if he were Lion.

"Too hot," Dutra said of the table. "I can't sit in the sun. It's a furnace outside."

"How about this one, then."

"That'll be in full sun in a couple of hours."

"And we're planning to be here how long?"

"Don't be so eager to leave."

"I'm not, Dutra, but since you don't care at all where we sit can you please choose a table?"

"So controlling, Ginny," he admonished as he dropped into a chair at the least sheltered, least intimate, most central and visible table, like planting his flag, in the act grandiosely extending his arm at the opposite chair as if I were the one who was picky—but I saw he took no pleasure in the gibe and might not even realize he'd said it. "I've been fired," he announced as I sat. "And blacklisted. I'll never operate again. At least not in New York."

It was possible my mouth was hanging literally open. Since we'd met on the sidewalk outside I'd been trying to ask him, hitting just the right note of alacrity, what had happened with Nikki, for I'd assumed that his crisis with her was the reason he wanted to see me. But the collapse of his marriage was miles downstream, far beneath our attention—not to mention my still-unannounced pregnancy, which I now couldn't manage announcing. "I had a hunch they would do it today," he went on. "Friday. Traditional day of the axe." He was deeply agitated. It was only by a Herculean effort of the will that he sat in his chair instead of hurling it and its identical brethren and anything else not tied down through the window. He kept twisting one way, then the other, jutting his long legs to alternate sides, and then twisting to check on the waitress, who'd ducked out of sight. "Excuse me!" he said.

"I'm sorry, you *what*?" I repeated. "How can *you* have been fired? Can they even do that?"

"Of course they can. Hel*lo*," he greeted our waitress with a psychotic sudden onslaught of charm as she ventured toward us.

"Oh, the wine list!" she exclaimed.

"Y'*know*," he stilled her with his voice, "you can forget about the wine list if you've got some Beaujolais you can bring us. You *do*? Oh, that's *awesome*. I don't want it warm," he warned her as she hastened to fetch it.

"What happened?"

"They wanted to get me. Real bad. And they finally got me."

"Who?"

"All the fucking nobodies. That's what they are. Fucking nobody, no-talent pricks hanging on to their power."

Friend of his childhood as I essentially was, utterly ignorant of the nature of his actual work, let alone the politicized hierarchies within which it took place, I was either the worst person or the best person in the world to whom he could unburden himself, given how much tutelage I required to follow the story. But in any case I was perhaps the only person. And it didn't make him impatient to have to explain every detail to me, but calmed him, to the extent he could ever be calm.

For years I'd assumed that Dutra, because so highly paid and sought after, must be highly valued as well, by anyone who could matter. This had been, it turned out, only partly true, but his troubles hadn't arisen from the fact that not everyone valued him equally. They arose from the fact that certain people valued him so highly, above everyone else, and that this favoritism coincided with a standing controversy. Dutra's field, like any field of science, was constantly riven by theoretical and practical disagreements, but all these disagreements, and their perpetrators, could roughly be sorted into one of two camps: the camp that left the paradigm of Western medical practice intact, defending it from all outside threats; and the camp that posed the threats—that sought, in other words, nothing less than a paradigm shift. The direction of shift, within camp, was not always harmonious, but by and large it tended east, toward China. I felt only momentary surprise to learn that Dutra not only threw in his lot with the paradigm shifters but was their prize specimen and their chief troublemaker. The surprise I felt because Dutra was, on his surface, so little a crusading world changer. He was a nonjoiner, a prankster and cynic who only recycled for money, who mocked vegans for their pious narcissism, who had never, to my knowledge, cast a ballot in any election because no candidate had ever failed to earn his contempt. But, as I say, all this surprise was momentary, because once he offered this alternate glimpse of himself, I realized what had always been obvious: Dutra was the only true idealist I'd ever known. He was intolerant to the utmost degree of waste, incompetence, disorganization, incompletely implemented knowledge, and wrongheaded priorities—he was intolerant, in other words, of human life, and all human-built systems, including the system of care at his hospital.

The head of Dutra's hospital—Dutra's boss, a category of person I'd not thought existed—was a hidebound Western-style traditionalist who disliked Dutra, finding him a loudmouthed irreverent prick, and was disliked by Dutra in turn, but the animus between the two men only made up a baseline and could have repeated forever. It was a third factor—external and wealthy—that provided the tune. The hospital's board of directors, as picturesque a collection of white-skinned and white-haired rich people as convened to do good anywhere in Manhattan, were for the most part ignorant or indifferent to such controversies of practice as Dutra had begun kicking up—for example, Dutra's declaration that a large percentage of the surgeries performed at the hospital, his included, were profit-driven and unnecessary; or Dutra's insistence that the hospital spearhead American use of supposedly uniquely efficacious Chinese traditional herbs. Either the board members knew nothing of all this, or didn't take sides, but one of them, a well-known philanthropist, got on Dutra's bandwagon and made it her own. She and Dutra twice traveled to China, and grew thick as thieves. At last she announced her intention of endowing the hospital with countless millions of dollars to establish a research institute. Its aim would be the reconciliation of the medical theories and practices of the East and the West, and its director would be Dutra.

"So you might say, Sounds pretty opportunistic, but believe it or not, and it doesn't matter either way, I didn't want her to pull the trigger on the institute. My contract with the hospital was supposed to be up at the end of this year and I knew I was leaving. No way I'd stay, even if I wanted to. I've been saying no to jobs all over the country the whole time I've been chained at that place because, idiot that I am, I didn't want to leave New York. But with the idea for the institute coming together I decided I had to get out. Find a real place, a real way to do this. Not a bullshit way to do this. So whatever Feshbach"—his boss—"wants to say, that I had this board member under my thumb, her going ahead with her gift is the proof that I didn't. Doing that, she signed my death warrant. Feshbach had to get rid of me fast, before my contract came up for renewal and I nailed this directorship. He had to bust ass to hang on to the money and get rid of me."

"But how could he? He needs you! Without you that woman won't donate."

"Of course she will. She did. Rich people are like that, they get excited and want to throw money around. She didn't need me to do that. The institute'll bear her name whether I'm there or not."

"But you're the whole reason for it! Isn't she loyal to you?"

"Shit no. She's putting distance between us right now. By five o'clock she won't ever have met me."

"But *why*—"

"Because of how they did it, Ginny. Not to mention I've lost all my power. But it's the *way* that I've lost all my power." His voice faltered abruptly, broke off mid-harangue, and he recrossed his long legs with violence and peered out the window. "They did me so good. The one way that, the more I fight back the more done in I am."

They'd gotten him on sexual harassment. The accusation and perhaps even the crime seemed equally unthinkable and inevitable, and for a damning moment my voice failed me from my fear it was true. He'd mastered himself again, whatever rivulets of moisture had ventured to travel his tear ducts had been scorched away, and he was watching me closely. "Never happen," he coldly assured me. "I don't shit where I eat."

"That metaphor's disgusting and doesn't make sense," I snapped, hiding my shame with annoyance.

"Then no metaphor: I don't fuck where I work. I don't fuck, I don't flirt, and I sure as shit never harass."

"I know that you wouldn't."

"Yeah, sure. But you can *imagine* me doing it, can't you? Come on. I know you can. You've known me a long time, you know me probably better than anyone else. You and Alicia. And you can imagine it."

"No, I can imagine other people imagining it."

"Short step. And don't think I'm wounded. I'm an asshole. I shoot my mouth off. I make people uncomfortable. Do I say rude, raunchy shit in the OR to put myself at ease and keep my brain from imploding? Fuck yes, I do. The stress I'm under, most people would die or they'd start killing others. I *save* people and in the process I sometimes crack jokes, fucking send me to jail. Bathroom humor, sex humor, whatever fucking humor I can find in there, they should be grateful—men, women, doctors, interns, patients, janitors, I hassle *everybody*, I fuck with *everybody*, I don't *exploit my position of power*. I don't *create a hostile work environment for women*. All my life I've been a loudmouth, all my career I've been a loudmouth, from the day I walked into that hospital I've been a loudmouth and people might not like it but they have to accept it because I'm great at what I do so tough shit."

But little by little, until fatally, Dutra's enemies at the hospital had come to outnumber his admirers, in a process having little to do with his jokes. It had never helped him that his most passionate admirers were his patients and their family members, who, because he did so well by them, dispersed. While his enemies—the surgical colleagues whose judgments he actively questioned or whose glory he passively, inevitably stole; the workaday inferiors whose lapses in hygiene protocol, and mishandlings of crucial equipment, and countless other health-endangering manifestations of incompetence or laziness he tirelessly reprimanded—stayed on, nursing grudges into vendettas. It had been remarkably easy, Dutra had discovered this morning, for Feshbach to find employees who were willing to swear, in signed but confidential statements, that Dutra had sexually menaced them, with lewd demands and plausible threats. Dutra's signature style—his big mouth—was not the crime so much as circumstantial evidence.

"You have to fight this," I begged him, for somewhere in the course of his telling I had seen him see himself: outmaneuvered, but above that, unloved. His face had gone gray with fatigue. A barely perceptible scrim—like the chic window shades that our waitress was now lowering, which did not shade the windows at all but did turn outside forms vague and dull—had come over his eyes.

"No point. They never charged that I fucked anyone. They know I could dispute that. This, I can't dispute without looking more guilty. A Chinese finger trap."

"You *can* dispute it," I said. "They're ruining your reputation. Smearing you."

"Yeah. I'll try. I made a call to a lawyer." But the effort of telling me this seemed the most he would make. Drained of his story, his bile, he was growing inert, though perhaps inertia was not overtaking him, but being willed from within. After we both had been silent a moment he reached for his wineglass and I saw his hand trembling.

"Wouldn't trust me with a scalpel," he said.

From the restaurant we went to a bar farther down the same block, my answer to his question, "Where can we keep drinking?" He'd never noticed he was drinking alone. I called Matthew clandestinely from the women's bathroom. "I need a huge favor. I'd never ask if it wasn't important, but I need you to come home and take over from Myrna. She leaves at two-thirty so you'll have to come now."

"What's going on? Where are you?"

All duplicity failed me. "At a bar. With Dutra."

"Jesus, Regina. You're asking me to cut short my workday so you can sit in a bar? With *Dutra*? You're not drinking, are you?"

"Of course not! What would make you say that? I'm sitting with him because he's been fired. I can't leave him alone. I'm afraid what he'll do."

"So take him with you to our house. For fuck's sake, Regina. I have meetings today."

"You have meetings *every* day, and every day, at two-thirty, I drop whatever I'm doing, and I go home to Lion—"

"Oh, is that what this is about? Is that what we're talking about?"

"Don't ask me to bring a blind drunk potential suicide who's been fired *and* is *getting-divorced-by-the-way* home to play with our child! Can't you please just get here? Have I ever once asked you to do this?"

After a pause Matthew said, through a locked jaw, "I'll be there."

"I'll get home as soon as I can. Maybe you can get back to the office by four—" I began to appease, but he'd already hung up on me.

At the bar Dutra said with impatience, "Tell the guy what you want. We've been waiting for you."

"I'm just drinking seltzer," I reminded him pointedly, as if this placed a limit on not just libations but time. Still, one hour passed, and then two, and we entered a third, discussing I no longer even knew what. I finally said, "Dutra, what happened with Nikki? Was there any connection?"

"With this?" He stared blearily. "No. Of course not."

"Then what happened?"

"She just wasn't the person I thought she was."

"Like she assumed a false identity? She was a criminal? She had a sordid past?"

"No. No. Just—she was disorganized. She wasted money. She made stupid decisions."

"But what do you mean? What sorts of stupid decisions?"

"Like that trip to Tunisia. She did most of the planning. The bookings and stuff. She was a travel agent for a while, before I met her. It was her idea we honeymoon there. I figured she must be savvy, know all the secret places. The good deals. The stuff it's worth traveling for. But the place she booked us, it was cheesy. So, okay, maybe Tunisia hasn't got something better. Then the next month I look at my credit card bill, this mediocre place she booked cost like four thousand dollars a week. She just—she hadn't even *tried* to find something good. She just took the first thing she found. And she's like that with everything."

"The pizza like cake."

"The everything. This is a woman who worked as a travel agent, real estate agent, jewelry maker, hair cutter, art-gallery sales whatever, publicist whatever, event planner whatever, lived in Tucson, Fort Lauderdale, Miami, Key West, Houston, L.A., San Diego, I don't even know where the fuck else, just randomly doing whatever. No choices. No thought."

"Just randomly choosing, say, you."

He shrugged. "Who the fuck knows."

"Dutra, Nikki pursued you from the far side of the continent. Two years after she met you. That wasn't random. She was crazy about you."

With head flung back he drained his pint glass. "I'm not divorcing her because she doesn't love me."

"So it's you, divorcing her?"

"She knows it's not working." He had summoned the bartender. "Double shot of Maker's Mark, rocks, and another pint of whatever this was. And whatever she's having."

"I'm having seltzer," I reminded him, and of his order, "Wow. The more things change."

"It's been a long time since I've had the freedom to drink to the full extent of my abilities."

"Maximize your potential."

"Finish what I've started."

"Why not do that with Nikki?"

"Because," he said, demolishing his bourbon, "she can't do that with anything."

"That's just a waste of ice, the way you're drinking."

"The next one I'll get neat."

"Have your feelings about her so totally changed?"

"Why are we talking about this? Even if I'd wanted to stay married this morning, this afternoon it would still have to end."

"Because this is the nineteenth century? Because you have to support your poor helpless wife in the style to which she's grown accustomed?"

"Nicely said."

"Why can't she support you?"

"That's an awesome idea. Can you guess how much debt she brought into the marriage? No? I couldn't either. It was really nice. I got to be surprised."

I called home clandestinely again from the bathroom, interrupting Matthew giving Lion his dinner. It was a pleasure Matthew rarely if ever enjoyed on his own—on the weekends we did it together. I could hear from the dilation of his voice, its rare musical lift, that he'd boxed up his anger at me. He would not let it spoil the windfall of a long afternoon with his son. "So," he said, between a stream of asides on the subject of carrots to Lion, "job loss *and* divorce?"

"And more. They got him on a bogus charge of sexual harassment. I'll explain it all later. I think he's coming to dinner."

Matthew loudly deflated. "That's not ideal. We've got steaks. Two of them."

"Can you cut them some way to serve three?"

"Jesus, Regina. They're T-bones." A dark pause. "I'll try. I'll make extra potatoes."

"It's just I get the feeling he's afraid to be alone."

"I think at this point you could forgivably hand him off to someone else for the rest of the night."

"There is no one else. I'm actually the only friend he has."

Through the phone I could almost hear Matthew's mind register this—a fact he would have never conceived on his own, but that was of course indisputably true. It explained a great deal.

"Bring him on then," Matthew said with exaggerated weariness, the degree of exaggeration a peace offering to me. And so I felt the relief of his forgiveness, and envisioned, once we'd hung up the phone, the parallel tracks of dismay and determination scored onto his brow as he embarked on our dinner. Matthew's annoyance at having two steaks and three people was a very separate thing from his habitual coolness toward Dutra. It would have arisen regardless of whom I'd brought home. Perhaps a legendary hostess of a previous age had transmigrated into Matthew, bringing with her a horror of impromptu or "make-do" arrangements, and an ardent desire to furnish each guest with precisely his keenest desires. Now that Dutra was coming, Matthew was annoyed that he didn't have a standing rib roast, or a contrasting first course, or exceptional wine, or an unopened bottle of rare Armagnac he could set before Dutra once dinner was cleared, for Dutra alone to deflower the seal. Matthew's lavish fastidiousness frequently came in conflict with my exactly opposed tendencies, my miserly attempts to make a meal for five stretch to eight, my noninterest in matching place settings, my "first courses" of olives served out of the plastic tub bearing the price tag, but little by little, in the years we'd been cohabitating, I'd found some of my impatience with him converted to admiration, and some of my admiration even to feeble emulation, so that, steering Dutra back onto the street, I stopped into the deli to buy bread and olives and cheese, and imagined preslicing the bread and the cheese, and presenting the olives in one bowl, with a second nearby for the pits.

I realized how eager I was to get home. The abrupt desolation of Dutra's existence felt threatening, as if it might spread. Where was my own generosity, my own tenderness toward him? I was less caregiver than captive, wondering, as I stole sidelong glances at him pacing stone-faced beside me, just how long it would last—and I remembered, as I hadn't in years, the girl who'd fainted off her feet at our party, and how cheerfully Dutra had hefted her into his arms.

At the corners I told him, "Let's cross," or "Let's turn," as if leading a blind man. Otherwise we had stopped talking. Dutra less followed me than was impelled by my movement, like a bit of detritus aligned with my slipstream and drifting along. Perhaps he less feared aloneness than had somehow forgotten about it. Coming into our apartment he received a glass of wine, a plate of food, a snifter of brandy, Matthew's undivided attention, and even, to my silent gratitude, Matthew's sympathy, as if it had all been arranged weeks before; and to my surprise Dutra did talk, relating to Matthew everything he had already told me, but with an altered, more remote and knowing style. It was possible for him to discuss with Matthew the disintegration of his professional life much as he might have discussed the malfeasance of the Bush administration or the financial collapse of the recording industry. But his persistence at our table, and the swiftly dwindling brandy, told the truth. I began to think I'd have to bed him down on the couch. Near one in the morning Matthew excused himself, rounding the table to shake hands with Dutra, which connection turned into a clumsy embrace and a clap on the shoulder. Then it was Dutra and I and a near-empty bottle beside Dutra's glass and Dutra still didn't move. "I've got to go to bed, too," I asserted at last, and like a paraplegic Dutra planted his palms on the table and hauled himself onto his feet.

"You have a cigarette?" he asked.

"You know I don't smoke anymore."

"Bodega near here?"

"On the way to the train."

In fourteen hours he'd consumed with no assistance at all four bottles of wine, ten pints of beer, and a liter each of bourbon and brandy, yet he perfectly bisected the doorframe and hallway. Feet neither wandered nor hands braced the wall. He only threatened to plunge through the floor with the force of a meteorite, as if he were made of cast iron. I'd find him smoldering in the subbasement, sunk to the neck in the poured-concrete floor. Outside he dropped onto the steps leading up to our entrance while I stood, debating. Sitting as well might suggest he was welcome to sit there all night, but standing was too dictatorial. I might have already told him I needed to sleep, but I wasn't some bartender tossing him out. I sat. The warm night was silken, its tenderness almost unwelcome; sharing the secret of such nights as this seemed a part of my youth I would never regain, this night and my discomfort in it the proof. All the numerous kindnesses Dutra had done me, those many occasions on which he'd maddened me with his arrogant competence, now presented themselves to my mind. I couldn't think of one kindness I'd done in return. Perhaps my acquiescence in his dogged belief that our friendship was deathless, at least not to be killed by betrayal or any other such finite cataclysm of feeling, had been my kindness to him. My declining to swear or hang up when he'd called that night almost a decade ago, what had seemed like so many years later, and what now was nearly twice that many years in the past. "Hey, Gin," he'd begun without the slightest preamble. "Didja know there's *five* Regina Gottliebs in the book, and you're the fifth one I called?" Having missed him so much I'd thought, All right, I'll play. I'll play along and pretend it's all right, and in this way obtain reckoning. But who had been playing—deluded—and who simply stating the facts? Hadn't Dutra, in calling, asserted the fact of our friendship, and in that way pried me loose of a chimera? For I never had stopped loving Martha, but Martha herself had been leached of reality for me, and Dutra far more than the passage of time deserved credit for that. The passage of time, left alone, burnished her and concealed her flaws. Dutra jettisoned her and forbade recollection. If I'd asked him, that first night in years that we spoke on the phone, "Have you also found Martha?" his reply would have been "Martha who?" But of course I did not even mention her name. I accepted the premise he offered. He embodied those years of my life, and if he didn't know her, she didn't exist.

I realized I'd gotten my reckoning from him already.

At this hour my unbeautiful block, with its broad deserted sidewalks, and its facing chain link parking lot now plunged into darkness like a secretive garden, and its restive ailanthus trees brooming their leaves through the pools of street light, had the feel of the deep countryside, as if that feeling came up all the time through the pavement, but could only be felt during near-perfect moments of hush. A delivery boy in cooks' whites and a white paper hat on his head glided by on a bike, as if towed by his handlebar freight of a great padded cube of stacked pizzas. From many blocks distant we heard drunken singing. Beside me Dutra metamorphosed. Dutra's steady ascent as the years slipped away had concealed the years somehow, his arrow and time's keeping pace. Now abruptly his fell and I gazed on a middle-aged man. Perhaps this was the relativity Dutra had labored so hard, and with such total lack of success, to elucidate to me, while sprawled on that scratchy orange couch we had shared. Two airplanes fly next to each other and onboard them no one gets old . . . I could not have it right. I longed to have something to ask him so that he could lord over me with his vast erudition. Instead I asked, "Are you taking the subway?" and with this he unfolded and rose to his feet, and I stood up also, now too close beside him to look into his face.

"I'll walk." When I protested he added, "What, you think Big Bad Brooklyn'll eat me? Don't forget I was born here. I'll survive."

"You were born in Queens."

"So much the worse."

"I just meant it'll take you so long."

"It'll take me an hour or so. I've got plenty of time." Without warning he crushed me against him. "I love you," he stated, as if bracing for a rebuttal. Before I could gasp out an echo he added, "I love you, I love my mommy, I love Alicia." He released me. His "mommy": mocking her, mocking himself, mocking all of us? Even with sarcasm he could not get the better of what he had said. He stood staring just past my ear, his eyes damp.

"Don't you love any men?"

"I love Lion."

"You hardly know Lion."

"He's your kid. I love him." Now he'd mastered himself. "You locked out?"

It was the moment to tell him, the first time in this long day and night that I'd felt I could seize his attention and turn it to me and the child I was going to have. Yet I couldn't. It would have felt like kicking him. Instead I said, "I've got keys in my pocket."

"Okay. Tell Matthew thanks for the food." He turned to go.

"I love you too," I said then, to his back.

"I know, Ginny. So long." And he sprang down the steps as if newly awake and strode off.

Not a week later Myrna greeted me, on my return home, with a look of rebuke and a phone number scrawled on a sheet of notepaper. "That gentleman called here again. This time he used up all the tape so to make him stop calling I picked the phone up." She looked much as I imagined she would after plunging her arm shoulder-deep in our hamper. "He asked me to give you a message. I had a great difficult time hearing him. It sounded to me like he called from inside a tornado."

In fact he had called from a rented convertible traveling west at high speed through the state of Wyoming. "That's when he calls to say goodbye: from *Wyoming*," I told Matthew later, aggrieved. Dutra had sold all his assets, or left them in somebody's care to be sold, and gotten onto I-80 with no clear destination in mind. At least, none he'd shared with Myrna. Just his mobile phone number. When I called I got a boilerplate message that the Sprint customer I was trying to reach must have strayed out of range.

T hat June a friend who taught French at Columbia offered me keys to her on-campus office; she was spending the summer in Paris. By then I was known in my circle of friends for my vagabond work habits, which gave visual expression, as I aimlessly wandered the streets with my laptop in tow, to the aimlessness that for years had afflicted my mind. Since Lion's birth, and his complete annexation of our cluttered apartment, I had "worked" on my third, as yet nebulous, book in the apartments of neighbors of ours when they went on vacation, in the circulation library of the local Catholic college until they expelled me, in an unheated, sawdust-choked former sculpture studio in an unheated, rat-infested loft building beside the expressway, and in any number of other unsuitable places which only had in common being neither my home nor a place that sold coffee. I could not even pretend to work at home or in public cafés, though I barely did better elsewhere; hence my ongoing quest. After all, I had a book many years overdue and a new baby coming, and amid this excitement of certain disaster my friend's offer seemed like a lifeboat: I'd have a manuscript finished by August! Even the commute to the office was fortunate. Much as I liked spending days in our neighborhood, I hated those jarring encounters that often took place, between Myrna and Lion and me, as I toiled with my laptop from one possible spot to another. Hated them no less if they took place at a distance—myself spotting Myrna and Lion, but remaining unseen—than if us three, heedlessly turning corners, were abruptly and queasily brought face to face. Unfocused enough as it was I became even more so, stung by the sight of my child getting on with his life very well without me. And so the train ride to Morningside Heights was a welcome adventure, like my own daily Paris, with its new rituals and refuges. I liked most my own newness: it felt like years since I had worn the city's anonymity.

Despite that it was just a few days before I saw Nicholas.

I was sitting on the traffic-median bench at Broadway and 112th Street, on the pretext, not that anyone would ask, of riding out a mild bout of nausea, but really for the view of St. John the Divine to my left, and of a framed square of the secretive lushness of Riverside Park down the street's steep incline to my right. I was on my way home, it being almost two P.M., the end of my workday, though the sun felt like noon and the day hardly started. I'd been doing all right in the office, amid the strident spines of the complete Irigaray and de Beauvoir keeping march around the walls, but with the commute I didn't even have four hours left for my work, and a good part of that was spent browsing the lunchtime selections on Broadway. Each day I'd felt more reluctance to pack up and leave. Today, dragging my feet, I'd skipped the subway station at 116th and kept walking, and now as if like my bench mates I had hours to burn was lounging on a bench two blocks shy of the next stop at 110th, between a bunion-tormented overweight woman and a small, birdlike man. The man was working a crossword I'd begun to spy on—I was just trying to read his next clue when I saw Nicholas clatter past with the traffic, so near I might have reached out and caught at his sleeve.

"That boy will get himself killed," said the woman, who had seen him also. Hearing this my shock turned to delight, and I started to laugh. The woman must have been well past seventy. I was now thirty-six. Which made "that boy," Nicholas . . . fifty-four? Whatever his age, he had changed very little. What I'd glimpsed of his style was different, but so akin to his previous style in flamboyance that the two ways of dressing together expressed more about him than either would have considered alone. He'd been wearing a three-piece tweed suit in a color that read, at that speed, as dark gold, with a bright green bow tie, polished caramel shoes, and some sort of elasticized bands binding up his pants cuffs. He'd been on an old black no-speed bicycle, with fenders and a rack to which was tied a briefcase of some kind. He'd been wearing no helmet, the probable source of my companion's comment, though she might also have noticed that he rode in precisely the least legal and least secure place, on the inside of the inner, fast lane, with the murderous cabs. Nor did he wear glasses or shades. I had seen, bearing toward me in all calm intentness, his narrow and elegant face.

I'd spent the greatest portion of my life now in New York, more years than I'd ever lived anywhere else. Here was the bedrock and topsoil, here the place seeds had sprouted and flourished or died; here I'd been young with some people who were already growing cantankerous; here I'd found my husband and given birth to my child and here the only world that child yet knew. I could accommodate my pre–New York life; four times a year I played host to my mother as she tirelessly circled the globe, and I continued to know people from my school days and even my childhood. But these threads had stitched themselves into New York. They were a part, however small, of the cloth of my life in this place. While Nicholas, by contrast, was not. He'd been severed from me totally. Yet it was far less his absence from me than my absence from him that to me made the difference. For him, nothing of my life—my real, full New York life—had yet happened! It was all in the future—how then could *he* still exist? He had not quite seemed to, passing by on Broadway. He must have been a phantom, or a prank.

I saw him again the next week, from a far more serene bench on Morningside Drive. It was true I'd been aimlessly walking the streets, aimlessly sitting on benches without so much as the newspaper for occupation, somewhat more in the interval. Perhaps I'd spent my working hours outdoors, far away from my laptop, because the weather was clear, blue, and hot, and because walking limbers the mind. But it was equally true I hadn't written a word since I'd seen him. I'd sat in the office relaxed as a fist, attentive to physical signs that I might need a bagel. The bench on which I'd paused now was en route to the famous pastry shop and literary enclave where such, unlike me, as can write in a place that sells coffee would sit hours on end, gazing loftily into their thoughts. I hadn't really wanted to go there. There were only a few passersby, the Drive otherwise quiet and sun drenched, a far cry from Broadway. We might as well have been alone. There was no avoiding the encounter, unless, rattling swiftly uptown again, energetically pedaling, he failed to recognize me. It was possible; I was fourteen years older. But he did recognize me, and even seemed gladly amazed.

"My God, Regina," he cried, at the same time as he swung a leg over his seat without ceasing to glide, so that he rolled to an elegant stop, perched upright on one pedal. He could only have mastered that trick as a boy, the devilishly handsome blond boy he had been growing up in Vancouver. Where I'd known him bikes had been pointless: everyone had driven up and down the escarpment, or slogged the stair-steps in the sidewalks on foot. Now I was surprised to realize that I, too, had been absent from critical parts of his life. I had never suspected he might be a cyclist, as if he'd been born onto pedals the way some are born into the saddle. And so my whole history with him coincided with a time of exile from his native conditions.

He must have been happy to be in New York, where the whole level city lies spread for the cyclist who isn't afraid of collisions. He clearly was not. Once again he did not wear a helmet, and once again he did wear a flamboyantly beautiful suit, just two pieces this time, no bow tie, bespoke shirt with a pale pink pinstripe.

"Do you live here now?" I asked, the greatest shock how unshocking it felt, to be standing before him again.

"Now? I've been here for more than a decade. Eleven years come September."

"I can't believe we've both lived in New York all that time. Although I've been in Brooklyn."

"As I know, having read the Author's Note of your book with the same delight that I read every word preceding. It's a wonderful book, Regina. How nice to get the chance to congratulate you directly. All the while I was reading it I kept thinking, What a good thing she's made! It must be satisfying."

I didn't protest his absurdly outsize compliment, just accepted with thanks—I'd learned at least one thing since last he'd known me. What I did linger over, in silence, was that I hadn't been absent to him after all. Any pleasure this might have yielded was obscured right away by the knowledge he'd known I was here and not contacted me. But why would he? I'd known where he was, or had thought that I did, and not contacted him.

We walked together, he pushing the old bicycle. I let him do all of the talking, which task he performed with easy, boyish garrulity, speaking of the neighborhood, of his apartment in a dignified building on 119th Street which within a few minutes we slowly went past, of his many terrible and few promising students, of school controversies and colleagues. In fact he knew my friend the French professor, but not at all well. "How smart of you, leaving your own home to write. It must give you such clarity."

"I hardly have a choice. At home there's a three-year-old boy who takes my efforts to write as a personal insult."

The disclosure delighted, but didn't seem to surprise him, and he didn't pursue me for details. Instead he said, with satisfaction, "I always knew you'd make a wonderful mother."

Now my heart did lurch into my ribs. "Really? Why?"

"Oh, of course," he evaded the question.

We came to the quad, then his building, within clear sight of the French department building wherein was the office I already knew I would not use again, and at last to his department mailbox, and all that while I felt eyes fix on me, as his companion, just as I'd felt them in the past. And just as in the past, he ignored the persistent yet guttering spotlight of furtive attention, performing his envelope errands, then leading me back as we'd come. His grimy Parisian building, with its worn-off gold numbers and sleepy doorman, once again was in sight. "Are you hungry?" he said. "Won't you come up for lunch?" And before I could speak, coded reassurance: "You'll give me a nice change from eating alone."

Still my heart shuddered and tried to escape as we mounted the three steps beneath the awning and crossed the tiled lobby to the ancient elevator and rose to the tenth, topmost floor. His apartment, at last, gave a tangible shape to the passage of time. Now even that glacial, underfurnished apartment of his postdivorce year seemed in retrospect meager, ad hoc, a place of scuffed walls and cheap kitchen utensils. Here was grandeur. Banks of west-facing windows gave a view all the way to the Hudson and Palisades, over the bowed heads of inferior buildings.

Enormous squares of art fenestrated the walls, each piece an oblique re-minder of the styles I remembered him loving, the unelaborate Inuit whalebone figurines, and Mondrian's bright demarcations, and Fried-rich's humbling fields of ice. On the walls that were not hung with art stood cliff-faces of well-ordered books, housed in beautifully joined, off-white bookcases, not heaped in man-high stalagmites on the floor. The expanses of cream-colored carpet were unworn and unstained, the soli-tude thriving and orderly.

Yet lost as they were in that gracious, impeccable space—how his twenty-two-year-old lover of the moment, whoever she was, must have swooned the first time that she saw it—somehow I spotted the few photos immediately. One, no more than two inches square, was set in a cube of gray glass that sat on a bookshelf, almost camouflaged by the bright spines. The other, an enlarged black-and-white, hung framed on the wall of his study. I glimpsed it down a long hall, through an open doorway, from a distance of perhaps fifty feet, but I would have recognized the subject had the photograph lain ten floors down in the street.

He caught me looking. "You remember these good people," he said. He picked up the glass cube and handed it to me with perfect simplicity, and there it lay in the palm of my hand: Martha, as I had first known her, in amber or locked beneath ice. Their son—Jeremiah? Johann?—was a featureless white-swaddled lump in her arms. She gazed steadily into the camera, ambiguity lifting one side of her mouth, as if she were afraid to show herself truly happy, or truly unhappy, but I couldn't decide which it was, what the truth of her feeling had been in that moment, and in this way she was just as I'd first known her, also. She even wore the oversize button-up Oxford, her wardrobe in all my first memories of her, the rolled-up sleeves girding her elbows like donuts. Of course, I realized suddenly. She had worn them to breastfeed. It was barely a year since I'd stopped wearing such clothes myself.

"I'm reminded this one is a photo of Martha," Nicholas was saying, now leading me down the hall to his study, as if I'd insisted on seeing both pictures. I still had the cube tightly gripped in my hand. "Which isn't to say," he went on, "I would rather not see her. Not at all. But for me, this is a photograph of Joachim." There it was, the high-minded, unsuitable name, somehow transmuted in the utterance, its alternatives rendered implausible, even before I'd laid eyes on the person the label denoted. As we entered Nicholas's study he turned to face me and in synchronized movement I turned the same way, so that I wouldn't have to look at the picture we'd come to regard. Instead I found myself facing the life of their son: that featureless, white-swaddled lump now grown the ripe, heavy cheeks of a baby; now the lengthening delicate neck of a toddler, air interposing itself between shoulders and jaw, strange composure saturating the eyes. It seemed that with Joachim, just as with Lion, that period of uncanny and ageless composure, of regal self-assurance and detachment—as if the child has already outlived you, or come from the past, from the charcoal of eons-dead stars—had peaked close to age two and a half. Thereafter the comical, treacherous world laid its snare, and the gestures of character covered that early quintessence. So that perhaps I was unsettled even more when the child of seven, or ten, or fourteen—the clown-child baring teeth to the camera; the proud, nervous child astride a small horse; the unaware child gazing out a bus window; even the child half-concealed by his own heedless sleep—in his thoroughly singular presence yet disclosed with sly flicks of the veil Nicholas, and then Martha, the longer one stared, although Martha a great deal more often, her unreduced presence in him like an optical trick. And though I hardly knew why, I abruptly remembered a trip I'd gone on with my mother, while I was pregnant with Lion, and she, for the first time in years of insatiable travel, inclined to revisit the country in which she'd been born. After my father had squired her away she had never gone back, through five decades of mind-boggling change, so that nothing at all looked the way it once had, which had suited and even relieved her. Then turning one corner we'd stumbled by chance on her grade school, with its humble colonial brick and its three cement steps she had climbed with small feet crammed in pinching "good" shoes shaped like little canoes. The forgotten and never-loved building seemed smaller to her, but not nearly shrunken enough not to wound with its merciless sameness, and she had bent herself nearly in half and sobbed into her lap as I drove us away. So perhaps it was her grief I felt as I gazed on this child not mine, and not even much of a child anymore. Grief not for him, nor for Martha exactly, but for all my lost selves, which I liked to imagine were still somehow there, waiting for my return. But those selves were long gone. I would never be younger again. This was so simple it went without saying, but unsaid, one could try to forget it.

"He's beautiful," I said. We might have been standing there silent for hours.

"He's fortunate in his resemblances. He's his mother's son in most ways."

This was my cue to turn around, and face that other photograph, and so I did, and did not turn to stone or to liquid, and my eyes didn't even subside beneath tears. I almost smiled. It was difficult not to, receiving that gaze, one of such serene love. I took a guess why Nicholas had called this one, also, a photograph of Joachim. "Did Joachim take this photo?" I asked.

"He did. And he sent it to me, as a sort of sly message. A flag for 'all clear.' There's a story. He sometimes spends part of the summer with me. Last summer my going-away gift to him was a digital camera. I'd known that he wanted one badly, but it stirred up a ruckus with Martha when he brought it back home. So this photo told me she had softened up to it. She'd sat for her portrait."

"What sort of ruckus?"

"Oh, Martha's very austere now. Or should I say, again. Very much as she was years ago when we met. Now she's found her way back."

I wanted to say, as if seizing the clue, *Back to where?* But instead I said, "I didn't know that could be done—going back."

"I suppose it can't quite. The place you go back to gets changed by your very returning."

"The time-traveler's conundrum."

"Exactly. But I'd say Martha's gone back in spirit. When I met her, her dream was to live in a tipi. Either that or on board a boat. Now she's got that, a little."

"The tipi, or the boat?"

He laughed. "Neither. But nevertheless, she appears satisfied."

What Martha had was a property in Mendocino County, some small, picturesque number of sheep, some comparable number of hens, a wonderfully typical rooster, all censorious pomp, and a wonderfully typical sheepdog, right out of the pages of James Herriot—or so went Nicholas's inventory of her household, downright puzzling to me in its eager affection until I understood that, like the portrait before which we stood, this manifestation of Martha manifested for Nicholas only his son. His son's eye, his son's world. "There's a great deal of shearing and carding and all sorts of wholesome nonsense—would you like to see?" he went on, hardly waiting for me to reply before turning his laptop around on his desk. There onscreen, at the ready, was a long-legged, lacy-cuffed sheep. "The spring lambs," Nicholas explained, scrolling. "Of course this post is rather belated. He begins it by saying, 'I took these shots six weeks ago.'"

Eleven years before, when Nicholas had started the job at Columbia, all three members of the erstwhile household had moved to New York, so close on my heels perhaps they had trod on my barely dried tears. Martha had come for an adjunct position at New York University that was beneath her, she had made it a point of remarking, as she had made it a point of remarking on every sacrifice, professional or personal, she was making to accommodate her ex-husband's career. At that time they still shared custody, Joachim's time divided equally between them to the minute, under the terms of an agreement it had taken them over a year of embittered warfare to work out. By the time it had been finalized Joachim was almost three, and within a year of its taking effect two developments had pointed the way to its being untenable. First, Martha lost her tenure case and consequently her job; and second, conversely, Nicholas's "light" book on Shakespeare and Eros became a mainstream best-seller, and he found himself offered, by Columbia, the best-paying job in his field.

Even before that grim spring of their starkly opposed job prospects it was already clear their careers weren't advancing in tandem. Martha hadn't published since Joachim's birth, not even essays that Nicholas knew were completed, let alone the first book that her chances for tenure required. She'd ignored a colleague's offer to publish whatever she had, even fragments, in the department's *Americanist Quarterly*. Meanwhile Nicholas had one admired book already under his belt and was in the last knotty stages of completing another when he'd decided, it seemed in the way one decides to step out for a breath of fresh air, to set his scholarly project aside for a couple of weeks and instead write "for fun" about Shakespeare and Eros. It was just the sort of book I'd expended such effort to not hear about, avoiding high-minded bookstores, and discarding the *Times Book Review* in the trash, for those first several years after failing to finish grad school. In the wake of the book's unexpected success Nicholas had been invited to do a thought piece on eroticism in everyday life for the opinion page of the *Times,* and enjoyed a small profile in *Newsweek,* and even been sent on a book tour, all heretofore unthinkable pomp in the dowdy, prim, penniless world of university presses. And so his stock had been high—very much higher, he unconcernedly told me, than at present or, in all likelihood, anytime in the future. Yet high as it was, Martha had complete power over him. Under the terms of their shared custody, he could not move away to New York unless Martha moved also. Martha had far less to stay for than he—he still had his old job—yet he'd known he would be in her debt if she did choose to go. Martha wasn't some camp follower. Her parents' deaths had given her a good amount of money and even then she'd been talking about buying land. And so she could have stayed put, and made him stay put too. But in the end, making clear that he'd owe her beyond his capacity ever to pay, she had taken the NYU job, and a spacious apartment overlooking the Hudson in Lower Manhattan, at the opposite end of the 1 train from where he would now live in Morningside Heights.

She'd made the move because she wanted to—Martha never did things without wanting to, even if the desire was fleeting—but it was useful to her to maintain that she'd done it for him, sacrificed so that he could advance, just the same as if they were still married. Nicholas had expected and hoped that this theme would abate once their life in New York had set roots. He was sure Martha felt the same way, that the tale of her sacrifice to him was only for face-saving. Before their marriage Martha loved New York. It had always been far more her city than his, something it had taken him years to understand, given their shared love of nature. But extremity and challenge were the things Martha liked, whether urban or wild. She was equally gratified by New York as by unspoiled backcountry. What she had no use for was the pastoral or meditative, which was why she'd so hated the storybook town where we'd lived.

Returning to New York as an actual resident, and the mother of a four-year-old child, she must have been dismayed, then, to discover she now hated it almost as much as that town, if not more. Must have been dismayed, Nicholas said, because of the effort she'd made to conceal her feelings. It had only been the depth of her Manhattan zealotry that prompted Nicholas, who still knew her so well, to suspect she was deeply unhappy. For Joachim and herself she subscribed to the Children's Playhouse and the Family Philharmonic and, at Christmastime, to multiple *Nutcrackers*. Afternoons and weekends she marched Joachim on an unending round through the Temples of Culture, not just the usual ones but the very obscure ones that native New Yorkers ignored or had not even heard of, the museums of Theosophy or of the Lenape Tribe, or the uncovered African burial grounds. She paddled a kayak off Battery Park, and broadcast her intention to moor a sailboat at the World Financial Center Marina. She grew tiresome about extremely local causes, giving her time away to them—to the persecuted South American fruit vendors, to the underfunded monument preservers, to the visionary bike path proponents—as if doing penance.

By contrast to Martha's frenetic displays of enthusiasm, Joachim's attitude to New York started off tepid and steadily lost temperature. He tolerated everything and loved nothing. His well-regarded public school—for Martha had also become a zealot about public school—was, each year from kindergarten forward, "okay," or "fine," or "all right." "Okay" and "fine" and "all right" were Joachim's workhorse adjectives, applicable to all the nuances of city life. The subways, the buses, their highrise apartment, the boats of all sizes pursuing their tasks up and down the great Hudson, the candelabra-palisade of the Metropolitan Opera as one crossed the great plaza dew-drenched by the spray of the fountains: all this was "okay." The view from the top of the World Trade Center disclosing—my God!—ancient stubs of the Ramapo Mountains, the fjord of the Hudson at Storm King, Jamaica Bay's islands adrift on the beaten-gold sea: all of this, equally, was "all right." No degree of Martha's enthusiasm could prompt Joachim to feel a passionate attachment to the city, and perhaps this was why her enthusiasm notched up evermore—because she lacked the attachment as well, and suspected he knew.

What did Joachim like? Peace and quiet. He remarked endlessly on the level of noise in Manhattan. What else did he like? Their old garden when they'd lived "in the country," which, even by age nine, he still hadn't forgotten. They tried to re-create it with tenth-story window boxes, but it wasn't the same. Their life in New York, even after five years, still felt

somehow provisional, and now came the fall of 2001, with Joachim starting fourth grade.

Having already learned how this story would end, I felt I hardly
needed Nicholas to tell me the details, which I could have invented myself. Nine-year-old Joachim Hallett-Brodeur, delicate of feature and pale
of skin, an uncombed hank of his father's gold hair hanging into his
mother's gray eyes, seated in a relatively quietish corner of the impossibly
hard-surfaced cacophonous school cafeteria at eight forty-five in the
morning, outsize backpack still weighting his thin bony shoulders on top
of his hoodie because like a soldier, or like a New York City schoolchild,
he's learned to hump half his weight on his back without thinking about
it. One small-palmed, long-fingered hand holding open the absurd doorstop of the latest *Harry Potter*, the other idly stickying itself in the morning's Free School Breakfast, pancakes with imitation maple syrup, the
usual and welcome Tuesday fare; Thursday, the other day he comes to
school early to sit with the kids from the projects and eat the Free School
Breakfast because his mother teaches an eight-thirty class, the entrée is
cinnamon rolls with icing. Beverage choice of chocolate milk or juice.
Martha forgivably sanguine about this nutritional nadir in Joachim's day
because she gives him whole grain cereals and fruits in the mornings and
wrongly believes that he gets the Free Breakfast at school just for show
but does not really eat it. This illusion, like so many others, will expire
today. Several hours later, when at last Joachim with strange slowness
comes into her arms, his face smooth of expression and absent of tears,
rather like that of a sleepwalker, his hand will still be tacky from imitation
maple syrup because, unusual for a fastidious boy who washes hands
before and after every meal without fail, on this morning he has never
been able to go to the bathroom. When the first airplane strikes, its vast
detonation just four blocks away making all the cafeteria's cumbersome
combination table-and-twenty-stool units jump slightly on their black
rubber wheels, Joachim is still subsumed in familiar aloneness, an aloneness made safe by routine. By the time the still-living bodies of people are
plummeting off the tower's crown to the street Joachim has been swept
into a dangerous crowd, of panicked teachers and children, all made
anonymous and vulnerable by the collapse of routine. Disaster procedures, such as they exist at the time, disintegrate beneath the onslaught

of parents rushing into the school to take children home. When Joachim tells the mother of one of his classmates that Martha is at NYU, teaching class, the mother takes Joachim with her. It doesn't occur to either of them, adult or child, that by this time Martha has canceled her class and rushed downtown against a tide of people rushing up, and that in fact she is in the school building, unable to find Joachim. Outside, on Greenwich Street, Joachim, pulled along by the mother of his classmate but paid no attention by her as she's too occupied with her daughter, walks looking back over his shoulder and has a clear view of the plummeting bodies, each as distinct to him as would be people on the subway or passing him by on the street. Some pump legs and arms in wild panic as if they had not meant to jump but were pushed. Some are strangely lumpy and thick until he understands that they're two people, tightly entwined. Some go down striking what seem like intentional poses, as if at a previous time in their life they had worked out a posture for this situation, like the teenagers at the Carmine Street pool coming off the high dive. One falls perfectly upside-down, one knee bent, both arms flush to the torso. From the distance it's hard to tell if they are women or men. Like most children, excellently defended by innocence, Joachim never imagines the falling are children like him. They are adults, to whom, he's remotely aware, death applies. When the mushroom cloud blooms from the top of one tower and the whole of it starts to cascade, with surprising, contained elegance, as if it too had worked out in advance just the right way to fall, it's Joachim's intake of breath that alerts his friend's mother. With a shriek she exhorts them to run, but just then some Korean store owners, standing aghast in the door to their deli, yell, "Children, inside! Come inside!" and they tumble inside as the wave of gray ash passes by.

At the age of seven Joachim had been a scholar of Pompeii as he had also, at various times, been a scholar of such things as the moon landing, Da Vinci, and dinosaurs, and in the days that followed, Pompeii was his template for what had occurred. Everything fit: the nice day turned horrific; the black column of smoke and orange flames; the fine rain of gray ash; and the plummeting black silhouettes of those headed for death, even in their last seconds of life rendered into abstractions, just like those sprawled, featureless statues one gazed on in books, Pompeii's fossilized dead. That a metaphor of natural disaster left no room for intentional evil seemed to Nicholas healthy, perhaps even miraculous, as did Joachim's other chief posttrauma symptoms, though they were not without irony. Joachim was suddenly an ardent, possessive, protective, patriotic New Yorker. New York was all he wanted to discuss: its history, its buildings, its street grid, its subways, its people from all the nations on earth. He'd grown abruptly alert to his fellow New Yorkers as if having discovered them under his bed, as if he were their sovereign now tenderly responsible for every aspect of their health and well-being. He would stand and talk to the doorman, Enrique, for hours if you let him. Every Korean deli they passed, he would want to go in. Bonds of friendship had bloomed all around him at school. It was as though he had fallen in love, was what Nicholas thought, but Martha, who saw everything differently after that day, saw this differently also.

It had to be one story or the other. All of us who had been there had chosen: disaffection for New York ratified by the awful events, or love for New York ratified—differently—by the awful events. I'd made the second choice, and so my life. Years of noncommittal cohabitation, of narcissistic foot-dragging, of self-righteous anti-marriage-and-child-rearing screeds, and—most stubbornly obstructive and thoroughly secret—of shameful bereavement for Martha, had come to an overnight end. Reader, I grew up. I married Matthew. To his speechless delight, as if doing a striptease, I saucily threw out my birth-control pills. It was a trading of the murky infinite for the well-lit and limited, and I would never regret it, but extravagance of action on the part of others—the assertion that plot twists remain possible—now excited in me mild scorn, the reverse side of envy. I would have felt this even if it weren't Martha, but given that it was, I felt it all the worse.

I felt it for Nicholas also, or something allied, as he wound up his story. Contempt/jealousy that he'd let her rewrite all their terms, and relieve him of shared custody, so that she could move from New York, taking Joachim with her. I didn't have any reason to doubt his motives, though it wasn't so difficult, standing there in his gracious, impeccable rooms, to imagine his sacrifice hadn't been total. But what did I know? There were his teenage son's photographs, beautifully framed. There was his teenage son's sheep-farming blog on the screen of the laptop. Still, something had altered in my estimation of him, or perhaps some unset intuition had finally hardened into permanence. Part-time, long-distance, aestheticized fatherhood suited him all too well.

"If he'd failed to adjust there was some thought he'd come back to me for high school. That's a point that we're still grappling with, I'm not thrilled with his schooling. But he has adjusted, remarkably well!—as you see. Should I write down the Web site for you? I'm aware I am biased but I think he does wonderfully with it. He's made it an art form."

"Please do," I said, and repented my judgments of him as, with a surfeit of pride more childlike than parental, he painstakingly copied the URL for me, down to the *http*.

Since Dutra's marriage announcement that spring I had noticed our home telephone sounded different, though it was the same dusty Panasonic cordless that Matthew and I had bought years ago when we'd moved in together. Now it rang with a strange obsolete gravity, like those fog bells on lighthouses no longer used. It seemed to know we would hear its portents with just half our attention, yet this made it that much more commanding. Perhaps it was just that I heard it so rarely. Since becoming a parent I'd begrudgingly gotten a cell phone, and like filings to the superior magnet almost everyone in my life now directed themselves to that number, especially as my life revolved mostly around other parents I'd met on the playground, or college-age night-babysitters, or the leaders of sing-along circles or wintertime play groups or tumbling-for-tots. Most of the people in my life now did not even know my home number, and perhaps this was why, when it rang, I flinched with foreboding as if at the sound of a siren.

It was Alicia, whom I hadn't seen in years, since long before she and Dutra broke up. "I know you're surprised," she cut short my confused pleasantries. "I want to know if you've heard anything from Dan."

There had only been the message he'd left from his car, and when I told her so she said, "I meant more recently."

"Why? What's happened?"

"Nothing—I mean, I don't know that there's any emergency. Um, okay. If we do need to talk you'll know why," and she gave me her number.

"Alicia, I need you to tell me a little bit more."

"I can't. I mean, it wouldn't be appropriate," she signed off, an evasion that would have addled the rest of my day if I hadn't heard from Dutra within the same hour, when the mailman rang my doorbell.

"Certified mail," he said. "You have to sign." The envelope had been sent from a town in California called La Honda, and it contained a short, jocular note and a cashier's check for ten thousand dollars.

"I've heard from him," I told Alicia when I called her a few minutes later.

Alicia had received an identical check, and a similar note, though tailored to their history. "Ali," it began, "do me a favor and deposit this check without getting all hung up about it. You know I've never cared about money except as a means to the most basic end. I have more than enough for that. What's left over is only a pain in my ass. You've put off grad school for years saying you can't pay for it. Now you have no excuse, get admitted and I'll pay the rest."

My note read, "Dear Ginny, I know that you care about manners so don't be ungracious and try to return it. I want you to have it. Put it in a college fund for Lion if that makes you feel better. In recent news, I've found a very peaceful place to live and there's even a cement Buddha by the front door that I haven't kicked over."

Alicia suggested we talk to each other in person. Since her marriage she'd been living in Bucks County but she offered to drive in to meet me, and she named a place at the bottom of First Avenue a few blocks from the little apartment she'd once shared with Dutra, the same apartment he had renovated "to the inch" in Italian Modern, and briefly lived in with Nikki, and finally sold.

When I came up the block from the subway Alicia was already there, looking the same as she always had, bone-thin and pale, her lank, almost colorless hair pushed behind her small ears, her wise-child's face gravely composed. She was leaning against an antique Chevy pickup parked in front of the café, and talking with a stout, powerfully built woman who faced her almost toe-to-toe, leaning toward her intently, with one meaty hand braced against the truck's body. The woman appeared much older than Alicia but this might have been an illusion caused by her physique. She had short, coarse brown hair and wore a pencil stub behind one ear, wire-rim glasses on her face, a white T-shirt, and Levi's held up by suspenders. Something in her bearing, an extremely compressed capability, suggested to me that she might be a butcher, or a construction foreperson, as well as a lesbian.

They stopped speaking as I approached and the woman sized me up until she was satisfied I'd noticed her doing it, and then she took her leave of Alicia.

"Bye, babe," Alicia said and kissed her on the mouth. I watched the woman go with what must have been visible puzzlement. "Let's go inside," Alicia said, and broke the silence once we were seated by adding, "You maybe don't know the whole story about me and Dan."

"Maybe not," I allowed.

"I know he let you think I was his girlfriend. It was the easiest way to explain me. But I wasn't—we weren't. We weren't like that."

"Like what?"

"Sexual. Romantic. I mean, we loved each other, and it was even exclusive, but we didn't have sex."

I must have looked, not as I meant to—receptive, nonjudgmental, for the moment all ears and no mouth—but completely dumbstruck, because her composure gave way and abruptly she said, "I was abused when I was little. By this guy that my mother was seeing. Intercourse, sodomy, the whole works. Starting when I was ten."

"I'm sorry, Alicia," I managed.

"Don't worry about what to say. I'm just trying to make it make sense. Anyway, that put me off track of, I guess you'd say, intimacy, for a pretty long time. When I met Dan, it's hard to explain, but he got it. It's like he saw me. And I saw him, too. The way we're wired up as people, it's hard to explain, but it matches. He's the first person I ever told about my mom's boyfriend. And he told me things too, that he's never told anyone else. So we were together—but in a way that was chaste. Having sex would have been grotesque somehow. A few times I tried to make him have sex with me. I really wanted—I was desperate to have love and sex in my life, just like anyone else. But he knew, when I acted that way, I was hurting myself— 'Come on, put your cock in me, fuck me'—I'd be goading him like that, like I was possessed. He'd just sort of hold me at arm's length until I woke up."

"You lived together," I said, after we'd sat in stunned silence a moment. "In a five-hundred-square-foot apartment."

"We did. And we slept in the same bed, and peed with the door open, and had big screaming fights with each other. But like siblings. No sex."

"Why?"

"At the time I would have said, to take care of each other. Having stepped back a little I guess I would say, codependence. It got us off the hook with other people, with trying to make something normal work out."

"But didn't you want something normal to work out?"

"I did. With him. I was blind, I refused to see clearly. You have to understand, all the time we were together, I never saw it this clearly, the way I do now. I would think, in a little more time we would heal each other. I'd stop being so frigid toward men, toward men's bodies, I guess I should say toward *his* body. And he'd put down his torch and start feeling romantic, toward me. But I was just nursing delusions. Dan saw us clearly. He always saw what we were clearly. He saw Nell, my partner, and her seeing me, before I even knew she existed. Nell lived in New Hope, a couple of miles from my mother. When my mother got sick, and we started to go there a lot, whenever we went into New Hope for stuff Nell would somehow appear. At the health food place, at the drugstore. She has a landscaping company"—*of course*, I thought—"and that truck's like her office, and whenever we pulled into town, Dan would notice her truck. Then he'd go pin her down, chat her up—you know how he is, like Attack of the Overly Friendly. As if he might actually be mocking you. And she *hated* him, later she told me he made her blood boil. But little could she have suspected. One day he says to me, 'That Nell's after your narrow ass, Ali.' And I said, 'Please do not be disgusting.' But over time he becomes serious: "You should let that dyke Nell make love to you. Just to see how it feels." I was livid. I threw things at him. I said, 'You're just trying to ditch me because I'm a burden.'"

"Do you think that was true?"

After a moment she said, "I had become a burden. But I also think he saw my chance to be happy, and was pointing me there, because it turned out he was right." She smiled down at her untouched cup of tea and croissant, made speechless a moment herself by the tale of reversals with which she'd stunned me.

"He told me you wanted to marry him, after you found out your mother was dying," I said, not to protest her story, but to ratify it, to give up what I knew for revision.

"It's true. I really thought, in my craziness, that getting married would fix me."

"And he said that he refused to marry you, until you faced up to your feelings about losing your mother, or something like that."

"He's such an honest person, even his lies come out basically true. He did refuse to marry me, because us getting married would have been a farce. And there were feelings I had to face up to, but they weren't just to do with my mother." She glanced at her watch. "Sorry," she said. "I don't mean to be rude. The truck's parked at a meter and I don't have much time, and we haven't even talked about the checks."

"I don't know what to say about them. I'll listen."

"Dan's impulsive. I guess you know that. He's also incredibly loyal, to ideas and people. He believes in love, he really does. Crazy lightning-bolt love, he would say that's the only real kind. In his life it's come twice and both times were disasters. Did he ever tell you about the girlfriend he dealt heroin with? Tanya. His first love. A very big deal. But he had this idea he couldn't let go of, that she'd betrayed him by calling the ambulance when he OD'd. She'd disobeyed orders. There was no way around it, he had to break with her. It's like a code that just makes sense to him, and it ruins his life. Then there's the second time, you know all about that. That time's even worse. Even more against code, so he gives that up too, but he never stops trying to replace it. Of course he would say you can't *try*, it's all fate, but he can't help himself. That's what happened with Nikki. Fuck, I still haven't dealt with the checks. It's this simple, he's asking for help. He knows neither of us would accept so much money, but he's forced it on us. It's sort of a power play, trying to have influence in our lives. I don't mean that the checks aren't a generous impulse. They are, but they're also so lonely. So needy. He sees our lives all taken care of, even I'm taken care of, and he's still alone."

As if to provide illustration, Nell now appeared on the sidewalk outside, checked the meter, then leaned on the Chevy and folded her arms.

"I don't know if you'll cash your check, or return it, or put it in a drawer," Alicia went on, "and I don't know what I'll do with mine either.

But whatever you do with the check, you have to do something for *him*. I don't know what. If it was as simple as get him a shrink, I'd have already done that. There's one last thing I wanted to say. I don't know if you knew that my mom was a suicide. That was awful but it wasn't surprising. Years before she did it, pretty much since I was ten or twelve years old, I was already thinking about it myself. I really believe it's genetic, the impulse. And not long after Dan and I met, I told him that to me, suicide felt alive. Like a friend, or an angel. Always there for me, if I ever really needed bailing out. Crazy as it sounds, I found that comforting. I still do. Anyway, I asked Dan if he'd give me his blessing—if he could tell me, truthfully, that if I did it, he'd bless me. He wouldn't resent me, or judge me, or be ruined by what I had done. You can probably guess what he said."

"He blessed you," I said after a moment.

"He did. I know that he meant it."

"Are you saying he'd do it himself?"

"No. I'm only saying that he doesn't have the hang-ups, the judgmental feelings or fears, that might stop other people from doing it."

"If he wanted to do it, he'd do it."

"I think that's all I'm saying. But—promise me that you'll worry about him. I can't be the only one worried about him or he'll really be sunk."

"I promise you," I said. "I don't know how, but I won't let him sink."

"Thanks," she said. "I knew you'd get it." Though Alicia sat with her back to the window she had sensed Nell's arrival. She turned to confirm, and turned back, and I knew that our meeting was nearing its end.

"Wait, Alicia," I said. "When was the second time? The second time that he had crazy lightning-bolt love. The time you said that I knew all about."

She looked at me oddly. "The time—how he met you. That whole thing when the two of you were both in love with the same person."

"Martha."

"That's right. That's her name."

"He loved Martha," I said, as if speaking a phrase in Sanskrit, the three words felt so strange in my mouth. "That's the torch that you hoped he'd put down."

"He wouldn't talk much about her. But he told me enough. That she'd been your lover, and then he fell in love with her, too. And she used him, to break up with you. He would say that was why he was finished with love. Because it wasn't just him devastated, but you. He had this theory, that from then on he'd break it down into components—friendship, emotional intimacy, and then sex. All totally separate. He wouldn't ever do all three, maybe not even two, with one person again. So far as I know, he hasn't. With me, it was emotional intimacy. With you, friendship. I know it meant so much to him, when you let him back into your life. After that he said he'd never give a second's thought to her again. But, you know, carrying a torch is a form of thinking. He couldn't help it." My face, like the tip of the iceberg, must have suggested to her, most inadequately, what I felt. "I'm sorry," she said. "I don't mean to stir up bad memories for you."

"Don't be silly," I said rapidly. "All of that was a long time ago."

"Not for him. People talk about time like erosion: 'give it time, it'll turn into dust, it'll all go away.' For Dan time is more like that clear shiny stuff that you paint onto things, now I've spaced on the name."

"Shellac. Lacquer."

"Yes. That. Every year puts a new layer on and the past just gets harder and brighter and more permanent. Thanks for the words for that stuff, not remembering that would have driven me nuts. Dan always talked about how smart you were, that you knew everything."

"I'm not so smart," I said. "In fact, I'm an idiot."

But not understanding my meaning she said, "It's okay. I used to resent how impressed he was with you but now I'm relieved that he has you. He needs to have someone he thinks of as smarter than him."

May 10, 2007 PARADISE LOST... and the angel Michael came unto them and said, "Guys, there was a brand-new Apple iBook laptop computer lying under that tree with a sticky note on it that said FOR THE USE OF THE DAMNED FALLEN ONLY and now it's like, GONE, and You-Know-Who says somebody called 'nudiecuties' is posting a blog about, like, gardening, and what to name your animals, and how fun it is not to wear any clothes and SERIOUSLY? Did you think you could do this without getting noticed? Get out! Hand over that Apple computer and GET OUT of You-Know-Who's garden! Shoo! Scram! On the double!" *It's official! Yours Truly is officially suspended from the Mendocino County Waldorf School for violations of the Home Technology and Electronic Media Restrictions! All I can say, Public, is Thank You, clearly one of you ratted on me, and I am so honored you'd bother to do that. Stirring up my Public to the point where they'd want to Betray me is more than I ever hoped for when I started this blog. Just so you know because Tone can be weird on a blog I'm not being Sarcastic. I'm never sarcastic, sarcasm is one of my personal Things I Don't Do, as I often remind HRH who, we know, thinks that Sarcasm gives her more Power.*

HRH [seeing not-so-clean kitchen]: Thanks for cleaning the kitchen after dirtying every last pan in the house. Wow, that's great.

Yours Truly: Are you really upset? Or just joking about it? It's so hard to tell when you're being Sarcastic.

HRH: I wasn't being sarcastic. Please don't lecture me on sarcasm.

YT: Not being Sarcastic is one of my Personal Goals.

HRH: How laudable of you.

YT: See? You just were Sarcastic again!

HRH: You don't know the difference between sarcasm and irony, Sweetie.

YT: Of course I don't! Because I go to Waldorf School!

But not anymore! Here's what happened. Earlier this year, when we received our Home Technology and Electronic Media Survey, we Fudged it because of some Lapses that all had occurred at the end of the summer, namely my Nikon Coolpix (it shoots video too!) and my brand-new iBook which knows how much I love it so doesn't require a shout out, and less sexy but very important our DSL line which I paid for myself out of savings and all of which brings me to you! Public! You remember (see Archives) that HRH felt some distress over this. We, HRH and I, share the unplugged all-wood-no-plastic Value System of the Mendocino County Waldorf School or we wouldn't be there. Right? Right? But didn't we also share the Value System that says Honesty is the Best Policy?

YT: Let's just put it all on there and see what they do.

HRH: Sh*t, what if they kick you out? Let's leave it off. It's not like they'll ever come up to our house.

Well, Public, you know the rest. Poor HRH is very Stressed, but at least there were only five weeks left of school and we have the whole summer to figure it out. Meanwhile you can enjoy the Improvements I've made in my new Leisure Time. Introducing the Hallett Farm . . .

LAMB CAM!

"Mommy, the song," Lion said when the lacy-cuffed lambs wandered into the background and couldn't be seen anymore. "The song" was another recent feature of Joachim's blog, a three-minute piece of rudimentary computer animation that superimposed orange and red, crudely drawn falling leaves on a still photograph of a sheep standing, passive and doomed, in a chewed-over field. The sheep, one learned elsewhere on the blog, had been killed by coyotes. Perhaps it was only the additions of the leaves, and the soundtrack, a continuous loop of the nonvocal violin part from the Kansas song "Dust in the Wind," that so imbued the image of the sheep with pathos, but regardless the sheep was intensely commanding. Lion stared at it, riveted, as the fake-looking leaves fell and fell, and the melodramatic refrain sawed its truncated plaint. After three minutes it didn't conclude, simply froze.

"Again," Lion said.

"Kitten, it's time to brush teeth."

"Again!" Lion cried in despair. "One more time, Mommy, please!"

It was a strange work of art; staring at it myself, hypnotized by its utter monotonousness, I was alternately blurting laughter and wiping the tears from my eyes. I knew that it wasn't Sarcastic and yet I suspected it purposely tempted the sarcasm of others, if only to shame it with unabashed sentimentality. It was very high/low, Martha might have said back in her Jacques Lacan/black leather days. But now she said, on the ladder of comments—finding her there made my heart lurch, as if I'd discovered her seated with me in the room—*Hi YT (my own JHB), thank you, sweetness. I'm so proud that you've taken your sadness, which I know is still so huge inside you, and turned it into something to share that will solace the sadness of others. You are my solace. No Sarcasm!—love, HRH (also known as your mother)*

The members of the Public liked it too:

beautiful! mist in my eyes. RIP Helene [this was the murdered ewe's name] *you will always live on in our hearts*

so few people understand the pain of losing an animal thank you thank you thank you dear YT you are a brave poetic generous kid

i know it is hard but try not to hate the coyotes. their just livin. doin what they haveta do

hi joachim its maya from school. your blog is awesome! i wanted to tell you! i'm not the person who ratted you obviously! hey rat: today i quit lurking to dare you to rat on me too!

Hi Maya, wow! Thanks for reading! And thank you for taking this risk, I'm so honored! E-mail or IM me and we can talk more!—YT (Joachim)

"Wow, look who's still not in bed," Matthew said, coming home at eight-thirty to find Lion slumped glassy-eyed on my lap, in communion, or perhaps it was now catalepsy, with departed Helene. "Is there anything here I can make us for dinner?"

"Um, no," I said, collapsing the browser window and hefting boneless Lion, too tired now to protest.

"Are we ordering in?"

"Um, sure," I said, pushing past him. I understood, better than a somnambulist, that after two hours adrift in that blog, my pupils were just slightly smaller than dimes and my mind was a blast crater, stupidly gaping. But I was no better than the sleepwalker would be at waking myself. In Lion's room I knelt in the darkness beside his small bed with my cheek on his chest, feeling it rise and fall, waiting for him to breathe into me ordinary perceptions and thoughts. *I can see why you wanted to keep the screens out of the house* I would e-mail to Martha. *I've been mainlining your son's sheep-farm blog and it feels pretty strange.* Perhaps I had still not returned to the world. I heard the door open and close, Matthew's swift angry tread on the stairs. By the time he'd returned with a bag of Chinese and a six-pack of beer, I had managed to put plates on the table and Dutra's check prominently between them. Matthew regarded it while roughly shaking glop from the takeout containers, which came down on the plates with a series of loud smacking sounds. "Is this what's the matter with you?" he asked after a moment.

"What?" I said.

"Don't '*What?*' me. That's just what I'm talking about. Your obliviousness and your incredible self-absorption. Every waking moment I'm with you, you look straight through me like I'm not even there. Lion says something to you and you don't even hear him. You'll stand blocking the refrigerator door until I take you by the shoulders and *move* you and you don't even notice. Can you try to have some basic awareness? Of your child, for example, who was practically asleep on top of you when I walked in the door, a full hour past his bedtime? Or of your refrigerator, for example, which is empty except for a bunch of tiny Tupperware boxes of mold—"

"Oh, so I'm not keeping house well enough? I'm not sufficiently managing *every* aspect of Lion's upbringing, and doing *all* of the shopping—" But I could never get away with this line and I was almost relieved when he cut me off short.

"Don't try that. We have both always done a shitload. I, for example, work fifty hours a week, earn a regular income, get our family health benefits, manage all of our money, insure our house and our car, do our taxes, and replace the fucking fire-alarm batteries every six months. *You*, very brilliantly and indispensably and even, until now, with much humor and grace, manage our household, care for our child, maintain our social life down to purchasing our friends' wedding presents and sending them notes when they have us to dinner, *and* you sacrifice your writing time to wait for the dishwasher repairman or whatever the equivalent pain in the ass, at whatever time it should arise. Don't act like I'm one of those husbands who don't notice things. You know I do, and you know that I've noticed that lately you don't do a goddamn fucking thing but read a blog about sheep." We stared each other down a long moment, too angry to laugh. We hadn't even touched the heaps of food, or uncapped the beer bottles. I heard the sound of our home telephone, though it was only in my mind, like the little red lighthouse in Lion's favorite book: *warn-ing! warn-ing! warn-ing!*

There were so many arguments we could have had at that moment, such oldies and goodies we might as well have had a player piano that did them for us. But none was germane, they were all just time wasters, the smoke in the eyes and the mud in the water. "Matthew," I said, "I don't want to go back to the life that I had before you." Wasn't that always the unspoken threat? I saw his eyes, so rigid in their sockets, glaze over with tears. Matthew cried easily, at the movies, during TV commercials, when told any sad story about a small child. It was something I loved, but right now his own tears only made him more angry.

"Why are you telling me that?"

"To save time. To not fight, and make threats, and then have to recant them because they're not real."

"Sometimes that kind of reassurance means the opposite thing. The very fact that someone feels the need to say it."

I couldn't deny this. I could only believe what I'd said, and hope that I was right. "I want to go to California," I told him, watching him watch me, from the back of the great distances that were somehow contained in his tired pale skin and his watery eyes. "For a long weekend. Three days at the most. I'll arrange babysitting. I'll arrange everything. You won't lose time at work—"

He made an impatient gesture: he didn't care about that. "To see Dutra?" he said.

I hesitated. "I'm hoping I'll see him."

"Is that what this is?" He lifted the check briefly. "Traveling expenses?"

"No. That's—a plea. For attention, or love, or something. We're not going to cash it."

"Of course we're not going to cash it," he snapped, sounding just like himself for a moment. Receding again, he asked thinly, "Are you sleeping with him?"

Then I felt such compassion for Matthew, that I could have so quickly grown so strange to him, that such an idea now seemed plausible. I would never have thought he could think such a thing, but what else would he think? I didn't flail or gape with affront. I only said, with finality, "No. Our relationship's nothing like that. But—when I knew him before we both moved to New York, he was really important to me. He, and somebody else we both knew. And we all had a misunderstanding."

"What kind of misunderstanding?" he demanded, aggressive again, lawyerly, for "misunderstanding," as both of us knew, is a baggy and cowardly word. Yet my reticence dug in its heels.

"Dutra did something for me. Gave up something for me. Because he thought that he should. Because it seemed like the right thing to him."

"Like this check."

"In a way. But this other thing he gave up cost him more. And I never even knew that he'd given it up, or how much it had cost, until now."

"I don't suppose you're going to be more specific."

"No," I said, as every kind of apology and appeal and self-justification and assurance to him clamored and canceled the others, until we'd been sitting in silence, absorbing my bald refusal, and it was too late to say anything else.

Matthew picked up the check and gazed at it; who knew what he saw. I knew he was trying to see me. Then he carefully quartered it, and put it in his shirt pocket. "Don't take it with you," he said. "I'll file it. You wouldn't want him to think you'd come just to return it."

Now I was in tears, though I'd never less wanted to cry. I didn't want to appeal to Matthew's pity, but to his reason and judgment and trust, and I grasped, all at once, that this was why I was married to him. We often sat together in a place of deliberation, where the temperature was cool and the atmosphere clear. In the past I'd thought it was a weakness, a failure of ardor, when it was the ark. It was where we'd survive, if we did. Perhaps there's no shame in my taking so long to realize it. I'd never had it with anyone else.

Through the blur of my undeserved tears I tried to climb in his arms, but very firmly, and equally gently, he pushed me away.

"When you come back," he said.

The etiquette of contacting an ex-lover's child to ostensibly compliment him on his blog is not yet codified. I am sure it will be, but I ventured without any guidance. I tried to be brief.

Dear Joachim, I wrote to his e-mail, *I've liked reading your blog. It was your Dad who first showed it to me. I'm an old friend of his and your mother's. Please say hello to her for me, and tell her, if she wants, she can write to me here or call me at the following number. Best wishes, Regina Gottlieb*

And below this, repeatedly typed and deleted and retyped and redeleted and at last after more vacillation but no true resolution a final time retyped and sent, an illogical warning, a warding-off gesture as ornament to the come-hither:

p.s. my three year old son loves the "Dust in the Wind" video of Helene

After fourteen years I perhaps wanted fourteen more hours of wondering how much or whether she thought of me, fourteen more hours to envision the curl of her lip at the sight of my name, to presume she discerned like an X-ray the contortions concealed in my prim little note. Perhaps I thought, having entirely remade my life on the plan of her absence, I still needed a little more time for doorknobs and a last coat of paint. Perhaps it was remorse, or intimation, but when, just a few hours later that morning, my cell phone, set to vibrate, began buzzing and scooting itself with the force of its own agitation the length of my desk, I first thought *please it can't be not yet* even as I smacked down on its beetling locomotion with the palm of my hand. I thanked God that Myrna and Lion had left for the zoo. I reminded myself that my cell phone rang daily, sometimes every few minutes, and that never before had I uttered my greeting and then heard the sound of her voice.

"It is you," she said. "Regina. My heart's in my throat. I don't know what to say."

"It is me," I echoed, having no better idea what to say than she did.

"You're in New York. You're in New York and you saw Nicholas and he showed you the blog."

"I've been here for years."

"I was there for a while."

"He told me."

"I want to see you," she said, as if no time had passed, or as if time had rewound its coil and I was that young girl again, who had not known that such things could happen. "I want to see you. But you can't travel, can you. You have a little boy. Do you have a husband?"

"Yes."

"A little boy and a husband," she repeated, as if reminding herself what these were. "That must mean you can't travel."

"I'm actually flying to Oakland next week."

"I'm a three-hour drive north. Could you drop in on me? Can you drive? You didn't used to know how."

"I always knew how. I just didn't have my own car."

"I'm sorry. That's funny: I misremembered. But you won't have a car here."

"I'll rent one."

"Of course. Right. All grown up!" She let out a wild laugh, as if slightly afraid. "All grown up, and a mother. You'll come? You'll drop in?"

"I'll drop in," I told her.

Flying west, I became middle-aged. All the cowardly, derisive ideas I had somehow absorbed in my youth of what middle age meant fell away, as can sometimes occur to clichés for mysterious reasons. That poor hunchbacked jargon stepped out of its clothes and stood uprightly naked and plain. It meant just what it said, nothing else. It wasn't a need for face cream or an interest in stocks or conservatism. It meant that one now touched both ends: that is what middle is. Middle age only meant that the least reconcilable times of one's life would in fact coexist until death. My youth—the demands of my young, able body, and my young understanding, whether able or not—was not going to shrink in perspective while allowing superior ripeness to gently replace it. My youth was the most stubborn, peremptory part of myself. In my most relaxed moments, it governed my being. It pricked up its ears at the banter of eighteen-year-olds on the street. It frankly examined their bodies. It did not know its place: that my youth governed me with such ease didn't mean I was young. It meant I was divided, as if housing a stowaway soul, rife with itches and yens which demanded a stern vigilance. I didn't live thoughtlessly in my flesh anymore. My body had not, in its flesh, fundamentally changed quite so much as it now could intuit the change that would only be dodged by an untimely death, and to know both those bodies at once, the youthful, and the old, was to me the quintessence of being middle-aged. Now I saw all my selves, even those that did not yet exist, and the task was remembering which I presented to others.

At the rental-car desk of the Oakland airport I allowed the young agent to sell me an upgrade: the miserliness of youth, the pride of young poverty, also die hard. One must give them a push. I asked for a sunroof, cup holders. Perhaps this was something like buckling my armor. I could have the Eddie Bauer edition for a mere extra twenty-five dollars a day, and I said I would take it. I could choose from their menu of types of insurance, and I chose the most pessimistic and costly.

That morning, when I'd woken up Lion to tell him goodbye, he had clung to me hard as he sometimes did now, and repeated his heart-piercing mantra: *I want to keep you forever. I want to keep you forever. I want to keep you forever.* I'd let him repeat it again and again as the cab honked outside. I'd felt he was casting a spell over me. Then I asked him for something to carry with me on my trip. He was at the age now where he constantly had some little treasure gripped tight in one palm, almost always some natural object, a pine cone or seed pod or stone. My request had electrified him, ceased his mantra, and caused him to lurch out of bed. "What should I give you?" he wondered, riffling through all the meaningful litter he kept on his dresser and in his toy chest. "Should I give you a chestnut? Should I give you this big dried-up leaf?" Wilted lavender pom-poms of clover, spiny balls from a sycamore tree; we had even considered some small, wilted carrots he'd swiped from the kitchen and hidden, perhaps weeks ago, it appeared from their softness. At last I'd accepted a feather, because I could keep it safe closed in a book. Now I had my knight's amulet, too.

Matthew had kissed me lightly, with dry lips. Neither punishment nor promise in them, as if to say *That's up to you.*

"I love you," I'd said. "I'll see you next week."

"I love you," he'd only replied, only certain that that much was true.

I'd felt him watching from our windows as I got in the cab. I looked over my shoulder, and after a brief hesitation he raised up one hand.

That was my second knight's amulet: the sight of him, letting me go.

I denied myself romance and drove on 101, not the coastal highway, but it seemed not to make any difference, scenery or lack of it, or perhaps had I chosen the fog chloroforming the hills and enhancing the scent of the frayed eucalyptus I might have been less overtaken by Martha, as if this drive, in its dull ugliness, had surrendered up its motion to the past. I had loved to gaze uninterrupted at Martha as she drove, her complicated hands so separate from her gaze, which was cast far out, past the veil of the road, caught on—what? What interior vision had transfixed her then, as my vision of her transfixed me? One summer day we had driven along the lakeshore to a town that was only a few little houses beside a deep creek that went down to the lake over massive square blocks like a giant's staircase; there had once been a mill. Now there was only a wild, profuse flower garden spread across the whole front of a falling-down cottage; Martha had discovered it some years before and admired it, and drove out every summer to perform clandestine observations. This was what she wanted to achieve: a flower garden that seemed to exist outside all human efforts. That day, for the first time, a tiny bent woman, the gardener, ventured out of her house to receive compliments. I remembered now the thrill of spousal impersonation, standing tolerant if silent beside Martha as she avidly talked about flowers and weeds. And I remembered now, too, my inadvertent youthful condescension, when the woman had said, apologizing for some information she couldn't recall, "I still remember the coat I wore when I was five, but I have no idea what I ate for breakfast today." I'd laughed and smiled in warm sympathy. How sweet, I had thought, she remembers her coat. She must have loved it not to have forgotten. But the coat wouldn't ask any effort of preservation. Feeling ninety, and no longer five, there would be the real effort. Telling that five-year-old girl, in her beautiful coat, You're all finished. Submerged. Obsolete.

We are ghosts of ourselves, and of others, and all of these ghosts appear perfectly real. Like the ghost coming down the dirt track from the house, as the ludicrous rental car bumps to a halt. I slid from the height of the driver's seat trembling, as sometimes now happened to me when I drove several hours at high speed. What had fourteen years taken away? Rancor. Some urgency, not all. The uniform gold of her hair, which was now a composite of silver and gold and exquisite, a far cry from my coarse, wiry gray that I slathered with hair dye, like tarring a roof. The years had taken something more from her skin, for she had that translucent pale skin that is easily weathered, but this imperfection had already been present when I'd known her before, and however much it had advanced, I couldn't measure—she so quickly approached me, effacing whoever she'd been. As if at a threshold, a scant inch of air left between us, she paused and we studied each other, she not without humor, that unruly right-hand corner of her mouth twitching upward, her gray eyes very active, like fast-moving clouds. They seemed to say, Do I dare? Isn't that why you're here? I felt her strong mouth again, wiping me clean, laying bare information; the shock of her body, to the eye barely changed but I now felt transformed, taut and hard with a life spent outdoors even down to the pads of her fingers. Then the inch of air sifted between us again, very different in quality.

"And pregnant too," she observed. "That's good. A reminder to handle with care."

Even notched tightly against her I couldn't believe she had known. "I'm not showing to anyone else."

"Then no one else is looking very closely."

"Aren't you the hippie earth mother, with all of your instincts."

"I always was. I especially always had instincts," she said, never ceasing to touch me, as we stood in the crook of the rental car's arm as if in the nest of her bed. But her "always," acknowledging time, tinged the air. She drew back a bit more, widening her perspective, and widening mine. I allowed her to study my face, all my own signs of age, as I took in the scene of her life, the gray splintering fence posts, the gray splintering barn with its cavernous mouth through which roosters and hens with unusual plumage importantly, aimlessly marched; I'd read something about them: each one was a heritage breed. A great golden mound of manure with a pitchfork stuck in it, all sorts of other enigmatic structures or monuments, a garage with its doors standing open, a shed, a greenhouse, an outhouse, a rust-eaten swing set, an inexplicable folly with miniature onion-domes seeming to house just a ride-atop lawnmower, all indicating or somehow affirming allegiance to the house, despite their haphazard locations—it was an unsightly yet organic whole, as if it all grew from one source like a forest of fungus. The house itself was large and unromantic and variously clad, and bursting its seams with pragmatic objects, and looking at it I understood, as I had been hesitant to, reading Joachim's blog, that she knew well enough what she was doing. And all around her, so abundant she need not honor, cultivate, or even notice it, the outsize gorgeousness of the land, which she must have liked most for its imperviousness to whatever she did.

I had arrived in the late afternoon, dinnertime where I came from, and the air was so still I could hear the sheep, dotted over a pasture uphill from the house, emitting their bland affirmations; apart from that only the wind.

"Joachim went into Willits with friends," she said, as if she'd sensed my inventory of the farm's living things. "He'll be back around seven for dinner. He's hoping you'll stay. He almost canceled his plans when he heard you'd be coming. He doesn't meet many people out here so he's named you the Grand Visitation."

"Who does he think that I am?"

"An 'old friend.' But he's probably guessed we were lovers. He's canny that way."

"He's seen you in other relationships."

"Sure. None that stuck. Yours has stuck," she said, after a moment, and it was strangely so natural, as she observed this, to kiss her again, and more roughly, some urgency creeping back in with returning acquaintance. "Can I give you a piece of advice," she said.

"That would be very ironic, in this situation, your giving advice."

"Be with me for the time that you're here. For the next couple hours, or a night. I won't mess up your life. I promise, Regina. I'm a lonely old woman who sleeps with two dogs. I won't do that to you."

"*You* won't do it."

"You won't do it either," she said. And so I passed through the screen and wood doors of her house, and climbed her stairs just behind her, the fingers of my left hand loosely hooked into the fingers of her right, our connection the feather-light kind children make when they realize control over adults can sometimes be achieved by mere touch, that they don't need to grip the whole thick adult hand in their little inadequate fist. The wooden treads of her staircase were as worn as the boards of some shack by the sea, the grain standing out in hard ridges I wished I could feel through the soles of my shoes. And Martha rose steadily two steps above me, so that I imagined the staircase removed, and her floating ahead at that slight elevation, like some supernatural guide. I faced the small of her back and took in the elaborate powerful scent, the faint blue-gray dusting of mildew baked dry by departed sunshine rising out of her jeans, and the moist confined hot pungency of her body, of collapsed low-tide sea vegetables, and peat moss, and her slick and metallic tartness I forever connected with lemon curd licked off a spoon.

It was not a long staircase at all, in fact must have been short, as the ceilings were low, but it seemed not just long but enormous, dilated in every direction.

She slept in a room full of ancient, hard-used furniture that had proved itself up to this point by not falling apart, and each piece seemed to feel entitled to provide commentary, so that as we lay on her bed, it set up a resonant hum from the depths of its springs, while the side table scraped on the bed frame, and the floorboards beneath us, though we'd hardly begun, popped and moaned.

She was devilishly sly in her virginal caution, for she let me, or required me, to strip her, without lifting a finger to help, and I did, in almost threatening silence, never taking my eyes from her face. In return her eyes never left mine, studying it with such peculiar absorption I almost thought all the years of my life she had missed must be on display there, like a silent movie, so that by the time we were finished, and her hardy old furnishings probably really done for, she would have come to the end of the movie as well, and would know the whole story far better than I could have told her.

Her body had changed. I thought of the tide going out of a marsh, that slow removal of repletion, and the tender exposure, so that beneath my fingers and tongue her skin gave slightly more than it had in the past, for the slightest moment longer held my mark—and so that I uncovered her that much more quickly, with a mercilessness that stole the human from her voice and the grace from her limbs, so a deafening animal groan tore from her and her drenched pubis, bucking at me, split my lip on my teeth.

"No permanent damage," she afterward said, repeating her earlier promise while kissing the blood from my wound.

We slept and woke up in near darkness. When I followed her back down the stairs there in the kitchen sat Joachim, a disembodied white face in the glow from his laptop computer. "Turn a light on," said Martha, proceeding to do it herself. I'd thought the photographs I'd seen of him would spare me any shock, but they might have increased it by misrepresenting his scale. Even crumpled as he was into a chair I could see he was taller than Martha. He was all legs and arms and the pallid and delicate face, and in his black jeans and a giant black jacket of thin shiny stuff, like a raincoat, which he'd pulled past his folded-up knees to midshin, he looked like an upside-down bat in repose. He had dyed his hair black and deformed Martha's mouth, which he wore slightly wider and fuller, with a thin silver ring. The sight of him filled me with tender amazement that the mold for the boys I'd pursued as a teenager still was in use, and I thought I should leave Martha's house before my numerous sins multiplied even more.

"The Grand Visitation!" he cried, seeing me, and with a struggle found one of his hands and extended it. "Thank you for reading my blog. You're my most far-flung reader I know of apart from my dad."

"Stand *up* when you're shaking hands," Martha said, lightly slapping his shoulder.

"Sorry, I've been raised on a farm and I'm very uncouth. So you live in New York? We lived there until evildoers assaulted our freedoms. Now we live here. Lots of freedoms."

"How was Willits?" Martha asked him as she handed me a beer. "Oops!" she said, smiling blindingly at me and taking it back.

"Oh, it was fabulous, Mommy. We watched the traffic light change. It has three different colors: a bright green, a sort of dull orangey yellow, and a really nice red."

"Joachim hasn't forgiven me for moving us out of New York. Even though he can barely remember it."

"Actually, I remember it perfectly."

"Actually, you remember everything perfectly."

"Do you remember me?" I said. "I met you when you were a baby. I even babysat you a few times." If it were possible he made himself even more handsome by blushing.

"I guess childhood amnesia is real," he said. "Tell me what I was like."

"You were very meditative."

"Oh, it's so nice how you said that! You mean I just sat there and drooled." Delighted, he made a brief hailstorm of noise on his keyboard.

"Are you blogging right now?"

"Just trying to catch up a little. Sorry, that's rude," and the tide of his blush rolled back in.

"It is rude," Martha said from the kitchen. "Please go do your chores."

"I don't mind," I said, "I'd just rather, if you were thinking of mentioning me—"

"The Grand Visitation. You'd rather I didn't? Okay. Of course." I could sense disappointment, and wondered what he would have said. "The glare of the Media Spotlight has been very stressful for Mom," he agreed.

"Our hired girl reads it," said Martha.

"You have a hired girl?"

"Two, actually."

"A veritable harem. What services do they perform?"

"Joachim, *do* your *chores*," she repeated, and this time he snapped shut the laptop and smilingly sprang from the room.

I had told Dutra, when I called from New York after booking my flight, that I was coming to the Bay Area for a couple of days to do some sort of "research." It was wonderful, leading a life of which any amount could be labeled "research." Having known me as long as he had Dutra didn't inquire what the research involved. My sincere research was generally fruitless, and most things that bore fruit were only labeled as research long after the fact, so that what I told him did not feel permanently dishonest. In any case, it only needed to spare him the offensive idea that I was worried about him, which, in any form, he was poised on the ramparts to soundly defeat. "You're not flying out here to give back the check? Because if you are you should save yourself money and time. Don't look a gift horse in the mouth, Ginny."

"Do you even know what that means? It means don't look to see if the horse has bad teeth."

"That's fine. Don't look at my teeth."

Earlier in the same conversation I'd already thanked him at length for the money, having to talk through and finally scold his impatience with gratitude: "Matthew and I were really touched and overwhelmed—"

"Yeah yeah yeah."

"Would you shut up and let me say thank you?"

"You're welcome! I'm not fishing for gratitude!"

"You still have to accept it, for fuck's sake!" I'd cried. Now, brushing gingerly again on the subject, I said, "I'd still like to talk about the check when I see you, but don't worry, I'm not planning to stuff it back into your pocket," and I silently thanked Matthew for his astuteness.

"There's nothing to discuss, it's just money. So when'll you be here?"

"I could see you on Sunday."

"Where are you staying?"

"I don't know, just some stupid hotel—I was thinking I'd come see your place. It's about an hour, right?"

"Nothing to see here. I'll drive up and meet you."

"Then I won't see the Buddha," I essayed.

"It's a concrete fucking Buddha from a garden store. I'll come up and we'll go to Ishida. It's the most unbelievable sushi. Once you eat there everything in New York'll taste rotten."

"That sounds great, but can't I come and see your place?"

"That's such a bore, Ginny. There's nothing to eat here."

"Then why are you living there?"

"For the peace."

"So. I like peace."

"I'll meet you at Ishida on Sunday at seven. Eighteenth and Mission. Your hotel concierge can tell you how to get there."

"Dutra, are you really refusing to let me come to your place?"

"I'm not refusing, it's just there's no point. You've seen places I've lived. You've lived in them. It's exactly the same, except it's in California, and there's a cheap Buddha next to the steps."

"Are you living with someone?"

"Are you flying out here to check up on me?" The temperature dropped very slightly. Either I responded with too much haste, or too much hesitation.

"Yeah," I said scornfully, "that's what I'm spending your money on, spying on you."

"Well, Virginia, that's a lousy investment, because there ain't nothing here to find out. I'm leading an extremely quiet life."

"Doing what?"

"Doing what? Doing nothing. Relaxing for once."

"You've never relaxed for one minute. Are you working?"

"Why the fuck would I work?"

"Volunteering or something?"

"Jesus, Ginny."

"Dutra, you used to fly to the third world in your spare time and operate on poor people who'd otherwise die."

"Exactly! So didn't I earn me a fucking vacation?" he shouted.

Through the phone I could hear him pacing, pacing, like he might carve a trench in the floor. A door slapping its frame and the aural expansion of insects and wind, the door slapping again and the room closing in. He had never sat still in his life. "Okay, okay, Dutra," I said, my heart clubbing my ribs. "Save your breath and you can yell at me in person." I wondered what image he'd held in his mind, fleeing west. Maybe his own Eastern medicine institute, bearing his name carved above the front door. Maybe a dazzling second career in competitive surfing. Regardless of what he had thought, it had just been a pretext. He had only been running as far as he could. I tried to imagine what Dutra in idleness looked like. Not peace but despair. Unlike Alicia I couldn't believe he would ever try harming himself. He too much hated waste, which included the waste of himself. But when we got off the phone I'd felt physical panic, as if it had bled through the wire. I had actually wanted to call the La Honda police.

It turned out there was plenty of work on a sheep farm, even on such a miniature, amateur, half-baked operation as Martha was running, to use Martha's words. The next morning when I came down at eight, she'd already been out of the house for three hours. "A farmer's work is never done," Joachim assured me, folded up in his chair at the table in front of the sodden remains of some cold cereal and his open laptop. "It's just neglected at times so the farmer can eat, sleep, and check his Facebook."

"Is that what you're doing?" I asked, pouring the last of the coffee. Joachim rose hunchbacked out of his chair, reached the empty pot from me, replaced the spent filter and grounds, filled the pot with fresh water, slotted and poured all ingredients into their places, and pressed the red button for "Brew," all the while never taking his eyes off his screen.

"Must keep the fresh java flowing all day for the Boss," he explained, climbing back in his chair. "To answer you, Yes, I am giving The Facebook a quick morning tend. It's like anything else on a farm. If you don't tend it first thing in the morning it starts making this loud MOOing noise, or it kicks in a fence, or it sprouts all these weeds. So much work!"

"Can I see?"

He shoved aside, making room at the table. "Dare I ask if you're on the FB?"

"I am not. I'm an old lady, set in my ways. I know nothing of your Brave New World."

"Pshaw! You've read my blog, so I know that's not true. And much older ladies than you are on Facebook. Oh, ugh! That came out really bad. You're not old at all." Blushing furiously, he clicked open a window. "Let's see some of my friends. Here's my not-really-grandma. Oh, look at her! She's been posting a storm." He leaned in, his face lit with pleasure, and I leaned in beside him. Onscreen, an appealingly overjoyed toad was embraced from all sides by a many-aged crowd of her obvious offspring. *Great-grand-baby Livia's High School Graduation!!!!!* exulted the caption. She hadn't aged a day nor faded a shade, and my amazement took the form of a Magnavox ad: *My puffy Nikes are brand-new pure white, my velveteen sweat suit with hoodie is vibrant fuchsia, my hair is the orange of an overripe pumpkin, and my eyelids, to the overplucked brows, are deep-end-of-the-swimming-pool aquamarine! If you're not seeing these colors, you're not seeing Lucia on Facebook in 2007.*

"Why, that's your old babysitter!" I said.

Joachim cocked his head. "I guess so. I guess she does watch me sometimes, when I go in the summers. She's cleaned house for my dad since forever. Since he moved to New York. And she cooks stuff, to keep him from starving. He says she's his excuse why he never remarried. Isn't that awful? As if people get married to get a house cleaner! But I think it's a joke."

I agreed that it was. "What's your mother's excuse?"

"*She* doesn't need excuses." We laughed like conspirators. Then Joachim reconsidered. "But maybe it's me."

"You're all she needs," I told him.

"Isn't that *eerie*? That's just what she says!"

Not until we'd walked out of the house did I glimpse her, far away up a steep bumpy waste of brown grass, baseball cap on her head with her silver-gold rope of hair pulled through the vent, sunk to the knees in her boots, at the head of a shuffling file of obedient bundles of wool. Joachim and I waved hugely over our heads, were not seen, and returned to my tour of the precincts. "The Districts of Fowl," Joachim announced, loping beside me. "The Armory: tools for plant Killing and plant Cultivation. Oh, this thing is crazy. This thing"—the structure with the onion-domes on it—"was built by the owners before, for their mules. Yes! The Mule Winter Palace! The people who owned this before had all kinds of great stuff. They had a nineteen-sixty-three four-door Mercedes sedan that ran on used cooking oil. Except it mostly didn't run, so they left it as part of 'as is' when they sold us the farm, and Mom tried to make it run for, like, years and she finally sold it for scrap. Mom always aspires to get rid of stuff. Anything that does not have Clear Use."

"All this stuff has clear use?"

"Most of these items are still being Processed," he admitted.

"You like it here, don't you?"

"You mean, as compared to New York? I like New York but I'm probably not fit to live there anymore. When I go in the summer I can't sleep the first couple of days from the noise. I get twitchy and weird. But then, here, I'm lonely," he said, with such simplicity I turned to gaze at him. I'd never had a younger Friend—not a substitute child, but a Friend. I was so pleased to identify him thus, that I Capitalized him.

"Joachim," I said, as we returned down a crooked fence line toward the house, where soon Martha would join us for coffee, "I'm hatching a Plan and I want to Enlist you."

"Oh, joy," he said. "You really are a Grand Visitation."

"I'm meeting a friend in San Francisco for dinner tonight and I want you and your mother to come."

"What kind of dinner?" he asked shrewdly.

"Sushi. Apparently really great sushi."

"That's promising. You might talk her into it. We don't get much sushi up here."

"Will I have to talk her into it?"

"She never wants to do that kind of thing anymore. No Clear Use. But I think she's just out of the habit."

"But you'd want to?"

"Yes yes!"

"We'll have to leave around four."

"Then I'll do my chores early," he said, in his eagerness bringing my tour to an end.

Waking that morning to the cool sheets, the cool, undisturbed air, the deep silence filling the rooms that told me Martha had long since gone out to her work, I had dressed without haste but without leisure also, had carefully gathered up all of my things, fouled underpants and linty balled socks fallen into the cuffs of her bed, my necklace and watch, the ring that had not left my finger, the feather from Lion, and closed the door on her room which I knew I would not see again. I had used to dream, when I'd loved her from such desperate disadvantage, of one day catching up, being not the naïve, needy girl she'd too fully ensnared but a woman, like her, with my own gravity. I'd caught up. Successful or failed, paired or alone, we were equal. It was hard not to wonder how things would have gone if we'd met at this time of our lives, and yet equally hard to pursue the thought far. It was too phantasmic. I could not even guess what her face would be like.

In the kitchen we drank mugs of coffee, the table between us. Finalities never occur, even after a fourteen-year wait, that aren't felt right away by all persons concerned. It was easy drinking coffee, immediate. The coffee was not a pretext or a symbol. After a while I said, "You remember Dutra."

Her face allowed itself full retrospection. "Sure. Daniel Dutra. He hated me. With good reason."

"He never hated you."

"He should have." It was possible to tip our hats to this and let it pass. "What's he been up to these past many years?"

I told her, not sparing details, and as I did, and as she exclaimed and protested and laughed—as I, frankly, enthralled her with the story of him—I was reminded how pleasant the game of seduction can be, even when one is technically on the sidelines. "We're meeting for dinner tonight down in San Francisco. Come with me. I think you might like to see Dutra, and I think he might like to see you. Besides that, Joachim's already counting on it."

"You're a very surprising minx, Miss," Martha chided, but laughing. I took note of the flush in her face, beneath which the fine lines of her decades of previous laughter and worry and scorn, all etched permanently, momentarily seemed to dissolve. She was in arm's reach of fifty years old now, so beautiful one might have called this her ideal age, but she'd probably look just the same when she turned eighty-five. I told her, "He still carries a torch for you," knowing she'd laugh at the old-fashioned phrase, as she did, but it didn't prevent her from blushing.

"In another life," she said, setting our cups in the sink.

"Then just come and have sushi. You don't get much sushi up here."

"That's true, but I can't say I find it a hardship." She considered. "Joachim thinks you're the bomb."

"Then just come for him. He'll have fun. It'll give us more time."

"Are you leaving tomorrow?"

"Tonight on the red-eye." Another decision I'd found I had made, on awaking that morning.

Joachim rode down with me—"I need him to operate the cup holder," I explained to Martha, "and make sure that I don't wind up lost"—and this time I did take the coastal highway, after dutifully seeming to listen to Martha's instructions for her locals' shortcut back to 101. Martha never looked back when she drove. At the opportune moment I slipped unperceived from the frame of her rearview and turned our course west. A river appeared to reward me and slid alongside. "Now we'll never get lost," I declared. "Keep the river on your right to the ocean. At ocean, turn left."

"We'll be late," Joachim said, unworried. "Where this river comes out at the ocean there's usually sea lions."

"Sea lions!" I cried.

"With their pups!" Joachim realized. "Is it summer? It is! They'll have pups!"

The sea lions, then, their lengths flung on the sand like so many superfluous sandbags, and sunning their lichenlike splotches, and at long intervals, as if hoping to shame you for prompting the effort, dismissively waving their flippers. And the busload of Japanese tourists dangling over the guardrail with cameras, in their effusions very like Joachim, who, delighted in turn, photographed them and thanked them and bobbed in response to their bows. Then we drove on again, the amusement-park road scalloped out of the bluffs like a practical joke. "This is the sort of road that would never be built nowadays," Joachim observed with satisfaction. "It's so dangerous. And erode-y."

"This is a road that was built when American arrogance hadn't yet found its limits."

"It's great that there's so much stuff like that for us to still use, even now that we're so conscientious. Like, the whole highway system."

"I know, there it is, you can't waste it."

"You can't. Wasting it's worse than having made it in the first place. Ooh! Barbecued Oysters. Have you ever had a barbecued oyster?"

"Is it good?"

"Scary actually, I wouldn't eat one, but I don't think it's something you'd find in the East."

Point Reyes now glimpsed through the trees to the west like a taunt, that the westernmost place had slipped out of our grasp. The sinking sun flashing a last telegraph, interrupted by fog. The fog dusk reminded us what we were doing, if we had forgotten. "Wow," Joachim said, "we're going to be *really* late."

"It's okay," I told him. "It's just dinner with friends. Your mom gets to catch up with a friend while they're waiting for us, which is what we were coming to do, anyway."

"That sounds nice. My mom doesn't actually have many friends." After a moment, as I was pondering this, he said, "Can I tell you a secret?"

"Of course."

"I'm moving back to New York for the rest of high school. At the end of the summer."

I thought of Nicholas's beautiful, ordered apartment, of which I'd seen only a handful of rooms. Down a quiet hallway, I now knew, was a room full of light, for his son. Herodotus and Shakespeare lined up on the shelves, their faded cloth spines harmonizing somehow with the top-of-the-line computer still off-gassing its scents of the future from the seams of its platinum case. In his father's world Joachim would be no less himself, but illumined by that world's lights in a quite different way. I asked, superfluously, "Your mom doesn't know yet?"

"No. I told Dad I wanted to tell her myself, but I'm chicken."

"Because you're afraid she'll be angry?"

"Because she'll be sad."

I glanced at him, gazing out the window. She was going to be many times sadder than she'd ever allow him to know. I thought how strange it was, that a child can seem such an intrusion on life, until the day that the child becomes life itself. "She'll be okay," I told him. "She'll miss you, but she'll also be proud and excited. That'll outweigh her sadness. I'm her friend and I'm also a mom, so I know what I'm saying."

I could see that he liked what I'd said even if he could not quite believe it. "I could visit you in Brooklyn," he realized. "Would you mind?"

"I'd be mortally offended if you didn't!"

Dutra called me at eight, while we were waiting in line at the Golden

Gate tollbooth, but the fog had been torn into pieces and vanquished, and the heavy gold light filled the car, and I knew, because it was a summer evening out there in the West, we had so much more time than the clock might have said. "We're almost there," I told Dutra, truncating his squawks of distress. "We're in town. We just hit the traffic."

"Who's *we*," Dutra cried.

"Joachim. Martha's kid."

"Martha's *here*, Gin," he said, and his voice, in its labors, suggested he'd worn a starched collar and a far-too-tight tie, though he'd never, to my knowledge, put on such clothes in his life.

"I know she is, Dutra. I brought her. She wanted to see you."

"Since when are you back in touch with her?"

"Since whenever. Is she sitting inside all alone?"

"We got sake."

"Well, go back in and drink it with her. Don't be rude. I've got to go now, I'm paying my toll."

Dutra emitted an odd, smothered sound, as if not being rude might be too much to ask. "Just get here."

"We'll be there in a flash."

But we weren't there for almost an hour. By that time, night had fallen. The restaurant glowed like a lantern, the center of which was their little square table. Across it they leaned toward each other, submerged deep in talk, neither laughing nor grave but as if they'd been talking for years. "There they are," Joachim said, Dutra seeming like someone he already knew.

"You go on," I said, kissing his cheek. "I don't think I'll come in. I'll be late to the airport." When he looked at me wonderingly I replied with that calm steady light of adulthood: he need not understand me, just trust me.

Taller than me as he was, he still felt like a child in my arms.

"See you in September," he said, shyly stepping away with one hand on the door.

I lingered a moment to watch their glad faces, as they caught sight of him.

Acknowledgments

In the course of writing this book I received invaluable assistance and support from the Fine Arts Work Center in Provincetown, the MacDowell Colony, PowderKeg, Molly Stern, Paul Slovak, Lynn Nesbit, Kenna Lee, and Pete Wells. Thanks to you all. In particular, two of the writers I most admire and cherish as peers, Jhumpa Lahiri and Jennifer Egan, set aside their own work to read my drafts and offer crucial advice and encouragement without which this book would not exist. All my love and gratitude to you both.